FOR MIKA—
MY DANCER
ALWAYS RISING

A SNOW LEOPARD NAMED MIDAS

S. L. COOK

A Snow Leopard Named Midas

ISBN (ebook): 979-8-9923589-0-2
ISBN (paperback): 979-8-9923589-1-9
ISBN (hardcover): 979-8-9923589-2-6

A SNOW LEOPARD NAMED MIDAS

PROLOGUE

IT WASN'T UNTIL LANDING that they could see the ground, sweating mauve dust under a smelt of smog.

Mexico City. Touches of beauty struggling to harmonize with all levels of hell.

Midas McKnight had been all over the world and he hated this corner—the heavy air, pleasant-faced women with haunted eyes squatting in the rank shadows of polluted alleys, catastrophe lurking around every corner. Apathy and fear the only currency, warding off curiosity and ambition. Though there also remained more than enough enticement for those of corrupt or gentrified blood—tonier suburbs and happier children, well hidden behind fortress gates patrolled by armies of well-compensated bodyguards. Black SUVs, the ubiquitous limos for the politically protected and all cartel brethren.

Midas had cleared customs first, pausing to scan through the grimy window into the haze outside the terminal. It all looked quiet. He turned to watch the crowds filing through the single gate from customs, pretending to look through his phone.

There were five on the current team, the Unit, their small group that ran clandestine ops when official channels couldn't be used.

Phillip Gillis was the next through, gangly and bookish, the smartest of them all and a formidable tech genius. Two minutes later, Kyle Palmer strutted through the one-way exit, sunglasses firmly in place, his smug grin holding court over his long linen sleeves and khaki shorts. Daddy's boy. Always the asshole.

The last two emerged twenty seconds apart. Team leader Conor Brennan first, looking more annoyed and focused than usual. Finally, Mason James pushed his way through the chrome turnstile, hesitating a moment before moving slowly toward the outer doors.

Midas and Mason had grown up together, the double-M twins as they'd been called, the offspring of families who'd worked together for decades. All these years later, the McKnights remained one of the most prominent broods in the San Francisco Bay Area. Maxwell James, Mason's father, was their indispensable partner, protector of the less glamorous sides of the business.

Midas watched his oldest friend cross the polished terminal floor. Only he knew how badly Mason was reeling. Guatemala had been a fiasco, and Mason continued to question himself.

The group walked outside as distanced strangers, toting small duffels or backpacks, never anything requiring checkage.

After reaching a pair of sweltering sedans parked fifty yards apart in an auxiliary lot, they slipped into them in prearranged groups. Brennan and Phillip took one; Midas, Mason, and Kyle, the other. The team preferred older four-wheel-drive station wagons, earth-toned whenever possible to blend in with structures and topography. Today, these primer-painted four doors would have to do. Beyond-factory tint shaded the two carloads of mostly white faces.

On the streets they drove the limit, Midas giving Brennan a four-car cushion. Ten minutes later they pulled in front of an undersized industrial structure. A weighted metal door rolled up with a grinding hiss. The cars moved inside, steering past several adult Rottweilers on chains sitting silent and menacing, flesh-and-blood gargoyles. The door came down again behind them.

The building measured about the same as two side-by-side tennis courts. It was essentially empty beyond a pair of picnic tables resting in a corner beneath filthy windows covered with black-widow webs. Two chunky middle-aged men materialized from a hidden room. Sergio Ortiz was the shorter one, a pencil-thin mustache across his upper lip looking right out of Hollywood casting. The other was Mario Marquez, darker and bald, slurping a hard-candy cinnamon fire missile attached to a plastic ring on his finger.

Midas knew neither had much use for gringos, but apparently made exceptions for the team and their US dollars.

"*Hola,* Mr. Brennan," Ortiz shouted, mustache rising over rotted teeth and the remnants of a jack-o'-lantern smile. He waved a greeting with two fingers—all he had left on his right hand, an appendage now useful for only fandom at death metal concerts.

"Ortiz," Brennan replied with dispassion, disembarking from the car and scanning the steel beams that stretched overhead.

Midas studied the room as well, pulling himself from the rear car to lean against the side fender.

Phillip stayed in his front vehicle's passenger seat fiddling with his laptop. Brennan strolled to the picnic tables, followed by Kyle Palmer.

"Mr. Kyle?" Ortiz said, liberally spreading sarcastic charm. "Didn't know you were attending this party. My ladies still talk about you."

"With good reason," Kyle said, never failing to brag about the strong impression he left with women. Strong, but not always good. His reputation was nothing to brag about.

Ortiz spotted the more formidable men hanging back. "Mr. McKnight, *mi amigo*. And the Sundance Kid, Mason James. Still using your same cover, Mr. Mason? Should I expect to read a new dispatch about our backward little country with your byline in the *LA Times*?"

"Maybe just a half-star review in the *Third World Traveler*," Mason said.

Midas felt his lips curl into a half smile.

"Still a snotty bastard, eh?" Ortiz wasn't at ease with anyone else's wit, derisive or otherwise.

"If we're done with nursery-school roll call?" Brennan barked.

Ortiz gave a bow worthy of a samurai.

Heavy canvas bags sat zipped up on the cheap tables. Brennan rummaged through each, holding up some of the contents and occasionally leaning in for closer inspection. Once satisfied, he motioned to the group, and they all moved to grab the merch and walk it back to the cars, placing the sturdy duffels in the trunks.

During the transfer, Marquez limped to the lead vehicle where Phillip was hunched over his laptop. He tapped his fire missile on the closed glass. "Good to see you, Phil."

Unlike Ortiz, Marquez's English was perfect, with no lilting inflections. He ran a block of houses in an area of the city catering to all forms of kink and other questionable appetites. Ortiz was his boss, higher on the reigning crime lord's food chain and taking a huge share from the houses along with pieces of many other such endeavors, as if no one could tell from the cowboy hat, boots, and gold buckle the size of a dinner plate.

Phillip responded with a middle finger, never a fan of middle-aged pimps or any of the other devious facilitators they were frequently forced to employ.

Back at the tables, Brennan and Ortiz held a final private pow-wow. Midas couldn't hear them but recognized the gestures.

Then Brennan was back in the lead vehicle's driver's seat. The cars inched forward as the heavy metal doors rose again. Once high enough for clearance, both peeled out into the muggy grime to start their three-hundred-plus-mile trek under the blinding sunlight and lung-sweltering heat to reach their target.

"The sooner we get those two assholes off the books, the better," Midas muttered without looking at Mase or Kyle. "This common-good BS is wearing thin."

"Agreed," Mase said, flipping on a pair of mirrored shades and adjusting his seat for the journey.

The team rolled into the outskirts of Guadalajara several hours later thanks to shitty roads and farmers' caravans. It was almost six p.m. and the sun was descending in a reddish-pink flare, though the pizza-oven temps would keep the ground and the city oppressive well into the overnight hours.

They passed through neighborhoods of shacks and rusted pick-up trucks. Farther inside the city limits the shanties became stucco multiple-family homes, where good living meant a sputtering wall-unit air conditioner and occasional warm water. Finally they reached the area that functioned as the city's center and show-piece, boasting well-tended roads and a circle of multilevel hotels nestled around a spouting fountain plaza teeming with foot traffic and hookers. Off the busier side streets, food carts sagged beside old men, taking up every free space. Green flags waved under a few of the canopies, signaling cheap heroin and weed along with the handmade tortillas.

Midas took a roundabout, changing direction and counting off a pair of blocks, then turned down another alley and came to a stop, squaring the car in neutral. He got out and walked to where it opened back onto the busy street.

Two blocks back, Brennan was slowly weaving his way through the pedestrians and weathered mountain bikes. He adhered to the few flickering red traffic lights, slowing well ahead of stops and caressing the brakes. Screeching tires wouldn't do. Midas observed Phillip's window lower and a kid of no more than sixteen amble up to it. Their contact. The kid handed Phillip a small piece of paper, palming five one-hundred-dollar in exchange. He was back on his corner before Phillip's window closed and the light flickered to green.

Midas jogged back to his car and pulled out.

A mile later he saw taillights swing out from a side street to follow. After a few more blocks, Midas turned slowly into another alley. Halfway down stood a plastic garage tent, open in front and back like a milk carton. There was enough space for both cars to slip inside with five feet of separation. A few seconds later Brennan pulled in behind them.

This time they all got out. The heavy bags were moved from the trunks onto the rear seats, and the contents divided, assembled, and checked. Midas shoved weapons and ammo into his pockets as they got back into the car.

Brennan walked forward and tapped on their windshield. "No ears on this until we're inside. His jamming is precise and, given their paranoia, they'll be listening. Stay together and tight. Kyle holds back and helps Phil."

Midas saw the profile in the back seat bob his understanding. Kyle Palmer wasn't averse to the front lines as long as the wet work was neutralized. He liked to tell himself he was more important behind the scenes. No need to play hero. His blue-blooded, well-connected daddy hadn't placed him in the unit to get his ass shot up needlessly. Whatever. At least he wouldn't be getting in the grown-ups' way.

"We've got a spot five hundred yards behind the fun house," Brennan continued. "Ortiz figures ten serious hires, so I'd expect at least twice that. Beyond Lupa, that is."

Pablo Lupa was a ranking member of the Mexican army who sported a pedigree reaching back generations into the old and corrupt Institutional Revolutionary Party, the political machine known as PRI, which had run the country for years. These days, Lupa was also the unofficial patron saint of Guadalajara, dispensing food to the needy and medical supplies to the indigent. All made feasible by his other rank within one of the country's leading drug cartels. Before a few weeks ago, Lupa had never mattered to the suits in DC. The truth being, despite full-throated Rotunda news conferences and internal DEA squabbling, no one gave a damn about drugs coming into the States.

Until they struck too close, that is, and some bureaucrat got emotional.

Midas leaned over the steering wheel and surveyed the tent's opening and the alley beyond. Apart from the bells and shouting from the busier drags, they seemed alone.

"Mase? You sure you're up for this?" Brennan asked, glancing over at the man riding shotgun.

Mason's anger flushed red in splotches over his fair skin. "Why wouldn't I be?" His voice was a coarse rasp.

Guatemala City had been less than two months ago, but it might as well have been the day before. Midas understood Brennan's concern, though he'd given up dispensing ill-advised counsel. Mason was needed. End of discussion. Hard truth overrode other concerns.

"Then let's do this," Brennan said, tapping the hood of their car with a fist before slipping back into his own.

Midas fired it up and headed out, careful to let a group of elderly shoppers cross the mouth of the alley before turning left, back into the crowded plaza and under the candy-toned lights dancing off the darkening street. Both cars moved deliberately, with enough space between them to dispel any thoughts that a caravan was rolling through. Eyes were everywhere, with loyalty in short supply and always for sale.

The necessity for this trip had arisen when a friend of the White House had called for a meeting of agency directors at one of the Capitol's exclusive caves pandering to politically connected aging assholes. After perfectly prepared sixteen-ounce rib eyes, Blue Label Scotch, and cigars, the friend in question produced snaps on his phone of a smiling twentysomething youth with a hoity gleam in his unkind eyes. One of the city's connected and pampered. The president's friend was the boy's father. According to Daddy's cleansed version, his son, along with some Georgetown Law pals, had been trolling bars for female companionship. The escort his son selected had chaperoned the kid to a greasy motel for a rough and cheap trip around her world. His father didn't mention that his son had also demanded party favors, and the hooker had delivered a dose of heavily laced black tar.

The kid never woke up. After a weeklong coma his parents had pulled the plug.

Family Pinkertons were dispatched, tracing the long and winding road of dubious smack back to the cartel in question. Pablo Lupa's. An old Yale buddy took it from there, leaning on Kyle's politically motivated father, Rawlings Palmer, to extract a measure of reciprocity for their son's death. The little shit's arrogance, poor judgment, and inbred stupidity never came into consideration. The final equation, after all, was what real influence was expected to buy.

Jasper DeMarco, known affectionately as the Old Man, was the team's rabbi and handler, having run the Unit for decades. He'd wanted no part of this op, but he'd been overridden by ignorant higher-ups, a sad power-play reality that was becoming increasingly common.

Now as the two cars maneuvered the noisy route toward the target, Midas allowed his mind to relax and concentrate on what would come next.

Pablo Lupa owned four homes in Mexico. Tonight's spread nestled on a small mountaintop to the south about five miles outside the city. Trees were a valuable commodity down here, and Lupa had imported an orchard's worth fully grown, planting them in symmetry around the gaudy pink palace, which, if lore were to be trusted, had once served as a turn-of-the-century bandito torture resort. Tonight, the drooping oaks would come in handy, providing the team with necessary cover and a small advantage.

The two cars pulled off the main highway and parked out of

sight in a sunken ditch, waiting for the last shades of daylight to turn to black.

An hour later, Brennan, Midas, and Mason set off for a precise point in the electrified fence circling the compound. A few days before and masquerading as homeless day laborers, Phillip's advance team had compromised a specific section during one of Lupa's frequent jaunts into Mexico City's underbelly, where he was known to peacock in full-dress uniform. The tireless populist soldier in service to his country.

The sprawling property was enclosed within reinforced cyclone steel, stained brown and green to match the surroundings. Brennan stood inches away, studying the wiring that was marked with a pair of fruit-bag twist ties. He pulled shears from his back pocket and tentatively cut the first link. There was a metallic *snap*. Five more snips and the three men scrambled through a tight hole, moving quickly over an unkempt knoll before halting in a crouch behind a smattering of planted shrubs. Peering between them, Midas could see the glowing yellow lights of the main house. Faint laughter and music carried through the stiflinly hot air.

For years, on the same Saturday of every month Lupa had been serving up an outdoor party for his private goons, always bragging about the soirees to the wrong people.

Thirty feet away from their position, most of the guests were assembled in one location, carousing near the heated Olympic-size pool. Men in shorts and Hawaiian shirts, the women in much less.

The floodlights' range barely extended beyond the patio's edge. Along the well-tended grass line a few yards from the house sat one guard in a wooden chair, an AK-47 resting between his feet, smiling with lazy ambivalence at the poolside antics. Beyond the red tip of his cigarette, he was barely a shadow.

Midas began to move forward. Mase and Brennan fanned out behind him, wary of sensors and other surprises. Midas crept up silently behind the guard, putting his forearms around the man's neck and mouth. Mase and Brennan were crouched nearby on one knee, silently counting. Ten seconds of mute struggle and the guard slumped forward. No one had noticed.

By the pool there were maybe twenty partygoers in all, an even distribution of drunken men and bikini-clad women, most in skimpy see-through frocks offering scant protection against the evening chill. By way of compromise, orange-coiled heat lamps burned, placed every few feet. Two women jumped topless into the shallow end of the pool to the sniggering delight of several loopy inebriates, who toasted their breasts while baptizing them from above with freezing dollops of shaken beer, eliciting feminine shrieks of phony delight.

Lupa was hard to miss, huddled in a corner near a sliding door, his medicine-ball gut hanging over a custom grill. His backward Padres baseball cap was soaked at the edges, and sweat fell from his face. He moved the roasting meat around with a long pair of tongs. Lupa was said to be forty-nine years old—a decent lifespan considering whom he ran with. Though like his stomach, the rest of him had long ago fallen from any semblance of shape, a final receptacle for too many plates of heavy consumption.

Brennan held up a pair of fingers, and the three slid on black balaclavas and night-vision goggles.

Moving together meant a specific division designed to slice the party into subsets of rectangles. Midas was in the middle and bolted first. Brennan and Mase fell in, with all hitting top speed at the edge of the manicured grass.

A woman lounging on a plastic chaise registered the first

glimpse of trouble. Her scream was lost under the music and frivolity.

A bullet hit the bartender just above the left eye, tossing him over his bottles. The team's suppressed Heckler & Koch assault rifles continued to spit, and two bodyguards dropped into the pool, spreading crimson viscera into the Caribbean-blue water. The element of surprise was now gone. Music abruptly ceased and pandemonium took over. Petrified women wailed, running on bare feet toward the massive house. Having been somewhat fortified behind the hood of the grill, Lupa jumped through a doorway just ahead of a string of shots that took out the glass and a few other bodyguards.

Having counted on the chaos for cover, the team followed their target through the same door, slipping inside just as Phillip cut the power from his laptop and all went dark.

They flattened on the cold tile floor, switched their NVGs to night vision, and adjusted their eyes to the green. Midas pointed silently and headed for the grand staircase, flipping on the flashlight attached to his rifle barrel. Mase went left and Brennan right, following paths marked by their own lights.

Reaching the second floor without resistance, Midas extended a small mirror around a corner of the carpeted hallway. Several doors but no movement. Anyone still standing would have armed himself. Their entry had been quick and precise, but what remained would undoubtedly not unfold as swiftly.

He caught a glint halfway up the hall. Beyond was :likely Lupa's primary bedroom—exactly where he wouldn't hole up. Midas rolled low on one shoulder into the hallway. Ten feet away a moving figure came into frame raising a long weapon. His angle wasn't ideal from the floor, so Midas fired twice into the guard's stomach and solar plexus. The man hit the wall with a *thud* along with a spray of blood and splinters. Midas crawled forward and waited.

Three more muted *pops* sounded from below. The miked bud in his ear cracked to life, comms silence ending with Brennan's voice: Two more on my side. They're done."

"One on mine. Also asleep," Mase added. "Ground floor's clear."

"I've got one down up here," Midas said. "Come up, and we'll spread the word."

Moments later the group was again together, inching forward, cautiously pushing inside and around each remaining door. Time was now the enemy. Someone from the party would have found a cell phone and yelped an SOS.

To the right of the primary's ornate double doors stood a smaller one. A closet maybe? The wood was cheaper and weakly locked. Mase kicked it open.

A young girl sat on a small bed that was covered with a pink Barbie quilt. She was dressed as if being escorted to her first school formal—a white princess frock with frills, socks reaching just above her ankles, and shiny black flats. She sat as rigid as a brass statue, mouth clamped through lips bloated with an excess of red lipstick.

Midas advanced slowly behind Mase's cover. Children were frequently forced into service as assassins. Though this one betrayed no hidden wires or traps. Her hands were flattened on the bedspread, appearing no more threatening than any other young girl waiting for a parental pickup. Only the eyes gave her away— far too old and missing nothing.

Midas pulled off his mask and NVGs, offering an unthreatening shrug, palms up, along with a "Whaddya think?" grin.

Her head turned silently in the direction of a flimsy shower curtain hanging in the corner.

Midas nodded with a knowing smile, lifting her off the bed with no resistance and walking her out of the room.

Mase let them get clear before moving toward the curtain and flinging it aside. Its screech along the cheap aluminum rod was jarring.

Midas turned to watch through the door, holding the girl against his shoulder to shield her sight line.

Pablo Lupa emerged from behind the curtain, his arms supporting a pair of open suitcases filled with American cash. He tossed them onto the Barbie bed, raising his hands surrender style above his heaving shoulders. His weathered smile was familiar—the ugly politician who twisted situations into malleability, nothing he'd ever failed to talk or buy his way out of. Lupa's smirk suggested this raid would prove no different, the only hint of fear the fresh salty drops rolling from his nose and cheeks.

Brennan moved a few steps forward and gave him a friendly pat on the shoulder. Midas put his hand over the back of the girl's head to keep her from turning to look.

Then Brennan pulled out a small automatic and sent a pair of slugs into Lupa's sweating head.

CHAPTER 1

LOS ANGELES, PRESENT DAY

MIDAS HADN'T THOUGHT ABOUT her for at least ninety seconds.

The ocean swells were benign. A gray-marbled moon threw strobing shards off the endless rolling current before vanishing beneath the smudgy jungle greens of the Pacific Ocean.

Tonight's three a.m. was no different from the previous restless four he'd spent atop his board bobbing in the silence. Tranquility didn't exist. The dark sky and tame surf had lost their touch. The vastness of the salty water and its shimmering tips weren't helping . . . or healing. The early hour meant sunrise was hours away, as were the stronger swells.

The truth was, Serena Cooper hadn't left willingly. That much he did know.

A woman like her would have communicated unhappiness, given him a chance to steady any tilting emotional ballast. Wasn't that who he was, after all—someone who fixed things?

"No," he said out loud, talking to himself and a school of dolphins frolicking thirty yards behind him in the cold ripples. The problem was his solutions came with a cost. It was why others were inert, and those like him necessary.

Such relentless introspection hadn't much mattered to Serena, the hopelessly upbeat and cheerful graduate student. She'd walked into his life a year ago, pulling attention and exuding more grace than was required for his modest surf bar with beer-stained floors near the Hermosa Pier. She'd needed evening hours, and they'd been searching for a bartender. What followed was a two-night tryout, a Friday-Saturday limbo within the suffocating presence of mother-issue inebriates five-deep at the varnished teak, screaming at sports on the large flat screens. She'd laughed and listened to their weak jokes and fabulist tales, eventually sending them on their wobbling ways feeling fine, watered-down masculinity intact, if not enhanced.

With Midas, she'd been more intrigued than intimidated, and owing to a lack of genetic defeatism, had over those early months proved a sweet-natured Cat in the Hat, radiating a ceaseless reserve of optimism he'd long ago stopped trying to question, and only recently surrendering to appreciate.

Normally, he made the most of these solitary overnight surfing sessions. Then again, what was normal?

Giving up, he waved to the dolphins before paddling in. His chest clenched as he stepped onto the shimmering sand, his feet leaving momentary backlit impressions as he trudged the hundred yards to his porch, board tightly secured under one arm.

The balcony door needed oil, straining against his effort to slide it open on skimpy tracks corroded by windswept sand and salt. Freed from the impediment of smudged glass, stinging wet air galloped into the living room until he managed to shut it again.

Once inside, he pulled a bottle of water from the fridge and took an extended slug.

A red light blinked from the end of the small kitchen counter. He picked up the phone, taking a deep drag of the lingering briny mist into his lungs before punching the button.

The voice was one he knew well. One of many mistakes that refused to fade, another survivor of an era that had harshly schooled them all in the brevity of joy and tenuousness of existence.

A package required his signature.

In Tijuana.

She'd been missing five days.

Dawn traffic heading south on Interstate 5 was sparse. Midas shared the road with other insomniacs and humps fortunate enough to commute during the early-morning hours. He kept his speed around eighty-five, hoping to avoid an unlucky pinch that would slow his momentum. His mind wouldn't leave him alone, vivid with images he'd vainly attempted to put behind him.

Five years was an eternity when polishing hatred.

He knew the package would be brutal.

At four a.m. he hit the US-Mexico border. Twenty minutes later he steered through the Tijuana tourist drags into a crumbling neighborhood no different from every other in rough-trade capitals. Three-story buildings shedding faltering plaster. Never-closed dive bars with specks of Christmas lights kissing grimy sidewalks through cracks in their decaying doors. No shortage of strollers, pimps, or pushers. The hour had cleaned the street of most business, but depressed armpits like this kept no clocks and never slept.

His eyes were sharp but still required two drive-by passes to see the small numbers scratched above a particular screen door. A by-the-hour no-tell. Behind the brown-streaked windows, a twitchy clerk's feet were propped on a grungy desk while he basked in the blue glow of an older-model television.

Midas left the car around the corner, setting the alarm but also giving a twelve-year-old dealer a hundred bucks to keep an eye on it, promising a hundred more if it were still there when he got back. The kid smiled like the old pro he already was.

The almighty dollar was still the currency of choice.

Behind the buildings was an alley, fetid and destroyed. Deep within crouched a well-hidden steel door with a rusted-out lock. He slipped inside, mindful it didn't slam behind him. He waited as his eyes adjusted to the dim gauze of a dank hallway stretching into more darkness, then stepped silently over discarded bottles, vials, hypes, and gum wrappers. Several feet beyond, the smelly tunnel opened into the soulless lobby he'd seen from the street. The TV was blaring. The amp freak behind the desk jerked to unheard music, resting in a battle-scarred office chair missing three of four wheels.

Midas moved forward without notice, grabbing two exposed burner phones perched near the clerk's feet. He leaned in to block his line of sight.

"What room?" Midas demanded, his voice sinking into the peeling walls.

The deskman's junkie tics were permanent, a quivering upper lip housing a smile of broken brown teeth, a jagged rack that required effort to showcase. His right eye was a drooping, broken marble taking measure of the balding, light-skinned black man confronting him. "Excuse me?" His mumble was topped with the attitude of someone protected, his English passable.

Midas nodded, making a fist and popping him just below the nose. The tweaker was lighter than a sixth grader, his bones already beginning to degrade. The force sent him over the back of his chair into the wall. He scrambled into a fetal position, seeking refuge. Pain would come later if he ever came down.

For the moment he was less defiant, surrendering his fading machismo to properly measure his uninvited guest. "You need a bed? For you and a lovely *mamacita*?" Attempted charm.

"Last chance," Midas said. "What room?"

Fifteen seconds later he was taking the stairs in silent leaps to the third floor. His friend in the lobby would sleep for about an hour and fight one hell of a headache when he woke up, though with all the shit in his system, he probably wouldn't appreciate it.

From above, the top landing loomed. Midas slowed to a crawl, regulating his breathing. The higher floor offered extra light, easier to maneuver but likely housing more eyes. These were apparently the best of this dump's accommodations, nothing more than oppressive hotboxes with plywood doors. Laughter and small screams drifted in unison with the decadent odor of drugstore perfume, baby powder, and sweaty sex.

The number he'd been given was at the far end, next to another filthy stairwell resting beneath more greasy windows, ones that likely hadn't ushered in fresh air in a century. The door holding the number was slightly cracked open, spewing patter from a televised soccer game. Excitable announcers and crowd noise were almost loud enough to cover an undertone of labored breathing.

Squatting down, he widened the opening of the door a methodical half inch, slowly placing a portion of his head into the sliver of sight.

Within the glare of a flat screen sat a man on a rickety cane chair with a frayed armrest, one hand holding the local sports page, the other cradling a cigarette. Dime-sized freckles of blood dotted his exposed chest and thighs. The rest of his torso strained against a leopard-print Speedo. A 10 mm Sig rested at his feet.

Whoever was having breathing issues, it wasn't this ape.

Midas leaned back, then violently slammed forward, splintering the door while rolling low into the room. In a flash he saw Serena on the bed, naked and broken. Then he was on his feet.

Dropping his cigarette, the minder snarled and reached for his gun just before Midas's jackhammer to the top of his well-moussed black mane scrambled his senses. He sprawled face down on the floor, stunned and useless. An instantaneous accounting told Midas there was no one else.

The commotion had done nothing to unsettle Serena, lying motionless on the grubby mattress, her breathing unnatural. The scrapes and bruises between her legs looked raw. Three infected needle marks sat fresh below her biceps. An odd assortment of purplish abrasions painted her arms and stomach, a few tinging toward yellow.

She had clearly suffered for several days.

Midas pulled a stained sheet up from under her feet, covering what he could. Her face was a mass of calculated destruction. One side had imploded, taking out an eye socket. The other, somehow still functional, measured him without recognition. Ketamine, if he had to guess. Matted hair stuck to the sides of her face, glued with a blackening layer of blood and dry sweat.

Rage and helplessness sliced into his gut. He forced it back down.

Minutes later the worthless guard sat pitched in front of a rancid bathroom toilet, hands and feet trussed behind his back with a pair of zips. With little resistance, Midas took hold of his head, using the gun barrel and enough crushing force to pry the guard's unwilling mouth wide open against the edge of the stained commode.

"Bite down on the bowl, or I'll snap your ankles."

Capitulation followed without protest. Gold teeth clicking against the porcelain. Breathing came heavily through a nose that had seen its share of fractures. He tried once to move his head, only to have his teeth painfully pushed back into submission with a thunderous slap.

"One question," Midas said. "When you boys were taking turns, was Kyle Palmer in the room?"

A shudder of hesitation. Even lower-level expendables were schooled in the dangers of giving up their bosses. The friends-and-family plan had entirely different connotations this side of the border.

Midas grabbed a handful of coarse hair, jerking hard enough to tear follicles from the scalp moorings. He followed with a sharp toe to the balls, the leopard-skin underwear quivering with the force.

The guard squelched out a meager scream chased with a garbled, guttural response. "He was the first one."

Midas instantly released his pressure, and the wounded man's neck dropped, his chapped mouth only too glad to reconnect with the smooth chill of the toilet. Beyond the diminished squabble from the televised match, all else went silent. The guard was too terrified to take his eye off anything but the gamy smears inside the bowl, no doubt briefly allowing himself to hope the worst was past.

Midas slammed his foot down on the back of the guard's scalp. The sharp *crack* could have been the bowl giving way, or sinuses breaking apart. Blood flooded from his face, draining in twin rivers through the jagged crevice of his battered mouth and the pulp above it. He slid to the floor, his forehead smashing against the dirty tiles, hog-tied hands and feet frozen and useless. Mounting pain brought him to the edge of unconsciousness.

Through the cloudy rage in Midas's mind came a metallic *click*, mushy and drawn out. Then a shallow *pop*. Fresh misery sprang to the guard's eyes. He gave in and gratefully passed out.

Midas stood above him before opening his phone. "Need you to meet me in the parking lot of that diner. Three hours."

Somewhere near San Clemente, Serena's disoriented head rose from the back seat of the car.

Midas watched in the rearview as she pawed at her wounded face with a swollen hand, then jerking it away as if on fire, still well under the effects of the drugs.

The freeway sliding past them in a blur, she leaned as far forward as she could, not trusting her own balance. Weighted words fell on his neck.

"Is that you?" she asked, shaky and wary.

"It's me, kiddo."

She tried to focus on him but was clearly lost. "What happened?"

"Talk about it later. Just lie back down and rest."

His words took a moment to register before she retreated onto the seat, pulling her knees up and turning to one side. Her good eye fluttered, then closed.

The sun was coming up. Daybreak. Normally the best time to wash away the sludge of a dirty night.

But what was normal, anyway?

CHAPTER 2

LOS ANGELES, TWO NIGHTS LATER

AS LOS ANGELES SHERIFF'S Department Homicide Detective Natalie Riiska drove through the misty shadows and chilly embrace of a heavy morning fog, the slippery darkness momentarily transported her back to her childhood in Iceland, a country cold in a different way. She'd taken the job with the LASD because of the cliché promising 330 days of sunshine—a game breaker considering a mere six months a year of sunlight was the norm in her native land. Los Angeles living was far from ideal, though she'd grown into it, even welcoming rare nights such as this, frigid dampness and all.

Her destination was just ahead, barely visible beyond the fog-shrouded swirling red and blue lights of local police cruisers.

An orange-and-white box functioned as the guardhouse. Inside stood a rent-a-cop projecting authority under a nondescript hat wrapped with a clear, rain-flecked, plastic baggie. He leaned out to check her windshield cred, and waved her SUV through the reinforced black gate. Narcissists were beyond predictable living behind their reinforced barriers—the modern version of castles, minus the moats. Then again, the Pacific Ocean sort of counted as a moat. A lot of good their security had done these two victims.

Pulling forward, she joined the crowd, veering right on a tight gravel road and passing several other official-looking vehicles. The crime-scene estate rose from the wispy clouds and shadows looking like a fortress from a Du Maurier novel.

Somewhere inside this two-story faux French stucco chateau was a pair of brothers in their early forties. Apparently quite dead.

Natalie maneuvered to a far corner off the circular driveway. An uptight asshole she recognized from the governor's office was holding a heated one-sided conversation with two overweight men. One was another state flunky intent on maintaining relevance while ungracefully hopping in place, moisture flying from the tassels of his ruined loafers. The other was her boss.

Bastard could have swung by and picked her up, she figured, though her comfort zones were likely not on his current list of concerns.

This scene was a Red Ball—what law enforcement types called situations of such magnitude that various agencies and departments were called out, each measuring dicks and fighting for turf.

Given their profile, these two deceased vics rated such a response.

She set the brake and popped the door, gratefully taking a long pull of the salty sea air after the stuffy warmth of the SUV. The wind slapped, stinging and unrelenting. Something else that reminded her of home.

Her boss, Captain Jay Brown, moved gingerly over the slick cobblestones in her direction. He'd been her superior at the South

City LASD for four years. Over that period, she'd helplessly watched him face-plant at crime scenes more than once due to an abundance of weight above his equator and an ankle crippled from an old football injury that had robbed his joint of strength and adhesion. Two competing shades of red and yellow rendered his hair an office joke, though tonight only a few loose sprigs were visible under the department-issue baseball cap. It took some effort for him to reach her, stepping around the oily pitfalls like a seasoned pro. All the same, she knew he was glad it was her catching tonight instead of one of the office burnouts.

"If you fall, there's zero chance I can pick you up," she said.

Jay's husky face widened, his blue eyes dancing and momentarily softer. "Screw you, Detective." He mimicked giving her a backhand, consciously widening his stance in deference to the rain and instability. He was an original, one of the few people in this pandering city she didn't register an angry desire to silence with a screwdriver through the forehead.

"So, why us? Out here, no less?" she asked.

Natalie lived to the south near Hermosa Beach, where she'd learned to read sounds in the surf, even when, like tonight, she couldn't see it. The roaring churn told her these guys frolicked inside walls only a few yards from the water. Or, they used to.

Serious Jay returned. "The Basmajian brothers are quasi celebrities, rating a substantial law enforcement presence. More to the point, this house is right on the county line between Malibu and Ventura. Making it part LASD and part Ventura PD—at least until we get waved off. Lost Hills Division is deferring to us on this one, being as we have the homicide staff and manpower."

In other words, the jurisdictional pissing contest was well underway.

She took a beat to appreciate the excess of scurrying humanity all vying to plant little yellow flags in some fragment of the embryonic investigation. And all answering to demanding, khaki-wearing little wizards with lanyards from Sacramento—FBI from the Westwood Federal Building, and God only knew where else. Along with most authority, Natalie also had issues with the town's endless pecking orders. Big-presence celebrities, B- and C-listers, social media influencers, and just plain trolls. Not to mention the publicists and personal assistants, all hanging on to what they could of diminishing status and credibility.

"You sure we'll get yanked?" she asked.

"More like downgraded. The younger of these two stiffs ran his own cabal. Pals with the mayor, governor, senators, congressional gimps, and other DC stooges. He'd been helping fund their campaign chests for years with clean money from real estate, malls, a few TV stations. Though the worst-kept secret in this county was where most of his family's coin comes from—big brother has been one of the country's most prolific smut kings since his twentieth birthday. From what I'm told, it's a very dirty enterprise. Which for us translates into nasty secrets the string pullers will want to keep hushed up."

"Political careers financed on the back of tit magazines?" she muttered, whimsy laced with disgust. "Tinseltown version of the Boston Bulgers."

"Which is why I want to get eyeballs on it all before we get the Heisman," he said.

She looked at him questioningly, pretending not to understand.

Jay groaned. "Do I have to explain everything to you? Before we get the stiff-arm. You really are a Nordic Philistine." She appreciated their never-ending jousts as much as his inevitable red-faced frustration. "You should know what the Heisman is. You've been in this country for years, and your boyfriend runs a goddamn sports bar."

On cue, she struck the iconic trophy pose, leg raised and bent into a right angle below a sideways lean.

Jay smiled, shaking his head with exasperation. "You're lucky I like you, though I'm constantly asking myself why."

A redwood-sized tube of jungle-green plastic tarp rolled by, shrinking and eventually flattening out between a pair of the dozen manicured hedges bordering the winding driveway. Someone was looking out for the bureaucrats, laying down a temporary path over the treacherous slippery stones.

Jay took the opportunity to make his move for the front door. She followed, marching past a pair of midsix-figure sports cars, metallic paint gleaming from their hoods under beaded rain. From a distance, the front door could have been a moody maroon, but within a few feet it focused into what it was—solid oak and fire-engine red. An English touch common to the glassy McMansions dotting the coastal beach communities.

Natalie was well versed in Jay's game mode, being focused on what he knew would be a shrinking window of opportunity.

She scampered to keep up. "Do we know anything?" she asked, welcoming dry refuge on the expansive porch.

"Only that there was no forced entry," he said.

A buttoned-up patrolman stood next to the bright door, showcasing the sleepy look cops are schooled to present when handed a menial task. His spine went rigid as they approached, his shiny shoes squeaking under a swift reapportionment of weight, visibly recoiling when Jay's six two, 260-pound figure stopped squarely in front of him.

"I'm Captain Brown, LASD. This is Homicide Detective Natalie Riiska."

They signed in, and she handed back the clipboard. "Pronounced *Reeska*," she said when the officer frowned at her name.

He grunted and quickly waved them in.

Considering how their fortune had been nurtured, the Basmajian brothers' home was tastefully understated. *Home and Garden* with no hint of new or dirty money. White walls, beachy watercolors, and polished pine banisters harmonized above gray marble floors. High ceilings hovered over the spacious entryway. Hardwood stairs wound upward from the middle of the atrium on both sides like great wings taking flight.

Jay picked the right and took the stairs two at a time. Natalie stayed behind on his flank. He still moved reasonably well when necessary. They passed an ocean-facing window only a few feet smaller than a stadium screen. Outside and beyond the double-paned glass lingered the dark sky and muscular precipitation. Beyond, the Pacific churned invisibly against the black night. On normal days it was a view likely worth several million all on its own. Though aesthetics and wonders of nature held no magic for Jay. He ignored the impressive architecture while leaning instead into a hard right toward the commotion and flashes coming from the second-floor family area.

Natalie followed, finding herself in another room that could have comfortably fit a good-sized wedding party. For now, it housed only two bodies, along with some fifteen cops, various other suits, a pair of forensics teams, handlers, and a half-dozen others who'd talked their way into the crime scene.

Her first impression was how peaceful the tableau appeared. The taller deceased sat on a puffy white sofa, his arm resting comfortably on an end table. His chin had dropped onto the top of his stomach, covering half the letters on a designer T-shirt. Had he been in better shape, the posture might have suggested a ballet dancer in a preroutine stretch.

To his right sat his brother, rigidly perched in the recess of a matching plush chair, gripping a TV remote the size of a cheese board between outstretched legs. He was apparently the older by two years. His head was slung back, Adam's apple jutting toward the ceiling like an anthill. The black stubble on his face was ragged and looked like scattered coffee grounds. They'd been watching a ninety-two-inch flat screen mounted on a wall built to take such an obnoxious size in stride. The TV was still on, the sound muted, and it wasn't family viewing. A woman was swinging a large dildo from a studded harness around her naked waist.

"Turn that shit off," Jay ordered, wincing at Natalie in apology.

Two uniforms jumped forward, grabbing a second remote from the surface of a small chest hidden under a lamp table. They punched several buttons with no result, finally moving to stand in front of the screen to cover what they could.

Natalie smiled, letting them know she appreciated the unnecessary gallantry.

Heavy clear plastic had been dropped to create temporary aisles around the brothers, preventing contamination of the scene. She followed one behind the couch, standing just above the defining grimace frozen on the older brother's face. His entry wound was dead center, an inch above the prominent black unibrow. There was no spatter, only a dime-sized hole fringed with a sticky circle of red. The floor and nearby bookcases also held no evidence of spray or residue.

"Could be a 22. Hard to know for sure until we get them on

the table." This from one of the FBI crime techs who was dusting for prints while also studying Natalie for her appraisal. He was grinning. Hoping to loosen the mood.

Natalie refrained from rolling her eyes. She was thinking 9mm but thought better of quibbling as she moved around to the front of the couch.

"Same with this one." The tech was ignoring Jay and giving her a guided tour. He placed a gloved index finger between the younger brother's drooped chin and stomach, tilting the face up. The forehead sported the same death mark, along with the same grainy transparency across the eyes. Above the lip sat an immaculate and undisturbed Fu Manchu. His smile included two racks of veneers, suggesting little brother had never seen it coming or had assumed he could bullshit his way past fate. This one had taken a moderate amount of pride in his appearance, the ratty T-shirt above his belt notwithstanding.

Natalie shifted focus to the third side of the furniture, arranged like a squared horseshoe. There could have been a slight depression in the cushion at the far end, though it was hard to tell. Custom pieces such as this were made to hold shape and snap back. Aesthetic appeal versus old-fashioned comfort. There were no visible footprints or scuffs on the hardwood beneath the plastic runners.

There wouldn't be much else to gather tonight. Too many hands and swaths of red tape, both expanding by the minute. On the way out, she surveyed the ground floor from the top of the stairs. Vast and colder than a church rotunda.

Outside, the rain was slowing to a heavy mist. She flipped up the padded collar of her department windbreaker, pulling the zipper to her throat.

Jay wasn't as prim, jacket hanging open and his fire-hazard tie snapping in the wind. "Well?" he asked.

"No struggle or signs of distress," she said. "Maybe they were all acquainted."

"And an opulent man cave, no question. What else?"

"The tech said possibly a 22, but my guess would be a 9. No evidence of the shooter standing that close, and a 22 will start to wander beyond a few feet. They were both hit dead center, so you gotta figure he pulled off both shots in about a second and a half. With extremely soft ammo to keep the mess to a minimum."

"Why would he care about a mess?" Jay asked.

"I don't know." She shrugged against the chill. "Maybe he didn't. But that kind of load? It's custom. You know what those things do inside a skull—marble in a pickle jar, inflicting serious intracranial damage, then fizzing out but rarely exiting. Harder to get decent ballistics. Or at least a quick read."

"You're all Icelandic heart. So, the shooter pops over, they watch some skin flicks, and then he decorates them both with a third eye? Pretty cool customer. It's plausible, at least."

Natalie was more interested in what she hadn't seen. "You notice there was no help around the house? No muscle?" She paused. "No girls either, which seems strange."

"Because along with their politically tinged philanthropic endeavors," Jay said, "they were also well-heeled deviants?"

She laughed. "Lotta syllables there, boss."

"I try." Jay chewed his lip, a tell when he was working through something. "But you're right. It doesn't make sense. Guys like this crave full-time company. Hugh Hefner disease—be seen and be held. Where *were* the women? Or considering their tastes, the makeshift stripper poles? And as you also said, no security? These guys are worth half a billion conservatively."

"And all their porn is legal?" she asked.

"What we know of is. I assume they wash the other cash through their numerous legits." He stopped. "Hold on." His expression turned reproachful, developed over years of playing the voice of sanity to the theories of underlings.

"What?" She asked.

He stared hard through the rain into her face. "You think these assholes might have had something to do with those Westside underground streamers?"

A few months back, LAPD had taken down an exclusive supper club in Santa Monica, one requiring word-of-mouth recommendations as well as a six-figure buy-in. Underneath the posh tables had come the discovery of a vaulted underground basement, complete with dirty mattresses, belts, chains, and rows of private viewing rooms. The warrants had come based on a tip from an angry personal assistant recently fired from the inner sanctum of a top studio producer—one whose name was well known these days following numerous sexual-harassment suits. One of the producer's three homes had turned up tapes, and behind that, the net had rapidly expanded, exposing several other so-called upstanders with their own, grimy diddle rooms. Even by hardened-cop standards, the entire cache had been wrenchingly horrific. Girls and boys abused and worked over in a multitude of inhuman, fetish-seeking filth.

Natalie's stomach clenched at the memory. Sex crimes were part of her earlier resume as a detective constable in London. She was no stranger to base brutality. But when it came to these children, each video was its own unique, soul-destroying spectacle. Death on tape for amusement. *Hunger Games* for pederasts.

Could this be connected?

"Maybe," she said, shuddering as she mentally returned. "If these Armenian freaks were a left coast hookup for the skin trade, they likely had serious partners. And steel-clad protection. Stands to reason they might at least have run in the same circles."

"It's ironclad, you vulgarian. And be careful dropping the references. Armenian gangs stick together and hate outsiders."

"Making them unique from the Russians, cartels, and our own gangs, how, exactly?"

"Don't get snide. We've got to stay ahead on this. Who knows what will shake out? You've got plenty to keep you occupied for the next few days." Jay turned to head back to his car. "Go home and get a few hours. I'll see you later at the shop."

As he trudged off, she opened her mouth to remind him about sticking to the tarp, but it was already too late. His black boots caught one of the mossy-wet cobblestones, and just like that, her boss was horizontal, suspended for an instant like an actor on wires in a martial-arts movie. He thudded to the ground, his back and tailbone taking the brunt in a heap of expelled air and profanity . . . less concerned with bruising than the possibility of someone bearing witness. He rolled onto his stomach and slowly pushed himself up and off the ground, his face glowing an extra shade of red.

Normal coloring returned when he realized no one had seen the flop. No one of note, anyway.

Natalie waited a few beats, then clapped with a chuckle, holding up seven fingers. "Decent execution but a nonstick landing."

Jay returned only one digit, suppressing an embarrassed grin as he made his way more carefully to the car, like a bulbous general carrying too many meals through an active minefield.

Several miles and lifestyles from the beach, a nondescript club nestled within the cheesy glitz and pasty do-over of the new-age Hollywood.

Kyle Palmer had started small, accessing dwindling family funds to scoop up a few decrepit properties when they could be stolen for nothing more than a smidge of green grease to the zoning department. Years later, he'd sold his piece of the block to a Chinese chain bankrolling luxury hotels. He'd worked a sweet deal, retaining a cavernous structure off a side street that would become one of the more lucrative and exclusive nightspots in the area. Nothing more to the naked eye than an address with an unmarked black metal door . . . and famous for what wasn't on menus. Kyle had traded up well, having a gift for sensing the future. Ten years earlier, those savvy skills had marked him as invaluable to his idiot father and his gaggle of assorted, white-collar pansies.

These days Kyle was a true CEO running a sheltered empire. The exclusive Hollywood club was only a minuscule contributor to his overall bottom line. But it remained his favorite possession.

The massive space felt roomier without the hypnotic lights and patrons. Glossy hardwood bars and racks of colored bottles bordered both sides of the open floor plan. Tables were scattered, none larger than a pizza pan. Nestled in the corners was a handful of booths. Black carpeting bordered a shiny obsidian dance floor that was laid out below an empty screen suspended on a far wall. Generations ago the place had been an elegant movie house. These days Kyle ran his own flicks, though nothing the Garbo crowd would have approved of. At least not publicly.

Conor Brennan ran all this through his mind as he walked into the frigid club.

On a corner stool near one of the bars perched Jojo Boudreaux, nursing a bottle of water while perusing the *Wall Street Journal*. Hillbilly with a portfolio. His tightly shorn hair was pitching gray at the sides. The fitted black thermal and baggy Levi's could have cataloged him as Russian muscle, but Jojo was all southern boy. Ex-army ranger, and for the last several years lead hammer in Kyle's stable of nutcrackers. He nodded listlessly as Conor walked past.

Owing to his need for grandeur, Kyle sat in an elevated, out-of-the-way booth, toys strewn over the lacquer—coffee mints and three cell phones, not counting the one he held to his ear. The expression was familiar, a child not getting what he wanted and plotting to make it happen anyway. He waved Conor to the bench opposite him, continuing an animated, one-sided diatribe before finally snapping the phone shut.

"How was Rome, Con? Didn't do any clothes shopping, I see."

Kyle never tired of pointing out his clothes were handmade, one of many compensations for his limp and crooked spine—the handiwork of an old acquaintance a few years back. Conor's jeans, T-shirt, and leather bomber jacket—his normal attire—would forever be a sartorial affront. Usually, he'd return a sneering verbal volley. Kyle was, after all, an angry toad doubling as a vindictive boss. A greasy, porn-peddling sack of shit.

But he also held the stripes within the unit.

"There were ITA airline tickets under my door at five a.m.," Conor muttered.

"Coach, I trust. Wasn't about to spring for your nondiscrimi-nating taste to fly twelve hours in business class." Kyle's grin was challenging. He was clearly feeling comfortable, making him that much more unpredictable.

Conor waited, stretching out a few long seconds. Finally, he asked, "Are you out of your pebble-sized mind?"

"No need to get personal." Sweat appeared under Kyle's skull-short cut, which clung to his head like a wig made from dying grass.

"So this was all . . . what? A lesson in impersonal temerity?"

"Always the poet, Con. I am sorry about ruining your vacation." Kyle moved his phones to one side of the table, leaning in while dabbing his sweaty forehead with a starched cloth napkin. How much had that navy button-up silk shirt with the mandarin collar set him back? Probably not as much as the plush slacks or grain-leather loafers. Like his patrician father—a serious broker within the Fort Meade merry-go-round—Kyle was sheathed with a genetic sense of how money should present. The same father who'd placed his son—the diminutive and soft pretty boy with too much time and cruel ideas for amusing himself—into the Unit's orbit. None of them, including Old Man DeMarco, the Unit's rabbi, had been given an option. Kyle's daddy had appeared one day all those years ago with a bagful of chits from DC's white-marble bureaucracy, and Kyle's placement had become a done deal.

"Con," Kyle said, drawing his attention back to the present. "Anything else we should be talking about? Pleasant conversation has never been your forte."

"Or subtlety yours."

"Touché."

Conor sensed a shift in energy, a presence on the move. Any audience with Kyle came with required theatrics, mostly in the form of his able-bodied stuntmen. Jojo was smart, tough, and capable. His counterpart—the overmuscled slab waiting silently in the opposite corner—not so much. Though both were well trained enough to know this was an opportune moment to shorten the distance to Conor. Each took a chair just behind him. Breathing set pieces to be seen and feared, seldom consulted. Earned or not, Kyle had the authority, and was out to settle a long-standing debt. Pushing him too far at this point wouldn't end well.

"It didn't need to happen like this." Conor heard his own fatigue.

"Sure it did." Kyle's tone slipped to acid. "It was inevitable." The last three words he spat out with reptilian hiss.

Conor felt his patience vanish. He wouldn't crawl, not now, and not to this asshole. "You should be proud, Kyle," he said. "Finally got your ball rolling. Though it was a puss move waiting until the Old Man's hooked up to a vent and roomful of chemo bags and I'm off the books in Europe." He snorted. "Who sanctioned? Anyone? Still Daddy's dirty-faced little urchin?"

Kyle shifted uncomfortably. "Fathers and sons, Conor. None of our tribe needs lessons there, eh?"

Conor clamped his jaw. "I suppose not."

A carbonation tank somewhere under the bar let go of a low whistle. No one paid any attention. Or moved.

"Indulge me," Kyle said. "All those moons ago in Mexico City. You ever wish you'd done a bit more to rein him in?"

"Which answer do you want?"

"Just the truth. Minus the tainted reflection. I don't have the energy for one of your sermons."

"Nothing wrong with a bit of reflection," Conor said. "But as to your question. No. I wish he had finished what he started. But he didn't believe in that."

Kyle's head bobbed in time with a throaty rumble that built into a howl and bounced off the club's tempered walls.

Conor looked behind him. Jojo wasn't smiling. Then again, he and his backup weren't directing this production.

"We are talking about the *Snow Leopard*?" Kyle said between bursts of firecracker sputters.

Conor allowed himself another brief mental fantasy . . . of jumping across the table's smooth surface. He pushed it away. This wasn't the time for emotional stupidity. "We never developed your taste for . . . final solutions," Conor said.

"Saintly pricks. And yet, here you are. And I've always wondered how he came to have that nickname. *the Snow Leopard.*"

"DeMarco. Allegedly it came from his teenage years. I really don't know why, and I've never asked. I do know he doesn't like people using it."

Kyle rolled this around for a moment. "All your buddies left the nest with that old fuck's blessing. But not you. Not charismatic Con. Why not?"

It was a real question, as it had been for the past five years. One with no decent answer. Even for Conor.

Midas and Mason had immigrated to Hermosa Beach to set up their bar and Mason's gym. Phillip Gillis had gone to the Palisades to move his well-layered accounts around and play with his kids.

The migraine over Conor's right eye had started flaring again, a holdover from no sleep and the long flight from Rome. The Valium had burned off. The debilitating pain was returning with force, roaring through his brain without restraint.

Jojo materialized at his side, reading signs he knew well, placing a bottle of water in front of him. Conor nodded thanks, which took some effort. His vision had reduced to pixels of blood-red film.

"Co-nor?" Kyle chirped, moving his squatty, gator forearms onto the table, the buffed surface flushing fog beneath redirected heat. "I'm talking now as a friend . . . which I realize is the wrong terminology, but who gives a shit?" He paused for a response.

Conor gave him nothing.

"Maybe you don't have the stomach for what happens next? That's okay with me and the bow ties back East. Why not start in on some of your own well-deserved, *permanent* rest? Expand your model-train emporium?" Kyle's words lingered as if spoken from another room or transmitted from a scratchy old radio.

Conor's skull thumped like a kettledrum. "I need to see this through." His own voice was damp, battling with what sounded like a torrent of roaring water in his head.

Kyle's open palm smashed onto the table with a deafening *crack*, blasting Conor's head with a new shade of heated color. Lights began to fade. "Want some Excedrin?" Kyle was clearly enjoying his moment.

Conor squinted through murkiness and film scratch. "Do it again, we might have a problem."

Jojo fidgeted off-camera. A warning, as if anyone needed reminding.

"No time for tiffs, Con. We've got to deal with our problem."

"*Your* problem."

"If you say so. But here we are. The genie's not jumping back in the bottle. You heard about my associates out in Malibu?"

Conor had been off the grid on a plane and hadn't heard anything. He slurped a slug of water, gently using both thumbs to rub his pulsating temples. "Why the girl, Kyle? Why Serena? Even your douche-weasel father and his candy-ass friends wouldn't have the stomach for that. Why not pistols at dawn? Or a cage fight? Hell, you could have had Jojo pick him off from a sand dune while he was surfing. It's not like he's been hiding. Instead, you kidnap and *brutalize* his girlfriend? A civilian, no less? Where's the sport in that?"

Kyle's mood and patience were often measured by the endurance of his surgically rebuilt legs, and he'd been sitting too long. Conor knew all his tells. The familiar ache was likely beginning its ascent, radiating through his lower spine while taking hostage of his moderately good humor.

Kyle waved a hand. "I'll leave hypocrisy and guilt to you Catholics. I have no doubt, given the option, an honorable sort like the *Snow Leopard* would have served himself up, even to me. But we're way beyond that now."

"I won't be able to talk him down."

Kyle methodically straightened his legs under the table. "I'm counting on it."

Conor slid from the booth, zipping his jacket. "You deserved worse."

"Someday you may get to address that. Or I'll simply adjust *your* attitude."

"I'm counting on it," Conor replied.

Kyle's lip twitched into a cruel smile, his neck jerking a dismissal. Conor backed away, not sure what to expect. Jojo casually pulling his 45 mm and dotting him a few times through the sternum? Maybe an unseen shadow player stepping out to halt his roll with a blade across the throat? Scenarios that made as much sense as anything else the past few days.

He reached the door without resistance. No surprises.

At least not today.

As the lock *click*ed and Conor moved back into the swirling fog of a dreary Hollywood afternoon, another door opened inside the club. The woman had watched the entire meeting from behind the one-way tint of the DJ cage. She slipped into the booth, kissing Kyle gently on his warm, flushed cheek.

"How much of a problem will he be?"

Kyle's eyes remained on the path Conor Brennan had just taken, as if there were a method of predicting motivation from carbon footprints.

"Time will tell."

The artery tracing most of the California coast was known as the Pacific Coast Highway. In the sunny and cheerful city of Hermosa Beach, the PCH moved farther inland and away from the sand, serving as the small municipality's main drag.

Midas maneuvered his under-the-radar Honda Accord in front of a new sushi joint that had only recently replaced a laundromat. A couple of kids whistled by on skateboards, all elbows, knee-length shorts, and tees touting bands he'd never heard of. Their only submission to February were the hoodies tied around the short boards under their arms. Balance and fashion most primitive.

He headed to a modest two-story building a few blocks to the south.

On the ground floor of Mason's gym were weights, machines, and heavy bags, with two regulation-sized rings nestled at the rear. Upstairs, in spite of the owner's dismissiveness—*"If you're gonna ride you should do it outside, and get somewhere"*—were three rows of gleaming silver spin bikes. Along with two rows of ellipticals and treadmills, a Pilates den, and a yoga room. Mason was decidedly nonconformist, sticking to a steady diet of boxing, resistance training, and extended road-cycling sessions. He'd groused about the new-age forms of fitness, but eventually bent to the steady money generated by those trendy and fickle followers who preferred sweating while getting screamed at by vacuum-packed instructors during overmodulated workouts.

The gym was in early a.m. bustle mode as Midas stepped inside. Clarion *dings* measured the bookends of timed rounds and *pinged* over the *snap*-patter and snare-drum rhythm of jabs finding padded mitts. The gym's manager was Carlo—a Muslim Spanish-Syrian hybrid, the orphan of parents butchered along with thousands of others by Assad's ethnic cleansing. He was dancing inside one of the rings, jerking targets above his shoulders for a first-time client, a new student embarking on hard lessons.

Mason James had been Carlo's first and only trainer, and now his employer. An army veteran and former mercenary, Carlo was extremely efficient with his hands, though he would never be on a level with the boss, whose fists could be brutal and far more lethal.

Midas found Mase lounging in his small rear office scowling at the morning paper. Being a holdout about that too, he still preferred the archaic print edition. His cluttered workspace featured three high-end road bikes sitting in a corner. Midas knew two others sat in his friend's garage at home. None weighed more than sixteen pounds. Mason was in his midforties, though with his build and blond hair, passed for younger. Friends calling him Mase was one of the few things that didn't seem to annoy him.

"Any coffee?" Midas asked from the doorway.

Mase scowled behind an eye roll. He hated stupid questions.

The steaming, stained pot was perched on a square table beside a box of Everlast hand wraps. Three glass mugs were neatly arranged on a pristine dish towel. Mase was a fiend about cleanliness and java, not necessarily in that order. His beans were the pride of an old friend's roasting house, specially shipped from Oregon.

Midas poured a cup and headed out through the back door.

The parking lot behind the gym was more of a narrow street with a few painted parking spaces, a portion of which had recently been converted to an outdoor dining area. Settling into one of the wobbly plastic chairs, he popped his retro Pumas onto the surface of an equally shaky table. White mist wafted from his cup before vanishing into the low fog hovering from the beach. It was, he had to admit, superb coffee.

Two of life's greater gifts, he told himself—caffeine and the ocean. Momentarily pushing aside more troubling thoughts.

The door flipped open and Mase emerged, setting his cup down while eyeing Midas's reclining feet. "You know I eat here," he said, frowning when Midas extended a middle finger.

Mase spread his sports page, ignoring the insult.

"How's Natalie?" Midas asked.

Questions, on the other hand . . .

"All right. I guess," Mase replied, unable to mask a slightly defensive tonal downturn, a habit he'd nurtured through years of muting emotional octaves. "Last night she got called out to Malibu on a homicide. Two titans of the porn industry. Brothers, apparently. Armenians. Friends of the mayor and shit. All over the local news this morning."

Midas felt a cold shard of ice pierce his stomach. He was momentarily stunned and did all he could to freeze his face into an oblivious expression. "I heard something about that," he casually replied.

Mase's eyes rose momentarily above the paper's banner. He must have sensed something, but left it alone. "And speaking of last night . . . as well as the past week and a half. What gives?" Mase was watching him closely but kept it light. "I seem to be the only one pulling duty these days at *our* bar. Not that I'm surprised. When real work is required, you become the invisible bastard. Like those damn Christmas tree lots when we were kids and forced into physical slavery."

The reference had the intended effect. The rickety table shook as Midas laughed at the shared memory. "What the hell made you remember that? You and your revisionist memory. Never accurate, but amusing just the same."

"Accurate, my ass," Mase said, hiding a small smile behind the paper. "What's to remember? I did all the work and was sore for days. Not to mention being grossly underpaid."

"The grown-ups did take their cut," Midas agreed.

"Fuck them, treating me like some damn coolie," Mase said, picking up steam, half-angry even while trying himself not to laugh. "And fuck you too, watching me sweat while you charmed the polyester off ample-assed, middle-aged moms."

"We all have our strengths. Yours is hardheaded manual labor, while I prefer charm."

So many years ago, their adolescent salad days in the San Francisco Bay Area.

Their fathers had rented an abandoned field near the racetrack with a scheme to convert it into the most abundant seasonal tree lot in the city's east bay. Midas and Mase had been typical renegade teenagers, smart-assed retorts and cynicism never out of reach. Both of them had been drafted for the escapade, under no illusions about what it all meant. Honest work, they'd been told, knowing better.

"Bastards," Mase said, as always unaware of the look that came across his face at the mention of his father, Max, a capable womanizer and professional rogue whose sixty-plus years were a Valentine to shadiness, scams, and when necessary, meting out attitude adjustments. How, as a youngster, the very white Maxwell James had fallen in with Midas's Black father and uncle would forever be a cosmic puzzle. And whatever Max had undertaken to prove himself their invaluable associate over the past several decades would also never be worthy of polite discussion. But the association had bonded the two families for life. Midas and Mase exhibit A.

"Our clans," Mase muttered. "Living testaments to ebony-and-ivory synergy."

"Some Berkeley liberal you are," Midas muttered back. When it came to the ethereal temperaments of Mason James, Midas knew distance and humor were the safe play.

The women who stepped up and into Mase's life were usually game and smitten, at least initially willing to overlook his intensity, moodiness, and lack of patience. His physical presentation, fitness, blond hair, and blue eyes held a generational sway of natural attraction. But Mase had never learned to relax, a downfall when relationships began to mature beyond the pandering stage. Many women had fallen for him, only to slip away quietly when the self-doubt and sadness eventually, inevitably, emerged.

Maybe Natalie would prove different. Then again, she was a cop, and by definition better off avoiding anyone outside the profession.

"How's Serena?" Mase asked, his voice soft and almost lost under the distant surf.

Midas sighed. "About as well as can be expected."

Mase would know better than to push. What had happened to Serena in Mexico was just the opening blast in a long-overdue dance, which, given circumstances and the sheer numbers at Kyle's disposal, would no doubt end badly. He was grateful to steal a few tranquil moments with his oldest friend, but he knew the storm was coming, and he wasn't sure they were still equipped to offer serious resistance. They'd been out of the Unit for five years. Skills such as theirs atrophied within a more sedate life.

"Well," Mase said, changing the subject again. "Because you've been MIA, I had to make an executive decision. I hired the kid for the door gig."

"Everyone loves him," Midas said, unperturbed.

"You only like that he surfs."

"I've tolerated people for much less. You, for instance."

Mase ignored the pithiness. "We were going over his routine. He had only one question."

"Let me guess . . ."

Mase leaned back too fast in the cheap Target chair, then shot forward to grab the edge of the table and avoid tipping over. After steadying himself, he ran a hand through his hair, taking his time. As always, relishing the moment.

"Yup," Mase said. "The kid wanted to know who the hell would saddle their offspring with a name like Midas."

CHAPTER 3

THE PLEASANTLY LUSH PASADENA foothills did nothing to dampen the storm in Midas's head.

Given the Basmajians' high profile and associations, and the fact they'd lived on the line between two counties, he'd assumed the feds would have taken over immediately. But LA Sheriff's Homicide? And Natalie somehow in the mix?

So fucking careless. The planning of an amateur. And a mistake he wasn't sure he'd be able to maneuver out of. All of his own making.

Somewhere along the line, Midas knew he'd gone soft.

Tijuana had stunned him, the severity of Serena's torture poking cruel mockery of his once methodically calculated judgment. Though there was no functioning playbook for such debts, he'd nevertheless been careless in naïvely assuming that when Kyle's bill came due, Midas would be the one called to the window. Him alone. Serena had allowed him to occasionally stand down from the baked-in vigilance of the past several years and imagine himself resting in an elusive long-abandoned desire for a more peaceful existence, even if he knew better than to trust such fantasies.

For a man like him, self-doubt remained lethal.

After the incident in Mexico, there had followed a self-induced sabbatical, along with a nasty struggle of attrition with his ex-flame Michelle, and finally the reckoning with Serena. His unyielding hard-bitten code had begun to fatally waver. Punishing himself over the methods of his self-defined nature.

Mase had called it a reckoning, while Conor had trotted out zen mumbo jumbo about the soul's stages of reinvention. Differing shades of the same unwanted insight from those he trusted, all volunteers in the same shitty club. Midas remained skeptical of neurotic self-analysis but had come to understand and appreciate time and distance for what they were—distractions. A four-corner stall. Mental hard drives could never be wiped clean. Normality was a myth, and existence was management of circumstance, nothing more.

Some were just better at evasion.

Still, Serena had been a tragic miscalculation. His latest failure, now on vivid display.

Halfway up a twisting tree-lined street, his destination came into view as the white antebellum-inspired home rose tastefully behind ornate, green steel gates. A few miles below were a few of Pasadena's rougher neighborhoods. But this was La Cañada Flintridge, where safety and angelic views were included with the property taxes. Surrounding the perimeter was a ten-foot-high fence, deterring unwanted visitors, curiosity, and gawking.

Midas punched the lone button on the driveway keypad. A slight whir from an invisible lens scanned his face. One side of the gate opened. He pulled the car inside, rolling slowly over the circular drive's pavement. His casual scan failed to pinpoint anyone on duty, though he knew there were at least three sets of eyes on him. Carlo had brought in some of his security to help, and Midas appreciated their value. He parked the car between a pair of marble columns, a match for the stairs and porch.

Dr. Julian Burgos slipped out the front door to usher him inside, dapper in dark jeans and a light green sweater.

Midas had been here several times and always felt as if he were entering a crypt. Clinical off-white coloring and the ever-present hum of air conditioning that ran whether it was needed or not. Inside, the walls supported a litany of black-and-white photographs of deserted streets from some of the world's most cherished cities. Burgos was a decent photographer but had made his reputation as a serious surgeon, one who'd done his share of rule bending and medical carpetbagging. He'd continued to occasionally work with the Unit well after Midas, Mase, and Phillip had been voluntarily retired. Yet it was Midas he'd asked to salvage his son, Alexander, a few years back from a San Bernardino meth house—an extraction that had turned into what the Brits liked to call a *nasty piece of business*.

"How's Alex doing?" Midas asked.

"Better. Back at Stanford." The doctor's comforting tenor complemented his attire. He could have moonlighted in commercial voice-over work and made a fortune.

Burgos led him toward the remodeled kitchen. Two glass mugs sat like disgraced orphans on an oversize island of black granite. He poured coffee, pushing one toward Midas, knowing better than to offer sugar.

"Glad to hear it," Midas offered.

"Even his mother is happy," Burgos said. "As always, I can't thank—"

Midas raised his hand, never comfortable with gratitude. "No need."

Burgos's smile shifted. "Then again, in his world, every day is a new temptation."

They talked freely for a few minutes, about the Lakers and anything else except the added security hidden around the house. Or the woman upstairs.

Midas stared through the French doors into the leafy backyard. "Tell me what I need to know."

More coffee was poured. Burgos pulled a chair and sat down at a small breakfast table in a corner, motioning for Midas to sit. "I'm afraid it's nothing you want to hear."

"Didn't expect it to be."

"You're no stranger to this. Physically, she's healing well. She's young and healthy, in great shape. All that surfing you're teaching her, I suppose."

Midas waited silently.

"No one ever comes back the same," Burgos said. "I'm not sure how extensive her injuries will turn out to be. At this moment, I can't say with any confidence she'll fully recover, at least not in a meaningful way."

Midas closed his eyes . . . as if darkness could make it any easier. He tried to shift his thoughts and recall better days. Serena the student shrink developing her couch-side manner on the boorish, entitled pricks who tried to get over on her at the bar. Mama's boys to whom beauty and conquest qualified as mutually inclusive birthrights. She had been overly polite and gracious, never wavering in her belief that even jerks possessed some glimmer of decency. Midas had never had the heart to set her straight, and now he wished he had. As if such cynicism would have made it easier for her to process what she'd endured.

What a grasping, inert fraud he'd become.

He opened his eyes, fixing on a decorative bench in the lush yard.

"We don't understand mental trauma nearly as well as we'd like to think." Burgos's voice sliced through the momentary serenity. "Certain incidents can be blocked by the mind but are rarely excised, and almost never from the subconscious, where suffering and grief are stored when not front and center. Serena doesn't remember much of anything from those five days. She's struggling to make sense of what feels to her like a fuzzy black hole. Her long-term memory is much stronger. She does understand, in a clinical sense, that she was raped and brutalized. But nothing much beyond. She's mentioned a few things, Spanish-language television, the crunching sound of candy wrappers. Other than that, she's a blank. I'm hopeful she'll be able to work through it. The drugs they used on her were inhuman."

"Maybe it would be better if she didn't get it all back," Midas said, witness to his own weakness and desperation.

Burgos seemed to recognize the protective default mechanism. He shook his head. "In the long term, that would be devastating. Pieces will continue to return. The only question is when. It could take a week, or years. Either way, she'll need real help identifying and processing those memories, and once there, who knows how she'll respond? But to ignore them would be to sentence her to a long and eventually fatal decline. Her memory will prove to be both savior and demon."

Outside the glass doors, Santa Ana winds shifted the ivy cling-

ing to the high perimeter walls. Midas caught occasional movement from the garden. The guards were as stealth as any he'd ever
known, but none was better than their boss, Carlo.

Carlo was a formidable ally, but even with weapons such as him
in the quiver, Kyle's strength was superior. Serena had just been a
flare.

"Can I see her?" Midas asked.

"She's been asking for you since the first night. It wasn't my
choice to keep you from her, but it was necessary. She needs to
begin remembering and healing, away from all she knows. She'll
need more surgery on her face. We addressed the immediate issues
and cleaned the deeper lacerations. She didn't lose the eye, but
the bones around it were badly damaged. It's a tricky procedure,
but we've access to discreet, talented people. The rest of it you already know. Pelvic displacement and genital trauma. Eventually,
she shouldn't limp, but for now she's a one-year-old learning how
to balance and take steps. Muscle memory should come back relatively quickly, though not without pain. And there's the broken
wrist. She'll have the cast for another six weeks or so."

The doctor had delivered Serena's prognosis as dispassionate-
ly as possible. Even so, Midas felt a new hole of despair spread
like dirty oil inside his chest. He'd always shunned the religious
and other such apologists as feeble-minded followers, desperate to
make sense of lousy timing, bad luck, and the generally unexplainable. But something about the law of averages, and even Conor's
insufferable nods to karma, were striking Midas with a strange
sort of sense of . . . what? Fate?

His failure was so unforgivable a million Hail Marys would
never atone for it.

"She's upstairs," Burgos said. "She prefers the room in back with a view of the yard and the mountains. Talk with her as if it's just another day, catch her up on light subjects. Anything else has to be something she brings up. She's very fond of you, and I don't expect that will ever change. But at some point there will be anger, and it will be severe. However, we're nowhere near there yet. So, be what you used to be. That's what she needs most."

Serena was in an old rocker near the window.

She flinched when she saw Midas standing in the doorway, then strained against the armrests to push herself up. Swaying against the unsteadiness, she placed the flat of her hand over the extended windowsill. Her broken smile went through him like razor wire.

Reading his eyes, she lowered her chin. "I'm kind of a mess."

"Not at all." There was a noticeable crack in his voice.

Hers had been remarkably clear.

Bringing her head back up took effort. A crooked grin tried to hide her broken teeth. The gentle slope of her cheek was now a lopsided dent, a lumpy tangle of swollen tissue and mangled bones. She brushed around her bad eye with a bandaged hand, the swelling obscuring its striking blue hue. She studied him now as though from within a murky well.

He stepped forward, his hands raised to imply no threat, before carefully and gently putting his arms around her. She jerked at his touch but didn't resist. It took a few moments before she began to relax. Muscle memory superseding judgment.

He helped her back into the rocker. The room was as heavy as southern summer humidity.

"How's the bar?" she asked.

"Fine. Someone always needs another beer, right?" He studied her as unobtrusively as he could.

"I miss it."

"It's not going anywhere. Whenever you're ready."

"When's that going to be?"

"Not sure," he said honestly.

She worked that over mentally, concentrating on the jumble that had become her new process. "What about school?" she finally asked. "I had papers coming due. I'll probably have to repeat those courses."

"Heal up first, then we'll worry about all that."

The room's air held the faintest trace of lilac and vanilla. A small candle had been lit on a nearby desk.

"Will I heal up?" she asked. The blue in her eye went dark, her tone one he'd never heard before.

Defeat.

"You will," he assured her, regretting the slight hesitation in his voice.

"You don't sound very convincing."

"I'm just a little sad. I'm not supposed to say that, but you know me too well."

"Do I?" Defiance wrapped with edge.

Her gaze drifted back to him from the pleasant wonders outside. It was too intense, even with the sagging face and broken eye.

He looked away, once again the shy kid in elementary school that Mase had protected until he'd become the boy no one needed to look after. But in front of her now, he was seven years old again. Frozen with guilt.

"It's not your fault," she said, softening in the presence of his unease, reading his mind. The anger and judgment he deserved from her would have to wait. Serena the pragmatist had returned, the conflict resolver. It was her nature.

Emotional muscle memory.

"It was *all* my fault," he said. "At some point, you will need that clarity to bring yourself back."

"Back to what?"

Questions with no answers were better left alone. "Just rest. You're safe here."

"You've always been a . . . capable man with serious friends. Probably assumed I never noticed."

"It will never happen again, I swear to you. Never. Carlo and his men are keeping an eye on you when I can't be here."

"*Serious* friends," she repeated, talking more to herself. A tear materialized and rolled down the pristine side of her face. She bowed her head forward and began to cry.

He moved behind the chair, wrapping his arms tenderly around her.

"I remember going out to get coffee, and then nothing till I woke up here. It's like someone just erased those days," she said on a soft sob.

"You'll get there. I promise."

Now he was a liar, too.

Natalie was leaning over the front deck's railing when Mason arrived home, her blue-black hair obstructing most of her face. An unusual color for an Icelander, which she'd told him was thanks to her mother being half-Welsh. From her father she'd been given a regally carved Nordic nose, along with long, strong hands, which tonight she was rubbing vigorously to keep the circulation going against the frigid bite.

As Mason approached, she took deep drags of the briny chill, fully in sync with the low rumble of the night surf. She had her own key, but sometimes preferred to unwind outside, even in the winter months.

After dropping his small gym bag, he pulled her hair back to one side to admire the deep jade green of her eyes and the long elegance of her neck, brushing his lips lightly below the frames of her black glasses. He found them complementary for her face, if somewhat severe.

She was, he had to admit, an alluring and jumbled package. Sharp intelligence waging a ceaseless battle with a personality that hated being front and center despite standing way past with a serious figure and cheekbones. Even so, she was a different species from the typical LA crowd.

Unlike him, she was not particularly athletic, though in her downtime loose shorts, she'd easily pass as a lanky ex-soccer player. Still, Natalie was way past the silly shoreside bunnies selling all they had to offer atop one-gear beach cruisers or in-line skates, vacuum-packed leggings, and sports-bra neuroticism trumping comfort.

"How're ya doing, slugger?" he asked.

Her thoughts were clearly elsewhere, floating out above the turbulent Pacific. He could read her tension, coiled like piano wire under the fitted navy blue blouse. He gave her hip a slight squeeze, sensing the energy subsiding as her shoulders slowly began to relax.

She turned his way with an expression of troubled hesitation.

"You got a glass of wine for me?"

There was little about Mason's Craftsman bungalow that shouted "home." A couch and pair of easy chairs facing the wall-mounted flat screen, a small coffee table, and a few bookshelves tucked near the sliding glass. The diminutive kitchen was functional but lacked the space and versatility now so revered thanks to home-improvement shows. Tonight, its only testament to the living was the breathing bottle of Sonoma red perched on the counter, one sure to be empty before long. Natalie had once said his neatness sometimes bordered on ADD.

"I am always impressed by your lack of clutter," she said, her floor-to-ceiling legs folded to the side of an overstuffed leather chair. Mason was staring at the curve of her knee, hidden under the sweats she'd changed into, bought online at some depot for the tall and slim. "Hello? Can I help you?" she asked playfully. He seemed as distant as she felt.

"Sorry." He laughed.

"I was saying," she continued, "you don't have much . . . stuff in here. At home, I can barely find my coffee cup." In that way, they were opposites.

Mason was on the adjoining couch, his feet resting on the low table and parted just enough to see the silent NBA highlights on ESPN. By way of compromise, the satellite radio was tuned to a schmaltzy station they both enjoyed.

"I'm not a sheriff's detective," he replied. "Only keep what I need."

"It looks transient." She took a sip of her wine. "Planning a quick getaway?"

"No decent place will have me."

She smiled, shifting for better position, and drifted toward the uneasy state she occupied when contemplating work problems away from the office. "I told you about this case I landed? The Basmajian brothers?"

"You went radio silent for a few days, so I figured you were chasing it down. That where you went on that midnight disappearance a few nights back?"

"Not as far as you know." Natalie hated rules, as he did, especially ones that said don't talk about open cases outside the chain, even with those you trusted, and even if he were no ordinary civilian. "You should have seen their spread," she said. "Back balcony hanging over the edge of an infinity pool. Ocean fifty feet away. Breaks so loud I wonder how they ever slept." The contrast was what had prompted her earlier comparison with his place.

"And it's your case?"

"As far as Sheriff's Homicide is concerned. But likely only for the moment, given locational geometry. Their home was right on the Malibu County line. We'll be sharing with a few other interlopers and jurisdictions before the feds steal it outright."

"Doesn't the FBI have better things to do than investigate a pair of high-profile porn slugs?"

She took a sip of the pinot and closed her eyes, not bothering to ask how he was always so well informed. Such questions resulted only in shutdowns and sullenness.

"Officially these two were well-heeled benefactors of various super PACs across the country. Think the Koch brothers, only this duo washed their dirty enterprise cash through political contributions, funneling big donations into various shells and other such portals. All legal. They've funded a fair number of careers, and because of that banked a serious vault of favors."

"And unofficially?"

She gave him a "you're-not-cleared" smirk. He said nothing and waited. She found his instinct and perception unnerving at times.

"Premier League-level smut kings. Beyond the normal degenerate fare, they've been quietly running more . . . *intense* material for years. I have no hard facts yet, but I'm pretty sure they were the bondage-and-torture pipeline to some well-heeled patrons. Tightly connected and disturbed individuals. These two got their skulls perforated with—what's that term you American tough guys love? Extreme prejudice? Very efficiently, I might add. By the time I got there the other night, maybe four hours after the deed, the squat-suited jurisdictional assholes were already on hand in serious numbers."

"Somebody's worried," Mason said, surmising.

"Several somebodies," she replied. "A pal in LAPD vice is convinced these guys had been bankrolling even harder stuff. Nothing they've ever been able to prove, of course. No lack of sick fucks into that sort of thing. But as you said, whoever did business with them has to be squirming."

"So," Mason ventured. "The usual suspects? Rich old white guys and God-squadding politicians taking their fetishes out on vulnerable kids?"

"You're talking to a lapsed Protestant," she said.

"No such thing."

She smiled. "It's a theory. One I'm sure I'll never get the chance to chase. Too many friends, favors, and Trumpian-level kompromat. Fear-induced lockjaw."

The wine was working. She moved to join him on the couch,

stretching her legs across his lap. She wasn't much of a drinker. On a few occasions, she'd battled through vodka-induced self-examinations of guilt and depression, though random enough not to be of concern. On nights like tonight when she felt like slowing down and giving in, red wine went down easier.

"All those vulnerable, scared runaways," Mason said, not bothering to hide his disgust. "Missing and then just gone. They've always been a target-rich environment for these reptiles. You'd think with all the advancements in mood therapy and technology, we'd be better at controlling those venal impulses."

She rested her head into the crook of his neck. Since he'd brought it up . . . "So who kept a tough guy like you from running away young? And on the righteous path?"

"No one," he said, looking a bit jolted a bit by the question. "I was a massive pain in the ass who drove my parents up the walls. Not that they hadn't had it coming."

She felt it was always too easy for Mason to dwell on his faults. Badly hardwired . . . much too young. "How so?"

She was vaguely surprised when he answered. "They split when I was a toddler. So my father's infrequent appearances. My mother's lifelong disappointment and distance. My stepfather's feeble attempts at bullying a young and angry teenager into line." He chuckled humorlessly. "One night I gave him a physical dusting that left the bastard dazed. One of my many defiant outbursts that my mother would never forgive."

Natalie didn't know what to say to that, so she remained silent.

"I didn't need much looking after," he said finally, the words sounding hollow and unfortunate. "And of course there was Midas. He was always around, and we kind of watched out for each other." He looked at her with a weak grin.

She smiled, not surprised as much by the revelation as the candor. She knew better than to reach deeper. This was their shorthand. Well-rehearsed evasions of sensitive whitewater.

"And how is our Midas?" she asked, her voice starting to dance gently, thanks to the wine.

"Fine," Mason said. "Just this morning he was saying you deserve someone better suited to your needs and overall welfare. I'm sure he thinks you'd be better off with him."

She giggled, catching a drift of perfume, recently applied, as she never wore it around the office trogs. "He is sexy," she said just to annoy him. It didn't work.

He grinned. "On that, I have no opinion. But I will admit it's hard to be around you two, chirping like a pair of yentas at a yard sale."

She turned her body into him, snaking one arm behind his neck as the other found his back, and burrowed a knee between his legs as she tightened her hold. "It's a shame, really," she playfully whispered. "I've always liked him more than you."

A flush crept through him. She loved reducing him to a fumbling kid on his first date.

"Everyone does," he murmured.

Natalie was sleeping on her side, hands together between her head and pillow. Her slightly twisted mouth hinted at a pleasant dream, while the moist glow of her skin bore evidence to the recent rigorousness of their needs. The sloping hips were an understated complement to the long, smooth legs, which she worked frequently with kickboxing and cardio runs through the sand.

Mason savored these moments, keeping watch and silently breathing in the predawn stillness. Overseer. It was one thing he could admit he did well.

He softly pulled the blanket up just below her chin.

Despite his light touch, her eyes fluttered open, momentarily disoriented, followed by a yawning, loopy grin. "Hey, you." Her voice was slumber low, relaxed. "How are you?"

He cursed himself for waking her up. And as her question hung in silence, his serenity began to shift.

First came the smoldering spasm of vulnerability rolling out to suffocate him with a brutal blackflash. These *fucking* incidents were happening with more frequency—dark, stealthy calling cards, attacking without warning, consideration, or restraint. His chest swelled violently, forcing him to sit up. He struggled to breathe, jagged colors invading his vision.

"Mason? What's the matter?"

He could barely hear her voice under the volcanic slamming his ears. There was no reason for these episodes. No trigger he'd ever been able to identify.

"Nothing," he croaked, knowing the only remedy was riding it out.

Then, just as rapidly as his airway had been assaulted, it engaged, gratefully refilling his lungs. He took a few moments to concentrate on his breathing while the heat in his head began to dissipate.

"Bad dream," he eventually muttered, unconvincingly.

She reached for his hand. "Tell me." Sometimes she could make it all sound so easy.

Yet there was no safe harbor for what he couldn't comprehend. Why, at seemingly calm and non-threatening moments he could be ambushed by looming anxiety and fear. Followed by untethered despair and shame.

What would she make of the faces that hid right under his eyelids, those with no future, smeared in masks of death? Features with black-bottomed eyes, from another time, that should have dissipated long ago like fine sea mist over the beach. The faces were appearing with more frequency, and beginning to reach beyond his tortured dreams. An arthritic old woman walking a dog, or even a young child at the park consumed with the singular joy of a favorite toy or swing. Innocuous images packed with disguised emotional triggers that could bring him to his knees. Buried reflections materializing with greater momentum and stronger footholds, always invading at inopportune moments. Taking him back to those years and events. Forcing him to live it all again.

As if he would ever forget.

"I wish I could," he said to her, knowing it wasn't good enough. How long before she tired of his sullenness and walked away to something better? As they all did . . .

The predawn darkness filtered through murky shadows with pale shades of silver. His heart was still working more than usual in his sweating chest.

He lay back down, turning to put his arms under her back and pull her tightly toward him, a gesture so consuming she began to weep, her weightless tears splashing off his shoulder. He could sense her wanting to offer reassurance, while not trusting herself to know what to do or say.

Sometime later, the room's shadows began to lift. His body had calmed, but his mind remained a morass of disoriented liability. Real solutions would never exist, and Natalie couldn't be expected to help carry his weight. As far as their life together was concerned, his intractability would never be healthy, even if it were necessary for self-preservation. If she ever learned about those years with the Unit, she'd have no choice but to walk away. Meaning silence and shame remained the best of a few lousy alternatives.

Though despite it all, he couldn't handle the thought of losing her, this woman he adored but would never deserve.

CHAPTER 4

AS USUAL, NATALIE HAD risen early, using cold and then scalding water to slowly bring her senses to full power. Stepping out of Mason's shower, she was pleasantly surprised by the mug of coffee on the marble vanity, its aroma curling through the condensation and steam. Someone had put it there. She'd been concentrating on her day, hearing nothing beyond the force of the needle spray. *Some detective.* She grabbed the cup and headed to the kitchen.

Three newspapers were laid out on the functional island next to a plate of egg whites and wheat toast. Not many read newspapers these days in print form. Mason had been a freelance journalist for years and couldn't break the habit. As usual, he'd vanished early for a bike ride or ring work, leaving her a protein-rich breakfast—serious cycling food, he'd once assured her, having never gotten over a morning at her place when he'd witnessed her down an oversize bowl of Fruit Loops.

She was also pleasantly surprised to find Midas standing by the sliding doors nursing his coffee while trying to spot waves out behind the fog. She hadn't been sure he'd received her summoning text. They gave each other a quick hug. He'd brought her a gift, a greasy bag filled with apple turnovers from Rosa's, the best bakery this side of Venice Beach. She reached inside, smiling a crooked line of guilt.

"I won't tell if you don't," Midas said. "I mean, who can eat the shit he leaves out for you?"

She returned a short laugh. "If I have to hear about food being fuel one more time, I might just slap him."

Midas nodded approvingly.

"Thanks for coming," she said.

"Anything for you."

She took a large bite, an instantaneous jolt warming her mouth as the cinnamon-and-apple goo worked its magic, a sensation so rich it made her tingle. She usually avoided sugar. After the momentary gratification, it dulled the thought process. But this decadence was worth it.

"It's getting worse for him," she said, wiping her lips.

Midas shifted, turning to pick up one of the newspapers and casually scanning without comprehension. Like Mason, he was one of the most reserved and mystifying men she'd ever come across. Taller than Mason by a few inches, but more angular with firm hands and a toned physique. He presented more sprinter than surfer, a seamless build of long muscle and nerves, perfect for clothes. His face was dominated by polished, linear dimensions, deep bronze like the rest of his hairless scalp. High cheeks and a forgiving smile. The eyes a little less so, deep brown and restless.

"Not sleeping again?" he asked.

"He won't talk about it."

He dropped the paper and turned to wash out his cup. "I imagine he can't."

"Why?"

"I couldn't say."

You could. But you won't. "He talks to you," she said.

"Never about this."

She moved a few steps into the living room, thought better of it, and returned to the kitchen island.

Midas was watching her. He innately understood that she and Mason were tethered by something beyond normal needs, at times as skittish and unpredictable as the currents.

"But you do understand," she stated, hearing her patience begin to slip.

Because Midas knew all. His wariness and scars might have been better hidden than Mason's, but they still cast their own imposing shadows.

"What happened to all of you?" she asked, probing. "You don't have to protect me. I'm in the business, remember? And under no illusions about either one of you."

No, Midas thought. *You really can't imagine, just as I can never know where you've been, or what you've seen.* Talking was a treacherous ordeal, exposing old truths beyond the controlled protection of memory.

With events now in motion, Midas also knew his habits and rituals would have to be amended. Kyle was a rabid dog. His taste for blood would not spare anyone who happened to be in the way, and the collateral damage could frag his friends, upending Midas's hope of a gentler existence for two people he cherished. He had to leave Natalie and Mason as far outside the cocoon as possible. Even if one wouldn't allow it, and the other was too tenacious to back away.

"I'm sorry," Midas said. "I really am."

She squeezed his upper arm. He flinched with the contact. "I know you are," she said. "But that won't help him. Or me." She brushed her lips across his cheek, gathering her bag and keys.

The door shut silently in her wake.

Meetings with the stripes were bad enough, but to have them this early was a big *Fuck you* to actual working cops. But Jay Brown had been insistent in his text. Thankfully Natalie worked out of Torrance, which was relatively close to the beach. Driving anywhere in LA was a punitive exercise, so any short commute was a golden ticket.

The sheriffs' South LA outpost was a two-story affair of shabby, washed-out bricks the pallor of dried blood, which was why it stood out somewhat in the heavily industrial area. She parked in an assigned space, adjusted her glasses, and headed in through a side door. The main bullpen was a dingy open-concept room. Empty at this hour. Most of the morning shift would still be down the block at the local grease pit splattering hash browns with watery condiments.

Natalie's father had loved large breakfasts. Once they'd settled in London, he'd taken her every Saturday morning to a favorite spot outside Soho, where a former Yank merchant marine had been running a moderate diner since the early eighties. Back then, she'd gulped her scrambled eggs, bacon, and toast, finishing with a pile of hash browns slopped in ketchup. Her father would frequently point out that she ate like a cabdriver.

These days, she avoided diners.

"Detective Riiska?" The distant grumble smacked of overdue reports and three decades of distrust. She walked to the end of a narrow set of partitions, leaning through the last doorframe.

"Boss?"

Jay glanced up, momentarily softening before catching himself and resummoning the hardened edge. Several years back, when agility was still within reach, he'd gained local notoriety chasing a serial killer through eight blocks of a government welfare dump outside Hawaiian Gardens, one of many downtrodden LA County unincorporated pits the sheriffs still patrolled. This particular gift to the species had raped and killed five suburban housewives. The foot pursuit had ended with a precell-phone-and-body-camera beating, turning several of the perp's organs into a soupy mess.

Jay had been canonized while his collar had taken a month to heal in county jail. He had then wisely parlayed his brief notoriety to climb over less adequate deputies in an ascent up the department's ladder, the only negative being that a life ascribed to overseeing schedules and mostly out of the field tasks had been an excuse to let himself go. Somehow, half of his hair remained as ginger copper as it had been during his glory days as a defensive lineman at Birmingham High out in the San Fernando Valley. The rest had faded to a blondish white. Overall, it presented as a disaster, as did his tan slacks, forty-four-inch waist, a light blue button-down shirt ample enough to cover the Redondo Pier, and a skinny striped tie that looked like a desk ruler, dangling below the folds around his collar. He didn't seem to care about any of it, or the peaks and valleys of his hardened gut.

It went without saying Natalie loved him.

"Grab some coffee and come on in," he said, avoiding eye contact while searching for a paper clip.

She had a good idea why she'd been summoned at this ungodly hour: Dooley Dolan, colleague and office shithole.

A few days earlier he'd put her front and center for one of his "goes," bullying jokes acted out for his cadre of washed-up hangers-on. A load of burnouts reduced to cackling, paycheck-stealing prairie dogs. Sexist pricks who hadn't been worthy of traffic stops, much less pension matches, at least not since the days of Rodney King. Dooley approached his jesting seriously, and when she ignored him without proper deference to his stale sense of humor, he'd asked snidely, "Are we having a *napkin day*, Detective Risky?"

The menstrual reference combined with his clever, deliberate mispronunciation of her name had elicited a fresh stream of nervous howling and grunts from his geek chorus.

She'd smiled politely before delivering a left hook into his rib cage. Dooley had taken an immediate knee, staring blades through his red eyes as the minions helped him back to his desk. He had convalesced the rest of the day, trying to remember how to breathe without pain. Natalie had chided herself for losing control but had also been moderately proud. She'd shown a lack of dignified etiquette, but at least her weekend sessions with Carlo were finally paying off.

The only downside was that Dooley had decided continuing to call her Detective Risky was a well-deserved punishment. She had a feeling the name would stick.

With her coffee secured, she backed inside Jay's small office, choosing the less splintered of two rattan chairs. His workspace—an American HR term she despised—smelled like stale tea and wintergreen Life Savers. She placed the mug on the end of his desk.

He gave it a quick look before returning to the open folder in front of him. "How are we doing with the brothers? How the hell do you say their names?"

"BAZ-may-gee-an," she said, pronouncing the surname.

"Where are we, Detective?"

"Their place was secluded for a reason," she began. "All we have so far are the slugs, pretty beaten after dancing around in their skulls. No hidden footprints, tire marks, nothing. Shooter must have parked elsewhere and hopped the gate. Though there's no sign of any such activity. So far, a ghost."

Jay brought his head up, either to study her more intensely with his cloudy pale eyes or to feign intimidation. One of their little games.

"Maybe he rang at the gate and was let in?" he suggested.

"Possibly. But there is no video, no trace, no security logs. And it was howling that night. Certainly a pro."

"You sure it's one person?" Jay leaned back, letting the loose stomach below his sinking chest spread between the armrests.

"No. Just feels that way."

"Instincts honed from those ice-hut natives in your ancestral tree?"

It was her turn to smile. "Beyond all that, we've got nothing."

He spun in his chair, an act requiring some effort, and fixated on the parking lot outside his inadequate window. "I got a call this morning. Five a.m. Take a guess who it was."

"The FBI?" she said.

He spun back, mouth pushed forward like a frowning clown.

"Bravo, Detective. These freaks peddled their smut nation-wide and probably beyond the borders. It seems they had serious friends, and their bankables financed some big hitters. I know you know all this, but indulge me. Naturally, the mandarins in DC don't want anything too compromising to filter out. Name-brand clientele and all that. I'm talking Heidi Fleiss times ten. Draw your own conclusions. But it means the feds are gonna be up our ass stealing any part of this for themselves. Play nice, but keep 'em at a distance. I want our hands to stay in it."

The pressure on him to back off she figured had likely started even before they'd rolled to the scene.

Jay put his hands behind his head and leaned back, projecting toward the ceiling and suspending his surprisingly small feet on the edge of his desk. "They're already talking mistreated local gangs, cartel retribution, or even a possible serial. Though at this point it's only the one scene. That we know about, anyway."

Natalie shook her head unconsciously, searching through her thoughts. "Skin peddlers with compromising pics and black books? Clipped the way they were? Doesn't play like a serial. The other theories make more sense."

"I think so to. Keep at it. And keep the other locals in the loop as well. We're all pretending we've got equal rights here. But they'll help to keep the feds off our back."

She got up, only to be halted at the door.

"Detective Riiska?"

She'd been so close to an escape.

"Dolan's a prick. And an aging pussy. You're in much better shape. So try to stay above it. He didn't file a report. No matter what you think, that was him doing you a solid."

"Okay, boss."

"Now get the fuck out."

Natalie poured another cup of coffee before settling into her desk. What she hadn't shared with Jay was a feeling that the killer lived somewhere in her city, owing to his familiarity with the area and terrain on an especially inclement night . . . at least by LA standards. Something about the way they'd come right up on the brothers and done the business. Had to be someone they knew. Possibly a woman? Probably not. Natalie'd had the same thought at the scene. The killings were too precise and clean, lacking any semblance of emotion. That alone would rule out any of the silly girls those two kept around.

Natalie decided she'd play more with that theory later if warranted. Meanwhile, she fiddled with her keyboard, straightening her legs under the desk. Across the room, Dolan had appeared and was trying his material on the new office assistant, a twenty-five-something Latina stuffed into a tight blouse and black pencil skirt. She had one of those figures that would blow up with the first child and likely never come back.

Natalie mentally chastised herself. It was time to grow up and stop letting ingrained insecurities manifest into judgments, especially regarding people she didn't even know.

Dooley caught her glance and grimaced, unconsciously massaging the ribs on his right side.

Hiding a brief smile, she refocused on the file. Why these brothers? And why hit them at such close range? To make a point, of course. Someone with this level of skill could have set up behind the pool house and popped them from distance with much less risk. And what if someone else had been in the house?

She'd have to go deeper into their backgrounds and dirty deeds, see whether anyone out of the ordinary shook out.

Her desk phone buzzed, the little green dot telling her it was an outside line. She picked it up, listening for a few seconds. "Sure. Noon. See you then."

The FBI poaching had begun.

Sunset Boulevard was in late-morning transition, rediscovering its usual pace. The overcast had cleared enough to entice the wannabes to street-side tables, most of which were littered with gourmet coffee, phones, and unread copies of *Variety*—props used for decades to brand themselves as players.

The scene ran in pantomime for Kyle Palmer, who was perched high above on his pricey deck overlooking Sunset Plaza and the sections of the city that still mattered. The low hum of traffic and occasional screeching of custom tires from the valet stands were the only sounds to puncture the otherwise sedate setting. He'd been watching this same play for years, conjuring the ins and outs of every conversation, inflection, and narcissistic twist.

The entertainment industry, like the rest of this plastic city, thrived on materialism and envy. Though bullshit was its lifeblood. Agents and fixers kept the gates manned with double-talk and innuendo. On the legendary street below, promises and favors came

COD, wrapped in phoniness and vapor. Any morsel delivered from a coiffed head with glossy business cards was devoured by the endless congregation of lightweights and nitwits succumbing to hollow promises with relish and faith.

Blow me in my Range Rover and I'll get you that meeting. Which might lead to another encounter, then several more before a dim light would finally flicker inside those pretty, empty heads, male and female. Some would eventually tumble to the sad fact that they were on a hamster wheel of one-way favors, fucking every fat Weinstein creep with his name stenciled on frosted glass and a tower of lousy scripts teetering on his Lucite desk.

The me-too era? Only if a person was stupid enough to get caught.

Kyle had been in this condo for several years and never tired of watching the Hollywood shuffle. Back then, his snotty blue-blooded family had wanted him legit and presentable, no distaste, no risk of scratching the old name. His father had demanded it, knowing Kyle lacked the decency and necessary patience for the white-shoe chicanery, the inevitable variations of lawn parties, cotillions, and never-ending hoity crap.

Instead, Kyle had discreetly taken a left turn far off the proverbial reservation. Oh, he'd put up with them all, relatives and customers alike, marking his time and planting his flags until he was too far beyond their reach. All the while harboring fantasies of parking a bullet into each of their decrepit domes while banging their daughters and a few of his better-looking cousins. Unfortunately, his minders frowned on his chosen profession, especially old-fuck number one. Daddy Dearest never missed a chance to convey his disgust with Kyle via condescending remarks or off-handed public dress-downs for the amusement of his siblings or company brethren. Pops liked it that way. He got to play the sage, the family's brilliant savior, while the prodigal was left to enhance what was left of the family fortune. Ensuring the favored and more acceptable inbreds remained flush enough to replenish their high thread-count sheets, faggy plaid shorts, and Keds.

Fuck you too, Pops. Relic prick. *One day you'll be dust in the breeze.* Somewhere inside the condo, a bell *pinged.*

Kyle slid the panoramic window closed and limped to the door. Like everything had since that damn night five years ago, it took longer than it should have. One of many things he'd been thinking about lately with more frequency and disgust. Once upon a time in another life, he'd been a point guard at Princeton, shunning the Palmer legacy and those muffler-wearing weenies at Yale. Back then, like now, he'd relished the sight of his father's tight, dime-hole mouth curled into disapproval. Rawlings Palmer had been fond of saying Princeton men were temperamental, while Yale men never allowed themselves to outwardly emote. In the end, his father's outdated horseshit hadn't mattered. Kyle had soon owned his corner of New Jersey along with the perks accorded an Ivy League jock and Palmer scion.

In the years after his salad days, Kyle had built his empire using monetary genius and a bit of Protestant luck to create a new path to fortune and independence. All on his own terms. Back then, the clan's lineage and ownership of textile mills and property had been decaying, as archaic and outdated as his father's loyalty to his arrogant clandestine career at the CIA. Still, the pipe smokers with their tobacco-stained files also held a certain appeal. Meaning Kyle had been savvy enough to obediently take his rightful place within the Agency, even if his motives weren't true-blue. While his father drank aged Scotch in segregated back rooms, Kyle had quietly become parser of his own narrative, shrewd and mockingly efficient. His outside interests were tolerated but never discussed. It had all been moving seamlessly forward . . . until the night of the *incident*. When his father had seen his chance and ruthlessly elbowed Kyle aside to resume leadership, not only of Palmer Group Investments, but also his standing within Langley. His father continued to relish the updated seating chart and his decade-long campaign to clip the wings of his profligate son. Within reason.

The following years and constant physical pain had served only to harden Kyle's mood regarding dismissive attitudes and meddling.

As he opened his front door, he heard the shower spring to life. Michelle rose late, having also become a night owl.

Jojo was standing on the Wipe Your Paws doormat. A joke of sorts, as Kyle had no dog.

His number two raised his head with a weary greeting. The capable fighter he'd recruited out of Camp Lejeune back in the day, a top-flight ranger who'd held no love for the army or its rules. Kyle couldn't, as usual, staunch a twinge of inferiority. He'd put on far too many pounds and Jojo never missed a chance to mockingly surveil his softening physique. Most of the time Kyle let it slide, but this was not one of those days.

"You got something you want to say?" Kyle didn't like rules either. Disrespect was another matter.

Jojo ignored the question, slipping through the doorway, formidable but, considering his frame, light on his feet. He tossed a bag on the coffee table along with a bottle of soda. "They didn't have your pink sludge, so you'll have to survive on plebeian cream cheese."

Snide. Like anyone with such skills reduced to running silly errands.

Jojo shunned the couch and pulled a hard chair from the dining table in the next room. He set himself up in front of CNN on the big screen, pulling the lid from his coffee and swirling in a pair of real sugars.

Kyle peered into the bag, ambling off with a fixed frown to get a knife from the kitchen. He returned and plopped onto the leather couch, offering the open bag to Jojo, who ignored him with a deliberately long drag of coffee. *Snide* and *a prick*.

Kyle fingered a plump onion bagel, breaking it into smaller pieces and smearing the first with an abundance of sticky white goo. "So besides my need of a gastric bypass, what else is wrong today?" He launched the schmear into his mouth.

"Can I just drink my coffee?" Jojo mumbled. "Before Typhoid Mary gets out here?"

Kyle suppressed a smile. "How about you do me a favor and be civil," he said between bites. "I know that doesn't come naturally to an ape, but I'd appreciate it all the same. And I think you know why."

Kyle could imagine what the big man was thinking. He figured his boss was a self-indulgent asshole and liked sticking his dick into a bag of snakes. Nothing else about Michelle Kelly made sense, and *now* it was reckless.

The first bagel was dispensed. Number two was a blueberry-nut mix. Three usually did the trick, at least until midday, when he'd start jonesing for a ham-and-cheddar omelet or a plate of huevos the size of a truck rim. Kyle had adopted the breakfast-any-time bug from Conor, who could eat the meal 24-7. Back when they all were still playing nice in the sandbox.

"We need to figure out our next move," Jojo said, flicking the remote through crime channels and various platforms of ESPN. "No way Midas is done."

"Astute observation. You realize I am capable of tactical thought? On occasion?"

"Then you should have known better," Jojo said, his eyes never leaving the screen, his passive contempt infuriating.

"I may not have sweated my balls off in a North Carolina basic-training swamp or made my bones chasing cutouts in a Mississippi swamp, but I got my ticket punched same as everyone else. You, me, all of 'em. We're physical animals first. It's what we were born to do. What would *you* do to someone who took all that away?"

"I was there," Jojo shot back. "Remember? It was me who got called in to pull you out of Mexico. Doesn't mean I haven't seen things from you that sickened me. But I'm still here, for better or worse. Don't ever question me on that. And Midas is not just any old sort. Mason either."

The chair squeaked as Jojo turned, his glare catching Kyle with his hand near his mouth, the latest morsel suspended. Jojo unnerved him, always had, the only one left in his circle who didn't process fear.

Kyle popped the bite into his mouth.

"You also don't keep me around to rubber-stamp," Jojo continued. "If something feels wrong, I'm going to say so, even if I assume you'll do it anyway." He turned back to the screen, inhaling and slowly letting it go, easing his tension.

Kyle knew there was only so far Jojo would ever be willing to push.

Meanwhile, the rich cheese was making his innards swirl. He shunned the rest of bagel number two and sat back on the couch. He hated his own lack of willpower, the inability to control himself with food or rage, constantly pining for the era of his younger lothario incarnation. Back when he'd been worth looking at. Banging coeds whether they wanted him or not. Eating what he wanted because he'd work it off. Doing whatever he felt like because he was a Palmer. Hell. Maybe he'd become a fossil of the past like his father, burnished and replaced with a lack of self-restraint.

His thoughts shifted back to the present and the woman in the bathroom. He probably disgusted her, too. Thankfully both now had something else to focus on. She needed him. Slovenliness be damned.

As the shower came to an end, Jojo bumped the TV sound up slightly, just enough to keep her out of earshot. "Conor wouldn't show up without an order."

"I didn't reach out," Kyle said. "Despite what I'd have him believe."

"Exactly my point."

"You think . . . ?"

"No. Midas wouldn't involve the old friends. Someone else is in play."

"Who cares? DeMarco is comatose, and Mexico was years ago. Well past time to make it all right." Kyle could hear the strain in his voice, lacking his normal conviction.

"Not like this," Jojo grumbled. "I should have stepped in earlier. The girlfriend was a bad move, and using those Tijuana yokels? Now we've got grumpy cartel hotheads who don't like seeing their guys sacrificed, as well as Midas, that bald, hooded cobra slithering around. All because you wanted to send a message by brutalizing a civilian."

"My call."

"Fine," Jojo said, weariness evident. "Get your Glock and do the ten-paces thing down on the Santa Monica Pier. That we could all respect. Especially him. But this? You've reactivated the Snow Leopard, and he's coming for our fish sticks and lunch money."

"The Basmajians weren't our only source." Kyle was trying to ward off an increasing sense of dread, something that always materialized when he riffed without the benefit of clear thinking.

"True," Jojo said. "But we're beyond simple math now."

The big man was a great soldier because he read scenarios as well as anyone. Kyle might have been rethinking the mess he'd created but not the reasons behind it. He also didn't care about recklessness, because the fallout would never be allowed to land on his porch. Kyle had to admit to himself he'd always been a physical coward, someone who demanded calling the shots but possessed a scared kid's reluctance to engage in true confrontation. Though he hid it well.

"What do you want me to do?" Jojo asked.

Kyle straightened. The browbeating was over. He started in on what was left of his second bagel and cracked open a bottle of Coke with a loud *hiss*, downing half with a long gulp. Breakfast of champions. He burped loudly, giggled, and popped another bite into his mouth.

"All's fair," Kyle said. "Make sure Midas's minions understand. He's on his own island."

"And Mason? You really expect him to watch from the balcony?"

"Hardly." Kyle was expecting that the Leopard's boyhood buddy would also go down with this ship.

Michelle came gliding from the bedroom, robe half-open, trailing a mixture of expensive soap and perfume, then diverting to the kitchen to start her own coffee. She'd been a gymnast in high school and was forever in a hurry. Her blond hair was wet and flipped drops where it hung just above her shoulders.

Kyle studied her. His new squeeze had proved to have several talents and inducements. Though being Midas's former paramour topped the list.

"You boys doing okay?" she called out.

"All good," Kyle said.

Jojo scowled, turning back to the morning news.

CHAPTER 5

MEXICO, FIVE YEARS EARLIER

THE GIRL THEY'D FOUND stashed upstairs at Lupa's hacienda told them her name was Alana, and nothing else.

Midas figured her for about twelve, and except for the empty eyes, could have passed for a few years younger. She sat stoically on the ride back to Mexico City, taking measured sips from the bottle of water clutched between her chipped, painted nails as the dusty streets rolled by.

He sat with her in the rear seat, with Mason slumped shotgun in front trying to keep his eyes shut against constant thumps in the highway. Kyle was driving, occasionally using the rearview mirror to steal a few looks at their passenger, then pulling away when he caught the cold stare from Midas. Kyle's creepiness was well earned. Typical old-money attitudes about everything, especially women. So far, he'd been smart enough to keep his activities to himself during his infrequent assignments with the Unit. Even so, he'd become a nagging source of skepticism for Midas.

Kyle colored outside the lines because he'd been spawned to believe he could. Midas recognized the symptoms. The difference being his own father had refused to favor or spoil his only child. Kyle had run banshee as a young man before ascending into Alphabet City with no talent and nothing more than his name, the latest generational gerrymandering of Palmer tradition.

Rawlings Palmer, the family patriarch, had been trying for years to bury the Old Man, their Unit's CEO, with a combination of gaslighting and underhanded favors owed from grateful influential friends. Palmer senior could never have outwitted or outmaneuvered Jasper DeMarco without that kind of backing. The Unit's effectiveness was a manifestation of his leadership, as well as the cohesiveness, loyalty, and the respect it garnered. Qualities no one of serious note would ever bestow on Palmer senior, his son, or his covey of cronies.

For the past few years, Rawlings Palmer had made no secret of the necessity for his own private squad, one with the operational freedom to run dark-corner ops financially beneficial for him and the rest of his followers. Though when it came to DeMarco, Palmer was well out of his weight class. The Old Man was a superior operator and an Ivy League equal, possessing not only his own crucial pedigree, but also the CV of a fear-lacking warrior who'd seen his share of battlefields and actual action. DeMarco, Midas, and the rest of the originals couldn't help despising Rawlings Palmer and his three deferments.

Like his son, Rawlings had no desire for dangerous situations of any kind—unless viewing black-site torture from a safe distance was on the menu. The Palmers and their ilk shunned the unwritten and rigid code DeMarco and his protégés demanded of themselves, instead preferring bully tactics to heavy lifting and the problems of aftermath. How he'd finally wedged his son inside their elite Unit remained an embarrassment for DeMarco.

Kyle's choice of private enterprise might have disgusted his new colleagues and even members of his own, extended family, but the ambitious son had become invaluable in the restocking of his clan's diminishing finances. Hypocrisy went back burner when it came to keeping those insufferable frauds in high cotton.

Don't ask don't tell had been a Palmer family mantra for a few centuries, well before the term became a PC buzz phrase.

But nothing to be done about it now, Midas mused.

After several hours of spine-crushing, potholed roads, Mexico City appeared through the grime beneath the brutal morning sun.

Back in Guadalajara, flatbeds filled with armed soldiers and bent cops were likely rousting residents. The early thinking on Lupa's demise would focus on rival cartels, giving the team the hours it would need.

Along the western edge of the country's capital city was a fortified community reserved for US diplomats and well-heeled families, boasting good schools, grocery stores, Little League, and all other accoutrements of self-contained, safe living. It also had a small army of US Marines stationed in front of the embassy and throughout the area to keep trained eyes on hardened generations of Yankee gentry, some of whom had been there for decades. Fortunes required nurturing even in the face of potential risk. Those who made the sacrifice were rewarded with shady compensation, tax breaks, and heavily armed security details.

Due to a slowdown in disappearances of foreigners, anxiety had abated over the past several years. The cartels had rewritten their playbook when it came to kidnapping and torture, concentrating now on targets and fear within the poorer local areas and municipalities, where it was easier to distribute and control their addictive, synthetic-laced products.

In the lead car, Conor turned down a tree-lined street and drove through an electric gate. The driveway stretched beside a tasteful ten-thousand-square-foot home, layered in off-white with sturdy beams supporting a second-floor veranda that wound around the entire structure, French Quarter style. The owner was an oil exec with ties to the agency, currently vacationing with his family in Switzerland.

Alana shuddered when Mason opened his door.

Midas carefully took her small hand. "It's okay. This is where we're staying for the night. It's nice and quiet, with a big TV."

She seemed to understand his dodgy Spanish.

The group moved inside, greeted by a pair of fresh recruits off the agency farm helping with support and transportation. Midas walked Alana into the kitchen and scoured the hulking silver refrigerator. Americans and their comforts. He set to making sandwiches with cold cuts and a few fresh tomatoes. There were chips in a pantry next to the stove. One by one the others filtered in, grabbing food and a few beers before heading upstairs for a few hours of downtime. Midas filled a large plate and grabbed a pair of bottled Cokes, walking Alana to the large family room, where another shiny recruit was watching a movie. He handed the remote to Midas and disappeared. Thankfully, there was an overstuffed and comfortable couch.

Midas offered Alana the remote, but she shook her head, so he went through the guide and chose a kids station. The cartoons and their vibrant animation seemed to relax her. She ate slowly, sipping her Coke. He settled back and made fast work of a half sandwich. By then she was asleep, her head tilted against his shoulder. He gently repositioned her so she could stretch out, and covered her with a blanket. He pushed the coffee table away from the couch and stretched out on the floor next to it, closing his eyes.

Later that evening, the team reassembled in a dingy downtown restaurant, sharing the space with a few tourists. Ortiz joined them, along with the two agency minders, but they had a table to themselves off to the side, listening without participation. In contrast to the surroundings and décor, the food was excellent. Near the front, another table housed four drunk revelers growing more boorish by the minute. Ugly Americans was a known species throughout the world, despised and tolerated.

The waitstaff brought Conor's table fresh bottles and left them to it, assured of a decent tip while also intent on keeping some distance from the imposing gringos.

By ten p.m., the other diners had vanished, as had the waiters and cooks. The owner had locked the front door and was sitting at a far table counting the evening's receipts, ignoring the men who remained.

Conor pushed aside the tequila bottles filled with nothing more than ginger ale. "They're still going door-to-door in Guadalajara. It'll take them another couple of days," he said. "Tomorrow morning at sunrise we head out for an airstrip fifteen clicks east. Leave all the toys. Marquez and Ortiz will take care of them. We jump and we're gone. Mexican radar is dodgy at best, and if we're on board and out quickly, it won't be a problem. We'll drop on a private runway outside of Dallas. From there, the usual. Separate cars to DFW Airport and connector flights home. Anything else?"

Midas cracked a fresh bottle of water, pouring a full glass. "The kid comes with us," he said, drinking deliberately.

Mason glared around the silent table, daring anyone to challenge.

Phillip spoke first. "Not a chance, Mide. We're not fucking UNICEF. The minders will get her to the right people."

Midas put his glass down as the air in the room went thin.

Phillip's breathing shortened, his forehead sweating despite the lowered AC. He tried again, taking the authority out of his voice. "You've got a good heart, but it's not what we do."

Conor looked for some sanity from Mason. At the other table, the company boys were silent. Doubtless, they'd heard the stories about this team.

Kyle's eyes darted around, seemingly pleased the adults were fighting. Midas could read his mind. Kyle hated their camaraderie, arrogance, and especially the way they froze him out of decisions and planning. As soon as they got home, he would likely tell his father about the great Snow Leopard ambling off the reservation, and how Phillip had wound himself up like a little bitch.

"We can't do it, Mide," Phillip said, more plea than statement, looking to ease the moment.

On the TV screen over the bar, Brazil and Mexico were playing a friendly. No score in the eighty-sixth minute. Midas had been momentarily distracted by a green-and-yellow-clad Brazilian striker cutting through the defense, before turning his attention back to the table. "You know how I am with regs, Philly."

"And what the hell do we do with her on the other side?" Phillip asked.

"Not your problem. She's on that plane."

Brazil was awarded a corner kick. Shanked it. Mexico's midfielder moved in, scissor kicking the ball away from his goal, players shifting direction to give chase. The announcer's hyperintensity intensified as the seconds clicked off the game clock. Midas had stopped paying attention.

The team stood to leave, tossing American dollars on the tables.

"Whatever you say, Mide." Phillip turned and skulked through the entrance door, slamming it so hard the glass panels almost gave way.

Outside, Kyle and Ortiz took one of the two SUVs, splitting off to go for more drinks. Midas secretly hoped the pair would get rolled in a back alley. Then they could leave the little shit behind and let Daddy send out a rescue party. He and Conor lingered near the entrance to go over a few final details. Mason and Phillip waited outside.

An hour later the SUVs pulled back into the enclave. Low visibility and deserted streets had a habit of darkening perceptions and moods, even in well-tended suburbs. The night after an op required contemplation, a process best managed alone and never discussed.

Later when he'd look back at that night, Midas could never place the moment he'd realized something was off.

It could have been when they'd left the restaurant, or at some point a few minutes later cruising through the deserted streets.

Something had been pulling at his stomach for hours, but he'd chosen to ignore it.

He jumped from the SUV as Conor slowed to make the turn into the driveway. He was up and onto the porch in a few seconds, thudding shoulder first through the reinforced wood of the front door. A brief search revealed what he already knew.

Alana was gone.

His mind went red. Kyle and Ortiz had been too casual about having that final round. How the fuck had he failed to read that?

In the kitchen, the lone company stooge-on-duty was making himself coffee. His eyes went wide as Midas pushed him into a wall, using one hand to brace his neck and cut off his air. The young man choked, flailing with no purpose, recruit training forgotten or momentarily ineffective.

"Where is she?" Midas said.

There was some sputtering and then a few broken sentences. "One of Marquez's crew removed her for relocation an hour ago. Told me it was on Brennan's order."

"And you didn't think to check with us?" Midas released two fingers worth of pressure, which was gratefully accepted with gulps of air.

"Brennan said no interruptions. You were there when he told us that."

So was Kyle, Midas realized, releasing the kid into a useless heap that slumped to the floor. By now Conor and Mason had run into the front hall. Midas passed them in a blur, sprinting outside. They followed, but he was already in the SUV peeling out too fast for any attempt at intervention. Midas hoped they couldn't see him through the opaque shadows of the tint banging his hand against the dashboard.

Beyond moonlighting with American spooks, Marquez and Ortiz had several other dubious sidelines. Among others, they were two of the most prolific pimps in the region. It was why, much like Kyle, the Unit found their services so valuable. The innate ability to ingratiate within circles and communities where men such as Conor, Mase, and Midas stood out like tulips in a desert. Men such as Marquez and Ortiz always offered a shortcut.

Midas continued to mentally lash himself as he hit the shadier part of town, skidding with too much speed over lousy roads. Small animals and rodents scurried for cover as he slammed through the deserted back streets. He knew exactly where he was headed, the navigation screen flashing the destination in blinking red letters. His mind recalled Kyle's predatory eyes in the rearview earlier that afternoon. He hadn't tried to hide his interest, but despite that, Midas had spiked any misgivings. Even the twisted Kyle Palmer would never consider such a play with him around, right?

When the fuck would he ever learn?

Midas brought his speed down as the address came into view along a deserted and forgotten city block, where cheap pleasures held a devilish luster during the overnight hours. Brothels were all over the city, though this one was special, tucked within the top two floors of a three-story walk-up, a multipurpose one-stop shop also serving as a drug, sex, and weapons den. Midas knew all this from one of Phillip's operational handbooks. It had the same, inauspicious dull tones as the see-no-evil flop apartments bordering it on either side. A few filthy windows glowed grungy yellow, the others dark and lifeless. He drove past slowly, holding his pace for a few blocks beyond to the north, reminding himself for the hundredth time how much he hated Mexico City.

He jerked the car to a stop with a gentle squawk of tires meeting a soft curb. He was instantly out and moving with renewed intensity through a small tunnel between two abandoned structures. In the rear, he turned into the darkness of a back alley that stretched for several blocks and crossed smaller side streets. The narrow, grimy passage was rank, a trash dump for an entire neighborhood of dingy flats and sweaty bars. He made his way silently, navigating the stench, overstuffed trash containers, rotting rodent carcasses, and empty beer bottles. Anything that, if disturbed, might announce his presence.

At the end of each block the pathway widened enough to allow some form of infrequent garbage disposal, though he couldn't imagine any trucks had been through in some time. Low-priority locations required extra greasing from slumlords who couldn't be bothered.

He slipped unseen along the two blocks, emerging on another side street, abandoned like everything else. Marquez's building was a few feet away. Unlike the other structures, this one didn't extend back flush against the alley. Instead, there was a rear common area paved in cracking concrete and cordoned off by a rusting chain-link fence. A man sat smoking in a dirty plastic chair, the only impediment to a peeling black door. He was strictly cheap help and probably not expecting overnight trouble, given Marquez and Ortiz's brothels were some of the most protected in the city.

Midas emerged from the shadows. The man in the chair stood, though lacked the reflex to block the short pop to his throat. He pitched forward, wheezing. Midas snuffed the noise and pivoted behind him, using a chokehold to put him to sleep.

Midas stepped inside and softly climbed the stairs, his stealth aided by the worn carpets and hum of overworked fans and window air conditioners. The taint of cheap perfume battled against mold and body odor. The fourth floor featured bulbs above every door, each a different color. The only sounds were rehearsed moans and running water.

Midas squatted beside the door of what he assumed was a common bathroom. The door pulled back. The other stooge from the safe house stepped out, obviously corrupted into Kyle's scheme. But he was far too raw, and his peripheral vision took a second to register the moving figure at his feet. Too late. Midas sprang, burying a fist in his sternum. He stumbled backward into the bathroom, his lower back bowing the wrong way when it met the suspended sink. Midas followed, cracking the man's skull into the mirror. He raised his elbow and drove two more precise whacks into the temple. The young recruit dropped into an unconscious pile on the cold tile floor. His first after-action report wouldn't be glowing.

Midas stepped back out.

Marquez stood in the hall, dead center. Strained female faces peered from under the weak bulbs of various doors. Marquez flashed a wide smile dotted with his corroded teeth freshly shaded from the new cinnamon missile attached to a plastic ring on his index finger, its sharp tip glowing with rank saliva.

"Mr. McKnight?" It was a stall. The call had already been made. "Where is he?"

"Surely I have no idea what—"

Midas whipped forward and secured Marquez's wrist, swinging it up and jamming the red cylinder of hard sugar into his left eye with enough force to puncture his sinuses. The pimp fell softly to his knees as if he'd just witnessed a religious apparition. His expression seemed to ask, "Why me?" He fell backward with his knees and legs folded under his torso. A single tear of dark maroon rolled from his obliterated orbital socket and off his cheek, splashing silently on the musty floor.

There were a few shudders from the women. Others thrust their chins forward in defiance. They were all likely hiding weapons.

Midas held his palms up above his shoulders. "No one but me," he said in his broken Spanish. "Just tell me where the gringo is. And the little girl."

He surveyed the mute faces, all weighing the options. Finally, one ventured out from behind her door, a double-edged blade in one hand at her side. She looked to Marquez, then back to Midas, pointing the knife at the ceiling. He nodded, heading for the top floor.

There were only two rooms off the upper landing. One faced the outside street, and its door was slightly ajar. Soft music drifted from somewhere inside. Midas gently pushed it open.

Kyle stood at the window surveying the streets below. He was proud of his body, on display tonight with a naked torso and white briefs. He was flexing gym-toned muscles into the reflection of the glass. Probably could recite his body fat down to the decimal. A tray of half-consumed food sat on a rolling cart, upscale and out of place with the surroundings. Strawberries, carne asada, scrambled eggs, an empty bottle of tequila, and a polished silver thermos of coffee. Opposite the king-size bed hung a flat screen tuned to a dubbed version of an American network procedural.

Alana was huddled in a far corner, wrapped tighter than a chrysalis in a stained red blanket she clutched with skinned fingers. Her big dark eyes were glassy and, if possible, even more vacant than before. Her face had been smeared with makeup, too much for a woman twice her age. She couldn't bring herself to look at Midas.

Everything slowed to a sluggish pace, as if oxygen and equilibrium suddenly held no bearing on tangible existence.

Midas's mind momentarily strayed to a suspended drift of the ocean, powerful waves that coalesced and bore down to smash whatever tranquility lingered in their path. The image never failed to reach out to him in such moments, a warning of imminence, a mental metaphor framing the necessity for the rebalancing of nature gone astray.

Kyle turned from the window, wreathed in self-satisfaction, incapable as ever of processing situational danger.

"It's the Snow Leopard," he slurred. "Want some food?"

His voice set off a violent round of trembling under the blanket as Alana's head disappeared under the scratchy fabric. Midas moved, placing himself between her and Kyle. She peered out with one eye, and after a moment tried to smile, likely wondering what was next, and whether she'd done something wrong.

Midas picked her up, light as a wounded puppy, and carried her into the bathroom. Her legs instinctively squeezed together. In the bathroom, a floral wing chair rested next to the sunken tub. Conor had once mentioned how Marquez had a thing about watching his women bathe. Midas settled Alana in the chair, grateful the fuckhead had added a second TV to the wall above the sink. He flipped it on, settling for a cooking show with a host who, for once, didn't possess a voice that could cut glass.

"I'll be right back."

She nodded and turned her attention to the chicken being prepped for roasting. He cranked the volume and closed the door behind him.

Kyle was still at the window, holding a cup of coffee, still admiring his physique. He never saw the silver flash or heard the muffled *gong* when the steam tray landed, denting the side of his head. Kyle spun to the floor in a blizzard of bacon and exploding shapes. More sickening *crack*s were followed by another sharp *snap*. His face registered blistering pain. His brain was trying to rebel, fighting to recognize anything.

Midas caught a glimpse of his own face in the window, twisted into a mask of rage. He continued to work with methodical efficiency, spreading as much damage as he could through the parts of Kyle's body below his waist. Then he went to work on his ribs, diminishing what was left of his consciousness.

Midas would never remember them pulling him off, nothing beyond the red-black screaming in his brain and a distant understanding that real trauma would soon pay Kyle Palmer an extended visit.

A few hours later, Midas and the girl took off from a second hidden runway. Phillip had managed to arrange another flight, for a party of two. Midas knew he'd left a crisis for the others to try to manage. He'd worry about that later.

Once airborne, Alana curled up and tried to sleep against the window. He watched her, rubbing his swollen hands and bloody knuckles as the engines whined with the increase in torque and speed.

Mexico City peeled away below like a festering wound.

CHAPTER 6

LOS ANGELES, PRESENT DAY

WEST OF KYLE'S WEST Hollywood condo, a low gray curtain hung over the Pacific like a painter's tarp. Given the time of year and water temp, the beach was nearly deserted. A smattering of full-suited surfers dotted the water-and-horizon line, patiently waiting above the heaving ebbs fifty yards out. An army informed by belief in the water, motivated by the endless search and pursuit of the next ride.

Midas sat along an edge of wet sand appreciating the simple pleasures. He'd been out earlier, the wind and a few worthy waves providing a decent workout, a ritual that not only cleared his head, but also made any day more manageable. Mase had his boxing and his road bikes. Conor was a lifelong runner. They all shared a connection with physicality. Kyle had as well, back in the day.

Behind his back came a flat-footed rustle making shin-high splays of sand with each step. He didn't move, even when the hands playfully grabbed his neck.

"What the hell's wrong with you? Snoozing with your back to the beach?"

Midas pointed to the mirrored shades half buried a few feet away, capturing everything behind him like a miniature movie.

"Bastard. I should have known better." Phillip Gillis released his grip, moving to the edge of the frothy surf. Slipping off his shower sandals, he daintily lifted and dropped the bottom of one foot into the frigid water, instantly snapping it back. "Freaking ice." He trudged back a few yards and took a grunting seat, brushing stray granules from his windbreaker and extra-long, fashion-challenged nylon shorts. Not that he had many athletic skills, but Phillip's passion was pickup hoops near the Venice boardwalk.

"Nice cuffs," Midas observed. "You steal 'em from some senior league giveaway table?"

"Better than your plaid, frat-boy cutoffs. You look like a sickly porpoise trolling garage sales."

Midas laughed, his first in days. Phillip's to-the-point wit never took a minute off. And when it came to planning, logistics, and the timely use of foreign currencies, there was no one better. Like Kyle, Phillip never had the stomach for the brutality of the up close and personal. Instead, he'd performed with distinction as the Unit's solitary eye in the sky, bailing them out more than once with clear-sighted efficiency and a heart rate that never strayed above fifty-five BPMs. It wasn't long after Midas's and Mase's exile that he'd taken his leave of the Unit as well. Of the originals, only Conor had hung in.

"Man, I do love the water," Phillip said, "not in the constant-motion *healing* way you do, but I love it all the same. Best thing about this crappy city."

"No argument."

A pair of teenage boogie boarders hit the surf near the pier and started to paddle out. Skipping a few afternoon classes to tame waves was common among South Bay teenagers. A swarm of gulls atop an empty lifeguard tower took their cue, rhythmically flapping to catch up with the teens. For a few moments the birds in the air and the boards on the water were in tight formation, an old-school squadron right out of World War II newsreels. Then the birds peeled sharply left, tracing the coastline toward Palos Verdes. The youngsters saluted them with a wave before turning back to resume paddling. Surfer respect.

"I'm sorry about Serena," Phillip said, invading the moment. "Not that that is worth anything."

Midas nodded. "What have you got for me?"

Phillip palmed him a small piece of paper. Because of his technical savantism, there were still things he refused to put anywhere near a smartphone, or any other electronic device, constantly scolding his friends about the danger of keystrokes.

Midas glanced at the scribble before shredding the Post-it and putting the scraps into his pocket.

"Conor came off vacation." Phillip's tone carried a slight hint of anxiety. "Right after your dance across the border."

Conor and Phillip had served as the Unit's ground-level originals, present at inception and later serving as shot-calling older brothers. Years before, the twenty-three-year-old Conor had taken on Midas as a late teen, after a recommendation from Nathan McKnight, Midas's uncle. Like most who gravitated to such callings, Midas had been forced to come of age well before he was ready, initiating a rupture with his father that his uncle had been powerless to fix. At the time, Uncle Nate had done the only thing he could, by throwing his nephew a possible lifeline. Conor Brennan had been that tether, channeling Midas into a talented, cunningly competent weapon.

Back then the Unit worked in the shadows, answering to the brilliant and capable Jasper DeMarco, who danced between the various agencies while keeping bureaucratic assholes like Rawlings Palmer away from his boys. The Old Man had been tapped to create a specialized cadre. Conor and Phillip had been his initial recruits. A few years later, Midas and Mason James had entered the ranks. DeMarco had referred to them as the Group of Four, a play on one of his favorite Sherlock Holmes adventures.

The team had fostered tangible results, hovering below the radar for several years.

Clandestine DC, however, like the rest of the city, would forever be a study in shifting political capital and alliances. The time had finally come when DeMarco was compelled to open his books to a new crowd, one that included the NSA and Rawlings Palmer—a red-tagged CIA dealer with the means to inflict his own agenda and change parameters.

By then, Palmer had already grandfathered his degenerate offspring Kyle into the Company's family zoo, and would soon inflict him on DeMarco and his gilded posse.

It was a few years later, with the Old Man's blessing and to the relief of the Palmer hierarchy, that Midas and Mase had pulled out. Phillip had soon followed. Under the ensuing turf war, and missing the loyalty and cohesion of his old mates, Conor had been flung around like a chew toy. Officially, he now took orders from Kyle. And if asked, indentured servitude would have been his stated profession.

"I'm still sorry Conor felt the need to hang around," Midas said.

Phillip was doodling in the sand with the underside of his sandal. "It's what he is," he replied. "Plus, he feels protective of the Old Man."

"We quit and left him there by himself," Midas said. "I've never been right with that."

"He understood. As much as we needed to leave, he needed to stay."

Phillip's words were becoming harder to hear. Midas sensed the approach of a new migraine, prepped to burst through his brain like an RPG. A creeping hood began to cloud his vision.

"Sleeping at all?" Phillip asked.

"Enough."

They watched the surf. After a few brutal rushes behind his eyes, Midas's head started to quiet down. He'd need to go home and sit in the dark for a few hours.

Phillip brought him back. "What's your endgame, Mide? You've got no cover. DeMarco's dying at Walter Reed, not even lucid at this point. Palmer and his father have the keys, and we can't fight city hall."

"You all should have let me finish it after Mexico. And taken the heat, too."

Phillip shook his head. "As it was, it took all the Old Man's juice to keep you breathing."

"You all went beyond the scope," Midas said. "I'm still grateful, but never wanted it that way."

A cloud passed over the pier as one of the boarder kids caught a nice gust, taking the wave from his knees, the afternoon shadows framing him in black and white, like a panel from a comic book.

"We're beyond all that," Phillip said. "But something doesn't make sense."

"Only one thing?"

"Humor me. Kyle has always been an unhinged prick. We all hated him, and he didn't give a damn. He was gold plated and knew it. Wasn't even competent at the menial stuff, but he had his hooks in, so we had no choice. But given all that, and his timidity regarding wet work, I've never found him to be suicidal."

Midas shrugged. "It's been five years. He thinks this is the time for his play."

"Maybe. But he knows you. And still initiates with an all-or-nothing move on Serena, leaving nothing for compromise or interpretation?"

"He's got the hardware, the personnel, the infrastructure . . . the favors. The Old Man's been sliding, but Kyle still waited for him to get sick enough to take his shot. In his mind, there's no real risk or downside," Midas said, surmising.

"Look at the entire board," Phillip said, playing again with the sand. "He's only ever *talked* a good game, but always huddled in the rear of the bus, getting out only once the risk had passed and the outcome determined. At his core, he's always been a puss, despite his constant fronting. You destroyed him that night, obliterated everything he knew or thought he knew. And put him on display for all of us, made a casualty of his entitlement and self-worth. Kyle with his finger on this current toggle makes perfect sense, but he's still who he is, that scared rapist you broke apart. He can have ten Jojo Boudreaux to protect him, but he's still that cowardly little shit."

"With the upper hand."

"You're missing my point. Serena made no sense on any level. He could have just had one of the mountain boys take you out from a rooftop. Or had Jojo's crew burlap sack you to some torture chamber. That would have made perfect sense. Not this. It's too . .

. I don't know. Out of character?"

"It had the desired effect," Midas said.

"Did it? My guess is he and his boys hunkered down and expected you to walk through his front door, ready to finish it. Because that's upright, and the way we'd all figure you to play it—straight ahead. Instead, you call an audible and napalm part of their bank."

"And I'm not finished," Midas added.

"That's obvious now to everyone, especially him."

"Meaning?"

"Meaning I don't think he's calling the shots on his own."

Midas had considered this as well. "His father."

"Too old-school. Bow ties and single malt. Aging white man scurrying around corners currying goodwill. Remember how De-Marco always laughed at him? Now, there's no question Rawlings Palmer wants you fried. But even he'd never sign off on a civilian."

"Who, then?"

"Don't know. But I'll start working on it."

Natalie couldn't help realizing downtown LA was fraying at the edges.

Despite constant new-money construction and upgrades, the city remained the decaying victim of sunny winters and harsh summers. Today it resembled any other urban sprawl heading out at lunchtime. Hotel workers decked in black rayon and exhaustion waited for traffic lights on their way to afternoon shifts.

There were skyscrapers and an aging sports arena where minimum wage flowed on game days. The hidden ones who scanned the tickets and made greasy food for pig-ass industry execs, accountants, and lawyers, all matriculating from their overpriced glass palaces and high-rise wombs to be seen where it counted, congregating in their write-off skyboxes and screaming inebriated encouragement and taunts at superior physical specimens on the floors and fields.

After dusk, the area coined LA Live transformed into a miniature-scale Tokyo, servicing a more discerning crowd under the neon as hoop and hockey fans stumbled off escalators to head home. A crowd that still believed it was safely protected from muggers and carjackers in the overcompensation of large-scale Mercedeses and Beamers. "Masters of the universe," Tom Wolfe had once called them. More like chasers and wimpy whiners, beholden to social media, jealousy, and comfort zones.

For the second time that day, Natalie frowned at her own cynical thoughts. She wasn't helping her mood wasting valuable energy analyzing the habits of deluded Angelenos, those convinced they ran this city, when in fact it was those taking care of their kids and scrubbing red-wine stains off polished hardwood floors who were the real influencers. Those whose worlds could come unhinged when a nanny called in sick.

Special Agent Collins had given her directions to a bland six-story structure south of the Convention Center, near some older construction off Flower Street. She pulled into the subterranean parking lot, taking the first available spot three levels down.

In the elevator she hit the button for five, and once there, veered left through a hall devoid of natural light. She paused near an unmarked wooden door, catching a hint of fast food and jasmine air freshener. The button on the wall blinked with a silent green flash. She braced herself for the inevitable tight-assed stiff in an ill-fitting suit and fed-issue haircut.

Her snobbery was somewhat DNA inspired. For a cop, her father had been something of a dandy, and she'd learned to spot third-rate grooming well before mastering math fractions.

The door opened, revealing a fit and tan midforties specimen. His faded old-school Montreal Canadiens T-shirt rested without tuck or obstruction over loose jeans. His sun-bleached hair hung too long to be regulation, with gray flecks covering the tops of his ears.

"Detective Riiska?" Correct pronunciation and all. *Reeska.*

"Guilty."

"Grant Collins," he said, shaking firmly. "It's an idiotic name, I know. Parents have a habit of saddling their kids with pretentious shit like that."

Natalie smiled. He was nothing like what she'd assumed over the phone. Instead, tall and slim with hardened shoulders. His attire probably an effort to disarm. She was sure he had several suits in his closet. And if so, they likely fit.

Collins led her through a maze of mostly unfilled cubicles, maneuvering her into an office with a few older chairs and one large window offering a view of cheap hotels and skid row. Behind a less-than-chic mahogany desk was a wall, empty except for two mounted remnants of a jaggedly broken surfboard. Natalie's own desk was so small there was no choice but to keep it littered with needed items. This one was immaculate. Men and their tidiness. Mason's condo was clean enough to eat off the floors.

Collins pointed to the chair, sitting down himself and closing his laptop, the only item on that pristine desk besides a lamp. He grabbed a bottle of water from a small refrigerator hidden underneath. "You want one? Or a cup of coffee?"

"No thanks, I'm fine. What happened there?" She pointed at the broken board.

"My one and only foray off the Oregon coast, a few miles up from Coos Bay. Ran into a nasty storm. Like a fool, I took it as a challenge. Damn board was brand new, too."

"You still surf?"

"Every day I can. You?"

He was not without charm. The playful spark in those greenish-blue eyes likely kept him well stocked with admirers.

"A few times, but I'm no fanatic."

"From what I hear, you leave that to your work."

His slight left turn lacked ease but wasn't a disaster. She'd never been at ease with compliments masquerading as small talk. The leather chair whispered as he leaned back. Fed bodyspeak intended to diminish tension. Quantico playbook.

"What I mean," he continued, "is you have a serious reputation for someone so . . . young."

"Or a woman." She was thirty-five, hardly young.

"No question there." Collins held up his hands preventively and smiled. He had a nice one.

"That kind of flattery usually work?" she asked. "Thought these days you all were working from the Me Too handbook?"

"Bad habit. Been living in this city too long."

She let that hang. "So . . . *Special Agent.* You didn't have me drive an hour and change just to flirt, right?"

"I wish, Detective." The sun was shifting beyond the window, shrinking the room along with it. Collins took a slug from the water. "Assuming you've been read in on everything new? And you were there the night they died?"

"Yes, to both."

"Okay. The Basmajians. What are your thoughts?"

Only the slightest hint of interrogation. He was smooth, mining her thoughts before presenting his cards. The muscles in her back flinched and slowly tightened. She was no lamb.

"Not much so far."

"Anything you care to share?" FBI types were notorious pecker measurers, thriving on the jurisdictional bigfoot. Like the buffoons USC spit off its alumni assembly line, feds and agents relished their own special handshake, blindly confident they knew more and knew better. Regular city cops would forever be freshmen crashing the senior prom.

But at least he had a few moves and didn't come off like the usual bureau asshole. She'd play along, for now.

"Competent," she said, starting slowly, measuring her steps. Was that a slight glimmer in his eyes? All trained associates she'd come across possessed a habitual tell. She'd need to identify his. "No sign of the shooter," she continued. "It was a wet night, the first in a few weeks. But no tracks, no marks or scrapes, nothing. Not even in the road's soft shoulders near the exterior gate."

He raised an eyebrow, feigning ignorance, universal cop theatrics designed to entice more details. He flexed long quadriceps under his jeans.

She could feel herself slipping into boredom at the tired antics. "My guess is this killer hiked," she said. "Probably half a mile or so. There's a shopping center closer to town. No security cams in the parking lot, unfortunately."

His unintentional squirm told her he hadn't tumbled to this theory.

"Almost nothing in the house either, except the two stiffs and small amounts of their blood. No gun, but it was a 9mm, as we'd figured. One shot apiece. Soft loads, exotic, likely self-made. Extremely precise. No threads or fragments of clothes, shoe debris, anything. A ghost." It was her turn to sit back.

Collins looked impressed. "That's a good call on the off-site parking. If he parked at all. Maybe he got picked up? Or swam in and out?"

"The breaks during that storm were hardcore. He'd had to have been SEAL level."

Collins smiled. She'd seen that kind of look before. Good-looking women were one thing, but sports or military knowledge elevated them to another plateau.

"But okay," she continued. "Let's say he did swim in. The brothers had elaborate surveillance from the rear of the hacienda down to the beach. High-end motion activated. All the bells and whistles, backed up by triggered floodlights. Enough to damn near service the Rose Bowl. He might have been able to skirt all that, being the pro he certainly was, but what would have been the point? No evidence this was intended as a silent entry. The brothers knew him. Because somebody let him in and brought him upstairs for coffee and whatever. No need for any surprise, stealth, or a dripping Body Glove wet suit."

"But if they were such security freaks, why nothing on the in-house, from the guard, or gate hard drives?"

"This guy somehow knew their systems. Everything from that night was wiped. We've got some of our forensic types giving it a once-over, but I'm not hopeful. He didn't come in through the front. The guard never noticed anything."

"You think the shooter's a hacker as well?"

"Not necessarily. But if you have some aptitude, it's not hard to wipe digital footprints off surveillance."

"And you think it was a guy?" he asked.

"Doesn't feel like a woman to me."

She watched Collins's wheels roll, multitasking between her theories and deciding how much to let her in on. He was likely realizing his recon on her had been right. Even so, he still seemed favorably impressed.

"Anything else?" he asked.

"You first, Special Agent."

He nodded, pulling a shiny folder from a side drawer. "The Basmajians aren't light reading. They had filthy fingers everywhere. Politicos, Wall Street, Fortune 500 CEOs. There were also PACs and back-channel money chutes. But you know that already."

"True, but you grown-ups have better access than us yokels."

He let that slide past. "The brothers were brazen. Never tried to hide who or what they were. It was all legal. Too legal for me."

"Meaning?"

Collins wheeled backward, resting one bent leg on the surface of his desk. "Let me back up a minute. Porn has always been a lucrative business, but now you've got big, mainstream studio films shamelessly showing it all. Pardon my candor, but blow jobs, literal penetration, women sitting around in naked circles discussing their labia? Makes the old days of overnight HBO and Cinemax look tame."

"Special Agent Collins," she said, cooing. "Were you paying attention in health class?"

His face went crimson beneath the tan, framing a bashful grin. "More than you'll ever know, Detective. My point is several years ago porn found its legs, so to speak. It may not ever be considered respectable, but it's not the dirty secret it used to be. Now I'm not saying everyone's streaming girl-on-girl on the same laptops their kids use for gaming. But the uptight brigade has moved on to other things."

Depends on who you talk to, she thought. "If you say so" was all she said.

"I do. My specialty is cartels, RICO, and, over the past several years, sex trafficking. Back in the day, beyond the bespoke pimps and free enterprisers in seedier neighborhoods, prostitution was a fringe benefit for cheating husbands. The Italians ran the show and used its women for the button boys to get laid when they needed to get away from nagging spouses. Anything beyond normal, transactional sex was considered weak minded and frowned upon. Then came the Asians and Russians with their new playbook. Going back for centuries, the shoguns and cossacks have used women to set up their banks. I don't need to tell you they snatch little girls and bring them in by the boatload. Have done so for decades. It's only the last few years our mandate has grown to make fighting human slavery a priority."

"Why now?" she asked with disgust.

"Two reasons. Despite all the shadowy, fear-inducing, Ruskie-Tong-Omerta shit, these girls flip on their minders much easier than *Law and Order* would have you believe. We protect them, one of the few things we do decently."

She could appreciate the self-deprecation.

"We're able to get them set up," Collins said. "In most cases, we can also rescue their families from the old countries. I'm not saying it's easy, but it happens, and that is good for everyone. Reason two is the other side. We can't keep up, and these groups know it. Too ruthless and mobile. But we still have to make them and everyone else believe we're trying. If you ever quote me on that, I'll take the fifth."

"The FBI admitting to impotence? Who'd ever believe that?" she drawling.

"Point taken."

Keep it civil, she thought, fixing her focus through the window at a greasy hotel a block away. "The brothers were mostly legit and had influential clients," she said. "So did the Mayflower Madam and Heidi Fleiss. So what?"

"The Basmajians didn't peddle strictly legit. They were in bed with some of the cartels. And we're not talking powder or pills."

"Trafficking," she said.

"Children, to be specific. Unlike the Russians, who are control freaks and run their railroads from beginning to end, the cartels don't care about what happens on this side of the border, at least not with these kids. They take a substantial cut off the top and they're done. The brothers were free to peddle their so-called merch in any way they wanted." He took a pause, clearly troubled and uncomfortable.

She found his reaction human, and against her basic misgivings, somewhat endearing.

"You've worked some vice," he continued. "I'd assume you're well versed in those repellent fetishes otherwise *normal* people keep locked away. These two provided the entire buffet, including tender-agers. Clientele like this believe they are entitled to whatever they want. The brothers gave them the means to delve into other worlds."

"All because they could. Those who never hear the word no," she said, more rumination than statement.

Collins nodded. "These customers present as normal, giving themselves passes by repenting one day a week under the Jesus-tinged stained glass, confessing in a wooden box, or holding their arms up in strip-mall parishes. Nothing wrong with sinning, as long as they take an hour here and there to feel bad about it."

"Lapsed Catholic?" she asked.

"Shamelessly, I'm still a true believer."

"With their history? Speaking of sanctioned prostitution."

"What can I say?" he said, trying to sound forthright. "I like to believe we're finally weeding out the evil. Plus, I like the pageantry on holidays."

"You could just settle for mood stabilizers and the feeb cantina."

"Nordic cynicism, Detective? I love the fiction and dark TV shows your homeland provides. All in the name of fighting a lack of sunlight and generational depression."

A cold chisel ran through her stomach. "Only when I run into some divinity school Dudley Do-Right with his head too far up his ass to address reality."

"Ouch." Collins's stiff smile betrayed he was more fragged than he let on.

"Sorry. That was over the line." She didn't know why she felt the need to explain, except that she'd found herself liking him more than she wanted to.

"Here's what I was getting at." He took her cue to move forward. "The brothers had a stellar group of proteans guarding their interests."

"I thought they were stand-alone? All in the one family. Black books and forced favors."

"So did we, until we started heavier cross-referencing. Turns out the Basmajians were only well-heeled fronters answering to what we believe are some even more seriously heavy hitters."

She knew he could read her sudden puzzlement.

"We've hit one wall after another," he said. "And since 9/11, that's not supposed to happen. We haven't made all the connections, but we know we're beyond a couple of Glendale-born, new-money, regional scumbags peddling dirty pictures. I think they were taking orders from someone with serious clearances."

It made sense, explaining how a pair like them could float with impunity, dancing between the raindrops.

"You think some governmental service is bankrolling human trafficking?" she asked.

"More like someone within. Truth is, I don't know. Not yet anyway. These guys were out front to keep the others hidden."

Whatever she had expected out of this meeting, the case had become an entirely different mountain. Careers were sacrificed for much less, making it all the more worth chasing.

"I've got a few ears at Langley," he said. "Don't judge me, but we went to prep school together." He dropped his voice as if someone else might be listening. "I'll poke around and see if they might point me in the right direction. The thing about spooks is they have no problem letting others till the dirt while they figure out which way the wind might blow as a result. I'm hoping you'll keep working it from your end. And I'd appreciate you keeping my theory to yourself. Jay Brown is a great cop. We've worked together a few times. But beyond him, I wouldn't trust anyone."

She gave him a slight smile, which this time came without effort. "I'll do what I can."

CHAPTER 7

DESPITE THE SEASONAL CHILL, the Hermosa Pier was buzzing, competing with the low roar of whitewater somewhere beyond the shore in the inky black. Jojo Boudreaux had always liked the beach, certainly more than the stained streets near his functionally mundane Hollywood apartment.

Locals were scoping out the lines at favorite venues, taking note of ingrates from the San Fernando Valley. Jojo had been in this city for five years and was increasingly finding it harder to distinguish authentic coasties. The beach was one of the few locations in LA where the housing market rarely took a downward tick, partly due to the migration of out-of-state Jethros taking over, just like everywhere else.

New money, strip malls, and never-ending traffic.

Pier Avenue, Hermosa's main street, had gone through a few moderate facelifts, though it had never been able to completely lose its sleepy and weathered roots. What had been victimized was

117

the old-school charm. Most of the surf shops had long ago vacated to the cheaper rent of side streets well away from the waves. These days Pier Avenue was like so much of LA, gaudy neon and trendy bars. Vegas West.

Unlike its surroundings, the bar where Jojo and his two associates were headed stood out for the wrong reasons. Fading kelly-green slats and crumbling gold accents bestowed a poor-cousin status compared with trendier establishments in the vicinity. The outdoor tables were half-filled, glowing under the warm orange of heat lamps. A battered sign painted above the main entrance read SHREDDERS, a term for hardcore surfers.

In his enlisted days, Jojo had done a bit of wave tossing off the Georgia coast. Yet those were puddles compared with the force of the rabid Pacific, especially around the beaches of South Bay, where Midas remained a minor surfing celebrity, revered as a breakers Buddha, relentless as the summer sun and hard as teak.

A hooded figure hunched on a stool near the door, eyes down and earbuds buried under ocean-streaked blond hair. His head came up, light brown eyes scanning a quick appraisal. Faint scents of salt, cocoa butter, and legal herb danced in the wispy air, the latter transporting Jojo back to those all-too-occasional silent nights in Kandahar.

"ID, bro?" the hood asked.

"I'm on the list," Jojo replied.

The beige eyes bore traces of the weed but remained somewhat alert. Their owner lifted off his stool, easily six one in flip-flops. The unzipped hoodie swung open, showcasing a Becker Boards T-shirt hanging over a flat stomach. Deep in the pockets of the board shorts, muscular hands rolled into fists. Jojo and his two companions were clearly nonregulars, and the jovial bar didn't

seem the spot for patrons like them, those with well-fitting bik-
er jackets and tight-cropped hair. The doorman was working the
possibilities over, likely assuming they were out-of-state hicks, the
kind who ordered Wild Turkey and smelled like gun oil.

"We got no list, pal." Beige eyes bounced a bit, rising anxiety
causing his legs to search for the balance wave jockeys were end-
lessly discussing.

"Then I guess we're not on it," Jojo said gently with some added edge. "But we're old friends of Midas and Mason. And we're
gonna have a beer."

He pushed past the lanky kid and stepped inside, navigating
the throng and good-time noise to a small alcove near the back
of the L-shaped bar. His associates followed. One posted himself near the waitress well, turning his back to the four television
screens suspended above the more expensive hooch. Jojo and the
other guy slid into a booth.

It took all of fifteen seconds for the amazing creature to appear.
Shiny brunette, perfect skin, skimpy clothes mostly covering ample curves. This was the LA impossible not to admire—the endless
talent. Half of it chasing the fantasy of acting, the rest living for
the weather and lifestyle.

Either way, they all came. Like Santa Monica, downtown, Hollywood, and even Studio City, the beach had its own vibe, sharing
in the commodity of beautiful people.

"What can I bring you?" She was friendly but hesitant. The
burnout at the door had obviously spread the word. Cocktail ma-
vens generally geared up under copious loads of war paint to hide
imperfections and weariness. This one was a ten with minimal
spackle. But Jojo didn't have the time or energy tonight. He needed to remain sharp, and could already sense the boy scouts in the

vicinity. They had a thing about protecting their people.

"Jameson neat for me. Whatever's on tap for him. And could you tell Midas we're waiting?"

She vaporized back into the low uproar of harmless patrons with their incessant inebriate bragging. Jojo looked around. Nothing like IPAs and long pours of eighty-proof courage to reinforce insecurities. Bring out the buddies for a few pops while glaring at broads who wouldn't give them an opening smile without a serious reason. Real interaction? That required an entirely different tax bracket. Self-delusion was an easier option, usually followed by a short walk or ride home to a fraying spouse in need of a Zoloft upgrade. And if these windbags were lucky, the possibility of drunken sex once every few months with the wife, though only when the youthful shelf stocker from Whole Foods was unavailable.

Wedded bliss. It would never be for him. Jojo preferred the company of those paid to leave. No shrinks or apologies necessary.

The waitress was back, moving their drinks off the tray with little fanfare, in a hurry to be anywhere else. She asked whether they wanted to run a tab. Jojo reached for his wallet, taking his time.

"And where's Midas?" he asked, firing up his big southern smile.

Her bottom lip started to quiver. Typical beach girl. Tanning booths and fumbling fucktards about the extent of what she was equipped to handle. "He's not here tonight."

It was a response devoid of the cutesy inflection normally employed to elevate the tip quotient. Jojo held out a fifty. When she reached, he maneuvered her dainty wrist between two fingers, pushing it down onto the table's polished wood. The corners of her eyes watered with distress and pain as she reactively squatted against the pressure. Across the table, associate number one offered a grim smile ... but failed to notice Carlo appearing behind him.

Before Jojo could react, his man was hugging the table and the waitress's wrist had somehow been freed.

Then his own face hit the table with stunning force, the back of his mouth quickly coating with coppery blood. Jojo became aware of pain and a kind of paralysis. Someone pulled his head up by the hair. For some reason his hands and arms weren't functioning, though his vision was clear. The bar seemed to be humming along, indifferent to his dilemma.

Carlo slipped into the other side of the booth and mashed an elbow into number one's cheek. Time moved without hurry. Jojo could feel his head falling forward again, the lacquered wood spreading to greet his face. He closed his eyes and braced for impact, powerless to resist.

A dull thud rattled his glass of whiskey and shook through his knees.

It must have been later when the distorted flashing webs started to clear. number two was on the floor near the bar. He was out. In the corner of their booth, number one was curled in a crumbled heap sleeping through a battered pattern of breathing.

Mason came into focus at his left, looking relaxed in a wooden chair.

Bastard still had lightning hands. What a fucking waste of superior talent. All those hours spent in his gym or tooling around the Palos Verdes Hills on that stupid bike like one of those skinny fags on the tour.

Jojo smiled through his discomfort. Mason simply stared at him, lost on any joke.

Sanctimonious prick never did have a decent sense of humor.

One hand was numb but somewhat functional. Jojo used it to

grab his shot and slam it down in one haphazard gulp. The burn tore through the ragged parts of his mouth and damaged sinuses. A single tear slid from the corner of his drooping eye, skimming jaggedly down over a swelling, fractured cheek. His nose felt like an old sponge holding too much water.

Mason held up his hand calling for another shot. He slipped Jojo's fifty back in front of him. "On the house," he said.

"Always the gentleman." De facto snide.

"Still have a way with the women," Mason observed.

"Fuck off. I came to talk to Midas."

"You can talk to me."

The refill arrived faster than the first. Jojo dropped it with less duress, the first having somewhat anesthetized his pain centers. He looked over at Carlo, who smiled in return. At least that asshole had a sense of humor. Big Syrian half breed they'd pulled from some African ditch. He'd be their lapdog for life, but a capable one, good in the street and with a punch like a packing press. Definitely a cut above the moron sitting next to him, still breathing with effort through an open mouth.

"Looks like talking was the last thing on your mind tonight, Jo," Mason said.

"If it had been my call, that would have been true." He met Mason's glare and held it. "But we're doing this politely."

"Serena wasn't polite."

Jojo rested his elbows on the table, lacing his fingers behind his head and taking a deep breath, holding it awhile before his shoulders deflated.

Retreat. For now.

"That was unfortunate," Jojo said. "I didn't find out until after it was all over. When Kyle decided to come clean."

"Yeah, you're quite the altar boy," Mason said, nodding to someone out of sight. This time it was the entire dark green bottle of Jameson getting placed on the table, along with a larger tumbler and a cup of coffee. Fresh steam curled toward a ceiling fan. Mason took a small sip of the java and poured him another stiff shot. "In service of being polite," he said.

Jojo held up the small glass in a defeated sign of thanks, sipping slowly this time as the fatigue of the last few days rolled through his bones. "Mase, you ever figure out how to sleep more than an hour?" he asked, the fiery whiskey loosening a reserve of sentimentality he normally tried to keep hidden.

Mason picked up his coffee, taking another small taste. He was a hard, coiled wire, in no mood to bond. "It shouldn't have happened, Jo."

"Can't argue with that," he replied.

The hum of the bar returned as the two nursed their chosen poisons. Old alliances and tenuous common ground now nothing more than memories.

"Where does Kyle expect this to go?" Mason asked.

Jojo wondered whether he was being rhetorical or just obtuse. "Only one possible scenario," he replied, rubbing his jaw. "Smart guy like you doesn't need me to spell it."

"Mexico was years ago."

"And you think that matters?" Jojo knew there was truth in that. Serena had been a collateral message, broken and damaged with the same sadistic efficiency Midas had once inflicted on Kyle. A ticking slog toward a preordained reality.

"Like I just said. The girl was a bad play." Jojo recognized that his background and training made him too willing to reduce human suffering to nothing more than a misguided coaching move.

123

"But the brothers?" he added. "Now that was inspired . . . though suicidal. You know Daddy Palmer's mantra. Have your fun, but don't ever think about touching my bank."

"WASPs," Mason said, momentarily deviating. "Protect the inheritance, punish the children."

"Ralph Lauren peckerwoods," Jojo agreed, relishing a moment of common ground ahead of the impending foul weather. "That old, oily prick is good at only two things—slapping the backs of agency buddies and spending family money. You ever wonder why Kyle's got such a long leash?"

Mason said nothing.

"They might hate each other, but junior's the family breadwinner. He brings in more coin than the last several generations combined."

"Classy, too," Mason snapped. "Nobody ever went broke pushing porn."

"We can't all be noble saloon keepers and beach bums."

"Noble. That's a laugh."

Jojo poured himself another three fingers. "You know, Mase, that's always been the problem. Too fucking hard on yourself, and by extension, the rest of us. Never could live up to your own shiny rules. Why do you think we're in this mess now?"

His freelance disappointments were showing signs of consciousness. Carlo slid out of the booth to stand and keep watch over them.

Jojo took what was left of his drink and flung it into his booth partner's face. "Wake up, dipshit. And nice work, by the way. Remind me to review your severance."

Mason moved his chair a few feet back. "Your boys could use some air."

Jojo slid from the bench. "Any damage?" he asked Carlo, gesturing toward the other one, who was still having trouble separating from the floor.

"Nothing a week off won't help," Carlo replied.

Mason leaned in, whispering, "If you feel like coming back, it better be heavier."

Jojo reached over for a handful of his partner's leather collar, pulling him out of the booth and upright. Carlo gathered up the other, bumping his head intentionally on the outer lip of the bar as he steadied him on his feet.

The three started to file out. Jojo was last and turned back before walking through the door. "Tell the Snow Leopard we need a meeting."

"I think he knows, don't you?" Mason said.

Jojo offered another half-hearted salute, followed by a partial bow for the offended waitress, now standing near the bar. He'd always liked Mason, mostly given his chafing around authority. But Midas's boyhood pal would be a problem, meaning both accounts would need settling. Nothing worth crying over. They'd made their choice. Brennan would kick and scream but would come around, yes-man that he was. Phillip was a geeky lost cause, no threat and not worth any effort.

Jojo stepped outside, ignoring the smart-assed look from the quasi, tough-guy doorman toking away on his wobbly stool. *Smile now, you little shit.*

The double-M boys had built themselves a nice piece of tranquility. Too fucking bad it was over.

He made a path through the dense fog as the sentimental pangs faded.

One thousand miles to the east and five thousand feet above sea level, pornographer Rudy O'Shea rested on his reinforced orthopedic mattress—the lone concession to his out-of-control weight—replaying the call he'd received that morning. Kyle Palmer had been adamant. Double his security. Yeah, not happening. So what if the Armenians had been snuffed? Rudy wasn't overly concerned. The two rent-a-cops trying to stay awake in the heated shack next to his driveway were more than enough insurance. Especially out here in the middle of nowhere.

The Baz brothers had been into creepy shit and had shamelessly recruited high-profile clients, any one of whom could have ordered the slate cleaned. Rudy's list comprised closeted old farts harmlessly jacking off over high-res pics and flicks. No risk.

He braced himself before pulling his frame up from the horizontal—no easy task. It had been ten years since the gimpy back had initially appeared, becoming full-blown arthritis within weeks. He shuffled off to the part of his home that affected assholes referred to as the great room. Tempered glass held in the heat against the outdoor Colorado snow and freezing temps.

His size eights—girl's feet, his mother used to say—were hiding somewhere under the abutment of his paunch. Gravity did the rest, creating extra work for his sagging chest and stooped shoulders. For the hundredth time, he half-heartedly vowed to get serious about the dusty elliptical in his swanky exercise room. However, the momentary commitment to self-improvement vanished once his feet touched the plush Egyptian carpet. Forty steps later, he was winded. He took a break, planting himself against the corner of his favorite floor-to-ceiling window.

Tonight, he felt positively regal in his boxers and wife beater. Remnants of harder times, long gone.

He smiled to the oversize, empty room. Kyle was being paranoid, and he was too smart to be a target. His self-made conglomerate was now well removed from those dank Los Angeles basements and videotape days. Back then it had been about servicing Hollywood D-list actors and the industry fringe, those who'd never score the fame that brought fuck-you paydays and ass-smooching staffs. Those who came to him as their conduit to delicacies polite and stable people were never supposed to seek.

A failed thespian himself, Rudy understood the inherent delusion and narcissistic necessity. Fornication with all the trimmings meant volume, never distinction. What kind and with whom were of secondary concern. Men, women, groups. Rudy made sure it was all within reach.

Including kids, his special forte. A talent well south of the decency line. He'd been known as the Facilitator. Best on the West Coast.

Right up until he'd been nailed.

He'd had been forced to throw all his cash and other holdings into a retainer for one of the city's big-hitter defense lawyers. Maybe the only smart thing he'd ever done. Minutes before his second hearing, the charges were inexplicably dropped, all because some assistant DA, a couple of cops, and a federal judge had been spotted nuzzling kids in a few of Rudy's pictures.

The afternoon of his release, he had jumped into his car and headed out of town, leaving behind his apartment and everything else he owned.

He'd spent the next six months where he'd grown up, in Phoenix. He was manning paint-shaker machines at an old friend's store, feeling like John Travolta's character in *Saturday Night Fever*, though with much less upside. The paint-store slavery had offered one decent perk—monthly parties at his pal's climate-controlled Scottsdale home. One night, his friend's wife had demanded everyone congregate in her private office. She had a new toy, something called a Macintosh desktop computer, complete, she'd pointed out, with the latest color monitor.

Rudy had been mildly amused, having never seen one outside a bank. She'd fired up the machine to something called the World Wide Web, taking them on a photo tour of the Paris Louvre. The bored crowd was enticed for about five minutes before heading outside to the barbecue pit and open bar. Rudy had hung back, spending the next hour transfixed and virtually touring anything he could find on the embryonic internet. It hadn't been a stretch for him to imagine what could be done with such technology.

Several decades later, his payroll now spanned a few hundred hubs throughout the country. Last year alone he'd brought in fifty million, before residuals and after paying off the Palmer clan for distribution and protection. Tax shelters and other details were handled by an old-school legal firm in Boston, Palmer connected, of course. The firm had recently opened a satellite office in Denver to keep Rudy even more insulated and out of trouble. Admittedly something that, considering his profile, was never easy.

Like tonight's fourteen-year-old.

She had been procured from a greedy social worker with a growing taste for opioids. Recently orphaned teenagers translated to few issues when it came to petitions for temporary guardianship. The judge who took care of the legalities was another friend . . . deep into his bookie. It had taken a few weeks, but now Rudy had a new roommate, if only temporary. Neat and legal.

He stood admiring the stately pine trees visible against the night. He had bought this remote mountain estate for the privacy and for what it represented. Its panoramic vista of the Colorado wilderness was a lifetime removed from his sweatbox in the grungiest recesses of Los Angeles.

The girl finally appeared, dragging a robe hanging over her slender frame like a fireman's blanket. She would be beautiful someday, though he recognized in the neurotic eyes and tight lips the signs of emerging psychopathy. She would be a handful, but thankfully for someone else.

Taking measure of his free-flowing flesh, the girl's expression shifted between disgust and hate. He dropped his shorts and pushed his hips toward her. She yawned, ignoring him and shuffling back to the bedroom, slamming him out behind the heavy cedar door. Deep blue flashes from the television licked at the hardwood floor beneath it.

Rudy smirked to himself. *Still got it.*

Without bothering to pull up his oversize satin boxers, he rested his bare ass against the chill of the window's glass. A sudden blinding blackness hit him like a curtain, snuffing out his senses.

He pitched forward, bouncing twice off the high-gloss oak floors.

Rudy was already past knowing that his brain stem had been shattered with precision by a long-range rifle.

In front of the house, the rent-a-cops were still playing cards in the heated shack, oblivious.

It would be hours before Rudy was discovered.

CHAPTER 8

PREDAWN IN FOOTHILLS OF Santa Monica. Coastal winds were standing down.

The public park was well tended. Clean seats, plastic slides, and metal hobby horses balanced above big springs. The north side was bordered by Sunset Boulevard, and across the famous street hulked mansions, secure and remote. Being four a.m., only one car had cruised past. Two scrawny coyotes peeked through the hedges of the homes, taking scavenger stock before crossing against a red traffic light. They were headed for a dumpster behind the strip mall a few blocks down.

A heavy *ping* from one of the gates announced Phillip Gillis's arrival as he stepped inside and walked with hesitation across the fragrant cut grass. He sat down next to Conor Brennan on a jungle-green bench beginning to show its age. Both wore black sweatpants and black hoodies, blending into the fading night.

"You couldn't have waited for breakfast?" Phillip said.

Conor was scanning the immediate area in and outside the gates.

"What the hell?" Phillip muttered, feeling cranky because of the hour. "Overnight meeting? London rules?"

Conor looked at him with something resembling regret, before turning back to his watchful diligence.

Phillip fought an unanticipated chill. His old cohort wasn't given to the jumps. And Conor was definitely keyed.

"Our pal went off the reservation again, about seven hours ago outside Boulder," he said.

Phillip blew out an extended exhalation. "Damn. Rudy O'Shea?"

Conor's hooded head bobbed affirmation. He leaned forward, resting an elbow on his thigh to support his chin.

Outside the gates, the intersection's streetlights changed with soft *clicks*.

Phillip dropped his head back against the splintered wood to stare up into the night bruising of blue and black. Without question, Serena had demanded a response. But the Basmajian brothers, and now Rudy, meant they were all headed for darker territory. He and Conor had discussed and dreaded this outcome for years, secretly hoping some unforeseen turn of cosmic fate would ward off the inevitable. Even if they knew better.

Midas was now assaulting the Palmer family en masse. There would be no winners, only survivors.

"It gets worse." Conor sounded beyond tired, his normally rich joking tones reduced to a defeated whisper. "Jojo took a couple of his fresh idiots to the bar last night looking to throw some hardness around. Mase and Carlo tuned them up."

"Oh, Christ," Phillip said, straightening up while jamming his hands in his jacket pockets.

"Uh-huh. The boys are officially fucked."

"Or Kyle and his crew are, depending on your take."

Conor's head dropped. "You know where this goes, Phil. It's a numbers game. Kyle has his platoon and the stripes. And he's every bit the defective code he always was. Making Midas wait all this time was calculated. So was keeping me on a leash. These past few years have been about ensuring we all slept with one eye open."

"We do that anyway," Phillip murmured.

Conor didn't seem to be listening. "Always there, hanging over us like a slow-rotting disease. Pulling our fingernails out by centimeters."

Phillip let him riff. Conor could easily slip into hyperbole when working things out. Though he wasn't wrong. And now they were all on board this leaking vessel.

"Is there anything worth doing?" Phillip asked.

"One thing. Take your wife and kids on a vacation."

Phillip closed his eyes. He was technically in good-grace retirement. Never considered to be the same kind of threat as the Unit's other three. All of which meant nothing now. The four of them had roamed for years as a tight element, not only the envy of the capitol citiy's agencies, but more importantly, a cohesive team of confidants Kyle had never been able to breach.

The real war had been between Old Man DeMarco and Papa Bear Rawlings, more about jealousy and patrician ties than competence or fundamental abilities. The Old Man ran the show while Palmer senior had spent the past decade chipping away at the team's lack of oversight, built meticulously by the Old Man to shield them from DC's bureaucratic tangle. By design, he had ensured he answered to and worked with only a tight and limited number of overseers. The rest he'd been able to dispatch with vague promises or a handshake.

Since their inception after World War II, the various alphabet agencies had always existed on power structures of sand. And over the past decade, much like the city, allegiances had changed hands frequently. The game's overlords had drifted away from the brilliant tacticians such as DeMarco, and toward the inducements and cardboard promises of Rawlings Palmer and others of his ilk. Decisions began to get worked out in cigar rooms. The better and the brightest suffered within their own potential and propensity to make lesser minds nervous.

Eventually, most of the old soldiers were quietly shown the door. Lofty mission statements designed to avoid politics and favors easily ignored.

Palmer and his less-than cronies took over, generationally watered-down bluenoses stealing chairs at the adult table. Hypocrisy became a commodity never beyond reach, as weathered, dusty, and necessary as their wine cellars. Shame and morality were best left to others.

"I'm not fucking around," Conor said, desperation in his tone. "Get away. At least for a while."

Phillip found himself not as prepared for or resigned to this moment as he had once hoped. "Can you help keep my family safe?" he asked. "My wife knows where all the pennies are hidden, so they won't ever have to worry. We've always had a plan, but I'd sleep better if you made sure they had some company for a few weeks."

"Of course. But you need to go with them."

"If they're coming for us, you'll need me."

"Fucking idiot," Conor said, his words sharp and choked. "This is no time for an Alamo."

The pair of coyotes returned, marking the perimeter of the park. They paused outside the gate, locking eyes with the motionless humans on the bench fifty feet away. Their noses furrowed as the long jaws settled into jagged grins, wired to sense vulnerability. Finally, they trotted off, across the empty street and through the same garden bushes.

Phillip stood, pulling his friend's hoodie-covered head into his stomach. "It's about time, actually."

Conor wordlessly wrapped an arm around his waist.

Phillip knew his friend wouldn't show emotion until he was alone.

They broke apart, and Phillip walked back toward the gate, stopping momentarily on the damp grass to turn back. "I mentioned a theory to Mide. I think someone beyond Daddy has Kyle's ear in this. Probably someone we know."

Conor stared at him, obviously thrown. "Who would that be?"

But Phillip had walked away, the creaking metal gate *clank*ing back into place.

Heading north on the 405 freeway, the world's *worst*, Conor's drive to Chatsworth was surprisingly fast. By LA standards anyway.

His chosen exit deposited him in an area still somewhat industrial, despite the never-ending creep of suburban expansion taking everything it could, like a virus. A mile in any direction and he'd be sitting in another ubiquitous, sepia-toned strip mall, fighting for dinky parking slots with the hybrids and SUVs. Starbucks, 7-Eleven, and greasy Thai food joints anchored every inch they could pilfer, pushing lifelong residents deeper into the abyss of expanding borders. One of the city's several synthetic-drug-producing corridors sat a few miles east, dotting a quiet neighborhood like a pimply faced teenager.

The atypically desolate stretch of Roscoe Boulevard was quiet, even for seven a.m.

Kyle had called a staff meeting at his studio, situated a few streets west in an unobtrusive concrete building nestled between a wrecking yard and a restaurant supply depot. A narrow driveway wove around both sides. Conor chose one and drove around the two-story structure to the parking area in the rear. Not surprisingly, most of the twenty spots were filled.

The full-court press had begun.

Conor felt more weariness digging into the tissue near his bones. He was on fumes.

Inside, he made his way across a long rectangle of a carpet, loose and bunched in spots with well-trodden holes. He needed caffeine, and there would be plenty in the conference room, which he slipped into without fanfare. Not that it mattered.

The low hum of mumbling fizzled as he grabbed a cup of coffee from a corner nook, ignoring the cream, sweeteners, and heaping plate of fresh Danish. He turned to find ten sets of eyes trained on him, glares intended to evoke menace. Overly eager hard boys recruited outside the channels. Hired goons. Types the Old Man would never have signed off on.

Kyle was perched at the far end of a long meeting table, striped shadows from the window blinds clouding his expression. Jojo sat to his right, serious and on point.

Conor took a seat at the other end. *Half in, half out.* One of the few choices he could still make. He flipped the lid off his coffee, spinning it airborne and landing it within range of the assembled group. Condensation splashed on a few of their arms. Most ignored it, though one squinted, likely contemplating some tough-assed response.

Conor tipped his head to the side, fixing his stare at an angle. An old intimidation tactic courtesy of a tip several years ago from an interrogator buddy. The message of his body language was unmistakable. *Problem?*

Squinty held his grimace momentarily, finally breaking to brush the drops from his sleeve.

A voice of ego mumbled in his head. *Another friend made, Brennan.*

Not smart.

"I said seven a.m.," Kyle said, taking measure of his tardiness.

Conor took a prolonged slurp from the cup, raising his eyes just over the rim while slowly swallowing. "Traffic."

The room's tension inched higher. The assembled crowd took silent notice of the adults circling each other in the sandbox.

Kyle rolled his shoulders with agitation. Conor sensed movement behind a corner cubicle. Some other clown? Ready with party favors?

More likely one of Jojo's more functional eye closers. Either way, not a good sign.

"Fine," Kyle continued, anxious as usual and retiring immediately behind their usual dance routine. "Anything you want to bring us up to speed on, Mr. Brennan? I'd have to assume you've been busy the last few days?"

"This is your show. I was summoned. So I'm here."

"And you have no idea why?"

"I try not to spend much time contemplating the thought processes of smarter people."

A fraction of a smile tugged at Jojo's mouth.

Kyle's pallor darkened. "Okay, smart-ass. Let's move on." He was now talking to the entire table. "We have a problem with an old member of the firm. Truthfully, we've had these issues for years, but this particular problem has always proved, for various reasons, to be somewhat . . . untouchable."

"And now?" one of the new crew asked too eagerly.

"Take it the fuck easy, Cordell," Jojo said, spitting out the words. "This is a serious individual. With serious friends."

The mouthy offender's head dropped like a twelve-year-old shamed by a belligerent parent.

Grim skull bobs all around. *Followers.*

Conor stood to refill his coffee, purposely keeping his back to the room while attempting to find some inner peace and regulate his breathing. This was the third straight morning he'd missed his run, the only useful means to keeping his head lubricated and his sanity intact. His mind was concentrating on what Jojo had just said. Had the big man slipped? Maybe his statement to the flunky was intentional. Normally, such appraisals were left off the table. No need to give the hired help more reason than necessary to be edgy.

Conor sat back down, flipping his second lid with less torque. It landed harmlessly a few inches away.

"This is about one man," Conor said firmly, setting his eyes on Jojo. "The others are off-limits. Christian rules, and all that."

"And rules are always followed, right?" Kyle's voice dripped with de facto condescension. "Unless the Snow Leopard is involved."

Conor measured his temper by the rising bile in his throat. Sun Tzu would have said, "Look at the room, son, you are severely outnumbered." There was no safe endgame, and Conor assumed it was a toss-up as to whether he'd walk out of this meeting upright and breathing. Kyle was like so much of the new breed taking cues from that pumpkin-faced fat ass who'd been anointed king. Blind loyalty and greed the only job requirements.

Still, Conor remained one of the Unit's active and well-regarded members. Meaning he had to play it out and keep it all straight. But he refused to stomach never-ending lies and bullshit.

"Midas has been a dormant saloon keeper for years," he said. "*You* poked the bear with Serena. At least sack up enough to admit it."

Jojo shook his head, silently imploring him to take it down. He and Conor held a healthy respect for each other, and Jojo, even as part of that loyalty gang, was still no fan of Kyle's. But the ex-ranger had made his choice a long time ago and now served at his pleasure.

"You archaic asshole," Kyle said, the phony smile turning rigid. "Fuck you, fuck DeMarco, and most of all, fuck your morality. In or out, Conor? Choose."

"Well said," Conor shot back. "And I'm here, aren't I?"

"Honestly?" Kyle sat back. "I'm never sure."

The moment passed, testosterone in retreat, followed by more stirring behind the hidden cubicle.

"Tell me, Jojo," Conor said. "Who you got stashed in the corner?"

The shifting and rustling immediately ceased. He conjured an image of another freelance tough guy freezing in place like a cornered raccoon behind the partition.

Kyle's eyes betrayed him, sliding to it and back, nervous.

"You're a bit too old to be paranoid," Jojo said dryly.

Conor stood again and started for the cubicle. "Even so, I'll just have a quick look."

Jojo and the rentals rose in unison, with two moving out to block his progress.

Conor halted his roll.

"Not today," Jojo said.

Kyle stood up, joining the fray only when self-preservation had been assured.

The others stood in place, feet apart, ready if necessary.

"I think the rest of us can take it from here, Mr. Brennan," Kyle said. "My order is this: You can go. Stay away from Midas and the rest of Spanky's Gang. It isn't a request. Jojo will be in touch with more instructions soon."

Conor scanned the faces one more time, committing them to memory. He waved with feigned assurance and walked out under the weight of silence.

Shit. He might have a day or two.

Midas couldn't shake the feeling.

Like so much else, instinct was prone to the detriments of age. Fortunately, his was still functional, and was now shouting at him to run.

His coffee had gone cold, staining the sides of the heavy white cup. He pushed it toward the center of the Formica table and leaned back, stretching his spine against the tight red vinyl of the booth. In an era of new construction and open floor plans, the suspended lamps and cigarette machines in this diner were refreshingly retro. Thanks to trendy touches and early Tarantino flicks, coffee shops had gone renaissance, easy access to be met and seen. This one sat at the base of the Hollywood Hills. Growling cars hummed past a few feet away on the busy 101.

Mason was fond of saying that LA was nothing but isolated villages connected by freeways, decaying streets, and orange traffic cones.

The attractive waitress stopped at his table with a silver pot. He placed a flat hand over his cup. "Can I have a new one?" Her look hardened momentarily, easing somewhat when he smiled. She might have been twenty-four, one generation removed from Honduras or El Salvador, with an assured and serene manner that had genetically bypassed the yoga crowd from the beach and rest of the Westside.

"You want anything with it?" she asked, pointing to a menu lodged behind the silver table jukebox.

"Coffee's fine, thanks."

She returned with the fresh cup. He sipped while surveying the clientele, a well-oiled habit of overcompensating through unease. Two fresh-faced guys with gel-spiked hair took turns marking a script with a red Sharpie. A few tables down, a homeless woman drank iced tea, diligently keeping an eye on her loaded, filthy shopping cart outside the window. Beyond that and the low hum of the oldies wafting through unseen speakers, the place was empty.

Midmorning was Midas's preferred part of the day, nesting between the antiquated rituals of breakfast and lunch.

There was a shift in the air. Midas felt his frame go taut and moved into a defensive position.

Conor appeared, seating himself across the booth.

"Midas," he said as if they'd been doing this as routine for years. He motioned to the waitress for coffee.

His old compatriot was something of a stranger after so much time, but his detached and slightly annoyed expression was nothing new.

Midas scanned the doors.

"I'm alone, bro. This is a social visit. Like I said when I called."

The years had changed little about Conor Brennan. His dirty blond hair was still thinning and pulled behind the ears. There were a few more lines around his mouth, and the leather jacket, soft cotton T-shirt, and Levi's were well-worn. Conor spent good money for casual clothes that allowed freedom of motion.

"Social?" Midas cocked an eyebrow.

"What's it been?" Conor asked.

"A bit. Guess I don't have to ask what you've been up to . . ."

Conor's eyes betrayed sorrow. "Not like you kept in touch."

More coffee arrived. Conor poked it with a spoon, trolling for grounds beneath the inky surface. He added a small amount of sugar from a hardened packet. "Artificial sweeteners," he observed. "One of many things turning us into weenies and the later generations into raving stone crushers." He chuckled at his own observation, taking note of Midas's straining forearms across the table. "Loosen up, Mide. This is off the books."

Midas studied the forced smile. Much like himself, Conor had always hated his nickname, *smiling Con*, though the polished cheerfulness had proved one of his many useful tools. In another era, it had served the team well.

"What can I do for you, Con?"

Conor took a quick slug, staring outside the window at the never-ending rush hour zipping past like slot cars.

Midas joined the appraisal, perusing the street but seeing nothing.

Conor's attention returned to his coffee. "Other than a couple of eggs, I honestly don't want a damn thing."

The pretty waitress ambled back, standing a few feet away as she took the order and disappeared. Conor inhaled deeply, his T-shirt stretching over his expanding rib cage.

The clock had run out on them all. Midas couldn't help feeling defeated about another compromised friend.

"Where's the chariot?" Midas asked, deflecting. Cars were an interest they had once shared. His old friend indulged in two passions, his 1970 ebony Cutlass S and his model-train store called The Freight Yard.

He'd once told Midas how he'd acquired his unlikely affection for small trains as a teenager, having previously written them off as clunky, battery-powered junk brought out of plastic storage bins during Christmas. His uncle's railroad appeared every year right after Thanksgiving. Conor had laughed at memories of his cousin reapplying glue to the underside of Santa's miniature boots so he wouldn't fall off the top of the caboose while spreading his jolly cheer.

Then one lazy Saturday in his senior year, a teammate from his high school track squad had dragged him to a model-train convention, and despite his whining and misgivings, Conor had been mesmerized by the colors, smells, and the sweet-tempered high whistles. There had been a serenity from the abundance of grown men in silly hats hunched over the oily tracks in the cavernous main hall. He'd been hooked, soon dispatching his understanding mother's Audi to the street in front of their home while diligently starting his own rail line in the garage.

"The Cutlass is up the street, around the corner," Conor answered with a cocky grin.

Unlike most of LA, Conor parked in sketchy areas with no apprehension. If anyone got nosy, he was notified by an app. Midas had no idea how much the security system had cost, but assumed it wasn't cheap... or legal.

Along with his trains, Conor loved his old Detroit muscle. Midas was a Jag man. His '75 XJ-S sat inside the right bay of his two-car beach garage, rolled out every few weeks to stretch the pistons. You couldn't pay him to park it around here.

"Pleasantries aside, would you be wondering how I found your new digits?" Conor asked, looking smug.

"I wasn't, actually."

"Still the sharpest bastard in the room."

"Phillip?" Midas guessed.

"I told him he needed to lie low. I don't think he heard me. You might want to reinforce the idea."

"I will. What about you?"

It was a direct question, one Conor responded to with subtle fiddling. A slow, meticulous push on the sugar dispenser. Scratching a dried-out cuticle. He could have been Brando working his way through the Method.

At length Conor said, "Remember all the fun we used to have?"

Midas shifted his eyes back to the street. Two guys in spandex and Dri-FIT were dodging traffic on Franklin Boulevard, which ran under the freeway. Once across, they pushed buttons on their watches and broke into a slow lope.

"I told you this was off the books," Conor hissed. "I've never lied to you, and it's a bit late to start now."

Midas knew he should have felt a measure of shame, but the sand had shifted, and Conor was still Unit. *Still inside.*

"You bring out my gruff nature," Midas said.

"And you've been a little busy. Amazing you can find the time between wave rides and the saloon."

Midas leaned forward, dropping his eyelids to half staff. Waiting.

"You went native," Conor continued. "But now you've re-emerged. Not that you didn't have a sensible excuse." He briefly held up a hand.

"And?"

"These hits? Are beyond the good-taste agreement."

"We don't have any agreements," Midas said, the slow boil of fury beginning to bubble. "Not anymore."

Conor's head cocked to the side again, eye contact designed to challenge. "I know you'd like to believe that. Problem is . . . well, you know."

"No," Midas said through a growl, reaching for his coffee. "I don't know."

The eggs arrived, providing a few moments of détente. Conor cut into them military style, bleeding the yolks into the hash browns. "I'd eat this shit three times a day if I could."

Midas realized the music had moved on from eighties oldies to a moodier set list in anticipation of the midday lunch crowd. Moby's "Natural Blues" carried hauntingly over the mostly empty tables. Conor shoveled the mess on his plate with edges of toast. Between bites, he laid out his agenda.

"The agreement, in case you've forgotten, was hammered out by the Old Man with love and care. You, Philly, and Mase were allowed to fuck off." He paused to wipe the corner of his mouth. "Kyle and his father? Were forced to stand down. Obviously, that truce couldn't hold forever."

"Serena," Midas said unnecessarily.

Conor halted his fueling, pushing the half-finished plate away, looking as if his gut was already turning sour. "I don't have any plays, Mide. As reprehensible as that was, I can't be your friend anymore."

"I appreciate that. But this isn't your fault or concern."

Conor shook his head. He refused to passively accept a freeze-out, alliances or not. "Everything is my concern. Five years ago, you all went walkabout. Someone had to watch the store."

Midas recognized the initial stages of a new migraine. His overloaded hard drive with no capacity for cleansing. Those years had taken from them all.

"Serena?" Midas whispered, the rising thunder in his ears making him wince. "That's what you call... *oversight*?"

Conor tried to smile, but it turned down. "What do you want me to say, Mide? Kyle kept me out of the room. I was in Rome, with a woman I'm sure has already moved on. Your passport popped at the Mexican border, and my phone *pinged*. Then you left that mess, and a few more since. You knew I'd get the message."

"Was it clear enough?"

"I'd say so."

Overnight insomniac vampires and frustrated thespians were beginning to file into the diner, hoping strong coffee and strangers' faces might jolt the creative neurons. The music was tilting again, this time in the direction of alternative. Early Depeche. Two more waitresses had materialized for the rush, older and frayed in that unique Hollywood sort of way.

The general hum was rising, giving them a bit more privacy.

"You've left a lot in your wake this past week," Conor said, tension lines tugging below his cheeks.

"It needed to happen." Midas noted to himself how tired he

suddenly felt. "But it doesn't have to be your problem, Con."

"Except it is. I've been told to sit back and wait for Kyle to perhaps summon me to the final party, whatever that ends up looking like. Till then, I'm on the disabled list playing with my trains and tuning up my car."

Midas shook his head, no remedy for his spinning sense of impotence. "You and the Old Man made me possible when my old man kicked me to the curb. If anyone owes, it's me."

"Then do me one last favor and back off. Dig a deep hole and cover up. Let me try to work something out. Kyle's a renegade and a compulsive prick. Given some time, he'll lose his leverage. Maybe DeMarco somehow rallies. But for now, with Kyle and his father drawing up the map, I'm sidelined. Not a place I like to be."

Lunch rush had officially begun. Most of the tables were full. Midas usually enjoyed the camaraderie of restaurants and bars, sensations of normality within packs of strangers. Not so much today.

"Everyone suffered because I lost it that night back in Mexico," he said. "We can both agree that Kyle should be off somewhere training sharks. Or worse. Except now he's branched out to selling kids. It all needs to stop, one way or another."

Conor shook his head. "Even if you take care of the Kyle problem, you'll be running forever. Rawlings Palmer has too much reach. Too many black ledgers and owed favors. So, officially, here it is. I spoke to Phil, and now I'm talking to you."

Beneath the polish and grimy bravado, Conor was still playing his natural role—that of the fixer. No matter how bad it tasted.

"I want to see Kyle," Midas said. "I need you to walk me in."

Conor slid out of the booth to stand, brushing crumbs from his jeans. "Not a chance. Get someone else to stand you up in front of the rifles and the bloody wall." He flicked a twenty from his front pocket onto the Formica. "You know what I think about a lot these days, Mide? Berkeley and Oakland. How much we all used to laugh. We were young, and we were friends. To this day, I've only had a few." He turned away, visibly not trusting himself to hold it together. "Don't count on me," he said, low but not enough so that Midas wouldn't hear.

Conor had a talent for vanishing—one of many things about him Midas could appreciate.

Phillip Gillis hated this trudge.

After shelling out the exorbitant day rate, it was a mile walk, all uphill. Though he had to admit, the city zoo did offer impressive sights. Orange flamingos, spider monkeys, a young pair of brown bears. He knew Midas had a love-hate with zoos—animal jails, as he called them—lamenting he found the caging of majestic beasts depressing, though he could understand the humane opportunities they offered families to appreciate various species they'd otherwise never get a chance to see.

Over the past few years, liberal and civic-minded donors had been generous to the Los Angeles Zoo. Winding trails and routes throughout the Griffith Park property were smooth and clean, and its inhabitants appeared well fed. Passing the croc and otter enclosures, Phillip ran through the conversation he was surely about to have. Despite Conor's warnings, he had no choice but to stay close, and move his information forward.

Today's crowd was dense despite the mild temps of the LA winter. Children were pushed in vividly painted elephant strollers or wagons with smiling pachyderm faces, rentable devices to make the visit more manageable for overwrought parents. He caught the weary eye of a mom heroically trying to keep up with the never-ending demands of her sugar-infused youngsters. Phillip had been here with his kids several years ago, moving from one pen to the next, praying there would be something fascinating enough about a group of gorillas, or whatever, that his girls would be smitten, and he could sit for a few minutes in relative peace.

To this day, both daughters continued to cultivate their mother's innate curiosity, soaking up such outings with unencumbered gusto. The younger, now fifteen, kept a photo of that zoo visit in her room, her excited face glittering from high on an observation deck right next to the long, rectangular head of a giraffe that had taken a liking to her. The popcorn she'd sneaked him might have helped . . . Phillip remembered his daughter's giggle when the big animal nuzzled her small hands. No fear, only the robust contentedness children possessed before filters of adolescence began to gum up the works. These days, at least she humored him, sweet enough at times that he could occasionally feel like a worthy father. But she was growing up, and the math was constantly changing. Much more whispering with her mother and conversations behind closed doors. Female talk meant exclusion. Her older sister had shut him out years ago, so he relished the moments when his little one still let him pretend. Pretty soon, he'd be begging her for five minutes of face time.

Normal, perhaps, but it still felt like encroaching abandonment. He'd never stop cherishing that giraffe's gentle touch, or his daughter's giggle.

Fifteen minutes and several detours along the black-paved path delivered him atop the park's highest point. The backside of the Hollywood Hills and Los Feliz perched in the distance.

Midas was leaning over a silver metal railing above a huge pit enclosing a low-yield, tundra-inspired domicile. A concrete-bottomed pool reflected the sun through an aqua prism, and a few blades of long grass floated across the surface. In the rear was a wall of deep, red-clay caves.

The inhabitants were out, stalking the perimeters.

Bengal tigers were magnificent creatures, 450 pounds of vivid orange and black stripes, with paws the size of watermelons. These two moved slowly, muscled shoulders and flanks flexing in time with each step. They stopped occasionally to look up, measuring the human rubes taking phone snaps while cooing with awe and fear.

"You know," Midas said, talking as much to the big cats as to Phillip, "there's something about those faces, the way they look right through us. In their world, problems are handled. No fuss."

"Given the chance, they'd likely rip us to shreds," Phillip said.

"It's their turf. I wouldn't blame them."

Phillip had seen Midas in this box before, searching for sense where none existed.

"Why the hell are we at the tiger pit?" he asked. "Shouldn't we be talking around the corner where they have the new baby snow—?"

Midas shot him a look, cutting him off. "Bad enough peering down on these fellas. Those would be too much."

"And you're *too damn sensitive*."

Midas tried to smile, instead working up a resigned slant that made him look twenty years older, mitigated somewhat by his smooth, shining eyes, buffed head, and cocoa-shaded skin that never seemed to sag.

The tigers started to playfully wrestle like a pair of common house cats. Even this they performed with natural grace. Midas was right. Higher reality.

"What couldn't be handled over the phone?" Midas asked.

Phillip bounced on the balls of his feet. Animal scents drifted past, courtesy of a light shift in the breeze. "I'm sorry, Mide. Things have gotten a little out of hand."

"Ya think?"

"Got a call early this morning. You realize that mornings are the one time of day I am granted occasional sightings of my daughters? I might as well be a kitchen stool these days. They're grabbing a juice, loading up their bags, speed texting. A good day is when one gives me a forced smile. A peck on the cheek might as well be Christmas. The young one complains I never shave enough. She's probably right. I hate shaving."

Phillip knew he was delaying, not quite sure of what to say.

"They love their dad," Midas said matter-of-factly. "Everything else can't be controlled."

"And we can never go back, can we? Or make things right."

Midas ran a hand over the polished dome of his skull. "Making things right is a myth. All we can do is try to be better."

"Where do the Baz brothers and Rudy the pimp fall on the making-things-better board?" Phillip asked.

"They don't."

"Don't ply me with that evasive, philosophical bullshit."

Three probable teenage gang members sidled up, girlfriends in tow. Cotton tees and baggy shorts billowing over long socks and puffy white kicks. The girls were dark brunettes with craggy blond streaks, painted with more foundation and eyeliner than runway models, and stuffed into jeans at least one size too small. One of the boys took the rail next to Midas, overtly studying the old-er man's relaxed composure. Competing impulses were obviously pushing the kid's wiring—fear and a need to properly front. He flexed one arm, a sleeve of tats.

"Hey, homes," he said. Midas gave him the corner of one eye. "Those tigers can fuck you up, eh?" He'd cultivated the Latino lilt, though this one was probably a fourth-generation Angeleno.

"Faster than a hollow point," Midas replied.

The kid straightened up, puffing his skinny chest and weighing options. Had he just been disrespected? And if so, what came next?

Phillip rolled his eyes, exhaled, and turned to face the rest of the group with a practiced and disarming expression. The alpha was looking to his posse. Thankfully, better judgment settled in, and the kid started to laugh. Soon they were all laughing.

The kid put a friendly hand on Midas's shoulder, recoiling a bit from the tautness of the cords under his fingers. "That's funny, bro." He wiped his hand on his XXL T-shirt. "I'm Victor."

"Hello, Victor," Midas said, turning his full attention. "You all enjoying your visit?"

Midas had a way, always had. People liked him, and more im-portantly, wanted him to like them.

Victor looked out again over the small vista below. "Animals are insane, yo?"

"I'd say they are," Midas replied.

A sharp *chirp*, Victor's cell. He motioned, and the gaggle moved to head back down the hill. "Take it slow," Victor said, then point-ed at Phillip. "You too bro." He fell back into line with his friends, and they ambled off like any other typical teenagers, laughing and good-heartedly roughhousing, generating small shrieks from the girls.

"Serena," Midas said, still possessing the maddening ability to pick up a conversation exactly where it had been halted, sometimes hours later. "Was that in bounds?"

"You know that isn't what I'm saying," Phillip said.

The tigers stopped wrestling, raising their heads skyward, as if sensing the presence of negative ions floating over their tranquility.

"Somebody reached out to you."

Phillip rummaged in his pocket, pulling out a pair of sunglasses and pushing them on. "Some guy named Grant Collins. A fed."

Midas unconsciously rubbed his chest. "Great," he said, his expression waffling between exasperation and inevitability.

"Wanted to know all about Midas McKnight. I played it straight. Said we'd once been business associates. But that was several years ago. He wasn't buying, not for a second. He ignored my tale and started asking the real questions. The Armenian brothers. Peddler Rudy. How the hell could he be that plugged into everything so fucking fast?"

"The Palmers," Midas said. "Covering themselves by calling in a favor. From what I've heard, Palmer senior has the FBI director on his cell's favorites list. Probably feeding them all just enough to get my name out there and let them do some heavy lifting. If Kyle can't play this out, he figures the feds can."

The bright winter sun was starting to descend. As it deserted the zoo and its blacktop paths, a slight chill took hold. Grateful parents pulled extra layers out of bulging totes and started back toward the gift shop and the exit. It wasn't long before Phillip and Midas were mostly alone with their two striped friends, who'd once again picked up the intensity of their wrestling. Dinner would be served around five p.m., and they were hungry.

"It cuts our options," Phillip said.

"So why did you really drag me out, Phil? Instead of a simple phone call?"

Phillip turned his back to the tigers. Resigned. "I did some extra excavating, called in a few favors myself."

"And?"

"Michelle Kelly."

Midas looked as though he hadn't heard right. Michelle had been a bartender at Shredders, and at one point for Midas, much more. Then she'd vanished, quitting both the bar and grad school. Midas hadn't tried to change her mind.

"What about her?" Midas asked warily.

Phillip couldn't fight the reluctance to continue, so remained silent for several beats.

"Michelle Kelly," Midas said firmly, more statement than question.

Phillip jetted out a breath. "She drifted into Kyle's world. I don't know how. But she's been with him for the past six months."

Midas seemed to physically shrink, taking hold of the railing. Phillip had felt the same way when he'd been told. The idea of the two of them as a pair was too hard to contemplate.

"I might have passed this off as Kyle making you squirm with a move on your old girlfriend . . ."

"Except for what?" Midas asked in a soft demand.

Phillip's mouth sagged, lactose surging through his quads and turning them into liquid. If he'd been standing next to an arthritic geriatric, it would have been hard to tell them apart. He rolled the heels of his hands over his shaking legs.

"Just tell me," Midas said, fatigue in his words.

A logistics man to his core, years earlier Phillip had forced himself to accept the realities of their lives. It had become his process for making sense of ambiguity, the strongest enemy. He was a strict left-brainer, avoiding nonabsolutes and nature in favor of numbers, finding a modicum of peace reframing dilemmas into patterns he could solve.

"Serena was taken after an appointment with a photographer," Phillip began, deliberately whispering even though there wasn't anyone else around. "Some guy who worked out of the part of the city called Palms. Has a studio over on Venice Boulevard. She wanted some tasteful shots from the beach. She was building a digital site for her eventual therapy practice. The referral for this guy came from Michelle Kelly, who apparently had stayed in touch with her after she'd split the bar."

"Serena never mentioned that to me."

"Why would she? Michelle helped her get the job. They were buddies from Marymount. And Serena had known Michelle a helluva lot longer than you. I figure Kyle used that, and then worked this photog to set up the grab."

"Michelle was the one who called it quits with us," Midas said despite himself, seemingly still not believing it all. "Said we would never work out."

"None of that matters anymore," Phillip said. "The Old Man's in a coma, and Rawlings Palmer is hovering. Father or not, he'll never be able to control his son. And as distasteful as junior may be to the clan, Kyle is the family money changer. He knows he can call his own shots. And now you've stanched his financial river." Phillip took a beat and briefly closed his eyes.

Even for a hardened operator like Midas, it was too much. "That was the point."

"You've got to get out of Dodge, Mide. Serena will be okay. We'll all make sure of that."

"You got GPS on this photog?" Midas asked.

"You aren't listening." Phillip heard the plea in his tone.

"I've been doing nothing but listening for the past week."

"Surprised you had the time."

Phillip hadn't expected to get through to Midas. And it wasn't like he'd taken the same advice from Conor that morning. None of them was going anywhere. He pulled a card from his rear pocket and handed it over, then walked away. He stopped midway down the path.

Midas was flipping the card through his fingers.

"Hey, asshole," Phillip barked, a flash of fond recognition passing between them. "Next time the aquarium, right? You know I love the otters."

CHAPTER 9

FROM ATOP THE HOOD of her car, Natalie strained to see a sliver of ocean under the early-morning fog.

The gunmetal overcast had been hanging around for days, relegating the sun to brief and infrequent appearances. At this hour, Playa del Rey's Dockweiler Beach was owned by the surf dogs, a sparse coven at this hour given the lack of decent waves. The fact that the summer swells were still months off didn't matter to the half-dozen souls bobbing like buoys forty yards out. They did have a small audience, a smattering of the resident coastal homeless huddled under makeshift tents next to the closed snack bar and fragrant public toilets.

Special Agent Collins had pinged last night requesting an out-of-office face-to-face, which would have been concerning had he not mentioned he surfed the Doc on occasion, and wouldn't it be easier to meet there? Closer to her office, and for him a chance for a quick morning session.

Feds. Never letting a chance go by to point out when they were doing you a favor. Banking some future chit.

Natalie hadn't seen Mason for the past few days, and despite misgivings, she found her thoughts drifting to Collins. She hated that he'd been on her mind, and what that implied. His text had amped her anxiety, tossing emotions into conflict. She didn't need a shrink to explain. Same profession, same confidence, mingled with that healthy measure of charm and grace.

Bastard even looked like that other cop she'd once known.

She took a few deep breaths and reclined against the windshield, closing her eyes as her mind retreated into the past. Ritual and process. All else faded, and she was back home, almost thirty years ago. Reliving what should have been just another day under the bleak Nordic sky . . .

October wasn't an especially cruel month in Reykjavik.

Her small family welcomed the fall, sitting inside on crisp nights with the fire and cocoa.

The bib skirt over long sleeves and trainers, along with a chunky red sweater, was more than enough for her quarter-mile walk home. Icelandic schools expected compliance, more so for the eight-year-old daughter of a celebrated local artist and a police captain. She marched through her days and lessons without issue, though was less self-assured when it came to youthful social skills. Her mother would describe her to friends as guarded, unable to give herself over to the normal pleasures and necessary silliness of childhood.

It was only three p.m., but the sun would soon be down, and her parents insisted she return home right after school. It would take her years to realize neurotic parenting parameters were extensions of the country itself, outwardly reserved, aloof, and genetically untrusting. A small nation muddling through the never-ending days of summer and ceaseless nights of winter.

Today, Natalie hurried her pace, unsure of what awaited her.

Miss Viitala had been in a sour mood and had taken it out on her. Her teacher was always grouchy, having fled a bad marriage in Helsinki to start over in Iceland. At least that's what Natalie had overheard her father once tell her mother. But this morning Natalie had made it too easy. Fridrik the pest had started in on her the moment they'd donned outerwear and moved outside for recess. He liked to pick on her. It gave him a measure of standing with the other young tyrants to take aggression out on someone whose father was an important man.

Initially she'd ignored him, taking her usual refuge on the freezing metal gym bars. All had been fine until Fridrik crossed the line. Standing below her as she pulled herself up and down, he'd made a crack about cops being stupid. She'd dropped to the ground, nearly slipping on the remains of two-day-old ice while responding with one of the three moves her father had taught her. She struck high on one arm, then low to the groin, both with a tight, closed fist. Fridrik's bullying smile faltered as he crumpled in place, slithering on the frozen concrete like a howling prairie dog just loud enough to victimize himself into an afternoon of service as teacher's pampered helper, complete with lunch perks that included candy and soda. Sugary treats were normally verboten—a German term her father used—but Miss Viitala kept a stash and lavished them on students who made her feel needed. The rest she likely ate herself, which could have been the reason that at the relatively young age of thirty-five, she was already surrendering the best parts of her fair complexion and moderate attractiveness to blotches and yellowing teeth.

Though, such perceptions and clear-eyed deductive thinking were still many years away for Natalie.

This afternoon she felt only anger and shame. Miss Viitala never passed up an opportunity to punish her. Today that had meant sitting her center stage on a small chair in the outsize room used for recitals and plays. She sat alone for four hours, the rest of the classroom day, allowed to do nothing but brood. Bathroom trips off-limits. No lunch, or even water. Miss Viitala was a sadist—another observation Natalie would tumble to some years later.

As she made her way home, she thought about the phone call that had surely already been made. Her mother, Elise, would have listened patiently, paying scant attention before beguiling the school principal into a less drastic course of action. Of course, her mother would agree, Natalie was a spoiled and precocious child and needed special handling. And of course, Elise and her father would have the latest of many stern talks with their daughter. But there was certainly no need to take her out of the gifted class in favor of a level below, the more benign track?

Natalie had been blessed with her painter mother's vivid visual sense. She could just imagine Principal Lekkonen—another unhappy transplanted Finn—perched behind his functional IKEA desk, a vile little ass-kisser with large glasses and a pointed, possum nose. He'd have played out the charade, taken his time feigning deep thought before agreeing that Natalie was a valued member of his school and simply needed a firm hand, both in class and at home. Elise would no doubt have gracefully thanked him for his insight and wisdom before inviting his family to her next show at a gallery on Laugavegur Street. She would ring off with best wishes for the overburdened Miss Viitala, and a vague promise to have that talk with her daughter. Crisis averted, as her father liked to say.

As she rounded the corner of her street, Natalie shuddered once at the imagined scene and trudged on.

Unlike most children, she wasn't one to procrastinate or stall the inevitable. Once home she bounded through the door, closing it with more authority than was necessary, ready to initiate the defensive strategy she'd been thinking about for hours. She waited for her mother's soft, angry summons, straining to hear the chair scraping over the polished hardwood in the back bedroom she used as her studio, the light brushes hitting the wooden easel followed by the sharp intake of exasperation Elise reserved for her daughter . . . and moments like this.

Natalie and her father called her mother by her first name. Even though there had been so many days she'd wanted to come home, snuggle up, and call her "Mommy." But she'd been told she was almost nine, far too old for childish things.

Though none of that mattered now. Listening carefully, what she heard was . . . nothing.

Strange.

Give it a few seconds. Maybe she was out back or in the bathroom.

Natalie passed through the kitchen like a cat burglar, doing her best to make no noise—a useless change in tactic, as she'd already slammed the front door. She'd passed Elise's car parked in front of the garage. But her mother wouldn't have walked to the store, not in the cold and so late in the day.

Natalie performed a cursory search of their modest house. There was no sign of her.

She moved back into the living room, stopping at the phone table. The red message button blinked like a fresh wound. She punched it. Lekkonnen's pinched voice came through hesitantly, fear in his tone. He was still groveling thirty seconds later when she pushed another button and erased the call. Screw Fridrik and Miss Viitala. Crisis averted.

But where was her mother? Something didn't feel right. She was never not at home when Natalie returned from school unless there was a special reason, and if that were the case, it would have been planned and discussed in detail the night before. Her parents were driven and meticulous, beyond careful when it came to their only child.

Natalie moved back into the living room. She tried a trick her father had taught her, designed to slow her thoughts when panic started creeping in, by counting the few pieces of furniture that saw use only when relatives or important people came over. It was no good. All she could focus on was how lonely and scared she suddenly was.

She started to recall her mother had been different the past few weeks, quiet and, by her own admission, "unfocused." Again, something it would take years for Natalie to comprehend. Though at that moment, the term absent-minded seemed a good fit.

She told herself Elise must have stepped out for an errand and simply forgotten what time it was.

Her thoughts began to shift from fear to opportunity. There was ice cream in the freezer, and in the pantry, sugar-sweetened cereal she was allowed only on Saturday mornings. Back in the kitchen, she poured herself a heaping mound from the box covered with brightly colored cartoon characters. After adding milk, she sat at the kitchen table and went to work on her bounty, assuming whenever her mother did come home, she would be forgiven the cereal indulgence because she'd been home all alone. The day was slowly getting better.

She was near the bottom of the bowl when she heard the unmistakable sound of her father's Volvo, several years old and desperately in need of maintenance. Natalie loved the approaching growl of his car. Unlike Ms. Viitala, and more frequently Elise, her father never seemed anything but happy to see her.

But now the nagging feelings were returning. He never came home before seven p.m., and sometimes well after she'd gone to bed. This was far too early. She ran to the front window. The car was in the driveway puffing white smoke from the rear muffler. Kristjan Riiska sat in the driver's seat, hunched and perfectly still. The cereal began to claw in her small stomach. Her eyes began to pool. He didn't look right, and she was suddenly frightened. It was for only a few seconds, but it seemed as if he sat for hours in the diminishing veil of the old vehicle's exhaust. For someone who always relished coming home to his girls, the delay was troubling.

Her father emerged from the car slowly, one leg hitting the ground, then the other, nothing spry in his measured tempo. Later she'd remember this walk as from someone much older than a man in his late thirties. His shape disappeared from view once he hit the front porch. She heard him fumble for keys and ran to the door, opening it. He was startled, his bright blue eyes shiny. He tried to smile and failed. She moved to the side, reminding him to come in. He finally did, cupping his large hand around the back of her neck and pulling her in for a long hug. For years she wouldn't remember any other small details, only the intense numbness that flooded her nerves as he picked her up and carried her upright into the living room, gently setting her down on a small wooden chair.

He descended to her level, taking a knee.

It reminded her of church—something else she hated.

"Natalia," he said, using her full first name that her mother had insisted on. His eyes dropped as his hands started to shake. He grabbed his knees.

"Daddy?" she chirped, hearing a choke in her voice.

"Elise has left us. She won't be coming back."

Natalie blinked, then started sobbing. She'd had only a few long moments to prepare for what she'd instinctively realized would be bad news, but, as she'd often heard her father say about his work, no one is ever ready for bad news.

"She's dead?" Natalie asked meekly.

Her father's face snapped up, tear streaked and drawn. The early hints of gray in his hair were harder to see in the low afternoon light. He smiled sadly but with warmth. "No, Natalia. She just decided she needed to go away. She didn't want to leave you, but she prefers to be alone, for now at least."

Relief came briefly, the weight in Natalie's stomach lifting as she started to understand. She would see her mother again. But then came the fear, with questions and blame for the only other person in the room.

"But we're her family," she protesting.

"Your mother needs time." He was talking as much to himself as to her.

"Why? What did you do?" she accused sharply.

She instantly regretted the words that brought fresh pain into her father's eyes. She felt shame but would soon come to realize that in a war of conflicting emotions, anger usually took charge, a protection against vulnerability. She straightened her back against the rear of the chair, folding her arms in a pose worthy of Miss Viitala.

"Obviously I did something," he said through the strain. "Because she's gone."

"Ob-vi-ous-ly!" Natalie screamed. They were learning about syllables in school, and that word had four. Launching herself off the chair to hide a fresh batch of misery, she ran into her room, slamming another door.

She stood near her bed waiting for the latest sobbing fit to pass. Her world had fallen into a deep hole and taken her along. What was she supposed to do now? Where had her mother gone? Shouldn't she have taken her daughter with her? Good questions that, even then, Natalie understood had no immediate answers.

Through the blur of tears, her eyes adjusted. The bedroom was as neat as she had left it. But there was something on her bed .. . one of her mother's paintings? She cautiously moved forward, each step requiring more effort. It was face up, full of the colors she'd come to understand mirrored her mother's moods, sullen while also vibrant. The painting was of an owl. Her mother had nurtured her love of animals, and Natalie's favorite was this mysterious bird of prey. Specifically, the snowy owl, mostly white with dark spots on the wings and parts of its breast, reclusive and rarely seen. Rounded heads perched above strong necks, intelligent eyes of black and yellow that, like her own, missed very little, more curse than virtue. She had found them fascinating.

Her mother's version possessed creator's liberties, soft at the edges, yellow substituting for the black. This owl stared out from the canvas, silently taking in her sadness. It was beautiful, like everything her mother did, but also restrained, lacking the detail of her other work. Natalie wondered whether it had been done in a hurry. It was the size of a small portrait. She moved to pick it up, and only then noticed the corner of something else hiding beneath it. She grabbed an edge with caution, like a burning match, and slowly pulled out a handwritten note. There were only a few words.

Natalia, I will see you soon.

No apology, or reason for leaving. Only a weak promise.

She read it three times, the rage returning, growing with each reading. Her hands worked furiously to rip the paper into the smallest shreds possible. She threw them onto the bed, then carefully rolled the picture into a tube, as she had seen her mother do so many times, placing it on the small desk near her bed. She dropped face-first into her pillows. As a fresh round of torment shook her entire body, there was a hesitant knock.

"Natalia? Natalia . . . ?"

"Detective Riiska?"

Her eyes opened, squinting against the cold wetness of the LA fog over the Pacific. She was disoriented, staring into her father's face. Except it wasn't her father.

Special Agent Grant Collins was studying her with something that looked like pity.

He leaned on the car hood, looking younger than he had in the office. The corner of his eyes ran smooth. The shorty wet suit was faded, and like his casual office clothes, he wore it comfortably.

She shook herself out of the memory and dredged up a smile.

He handed her a warm lidded cup. He'd brought coffee from Dogtown, a local favorite in Santa Monica.

Not too bad, she figured. For a fed.

For a few minutes they basked in the breeze and release from the caffeine, enjoying coastal sights still unencumbered and free.

"Coffee okay?"

"Great. Thanks for the service."

He shrugged it off, obviously not one for compliments either. "So, if I can ask? Iceland to LA law enforcement. Not a typical progression."

She swirled inside her cooling cup with a pinkie, the movement slightly hypnotic, creating a small tempest. She hunched forward and took a deep breath.

"Not as atypical as it sounds. My father was a Reykjavik cop. We moved to London when I was a teenager, after he took a job with Interpol. He died six years later, after I'd finished college and was working with the Metropolitan Police out of Islington. A few years after that, I accepted transfer to the Seattle PD. Five years there before transferring here."

"So why LA?"

"Got tired of the Northwest winters, the gray and gloom," she said, with an ironic backhanded wave at the overcast hanging strong over the building swells.

He raised his cup, peering at her over the rim. "I wouldn't be doing my job if I didn't run your creds, Detective."

She felt her defensiveness rise, hoping to avoid a conversation with details few knew about. "I really don't need some busybody checking up on me. Or running games on my head."

Collins's expression told her the words had stung. *Again.* He put his coffee down on the curved hood, straightening up and looking away.

"Sorry," she said, meaning it.

She'd run him, too. SOP for anyone and everything involved in this kind of case. The difference was she had no access to the same clearances, and had uncovered little beyond his basic vitals. She also didn't believe in using personal prying as a conversation starter . . . even if his intentions were probably more honorable than she wanted to admit.

She took a long breath to tame the sudden anxiety. The tension in her long arms began to relax.

"My life was, and is, something of a mess," she said. "Having anyone peek under the covers never fails to feel intrusive." That was about as naked as she was willing to get.

The ocean was changing color, deep green giving way to pale blue as the sun began to win this morning's tussle with the low ceiling. The wind was also picking up, and behind them traffic was tightening on PCH.

"No one's life is Candyland, Detective. I was just making conversation. Sorry it came off badly." Reluctance peppered his second attempt at an apology.

"I know." She managed a sincere smile. "And if we're gonna work together, you should call me Natalie."

He nodded. "I prefer you stick with Collins."

"With that first name, I don't blame you."

He chuckled and they held a momentary truce, which wasn't unpleasant. A few yards away, a pair of mothers and several small children bounded out of an extended van. The group had a trunk load of gear—coolers, umbrellas, and baskets of plastic toys. The kids ran toward the sand, oblivious of the concrete bike path they crossed on their way to the water. Thankfully, the closest cyclists were a hundred yards south, hunched over while cranking out their grueling morning miles.

"Another prolific porn distributor got clipped night before last." Collins marked his words, eyeing the group making its way to the water. "Small town high in the Rockies, a bit outside Boulder."

"How?" she asked.

"One shot to the back of his head. From distance, with a high-powered sniper rifle."

She chewed on the new twist. The additional murder, connected or not, rendered her and LASD's jurisdictional role more tenuous.

"Different MO," she said. "Not that it means much. We've still got no trace or leads on the brothers' shooter."

Collins nodded. A renegade ray of sun splashed across his forehead, making him appear tired and frustrated.

Two old cars screeched into the parking lot, tail ends of short boards jutting from their open rear windows. A few feet away, the large, rusty security shutter protecting the snack bar began to crank open. In the distance, a red lifeguard truck approached its tower, bouncing on sturdy struts over the dunes of uneven sand.

"We have reason to believe the Colorado murder is related. Anything more from the Malibu scene, beyond what I've seen through the internals?" Collins asked, eyeing the kids congregating near the water.

"Not much," Natalie said. "I did the circuit with my vice friends from surrounding PDs. The Baz brothers, as we've talked about, were serious functionaries. Back doors and dubious accounts. They filled a lot of sleazy coffers for some of our finest citizens, mostly politicians and judges. Doesn't take Mensa to draw a map of what was going on. Ever since the net and streaming became the preferred vehicles for delivery, they've needed favors from those same assholes to keep the FCC and other watchdog do-gooders out of their backyard."

"The pool goes well beyond them," Collins said, picking up the thread. "Various celebrities were balls-deep—sorry. Into the brothers as well. For them, it wasn't about funding as much as product."

She knew he wasn't sure it was wise to give her a total account-ing of what he'd learned. He'd likely already said too much, like an anxious schoolkid who couldn't control his need for approval. But there was more than that. She also couldn't miss the warming attraction he was trying to suppress. It was a nonstarter, but the least she could do was to try to be civil.

"This new body up in Colorado?" he continued. "Name was Rudy O'Shea. He'd been doing his thing for the past twenty-five years, an army of lawyers and other enablers on his payroll. Pre-vious to that, he'd fallen off the grid for a few years. And before all that? He'd been one of the filthiest facilitators of hidden-room secrets Los Angeles has ever seen. And back in those days? His clients were all celebs of one ilk or another."

"What are we talking about?" she asked, though she had an idea. One that ushered an unwelcome flush to her face.

"Pretty much whatever they wanted, from barnyard animals to kids. Runaways or kidnaps—what they used to call it before traf-ficking became the PC term." He looked to the ground in disgust. "And sometimes much worse. Porn's version of the third rail."

"Jesus," she said, more to herself than to him.

He straightened up, motioning for her to follow. She slid off the hood. They dumped their cups in a nearby dented bin and walked toward his bureau car, a four-door SUV. His stride gave away old injuries, somewhat belying his age and outward physicality. He unconsciously fought to hide the tic in one knee, paddle-toned shoulders moving in sync with each step. He chirped his fob twice and opened the back door, leaning inside and reemerging with an Apple tablet.

He thumped his fingers a few times over the surface. "Our techs got this from Rudy's closet safe. It took a few hours, but they were able to break the security protections. Three videos were deeply buried on a hidden drive." He paused a moment, then handed her the device, resting one of his feet on the truck's running board, visibly bracing himself.

The screen flashed three icons. "Which one?" she asked.

"Doesn't matter." They held each other's eyes. "I'd totally understand if you'd rather not look. It's ugly."

She paused. Then touched the top red arrow.

The screen instantly went full. A wide, panning shot of a blazing white room, sparse beyond a set of floor-length curtains dancing in the swirl of an open window. The shot steadied, remaining motionless for several seconds. She pulled the screen closer to her face. The camera was moving again, slowly to its left, settling on a naked figure facing a wall, her extremities stretched and chained, like something out of a medieval dungeon. Given the angle, her face was hidden, though not the strawberry-blond hair, cemented dull with bloody grime and sweat.

Natalie swallowed bile.

The camera panned in the other direction, to a door with no knob that opened from the outside. Five men in elaborate animal masks walked in, single file, all naked, dragging their fish-belly stomachs, chicken legs, and dangling members. As they approached, the girl started to sob, whispering indecipherable words. The men formed a half-circle around their victim, striking a few muscle poses for the camera. Then one gave his groin a few tugs and the girl disappeared behind his bulk.

Natalie shuddered and paused the file. She raised her head, handing back the device.

Collins grabbed it and tossed it back onto the seat. "All told, we counted thirteen forms of rape." He slumped against the edge of the door.

She leaned against the back fender. "Christ."

"It went on for over an hour, and the camera op made sure to get as many close-ups and tight shots as possible. Enhancing the value, I guess. For the first bit, it's her screams against their laughter, taunting one another on. An hour in, she passed out, just hanging there while they finished up. But before they brought her down, the bastard in the demented lamb mask reappears in frame with a short Japanese KA-BAR... and cuts her up. Enough so she just passed out."

Natalie heard every word, but his voice was so drained it was almost lost in the morning beach noise.

Several times during her career, she had questioned herself and her chosen work, along with the distance demanded to remain functional and in the moment. That wasn't an issue now. Her mind screamed, fueled by helplessness and inadequacy. She was merely a witness after the fact, with no idea who the young girl might have been. A neutered voyeur, incapable of rendering anything beyond disgust and useless empathy.

"Is there anything more you know?" she asked.

"We believe Rudy and the Baz bros had some sort of connection, either to a larger master or an indirect chain of loose parts. As for who might be pulling off these recent hits, my money is on one of these kids' parents, someone with the resources to put the puzzle together. It's too coincidental otherwise. But whoever it is, they seem be working off serious intel. Rudy and the brothers ran in unique and separate circles. From what we can tell at this point, if they knew one another, they had no interaction. Ever. But that doesn't mean they weren't branches on some larger tree."

"A deep state for degradation?"

"Not that ingenious. More the normal variety. This stuff remains an out-there trade, one that still frightens almost everyone. Most will go right up to the edge but draw the line at finales like what's on that drive. Many fake it, calling themselves artists. Sick, but mostly legal. My guess is this is something that was kept around to show only selectively when the situation dictated. It might also have been a personal project, something kept hidden from the rest of the group."

"Rogues within their circle?"

Collins lifted a broad shoulder. "I really don't know. But it wouldn't surprise me. These guys are just like any other sociopathic crime organization, someone always trying to get ahead or pulling side deals outside the scope of the bosses, with the entire group living in a perpetual state of paranoia. 'Et tu, Brutus?' and all that."

"So the problem remains. Most of what they both distributed wasn't illegal," she offered. "Except for those videos . . . and even if the vics someday surfaced, we'd have a hard time charging anyone with anything."

"We'd have had enough. Tender-agers were involved. O'Shea was shacked up with a fourteen-year-old girl. Who, by the way, he'd legally taken guardianship of a few days before."

Her jaw slipped. "How the hell does a sheeted pornographer get his hands on a young girl?" She immediately realized how naïve she sounded. "Let me guess, Children's Services on the payroll? O'Shea had something on someone?"

"A judge, we think. Like hedge-fund managers, enough is never enough. If something's available, it's to be exploited, taken, and used. It's the way gangs become industries. It's also their rush, way beyond the dollars payoff."

"For a pleasant-looking beach boy, you are one bitter fed."

"You have no idea, Detective."

She pulled out her phone. "I'll keep digging into the brothers' patterns and friends. See what I can shake loose."

"Okay. I'll be in touch," he said, walking to the rear of his ride and raising the hatch to retrieve his weapon of choice.

She stopped halfway to her car. "Still going out, huh?"

He slammed the window shut, tucking the short board under his arm. It was a dirty shade of light blue, the color well faded. "Need the water more than ever about now." He gave a half-hearted salute and jogged away, the tethered leash slapping against his tanned calves.

Mornings were always brisk at Huntington Memorial's emergency room, but today had been worse than usual.

During his first rotations, many years before at County USC, Dr. Julian Burgos had tried various methods for anesthetizing himself to the grim and fragile absolutes of his profession. His mentors had preached that grief shouldn't be carried by doctors when dealing with patients and families. But after decades of bearing witness to various levels and forms of death, Julian could still be emotionally felled by the suffering of those left behind.

Shrinks liked to argue that upbringing, parental influence, and early hardwiring cultivated methods for coping that only hardened over time. Researchers preferred hiding behind theories of tainted DNA, a clinical catchall justifying what most didn't have the patience or emotional sensibility to understand. Julian believed neither school could claim superiority, and that the true nature of most humans reached beyond both hardwiring and DNA.

For the past two hours, he'd kept a concerned watch on the family of a stabbing victim and a dead college student's girlfriend. They hadn't moved, withering in seats separated by ten feet and silence. Anything he could say wouldn't be heard, and later would ring as hollow and contrived. Being prepared if they needed him for something was the best he had.

At length, he went for a much-needed break in the employee lounge down the hall. He put his hand on the cold pot of stale coffee before starting a new one. Outside stretched a thriving garden designed to inspire serenity around illness and demise. He sat with some effort, more drained than he'd realized, and quickly nodded off.

Minutes later he woke with a start, a hard tingle working over his skin. Scientifically speaking, it was merely the redistribution of loose molecules, a lofty way of realizing he was no longer alone. This room was climate controlled into the high sixties. Even so, a warm flush of adrenaline passed through him.

Midas was the only man who could simultaneously make him feel safe and uneasy.

"Doctor J." The statement came from behind him, searching for an approachable tone.

Julian clinically noted that his stomach was beginning to turn with nervous heat.

"You okay?" Midas asked, walking around the table to face him.

"Fine, sorry." Julian reached out to shake his hand. "Been a long morning." He followed Midas's eyes as they glanced through the window in a never-ending search for possible trouble.

"You called?" Midas asked.

"Sorry it was so early." Julian wasn't quite ready for this conversation. "Let's get some better coffee."

Midas followed him out of the lounge like a weak employee about to get a lecture from his boss. On the walk, Julian tried small talk, but Midas's usual sociability had taken a deep dive. The hospital cafeteria was on the same floor as the ER, and Julian filled two cups from the large urn. Midas offered to pay, but the cashier just smiled condescendingly. Julian winked, dragging his ID over the red scanner, extracting a snappy *beep*. "Free java," he said. "Spoils of the early shift."

Midas nodded and followed him to a table in a far corner. "Why do you still work the emergency room, Doc, patching up head wounds and bangers?" Midas didn't seem eager to get on with it, either.

"Mainly for the exercise. Skills fade if you don't stay sharp. No better place for an MD than the emergency room. One day a week is a pure tonic." He smiled. "My form of surfing."

"I would think it takes too much. Out of you, I mean."

"Anything worth a damn does."

Julian watched Midas bring the cup to his mouth, taking a long pause, not to savor the smell but to scan the room. *Speaking of skills.* He took a short sip, setting the bulky white porcelain back onto the table before resting his elbows and turning his palms up toward the ceiling, an invitation for the doctor to proceed.

Julian nodded. "A few nights ago, Serena started remembering. Bits at first, then extended fragments."

The dark eyes holding his focus lasered in.

"It got bad very fast. She was severely brutalized in captivity, but there was an added element, which I can only compare to psychological torture. Rape and bondage are used to degrade. But in between their...sessions...they must have worked on the things that made her special. It went beyond mere humiliation, and presents like calculated, mental destruction. She'll be questioning who she was, and more importantly, who she is now, for some time. I had to sedate her."

Both men had heard the stories. According to Conor, Kyle had built a side team over the past few years for just such a purpose. This deviant who'd probably grown up pulling wings off flies, kicking stray dogs, and maiming cats. There was no shortage of psychopathic and socially inept CIA contractors, and Kyle's group was now dubiously regarded as one of the most effective and ruthless bands of interrogators alphabet city had ever blindly sanctioned. With no oversight, Kyle had become everything DeMarco and his diminishing band of loyalists had labored to keep out.

Across the table, Midas was looking drawn. He'd once confided in Burgos about the migraines that could flare up like a galloping horse. He now looked as if he were doing his best to hide one.

"How severe will it be?" Midas asked.

"A huge challenge," Burgos replied. "So much remains up in the air, and will depend on how emotionally strong she turns out to be. You know better than anyone that there's no playbook for this. I can't even tell you when the real work will begin. Right now, all we're doing is identifying issues, bringing the poison to the surface, while reinforcing the structure of safety. I'm encouraged it took only a few days for some of this to come back to her. Such severe trauma can sometimes remain buried forever. Many patients do resume their lives. Some even try to start new ones. Ultimately, most learn to function, some decently. But PTSD is a life sentence. Those who learn to steadfastly deal with it are the lucky ones."

"But what about triggers, those moments we can't control?"

Midas asked. "When something inexplicably brings it all back, forcing us to admit we'll never . . . be all right?"

"Most who make a conscious choice to try and move on learn the skills needed to adapt to such land mines. But yes, you're right. Depending on the severity of the incidents, triggers can never be completely managed, and certainly never overcome. With practice they can be somewhat . . . manipulated. But it requires a rare form of discipline."

Midas nodded. "Maybe someday I'll try it your way, Doc."

Julian smiled, as ever in awe of his complexity and perception. Midas missed nothing. Including Julian's not-so-subtle hints. Side-door inflections and rhetorical posturing were useless against his penetrating carbines. Over the years, Midas had never shown a willingness to tackle the incidents holding sway over so much of what he did and thought. Incidents that continued to consume him. Because he believed himself unsalvageable.

Perhaps he was.

"This is friend-to-friend," Julian said.

"I appreciate it. But we've got bigger problems."

"I'm not so sure."

"Meaning?"

"Since the night you brought her to me, Serena has had one constant mantra. That this wasn't your fault. We both know that isn't true."

Midas leaned back, his eyes registering more than simple regret.

"They broke so much, though apparently, not her feelings for you. Some lash out at anyone and everyone, which can be a healthy form of intense healing. That need and capability for emotional anger release. But so far, not her, and not with you."

"What does that mean?"

"That at some point, she'll need to focus responsibility where it lies. Right now, there's too much coursing through her, and she's not willing to loosen the bond. You might be the one tether keeping her from going into the depths of black ice. She also knows you well enough to know you're hammering yourself. My opinion is, she's trying to let you off the hook."

Midas looked away. "She's so much . . . so much *better* than I ever was. That's the part they couldn't take."

"She's dealing with a mountain load of shame and humiliation, and asked if I could help you to understand. She says she can't see you right now. I called Mason. He's at the house."

Midas leaned forward, weaving fingers behind his glossed skull, knuckles displaying a tense stretch. "I don't blame her," he said, his voice fading. "Don't blame her at all."

Julian's home was as frigid as usual.

Midas found Mase watching an early edition of "SportsCenter" on the kitchen TV.

"Fucking Lakers," he snapped. "Can't finish games worth shit these days."

Owing to his phobic fear of LA tap water, Julian kept a healthy supply of the bottled variety in his Sub-Zero fridge. Midas pulled one from the rear before taking a free stool at the granite island, while the sports anchors narrated highlights and scores mechanically from the screen. Almost any game or form of competition had the ability to hold Mase's interest. He might not have inherited his father's degenerate fever for wagering but did possess a knack for handicapping.

"You look worse than usual." Mase delivered the news flash without taking his eyes off the screen.

"She doesn't want to see me," Midas said.

Mase muted the sound, pulling his legs off the countertop. His attention turned to the leaf-covered back terrace, a luxury lost on most beach dwellers used to tiny lots. The two of them had grown up in the northern San Francisco Bay Area, notorious for microscopic lots. Both could appreciate a roomy yard. Even in the more exclusive sections of Santa Monica or Manhattan Beach, only the semblance of a yard was usually possible. Of course, such property required serious money, or at least the jealousy gene most materialistic Angelenos triggered to finance lifestyles beyond their means. For the past several years, financial experts had assumed most of the city's foreclosures were driven by lower-rent suburbanites and the bottom income brackets. In truth, it was the legions of envy chasers and their compulsive lack of restraint keeping the repo banks busy.

"She's dealing with more than she can handle," Mase offered. "Seeing you complicates it all."

"Complicates it? She said that?" Midas said with a catch in the words.

"It's the way it is." Mase bowed to no one, including his best friend. A simple fact that hadn't changed in forty years. Something everyone around him eventually learned, sometimes reluctantly.

Mase had been a serious jock, drawn to basketball, but a wizard on the baseball field, good enough for sniffing pro scouts and a full ride to UC, Berkeley before it had all vanished behind a bad injury.

During their senior year of high school, the baseball team had played a tournament in the city against a derisive prep school. The rival catcher was a moonlighting three-sporter, an all-league offensive lineman who stood six-foot-three and checked in around 240.

During a bang-bang play, Mase had rounded third as the opposing cutoff whirled to throw home. Approaching the plate, Mase launched himself, coiling his flying, prone body like a missile and aiming his shoulder for the catcher's solar plexus. In the ensuing and frightening collision, he reached for the plate. The big catcher had gone down, and the ball had squirted free.

The benches had immediately cleared, and one of the catcher's teammates confronted Mase with a screaming tirade as he dusted himself off, followed by the mistake of an aggressive push. He never saw Mase's punch coming. An ump had then grabbed Mase by the flap of his torn uniform, putting his finger inches from his face, and tossed him out of the game.

Mase had stood silently, staring at the two stunned players still sitting on the ground. Then he'd raised himself on his toes, putting his face inches from the ump's jutted chin. "I was fucking safe, you dipshit."

Mase's manager and two coaches had to pull him off the field. As they led him away, he'd flipped off the ump before ducking his head into the dugout's musty darkness.

Midas hadn't been at the game but was given a full accounting from teammates later that night over pizza and Cokes. He'd laughed so hard he'd barely been able to eat. Mase had sat sullenly in front of untouched pepperoni, occasionally piping up with the same few words. "I was safe."

When it came to sports, and later more perilous pursuits, Mase played hard, even mean, but usually fair. In that sense, he was the perfect teammate. Midas had never seen him back down, even when losing or beaten.

"You've got to trust me, Mide." Mase was staring at him. "And the doc."

"I do. Doesn't make any of this easier."

A light breeze rustled the mature leaves on the backyard California oak. After a few minutes, Midas asked, "What can you tell me?"

"A few things."

Several minutes later, Midas's phone chirped with an urgent text from Phillip.

He punched in a response, then moved to grab another water, softly shutting the fridge's heavy silver door. "Gotta go. Just keep me in the loop on her progress."

"Sure. One other thing," Mase said.

Midas stopped and turned.

"Let me help you with all this."

Not a chance in hell, he thought, but said, "I'll let you know if it comes to that."

"How can it come to anything else?"

CHAPTER 10

CONOR'S MUSCLE CAR MADE its share of noise in the morning traffic lumbering down Culver City's stretch of Sepulveda Boulevard. Silent electrics and hybrids waiting for a light shook next to the four-barrel, 350 GM engine.

His first car had been a 1970 Oldsmobile Cutlass Supreme. He'd picked up the same year's Stoo model a few years ago at an auction in Alabama. The lines of old Detroit cars spoke to him in ways the mass-produced plastic turds dominating today's streets never would. A few times a week, he brought this one out for a stretch, a relatively painless poke between his Mar Vista townhome and his store, The Freight Yard. The rest of his driving was done behind the wheel of a ubiquitous BMW 5 Series, which in Los Angeles would never stand out.

Normal foot traffic was scurrying from the corners of long-wait lights. Over the years, the yuppie influx had transformed the once-fading area into a shopping and nightlife destination. No shortage of craft beer and overpriced chicken wings.

The neighborhood also remained home to the historic MGM studios—currently flying under new and ever-changing owner-ship—where *Gone With the Wind, The Wizard of Oz,* and other classic films had been produced. These days, the legendary back lots were mostly used for television production and audio sweet-ening. Louis B. Mayer, the ironfisted chief who ruthlessly built MGM into a global brand back in the 1930s, would recognize nothing from his old neighborhood, including the million-dol-lar-plus asking prices for its two-bed, one-bath retro bungalows.

Conor turned his revving beast into an undersized one-way parking lot that fed out through a back alley, wedging it between his store and the latest inhabitant of the space next door—a coffee roaster called Pour de France. Fittingly, it was run by and catered to a clientele of arrogant cyclists, many of whom had settled today, as on most mornings, onto its outside chairs. Outfitted in brightly painted Lycra that stretched over skinny shoulder blades, the spin-ners were mainlining potent caffeine before heading out to pound their miles.

His old friend, Mason, was what most would have called an elite rider, ringing up 150 miles a week, but Mase also hated the culture that came with it. He attacked his routes alone, shunning the social aspect of group-route clicks. Mason had once told Conor the never-ending discussions of watt meters, pitch perspective, and superfoods were relentless, as well as boring and a waste of time. "Serious cycling is the only subject they feel comfortable dis-cussing," he'd once said between bites of a burrito with white rice wrapped in a flour tortilla—sacrilegious fuel for a serious roadie. "They're like roadside ministers. Judgmental and vain pricks who never let you forget they believe they've found the key to life."

Conor parked in the marked spot he'd paid to have expanded to fit his Cutlass. He got out and clicked his remote. The expensive alarm was the pristine car's only necessary add-on. This was still LA, no matter what or how little you drove.

He detoured for some coffee. Biking monkeys or not, Pour de France java was superb.

Conor's store was dedicated to model trains. The Freight Yard was now twenty years old, bought thanks to a loan from his father, who hadn't been in favor of a low-yield venture but believed in tacitly supporting his son's vision. Conor had already been well into his covert work but had needed a distraction for down periods. Most guys in the Unit had them in one form or another. Outside hobbies kept off the books, and by long-standing tradition, off-limits.

As he passed the jabbering cyclists with his twelve ounces of overpriced Somali blend, an unease took hold. A large, dark sedan was sitting on the street beside a one-hour meter. No one browsing or buying coffee beans parked on Culver Boulevard.

He approached his front entrance with a timeworn sense of readiness, stepping cautiously inside. The faintest hiss of a small engine echoed from in back.

Hobby stores were as cramped as a shoe salesmen's closet, and his was no exception. Walking space was limited to narrow paths between elaborate miniature cities, all with the common denominator of chugging Sante Fe or CSX diesels pulling ornately painted cars.

The rear hiss turned to a whistle—a vintage Lionel engine singing along its circular journey. He made his way through the maze of eras represented by the Smurf-sized wooden cities, his Smith & Wesson single-sided utility blade within reach and a comfort in his pocket.

Behind the numerous displays, the store opened to reveal a cash register, plastic cases, and, further removed, a door to his small office. The intruders came into view—a pair of well-dressed Secret Service washouts, fancy suit jackets buttoned, flanking a stooped older man. He too, was smartly dressed . . . and tussling with the gearbox from Conor's 1957 collector's edition, one of the showpieces of his fleet. The post-Civil War engine was pulling its load with ease, happily chortling its signature trill.

Rawlings Palmer's smile was that of a child transported back to an uncomplicated age. His full head of gray hair sat tightly styled above black tortoiseshell glasses framing gleaming eyes as mean as they were calculating.

"Conor Brennan," he said, straightening up to full height, which at six-foot-one was at least five inches taller than his son. "Did you know Culver City was first inhabited as a whites-only enclave?"

Conor rolled his eyes, pretending not to be surprised or disturbed by Palmer senior's sudden appearance.

A minute later, they were sitting in his cramped office, barely room for two chairs and a small desk. Palmer's handmaidens had declared it safe, having cleared it for hidden exploding trains or any other deadly threats.

Palmer wiped his glasses with a red pocket square. "I've always found establishments like this fascinating. No real money to be made, and not even a decent tax dodge."

Conor tried to remember the last time he'd seen the senior Palmer. A few years back, during a status update in DC with the Old Man?

"So why bother? With this . . . low-level sidelight?" Palmer continued, pushing his glasses back in place.

"I guess I need the eggs," Conor said.

Palmer's lizard mouth curled. "Very nice. Woody Allen. My ex-wife loved him too."

"What do you want, Palmer? I don't open till ten. You're trespassing."

"Really, Mr. Brennan, this is pathetic. I'm sure we could find you something . . . appropriate . . . to consume your downtime." His voice was a Waspy combination of genteel farmer and Eastern Seaboard law professor, varnished by aging Scotch and rare cigars. Cultivated confidence crowned at birth. Rawlings Palmer's existence was a blueprint for fading white power and arcane privilege. An entitled pedestal with singular purpose—schooling yes-men and followers with an infallibility beyond laws and rules of decency. But as Conor also knew, hubris created weakness. And Palmer's tangible, viral load of insecurity was one of many gifts passed on to his son.

"Again," Conor said. "What do you want?"

Palmer's perfectly veneered teeth slipped into hiding. The scowl was another trait passed down. He leaned forward, the line of his suit tightening.

"The Snow Leopard has been hunting outside his habitat."

"So I've heard. And you really shouldn't call him that."

The coiffed head—a $400 trim from the K Street barber he shared with other such assholes—moved vertically as if in prayer, rocking with silent rhythm. Flinty eyes flashed over the top of the rounded specs. "I don't care what you've been told. I'm here to figure things out, starting with the score." Palmer senior loved baseball. And like most from his corner, he was a Red Sox fan.

"Why don't you ask Kyle? Isn't he calling the shots?" Conor smiled guilelessly.

"Don't be a sap."

Conor pried the lid from his cooling cup, using a napkin to mop up condensation before snapping it back in place and running a finger around the rim to be sure it was secure. Bitterness washed over his tongue, and it wasn't just the coffee. Kyle and his father were reptiles. Making Conor the mongoose with conflicted loyalties.

Conflicted because Conor had been DeMarco's right hand in the field for a generation. This despite his age, which had once been considered green by the bow ties with old-money standards. Still, Conor's dedication and abilities had garnered him more than a few favors. The Palmer family needed him inside the tent, pissing out, perhaps, but inside. They were banking on his loyalty to the tradition he'd helped construct. Something especially true now, with his mentor in an induced coma and, from all reports, on his final glide path.

As much as Conor might despise the current hierarchy, he didn't believe it was in anyone's interest to see the Unit burned down.

"I'm listening," he said, distaste swirling. "But I'm certain you don't crank up the G-Stream for a five-hour flight unless you need something."

"Jasper DeMarco." The name was stated without emotion. "Your martyr is dying." Palmer was smiling at the disgust on Conor's face.

Palmer's casual and condescending use of the name Jasper instead of just J, which Old Man always preferred, grated like an out-of-tune string section.

"He's been your rabbi since the Unit's inception, raised you up from a seal pup. You did well by each other, yes? You're a superb soldier and tactician, and we all know you're committed to your work. The same can't be said for a few of your old pals, including the Snow Leopard. Sorry, Midas. Which is why I'm here."

Conor kept his face blank, waiting.

"Kyle has very few strengths and several weaknesses," Palmer went on. "Not news to anyone, especially you. He's buggered this badly, more so than usual. Now the grown-ups need to stop the bleeding."

Conor was mildly surprised. "I don't think your boy sees it that way. His torture posse kidnapped and repeatedly raped a civilian simply because she was close to Midas. And now you're all worried about repercussions? Little late ... *Mr. Palmer.* There was a reason the Old Man kept your inbred spawn at arm's length, despite having the pair of you shoved down his pipe."

"Mr. Brennan. Please don't think for one minute that you have standing in any of this. I'm here because you, at least, remain capable of levelheadedness. Unlike Midas. You know this trajectory ends one way, and what that means for your former playmates. I'm here to do the sensible thing. Late, yes, but here nonetheless. So spare me the idealism. Or would you prefer I call in the boys and we start this cleanup with you?"

They measured each other. Conor mentally venting about taking his chances and breaking this prick's neck, which wouldn't help beyond momentary gratification. Plus, Midas was counting on him to do what he could to keep Mason and Phillip off the list. Minimize the imminent damage. He kept silent.

"My son won't like this, but I am willing to call it all off. That is, *if* you can get Midas to the table for a meeting." Palmer leaned back in the cheap chair, letting his arrogant generosity marinate.

Conor wasn't completely surprised, having expected some sort of truce proposal the second he'd seen Rawlings Palmer fondling his trains. Kyle's father could easily have stayed home and called the next play from distance, putting Midas to sleep along with anyone else who was a threat. Yet he was here. Meaning for whatever reason, that option wasn't currently on the table. Perhaps too many political hurdles, despite DeMarco's worsening condition? Even so, Conor knew this was no retreat. More a calculated pause. Palmer senior was certainly working his own plan for Midas's demise, rendering this proposal nothing more than a stall, an uneasy postponement—one which Conor grudgingly had to admit made some sense, as it could create more time and room to figure the angles and lower the temp. He didn't believe one word this patrician dickbag was peddling, but his options were limited.

"Your son won't stand down," Conor said. "He'll say you can't afford to let Midas continue to cripple the empire." Conor used the c-word deliberately.

Palmer's eyes narrowed dangerously. "Kyle will do what he's told. The question is, will you?"

"Depends on what I'm asked to do," Conor said calmly.

Palmer stood up, leaning over slightly to avoid banging his styled head on the low ceiling.

"Bring Midas round for a little chat. Kyle's club tonight, after hours so no one gets stupid ideas. Feel free to bring a couple of friends if it makes you feel better. But no more than two, besides yourself, of course."

Conor stood to face him. Never let anyone loom over you. A street fighter's rule. "And what do I say? To help Midas see . . . *reason?*"

"The truth. That this is his only play."

He followed Palmer out of the office, eyeing his flanks. The stockier of the two shadows was standing in the aisle. The other was pawing the pre-Civil War engine, tossing it in the air a few feet, then catching it roughly on the way back down.

Conor stepped forward and held out his hand.

The man looked between Palmer and his partner. Neither moved nor said a word, enjoying the show. He brought the engine behind his ear like a quarterback eyeing a receiver slant before slamming it down into Conor's waiting hand.

The few wheels still intact had been pulled apart and hung at a crippled angle.

Conor delivered a debilitating liver punch with his free hand. The bodyguard folded like old newspaper, curling on the floor in a moaning trance. Conor reached down to grab his ear and twisted it harshly. A weak howl of pain sounded, along with the *click* of a Glock close to Conor's head.

Ignoring it, he leaned into the agonized face and tightened his grip. The goon's ear turned deep maroon. "You'd be better off wrestling Samoans than fucking with my stuff," he growled, releasing his grip with a push.

He turned to Palmer. "Take your day laborers and get out. I'll be in touch."

Two hours later, Rawlings Palmer sat in his town car, parked off the street in a shabby Hollywood back alley. The end of the meeting with Brennan had left him shaken . . . as well as down a man. His injured minder had been abandoned to the supervision of a Westwood doctor on the company's approved list. He'd be laid up for at least twenty-four hours and would require monitoring. *Imbecile.*

The older man scowled to himself. There had been something about Brennan, beyond the ferocity of his action. Rawlings had built his career and reputation working above such lesser men, issuing orders while maintaining a healthy distance. Those of his station spent their lifetimes staying insulated against the foul and the violent, paying others well so real danger never invaded their world. But Brennan could easily have hit *him* instead of the idiot bodyguard. That fact was a demonstrated reminder of Rawlings's weakness and vulnerability, one that had induced anger and resentment.

And as usual, most of the problem could be traced to his son.

Five years earlier, Rawlings had been ordered to DeMarco's cave, nestled trog-like beneath humanity in the hidden basement of a weapons depot a few miles from the Pentagon. As he'd walked down a flurry of stairs and through the jumble of winding concrete corridors, his trepidation had risen. Rawlings's own office was a few miles away, welcoming, warm, and above ground. No shortage of natural light. DeMarco's felt like bowels of Lubyanka, the infamous Moscow prison few survived.

On that day five years ago, Rawlings had knocked on the nondescript metal door and walked in without waiting for a reply. It wasn't his first visit, so he wasn't surprised when assaulted by the competing scents of coffee and fresh fruit. The man inside motioned for him to sit in one of the two chairs facing his undersized but tasteful cherrywood desk.

Despite his advanced age—near seventy-five if the rumors were true—Jasper DeMarco, J to insiders, remained a formidable enigma. An image cultivated since his pioneering days at the Company running resistance for various directors and their restless savages. DeMarco was just under five-foot-eleven with thinning white hair and a knowing face, devoid of lines save for a pair of worry troughs bordering the sides of his mouth.

Word was he'd been married for years to a surgeon, one of the first females to be granted elevated privileges at Walter Reed. The lore was she'd been on crisis duty at Dover Air Force Base when he'd been brought in after one of his many brutal missions. They'd married soon after, had no children, and until her death a few years ago, she'd continued to work surgery at Johns Hopkins while also serving as a revered professor at Georgetown Medical. At least that was the story. In an existence ruled by legends and secrets, few knew DeMarco existed, and fewer still anything regarding his personal background.

"Appreciate you coming over," DeMarco said, as usual shunning small talk with his world-weary burr. "We've got a problem."

Rawlings knew the reason for the summons and had prepared himself for what promised to be unpleasant. It had been a month since Mexico City. Kyle was still laid up, facing months of rehab. Both legs had been broken along with several ribs and his lower back, which they said would remain permanently out of alignment. Midas had made sure Kyle would never walk properly again, or at least not without significant pain.

Rawlings knew he had to tread cautiously. And sitting across from this Catholic bastard only made it all the worse.

"This problem, I suspect, regards the Snow Leopard and my son," he said.

DeMarco simply stared back at him with his de facto expression of tolerance.

"If this is yet another lecture about m-moral imperatives, you can save your b-breath," Rawlings said, beginning to stammer.

The Old Man waited. Interrogation shorthand. Set boundaries.

Make all rules. Intimidate when necessary.

"Your son," DeMarco said at length, "is lucky to be breathing."

"I've read the report."

"Not mine."

"Meaning?" Rawlings leaned forward, his cuff links shifting into the open.

The office seemed to be getting smaller, symptoms of panic and fear, a state to be avoided whenever possible. He reminded himself to breathe normally and face the threat as unemotionally as possible. Give in to nothing. At least outwardly.

"Like I said, we have a problem." DeMarco rested his wiry forearms on the flat surface of the desk, taut and toned.

How much damage, Rawlings wondered, had those rough hands inflicted?

"Midas is looking to leave," DeMarco continued. "I'm not happy about that, but it's the only sensible alternative. All things being equal."

"Equal?" Palmer spit, the word hanging like smoke. "My son is looking at life as a damn cripple. Someone needs to answer."

A ripple moved through DeMarco's shoulders. He focused on the wall behind Rawlings's head. "Your boy kidnapped and raped a twelve-year-old girl." His voice was soft and laced with bitterness. "On my watch, and on our payroll. Answer for *that*, Palmer."

"That's your version." Rawlings surprised himself with the deftness of his prepared defense. Then again, he'd been talking himself and his son out of minefields for years. It was a strength that had helped punch his card within alphabet city. His confidence began to reemerge. This was no more than the Old Man flexing and reestablishing boundaries.

"The version our friends around town will believe," Rawlings started saying, "is that the Snow Leopard went off the reservation. Yet again. And only a month after Mason James, one of your other favored children, botched Guatemala City. They'll believe it because they have no choice. And because I'll be the one providing the analysis, given your aversion to departmental schmoozing. You'd do well to remember that your little section continues to exist because of me."

Rawlings usually resisted poking a dragon. But desperate times had left far too much at stake. Things well beyond the survival of his troublesome son. DeMarco sat stoically, the lids of his eyes lowering to the point of almost closing. If Rawlings didn't know better, he'd have thought the aging bastard had fallen asleep.

"Your son is a candy-ass," DeMarco stated. "Just like his father. The two of you are clones of our fat-assed king. Bullying while standing safely behind others when the heat rises. Neither of you ever served, nor have even been in a decent street fight, something that might have allowed your testicles to descend. The fact that you used favors and politics to worm your way into my department and somehow get Kyle placed into operations remains an enduring failure on my part."

Rawlings squirmed in the uncomfortable chair. The lack of respect burned through his brain. He was obligated to speak, to defend himself, but for one of the few times in his life, words escaped him. Even so, DeMarco had to be acutely aware of the trouble he was buying.

"Was it your intention to raise a sociopath, or was it a bonus of restrictive breeding and wealth? Your son funds your dwindling family empire with hardcore and explicit pornography. You think I didn't know?"

"Never really thought about it. Or cared." Rawlings's nerves were failing him, but he refused to wilt. "My family's business is no concern of yours, or anyone else's. You'd do well to drop the subject."

The Old Man smiled. Rawlings tried to read his thoughts. It likely wasn't the first time the geezer had been told to back off, no doubt by someone more substantial than a colleague he'd summed up as a quivering fool. But DeMarco also had to know there was an internal and prolonged war on the horizon with too many years and favors working against him. The Old Man should think about protecting what he could, and manage the rest.

"Rawlings," DeMarco said, "I couldn't give five squirts how your family operates or holds its place in the sun-freckled gatherings of elegant society. You're all decency-lacking whores desperate to keep your summer homes and private beaches. My guess is almost everyone in your realm knows how Kyle props up the family trust. And they couldn't give five fucks, as long as his fecal taint never fouls the holidays or their fancy soirees. But the problem I do have? Kyle likes to kick small animals. He enjoys hurting vulnerable people."

Rawlings snorted. "Kyle is no better and no worse than your hard-hearted flock of assassins," he said. "You're every bit the hypocrite we all are, despite those who consider you some sort of guru."

DeMarco shrugged. "Maybe. We've all learned various methods to justify what we've done. To a fault sometimes. But Kyle doesn't possess that gene. He's destructive without the filter of self-doubt. I can't have that anymore."

Rawlings smelled something of a retreat. He'd play along. Yale debate team rules. Ignore the negative. "I would agree that we need a reshuffling."

DeMarco stood up, stretching an aging frame that, despite diminishing muscle tone, still appeared formidable. He turned for a bottle of water from a minifridge resting on the metal cabinet behind his chair. He held up a second bottle.

Rawlings shook his head no.

Cracking the seal, DeMarco took a long pull, then sat back down with a weary *thump*. "Midas will walk away, with my blessing. I would expect Mason to follow. Connor Brennan will continue to run the team."

"And Kyle?"

If the Old Man were struggling with compromise, his only tell was a momentary hesitation. His eyes glowed against Rawlings's glare. "If he heals up well enough to want to come back, he will be given a supervisory role. Out of the fray. He won't return to the field, under any circumstances."

Rawlings took a deep breath. There would come a time . . . but this wasn't it. "That will be satisfactory" was all he could manage.

"You need to hear me, Rawlings. And make sure Kyle gets it into his thick head as well. Midas and anyone else walking away will be out. And left alone. No reprisals."

Rawlings's answer was a single slow nod of acquiescence. He pushed himself up and walked out. Making his way back through the cold, musty maze of passageways, his mind started formulating the outlines of an endgame.

He had been thinking and planning ever since.

However, today, half a decade later, not much had changed. There were no good solutions, and Kyle still needed adult supervision.

Putting aside the memory, Rawlings opened the car door and got out, hopscotching around grimy garbage, pill bottles, and used condoms. His remaining man fell into line as he passed through a nondescript door. A few steps later, he arrived at the main floor. He was no stranger to his son's club or its topography.

Jojo sat at the bar, two of his elves nursing drinks at a side table. Kyle was tucked in a corner booth along with Michelle, a woman Rawlings had never met in person but knew just the same. His son stood to awkwardly greet him. His father slid a chair from a nearby four-top while ignoring the strained pomp. Kyle took the hint, slumping back onto the booth's vinyl bench. He looked awful. Tired and wound up, his red-ringlet eyes smudged with the likely assistance of some form of stimulant. He must have put on thirty pounds since their last meeting—not flattering on someone five seven and already calorically challenged. He knew Kyle could read his disgust, so he moved his glare to Michelle, who gave him little reassurance beyond eye contact.

"Brennan will take care of getting them here," Rawlings said, skipping any preamble.

"This is a mistake. I can fix it." Kyle was pleading. Pathetic.

Rawlings motioned to Jojo for a drink. "You'll fucking do what I say."

It was just after seven am when Conor made his way into Shredders.

Midweek crowds were mostly quiet locals, as opposed to the rowdiness of weekends. He'd called ahead so there would be no surprise. Midas and Mason were waiting at the bar. The three old friends exchanged a restrained greeting.

Conor wiped the mist from the sleeves of his jacket, signaling no to the offer of a drink.

"Boys," he said, "how's this pile of bricks treating you?"

"Keeps the lights on," Mason replied, as ever the on-point existentialist.

Midas smiled. "Good to see you, Con. Been too long."

"Wish it could have been a bit longer," Conor said.

The Lakers and the Kings were playing on several screens above the bar. Bar noise dropped to a low hum as the friends circled closer for privacy.

"Give me the headlines," Midas said.

Conor peered through a window toward the ocean but saw only darkness beyond the flickering lamps along the strand. "Rawlings Palmer paid me a visit this morning. Wants you for a face-to-face tonight at Kyle's club. After hours."

"Fuck him," Mason said.

"What do you think, Con?" Midas asked warily.

"It won't be like Michael Corleone at his niece's baptism. Palmer assured me as much, for what it's worth. Beyond that, I don't know. You've cocked up his supply line, the part they assumed none of us could ever touch. And if I can see Phillip's fingerprints, so can they."

"Keep Phillip out of this," Midas said. "I told him to disappear."

Conor raised his palms in capitulation. "I told him the same thing. Don't think he's listening."

A group of five young women nestled up to the bar, tight skirts and tops offering little protection against the beach chill, though it was passably warm inside. Conor saw one of them order while another took aim at Mase and Midas, still huddled in conversation. She flicked on the maximum wattage, pushing her full lips into a selfie pooch brought home by the glowing deep maroon of fifty-dollar lipstick. Smoky mascara and Bijan perfume should have completed the assault.

But her targets weren't paying attention. Conor almost smiled. She might as well have been an empty chair. They're probably gay, she was no doubt assuring herself, already turning her interest to a fresh mojito.

"After what that fat midget pulled?" Mason was muttering. "Why give them anything?"

"It's a play for time," Conor replied. "Rawlings is nervous. Even with the Old Man out of the loop, he still answers to his cadre in DC, and I can only assume they've told him to get his house cleaned up. None of this has gone unnoticed, despite happening outside the charter. Remember when you both left the Unit? The Old Man told you that everything is personal, and at the same time, nothing is? Once in, you're never *really out*? You knew that, Mide. Yet you still went ahead with all this. I understand the reasoning, but accounting will be required. Though for now, Rawlings wants the bleeding to stop."

"And then what?" Mason demanded, channeling his usual bad mood.

Conor studied them both. Any play for Midas required factoring in Mason. Despite their Bickersons routine, the pair had been watching each other's backs for most of their lives. Rawlings Palmer and the other suits understood what both were capable of, even if Kyle didn't.

"I wouldn't expect détente to last more than a week or so," Conor said.

Carlo appeared with a fresh keg hoisted over one shoulder, fist-bumping Conor while moving behind the bar. Once he'd secured the metal barrel and tightened the pumps, he pulled one of a long row of levers, clearing the hose of remaining air and carbonation. He drew the first tap into a tall glass and handed it to Conor, who took one sip and reluctantly handed it back. Strong and hoppy, probably a double IPA. This was not the night to appreciate it.

Midas had other ideas, signaling his bartender. She reached for a familiar green bottle, laying out four sturdy tumblers and filling each with a robust shot of Jameson.

"Better days," Midas said, draining his first, as the others followed. "Guess we'd better go see the little shit and his daddy."

Mason looked pissed. Carlo shrugged with determination.

Conor's apprehension was bottoming toward resignation. The salvo of a fresh migraine was trying to creep into his skull, the wicked equalizer that never called ahead and owned a piece of them all.

Homeless enclaves around Los Angeles were insular villages, requiring tribal background checks more ruthless than large corporations ran for potential CEOs. It could take years to locate the right environment, and then several more to garner respect from the neighbors.

Ronnie had been surviving on his patch just off Hollywood Boulevard for almost a decade.

The result of a severe drinking habit that had forced his wife and two sons to disappear one morning years before. Ronnie hadn't seen them since, not that either side had done much looking. Because his wife's supervisory role with an insurance firm had supplied the majority of their living expenses, her loss and his lack of initiative had eventually put him on the street. That being after the six months spent in his car, which he'd finally hawked for $300. From that payday he spent only a few dollars before getting rolled for the rest, and beaten with a bottle of Johnnie Walker he'd nuzzled up to on a side street near downtown.

His great migration to this alley had been all of seven miles from that midnight pasting. How many years it had taken he couldn't have guessed. Jack Kerouac he wasn't. And now, having found a group and situation that suited him, Ronnie was finally able to survive with some form of purpose.

Earlier this evening, Coco and Gabe, his two best friends, had ventured off in search of "the toss." That magic hour when the local restaurants dumped all their half-eaten plates after final seating. Some nights were better than others.

Ronnie had remained behind to keep watch. Of the three, Gabe had the best stuff. A moderately new sleeping bag and a rusted but functional Coleman hot plate. He also had an antique box radio, requiring stolen batteries every few weeks. Tonight, its small speaker crackled out a classic rock station. Bunny-eyed Edgar Winter was singing about a "free ride." What a laugh. No such thing. Ronnie squatted down, turning the tarnished dial. Had to be something better on—maybe some Temptations, or Funkadelic?

Ronnie felt movement. His once-dormant sense of survival had one day just reappeared, after so many nights of fitful sleeping over steaming steel grates and concrete.

Four figures crossed his path. They took note of his presence but said nothing as they floated by. They weren't thieves or muggers, or even the young gang members who occasionally stopped by to kick him and his friends in the face while they tried to sleep.

This group crossed the alley and vanished behind trash cans and festering piles of gritty garbage. An involuntary shudder coursed through his stomach. There was something about them that radiated danger. Ronnie was glad they were gone.

Conor was on point, leading the others along a route he'd determined as being the least visible to any security Kyle's crew might be monitoring. Like the others, he'd pulled his no-logo black baseball cap lower over his forehead, just in case. They'd walked by an itinerant man and passed numerous rickety cardboard boxes and ripped blankets doubling as tents. Homeless gentrification. The evening carried the fragrance of baked-in body odor, cheap booze, piss, and stale pot.

The team moved neither fast nor slow, bundling closer as they approached the rear entrance of Kyle's club. They all loosened their tension, to better blend in with the eager crowd of club-hopping rousers hanging around the door.

The lone bouncer was beyond his depth, appraising them without fear. Just another bunch of dipshits eager to spend money.

Carlo stepped to the front, showcasing his best inebriated half smile. He was easily the tallest of the group, and even so, the bouncer had a few inches on him.

The doorman held up a hand. "Main entrance is on the other side of the club, fellas. This is for VIPs."

Conor stifled a smile.

Carlo snapped out a smart uppercut to the bouncer's chest, doubling him over, then another punch to the side of his face. Lights out. Mason caught him as he lurched, gently guiding him to the ground and ensuring he didn't bang his head on the pavement. He also pulled the doorman's earbud loose and secured his cell from a side pocket.

Conor walked through the door, followed by the others, taking an immediate right. Another door, this one requiring a lock code. The back way for hired help. He tapped a few numbers onto the small screen, and a light pinged green.

The group walked in tandem through darkness broken only by a few exit signs.

The walls started to narrow, and the floor began to rise. Soon, they arrived on the upper landing, passing a handful of open doors and empty spaces with couches, tables, and tinted windows. All configured for observing the action on the main floor. Debutante rooms with a view. Near the corridor's dead end, they arrived at a closed door. Conor motioned for Carlo to stand guard outside, then he gave a short knock, and without waiting, pushed the steel handle down and strode inside. Midas and Mason followed.

This expanse was twice the size of the other areas they'd passed, with two leather sofas, five overstuffed living room chairs, and a full bar in the back. One wall was a curved, panoramic sheet of smoky glass overlooking the busy club below. Motion inside the room froze as Mason kicked the door closed.

Jojo stood at the window planted like a redwood, whispering into an unseen mic. His right hand rested inside the breast of his nylon bomber jacket. Rawlings Palmer was perched on one of the soft chairs, showing off a nonplussed grin. Kyle leaned forward from the middle of one of the couches, gripping his knees. He looked smaller than usual.

Midas stopped to stare pointedly at the woman sitting next to Kyle. She looked younger than her thirty-seven, streaked blond hair long and full beside her fine jawline, framing a face that turned from soft to hard in a whisper.

The deep-set brown eyes glared back at Midas, who suddenly looked defenseless. He slowly crossed his arms, as if fighting an overwhelming curtain of regret.

Mason had locked on her as well.

Conor grimaced. Michelle Kelly? What the fuck? Could this get any more complicated?

Mason took a step forward. Jojo's hand tightened under his jacket.

Mason sneered at Michelle. "Aren't you the filthy one?" His statement was laced with condescension.

She gave a proper beat before thrusting her formidable chin forward. "If it isn't the three stooges," she drawled.

"Enough." Rawlings Palmer decided to join those standing. "We did say *after* hours. I'm having my doubts about you, Brennan."

"I told them," Conor replied.

"We like to control our own narratives," Mason said.

"This is between Kyle and me," Midas said. "Why not give Con and Mase drink cards while the rest of us get down to business?"

"We can do that," Jojo said.

"All the same, I think we'll stay," Mason said, lowering himself to sit on the arm of a free chair. "After all, we come in peace . . . with apologies to the sleeping stiff at the back door," he added with evident satisfaction.

Conor watched as Jojo whispered into his hidden mic with more urgency, cocking his head to hear a response that wouldn't be coming.

"Where's Carlo?" Jojo asked, knowing them a bit too well.

"Waiting outside," Conor said. "Not inclined to join this party, as long as it's civil."

"I'm not gonna forget this, Con," Kyle hissed, white knuckles still clutching his knees, looking as though his nerves were responding to old signals of trauma.

"Do shut your mouth," his father said. "For once."

Kyle tried to hide a pout behind an expression of belittled anger.

Mason's judgmental grin only added to his embarrassment. Conor could almost hear Kyle's brain working through his shame, pleading with an unseen power to help the great Rawlings Palmer do him a favor and croak. Hopefully in debilitating pain.

Midas shifted on his feet, his head glowing in the low visibility of the posh lounge. "You know what your boyfriend here did to Serena? The two of you were friends, Michelle."

A look passed between Kyle and Daddy Palmer. Jojo squirmed but held position.

"You and I were friends, too," she shot back. No attempt to defuse the bitterness.

More than friends, Conor knew. Midas wouldn't need reminding.

Conor couldn't ignore his own feelings of loss for them both. After a lifetime of working against the tide, of dealing with problems that ended with only bad solutions, Midas had called an audible and come in from the storm. He'd quit the Unit and moved into the barkeeping business with Mason. Though after so many years on the fringe, normalizing proved impossible. Michelle had been a pleasant distraction, but being Irish and Catholic, she'd carried her share of preordained guilt. They'd stopped seeing each other over a year ago.

So how did Michelle end up in Kyle's orbit, Conor wondered.

"We're not here to discuss how the world turns," Kyle said, turning to her for emphasis.

She seemed on the verge of a retort but thought better of it, shifting her attention to the strobing colors from the revelry below.

"But we are here to come to an agreement," Palmer senior added.

"No idea what you're talking about," Midas said, his focus repurposed and intense.

"We're prepared," Palmer continued, "to do whatever is required to make that happen."

Kyle gave a snort. Obstinate posturing his father chose to disregard.

"So how do we get there?" Palmer asked.

"Last time I checked, Silver Fox, you weren't calling the plays," Mason said, pointing a finger at him.

Conor managed to hide a small smile. Mason never made anything easy.

"Actually, *Mr. James*, I am. And my charitable mood will soon expire."

"Charitable?" Mason chuffed. "I didn't realize you or your sniveling, feeble mistake of an offspring had that word in the family dictionary."

Kyle was on his feet in a flash, impressive for someone with a large waist and gimpy legs. He'd transformed into a blur of temper and steam.

Jojo cut him off with a bear hug one step before he reached Mason, who calmly remained seated, not bothering to flinch.

Jojo held his ground as Kyle's fury ebbed. He finally surrendered to the inevitable and broke free to retreat to the couch. The cheap leather groaned as he hit the cushions.

"Now *that* was what I call charitable." Mason reached up to pat Jojo's shoulder, which was roughly shrugged off.

"Can we continue, or do you have any other smart-assed observations?" Palmer senior asked.

Mason clowned his face into a quizzical expression, pointing an index finger at his cheek as if in deep thought. They all waited until he shook his head, holding up open palms. "I got nothing, Jeeves." Momentary capitulation.

"I'm leaving for DC in the morning," Rawlings Palmer stated. "What I'm proposing will be distasteful for all, but practical. The basic facts are not in dispute. The Snow Leopard declared war on old friends, the current Unit, and the Palmer family. Actions that were triggered by the unfortunate events in a Tijuana flophouse."

Midas stated his own version. "A few lewd peddlers took early retirement. So what?" He locked in on Kyle. "Didn't need to happen. But neither did Serena, *nor* a little girl in Mexico City."

Michelle glanced sharply at Kyle. Obviously, there had been omissions in the life story he'd shared with her.

Midas continued. "I'm sure you both took some physics at those Ivy League pajama parties you call higher learning. For every action, and all that . . ."

"You should be compost," Kyle mumbled.

"Yet here I am," Midas said, walking to the bar. He grabbed a bottle of Jack Daniel's and held it up Olympic-torch style. No one acknowledged the offer. He twisted off the cap, filling a glass with a healthy shot and dropping it in one prolonged gulp.

Conor could feel the whiskey fire as if it were in own his gut, crawling like a hungry colony of red ants. Combined with the lack of sleep, he was beginning to feel as if he had a weak fever.

Kyle started to speak but for once held himself in check.

Michelle shifted nervous attention between him and his father.

"The Brits would call the past few weeks a spot of nasty business," Palmer senior said. "But whatever this is, it needs to stop. *Now.* Everyone involved walks away. Against my better judgment—that includes you, Mr. McKnight. Brennan will ensure everyone plays nice, won't you?"

Conor had no such intentions but slowly nodded anyway.

"We're actually supposed to trust you?" Mason said, glancing toward Midas, who was refilling his tumbler.

"What choice do you have, Mr. James? You don't expect Conor, here, to shave any points, I assume? Unlike you, he understands relevant objectives. It's either that or we all retreat and start making other plans. And should that happen, who do you think keeps standing? Without question, you are some of the most accomplished operators I've ever known. But you're also an isolated and tiny country. The Snow Leopard mentioned physics. For me, it's more the science of attrition. I hope, Mr. James, you are getting this through that thick jock skull. No reason this should end like Butch and Sundance in Bolivia."

Somewhere below, an expensive DJ was blowing up the intensity. Bass beats pounded through the walls and floor. A time-tested saloon strategy. The more they danced, the thirstier they got and more they drank.

The situation was now on the clock. Instincts flashed to crimson. Trust wasn't an option. Conor knew Midas had a need to ensure what safety he could, at the very least to get Serena and his friends beyond his jackpot. He'd already decided none of them deserved the fate he'd preordained for himself.

"Guess I'll go with option A," Midas said, and added, "One other thing? Do yourself a favor and never use that nickname again." And then he was striding toward the door.

Quick as ever, Conor thought, following behind him, with Mason picking up the tail. Back in the low-lit corridor, Carlo jumped into the lead as they briskly descended the ramped hall and emerged back outside.

Three men had replaced the lone bouncer still snoring off Carlo's mallet shot. The new group tensed, leaning forward on their toes, but made no other threatening moves. Word had filtered down.

Midas's cell buzzed from his pocket. He studied the text without breaking stride.

Five minutes later they all drove away in separate cars. For the sake of caution.

Back inside, Jojo sat down, spent.

Michelle was silent, an angry sheen rising from red patches on her cheeks.

Rawlings Palmer was mixing a drink, the only one not looking as though he'd been through an industrial spin cycle.

"We need to finish this," Kyle said. "Kicking the can down the road presents as a weak retreat."

"For once, try to get out of your own way," his father replied, tempering the lesson with less scorn. "I have no intention of standing down. You've made that impossible. And yes, I do have plans for the Snow Leopard beyond your base need for revenge and momentary gratification. All of which you will ultimately have, be assured. But not before I decide the time is right."

He took a small taste of his drink as Kyle frowned.

"Trust me, it will be worth the short wait."

CHAPTER 11

IT HAD BEEN YEARS since Midas slept with regularity. Two hours was normal, four was decadence. Zombie hours were the most unforgiving, between midnight and five a.m., the circadian zone too often startled by his cerebral intruders.

The red digits of the bedside clock blazed 1:30. The meeting at Kyle's club had been twenty-four hours ago, followed by radio silence.

On nights when the foul weather of the past took hostage of his mind, he would set out through the inky ocean darkness for a spot close to waves, where he'd stretch out on the sand. The proximity of the raging overnight surf sometimes proved calming. Eventually he'd drop off for a bit, waking later to the bustle of lifeguards and their early sweeps.

After pulling on a Wet Seal shorty, Midas took one of two boards off the wall mounts and locked his door—as if that mattered—and made his way toward the water. Tranquility, that word that kept appearing in his mind, remained a saber of the wellness crowd. Nights next to the ocean were as close as he would ever get, marking time with the ceaseless bubbles popping beneath the froth and the diminished glow of visible stars. He reached the shore, and the Pacific stretched before him, a rumbling wall of power and muscular currents with no rules. He buried part of the board vertically in the sand to brace his back before he sat. The wind bit against his exposed legs, naked below the knees. He craved sleep, but it was a waste of time to try.

The memories flooding his mind after the meeting wouldn't allow it.

Michelle Kelly, of all people.

She had sauntered into Shredders four years ago, just after he and Mase had gotten the bar up and running. A graduate student recently cut off by her provincial and controlling father, she'd taken a job moonlighting for a couple of local craft-beer brewers. The part-time gig paid enough to supplement the student loans she'd taken out to finish her doctorate in psychology. That first day, she'd walked in before hours and asked to test all their tap offerings, each of which she'd appraised as subpar, and then naturally signed them up to try her boss's brews.

She'd given no ground to members of the striking plastic beach set that made the South Bay its home. Midas would soon identify Michelle's long blond hair pulled into a ragged ponytail and the intense brown eyes hovering above a naughty grin as her stock in trade. Her features were more midcontinent European than her Irish surname. Beyond a dusting of lipstick, she shunned feminine staples. No mascara, eye shadow, or perfume. Her presence was undeniable, and the well-bound energy required an outlet.

The easier money would have been as a waitress or bartender.

But Michelle declared she was fine brokering small deals for up-scale beer and had no intention of wearing shorts, tight T-shirts, or stroking inebriated male egos, regardless of how much they might tip. A few years later she recruited her psychology school classmate, Serena Cooper, a sunnier flower who'd been more than willing to tend bar despite having no financial need for the fast cash, declaring it a perfect way to study human dynamics in an environment men and women felt free to act uninhibited, if not completely childish.

Time and hindsight had the advantage of sterilizing filters. Midas could now see Michelle as he hadn't then—overly headstrong and frequently angry. Because the bar was still a new venture that benefited from her presence, he'd chosen to ignore the warning beacons. Within a few weeks of that first meeting, she'd taken over the books, ensuring the boys weren't getting fleeced by markups, nonexistent spirit taxes, or shady delivery schedules.

Even Mason had grudgingly agreed her skills and organization were a decent fit. They'd promoted her to manager. After getting the accounts straight, she'd gone to work on the staff, weeding the burnouts, giggly coeds, and other unreliables in favor of better employees and those who truly needed the job.

Somewhere during those first six months, she and Midas had initiated a casual relationship. He'd assumed parameters were clearly defined. She had concluded something else. She harbored expectations, and when authenticity intruded to install barriers, she chose to ignore them. Theirs became a battle of physical ne-cessity versus obstinate erosion. "Damaged souls, and all that shit," she would casually scoff, conceding their dependence was nothing beyond fatalistic connection and sexual desire. He'd gone along, hungry for companionship no matter the trepidation. They became bitter lovers, purifying necessary needs. If they weren't fucking, they were arguing. Or at least she was.

He preferred silence to her need for conflict, disappearing for a few days when it became too much—something he could now admit was a weak, passive-aggressive deflection. He never understood why she'd chosen psychology, given that the nurturing gene had seemingly eluded her. She was bright, at times brilliant, and engaging when she chose to be. Though for a future shrink, she wasn't a healer or empathizer. She also wasn't comfortable with critical self-reflection.

What they shared said more about him and his attempt to grasp an elusive form of sanity. Over time, their partnership became a cliché, businesslike and clinical, emotionally distant. When nothing remained worthy of salvage, they'd shared a final drink, pledging to remain friends, that shaky crutch of a relationship *bon mot* easier to handle than backing away to neutral corners on lousy terms.

A few months later, Serena had shown up.

She'd spent three years in Italy trying to make her way as a painter after securing a degree from a tony New York art school. But the romance and inspiration of the great masters had diminished, and she'd found she wasn't suited to the isolation of an artist's life. Too many hours spent alone. Humanity was far more enticing than canvas. So, she'd come to LA to spend a summer in a friend's Malibu beach house before enrolling at Loyola . . . as much as to avoid her old-school Episcopalian Boston Brahmin clan on Beacon Hill. Serena had met Michelle a few months into the semester during a weekend seminar. They'd become study partners, and Michelle had liked her well enough to offer her a shot as a bartender, figuring it would prove a short-lived experiment since she didn't need the paycheck.

Serena's layered demeanor and dark-haired beauty initially worked against her at Shredders, though Michelle had been pleasantly surprised at her protégé's latent toughness and her uncanny talent for disarming even the most hormonal of aging, drunken adolescents.

Midas couldn't help now going over those days, again and again.

Beneath this morning's blemished sky, the first fragment of dusk spread a rheumy eye on the horizon. There was a short, muted pitch of a boat horn, followed by three others in quick succession, then laughter out beyond the swirling currents. Owners of the bigger vessels liked to troll the a.m. hours around the South Bay when the lights of the seaside homes were brilliantly condensed and the tides more forgiving. Midas had spent many similar nights atop his board, out on the bobbing sea studying the low hills of Manhattan, Hermosa, and Redondo, a passable imitation of some of his favorite European coastlines.

Michelle had hated the ocean, seeing only monotony and unpredictability. Serena had begged him to teach her to surf.

When it became clear what was happening between them, he'd purposely kept himself away from the bar, making short and infrequent appearances. No need to borrow trouble. In retrospect, another weak move of avoidance, and unnecessary. Michelle had understood what was unfolding well before they had.

Then one day Michelle was gone without notice, abruptly quitting school as well.

The sounds of the other early risers out beyond the waves had died, a victim of a stiffer wind that rattled the zipper of his track jacket like a wind chime. He took a deep pull of the ocean scent, recalling a favorite image of Serena laid out straight on her longboard as it rolled over soft waves beside his, the dark, wet hair on her back belying hints of curls. In those moments she would turn to him and smile. Not to be sure he was still there, but to share the camaraderie. They would gently rock and weave for hours, never passing a word.

The pleasant picture quickly melted into a red mass against the shards of her broken face. A garish reminder of her spirit and trust, forever destroyed.

He put his head between his knees and wept.

Two hours later, Natalie stood just off the strand watching Midas emerge from the smaller waves.

He moved with the precision of one in control, a physical genius, halting momentarily to thankfully appreciate the water, the board loosely held at his side. He always confessed to not being a natural athlete, on his better days maybe half the jock Mason was. But as Natalie studied him in his elemental haven, she knew his skill couldn't be questioned. Like that English writer who'd once said talent was the one thing that couldn't be faked. Midas's form was a testament to thousands of hours of work and crafting. The stroke, muscular arm turns, followed by the pop-up to complete the ride with steadiness and vigilance. Again, and again. Few looked as sturdy or as nimble when skimming over the water.

She wondered whether Collins the fed looked half as polished on his blade.

She shook herself out of that thought, settling on what she had to do. Natalie forced herself to begin moving above the uneven sand. Walking over the mounds took time and effort and imposed its own organic concentration. Healing protocols. Beach zen.

Sensing her presence, Midas turned and started toward her, as always scanning the area to be sure she wasn't being shadowed. "Little early for turnovers," he called.

As their distance decreased, he must have seen that she had been crying. He tried to smile gently but managed only a stoic grimace. When she rested her head on his shoulder and wrapped her arms around his neck to pull him closer, his body went cold, and still.

"What?" he asked, panic seeping into his voice.

"I need you to come with me."

Playful dolphins were hard to miss, especially when captured with pastel vividness on an outside mural three stories high. If not for such colorful touches, the Long Beach Aquarium could have been mistaken for a bottling plant or a modern high school, with its cylinder shape and contemporary architecture reveling in a distaste for right angles.

Midas remained silent, fixated, restless as a spirited Thoroughbred in a starter's gate. Natalie pulled her car into the four-level parking structure, slipping into a spot on the ground floor next to several black-and-whites and a beige coroner's van. They got out and made the short walk to the ticket window and entrance. The only normal activity at seven a.m. was the two cafeteria delivery trucks, today augmented by a gaggle of cops. Rope barriers sagged around the entry, where the glass doors were propped open. She paused for a few words with the uniforms stationed outside.

"It was a strange enough crime scene that everyone kept it off the scanner," she had told Midas on the drive down. "But it also came across our encrypted text service, meaning his name had popped somewhere important. The local Long Beach PD is coordinating for now. They want to get it all swept before reopening the aquarium to the public. I leaned on my boss to claim professional privilege. So they are letting me nose around, unofficially. But they'll probably have trust issues."

She turned and led him inside, her badge clearly visible. There were a few suspicious glances and nods of recognition.

Inside, he barely took notice of the impressive atrium, a museum-worthy space capped with a forty-foot painted ceiling, or the reinforced-glass-encased habitats that had been carved into the curved walls. The handful of openings for well-marked tunnels, tourist access to UV-lit displays, had been blocked off. Beneath the scale-sized blue whale suspended overhead by durable metal wires buzzed a subdued hum of humanity, lowered voices, and pinging cell phones, conversations indecipherable over the pressurized bubbling of a vast shark tank. Two of the uniforms stood next to it, transfixed, their faces close to the thick glass as mako, thresher, and hammerheads swam with an agitation caused by the unusual early-morning activity.

Midas continued to ignore the abstract minutiae, dread churning through his fibers.

Natalie put a hand on his arm, guiding him toward one of the darkened passageways blocked with the yellow tape. They slipped under it, leaving behind natural light for a narrow, twisting path framed by colorful underwater creatures swimming in clear enclosures. Winding through the man-made reef, their path opened to an observation room with more wall-mounted rectangular tanks.

A two-sided wooden bench stood in the middle of the room,

the floor around it empty except for a mound under a pale blue plastic covering.

Natalie looked at Midas, who said nothing.

She nodded to the detectives and one of the forensic techs, who rolled the plastic to one side.

Phillip Gillis's face appeared serene. His right arm was thick and useless, badly swollen below the elbow and colored by a mixture of deep blue and plum, a violent mesh of hues that could have been a stormy sky. His khaki chinos and old-school Adidas were clean, as if just out of the closet.

Midas swallowed, holding back the rage, and fell into a squat. The weak hum of electricity and air bubbles were the only sounds … other than the blood of fury pounding in his ears.

Natalie was having trouble keeping it together. Her sight suddenly betrayed her, becoming nothing but tears manipulating shapes and fuzzy outlines. Her chest tightened as she tried to control her galloping heart.

She stepped in to offer Midas support, but he waved her off sharply. Instead, he grabbed for the edge of the wooden bench, struggling to brace his trembling body.

She replaced the plastic and sat down beside him, her thoughts spinning without restraint. Time dragged and she gradually regulated herself, the anguish retreating to a bearable level.

Midas got to his feet, taking a few unsteady steps forward to lean against the damp glass of a tropical exhibit. "What did they do to him?" he finally asked.

She jammed her shaking hands into her jacket pockets. Notifications were a routine part of her job, but this morning she might as well have been a rookie. "He was poisoned," she said. "From the marks on his arm, the coroner thinks it was a large amount."

Midas's head pitched forward, chin to chest. "Tortured," he said. "They followed the manual on that, too."

She was puzzled by his statement but didn't ask.

A middle-aged man in cargo shorts and a short-sleeved polo with tanned arms and leathered hands slid under the tape. He stopped to sit beside her, tension in his face. She whispered through a brief conversation with him. "Midas, this is Dr. Ray Haden. He's the expert here."

Midas moved forward so they could solemnly shake hands.

"I understand he was your friend." Haden's manner was respectful. "I'm very sorry. Never seen anything like this."

Midas nodded, his expression indecipherable. "What can you tell us?"

"First of all, it's shocking to realize someone could actually *plan* something like this. I've never heard of death caused by one bite, so it must have been multiple and sustained bites."

"Bites?" she asked.

"Your friend was bitten by sea snakes. Several of them. The species possess one of the most toxic poisons known to humans. But they're also a mild-tempered group, and generally avoid trouble. Not aggressive unless threatened. And given their habitat here, that would be rare." Haden paused, surveying the room with a practiced eye.

"Which means . . . ," she said, prompting him.

"Someone disabled our security," he said. "As far as we can tell, they brought him through one of our rear entrances before somehow getting into the tank over there. From the look of it, they held his arm inside, thrashing it around enough to rile up the creatures. We have eight sea snakes in that tank. And like all our displays, it can only be accessed from feeding stations behind the walls."

She and Midas walked over for a closer look. Like the others, the tank used interior illumination, still visible despite being covered with another piece of the blue plastic. Midas approached, pulling the covering to one side.

She stepped up to him and said, "The aquarium is naked between eleven p.m. and five a.m., between the evening and morning feedings. I'm told there's supposed to be a guard on the property. At the moment, he's missing. And as Dr. Haden said, security was disabled. LBPD confirmed nearby traffic cams were also hacked and jammed overnight for several hours, so we don't even have visuals of potential vehicles around the area. There was an anonymous nine one one call around twelve thirty a.m. He was discovered a few minutes later."

"Preplanning," Midas muttered.

"It looks like after he'd been infected," Haden said, joining them, "they brought him out here. So he could face the tank as he died."

"How would the poison manifest?" Natalie asked.

"Sea snakes," Haden said, "have small fangs but can strike more than once. A dose like what this appears to be would have taken over his nervous system very fast. He must have been carried out here. His motor functions wouldn't have held up for more than about forty-five seconds. Everything shuts down rapidly with that much venom. It's doubtful he lived more than a few minutes. I'm sorry to have to say it, but those minutes would have been excruciating. At the end, one is paralyzed as the airways close. Basically, you suffocate."

Letting all that sink in, they wordlessly studied the tank.

There was no discernible movement within. For a moment she thought it was empty, that the offenders had been relocated. Then she saw them hovering at the bottom, camouflaged against colored rocks. They were each barely a foot long, black with yellow-striped bands across flattened tails, as skinny as baby garden snakes. The heads held no shape or distinguishing marks.

A deceptively innocuous congregation of silent killers.

CHAPTER 12

MASON WAS SITTING ALONE, trying to remember when crying had become a fashion statement. No less than three of the morning news stories had featured weeping witnesses to various crimes.

He was also having trouble trying to distract himself.

It had been over twenty-four hours since the tense meeting at the club, and he hated nothing more than lying low. It was almost as though he could feel his mind and body losing elasticity. He was best when moving. Inertness offered openings to shadows he was better off avoiding.

His mind locked back on the current crisis.

Mason knew Midas was too careful to ever be connected to the Basmajian brothers' and O'Shea's demises in the usual ways. But Natalie was relentless, and her new FBI buddy had a drawer full of better resources.

She had been distant since taking lead on the case, so he'd also been bracing for the inevitable. His perceptions were microtuned, and he could sense her pulling back. He assumed she was contemplating their existence together, more so than usual lately. He was also convinced she was thinking about this fed beyond being cops working the same beat.

Such thoughts wrecked him. But he was the first to admit she deserved much more than a guy who couldn't be what she needed because of an inability to outrun demons he had to face alone. Though in this isolated moment, the thought of life without her was beyond anything he could grasp, even if it was the only solution.

Instead, it was better to sit and wait, and wonder why so many people interviewed by local news twerps felt crying branded them as more deserving members of humanity.

Watching them tearfully emote for the camera made him feel old and untethered. He had grown up reserved, like Midas the only child of a limited and closed-off family in which physical displays of joy and emotion had been deemed suspect.

All this current schmaltz had to have started a few generations ago, when American social dynamics shifted to being more demanding while also enabling the homogenization of the sexes. Truth was, beyond the physical, he couldn't tell most men and women apart these days. Both communicated with an annoying, exacting, vocal-fried inflection. Avoiding the hard edges of living in favor of what they referred to as *their own truths*. Using lessons in me-first to complain and be heard while sharing the endless numbing facets of their insular orbits. Certainly never passing up a chance to share their pain in a public display of tears. As if such exhibitions were a gateway to a favored form of sainthood.

In the last few decades, spurred on by social media and especially what now passed for journalism, restraint and critical thinking had been lost, casualties to less rigorous and intellectually challenging tells. Anchors and reporters had become tepid followers, incapable of demanding hard truths from those they chased and certainly not from themselves. They'd chosen instead the route of mindless cheerleaders and stenographers, blindly repeating what self-anointed tastemakers and influencers chose to scatter like weightless glitter over various platforms. It was the expanding culture of correctness taking prisoners . . . but beyond something more insidious.

Gaslighting, masquerading as community and psychological nourishment.

When Mason had worked as a freelance writer, journalism was a fading ideal but still held some claim as a meticulous calling. He had sadly watched as the transformation from creative and insightful, serious newsgathering had eventually been shed in favor of emotional bargaining and choked-up codas. Delivered by bland and maudlin *personalities*, in an all-out assault on evenhandedness and impartiality. What passed for news these days was nothing more than a group weepfest, grief therapy for the masses. Equal parts ebullience and shallow sadness.

The buzzing of his phone startled him. He saw it was Natalie, and given the time of day, it felt wrong.

"Hey, slugger," he answered, trying to take the weight out of his words.

In short, broken sentences, she gave him the sickening news about Phillip, apparently not trusting herself beyond the straight facts, soldiering through most of it before her own voice started to fade. She tried to cut it short, clearly not trusting herself to continue, probably hating herself for having to make this call.

He was too stunned to feel anything, instead reverting to op mode. "Where's Midas?" he asked hoarsely.

"He left about an hour ago, hopped in an Uber. I've got to go. I'll call when I can."

The line went silent.

Mason threw the phone onto the floor as his head swirled. It all landed on him in an avalanche. He felt like what he was.

A hostage in a locked box. A room with no walls.

Sometime later came the rustle of shoes crunching the sand on Mason's front deck, followed by a weak knock. He had no doubt who it might be.

Midas's eyes were as ashen as the morning fog, his face a mask of anguish and agitation, his legs quivering but somehow planted firmly like a soldier at his post. He seemed more apparition than human.

Mason reached forward to gently guide him inside.

An hour later a bottle of Jameson sat empty on the small table between them.

"Has Conor checked in?" Mason asked.

"No."

Con was one of them, a good friend and dependable partner. But he'd also chosen to remain with the Unit. Stuck between the Palmers' sinister blueprint and the Old Man's commitment to necessary objectives, Conor had been forced to dance between his two masters. His loyalty and character were as firm as granite, but he was also a survivor, and may have been forced to make an impossible, if not Faustian, bargain.

"Have to assume he knows," Mason said with caution. "Should

we be gearing up for him as well?"

Midas didn't seem surprised by the suspicion. Mason had been forced into vigilance mode in which only two parallels existed—threats and safeguards. Those requiring protection, and those in need of other resolutions. Mason was finished with standing down.

Midas wouldn't like it. But Midas could no longer allow himself to wonder about the what-ifs or working unseen angles. He had surrendered any such rights behind his miscalculations and careless mistakes . . . however righteous.

There was only the finality of what remained to be done.

"Con wouldn't sell us out," Midas said. "He thought he had a few days to pitch DeMarco's remaining allies, force Kyle and his father to stand down. Rawlings told him we had a week. I still don't know why Kyle didn't come after me faster, but my guess is they're still afraid of the Old Man, deathbed or not. Rawlings needed that week to shore up and secure his seat within the eventual post-DeMarco world. But as usual, Kyle can't be controlled and jumped the gun. Conor will revert to training. He's lying low, doing what he does best—reading the wind and his own recon. He and the Old Man have kept me sheltered from this for years, but the bill is long past due." Midas glanced at him wearily. "I need to ask. Any chance you'd consider sitting this one out?"

Mason responded with a prolonged glare.

"Okay," Midas said, unable to hide the defeat in his eyes. "But it's my mess. Because of it, you're all targets. Nothing remotely right about that." He moved to the sliding glass doors, heavily shaded to make it difficult to see inside without proper toys. He scanned the mostly deserted beach.

A few joggers were pounding workouts on the strand path's smooth concrete. Farther out, a lone surfer waited for his set. Beyond that, nothing of much concern.

Mason studied his oldest friend and ally.

Midas had never struggled with or questioned his own motives or character when it came to the team and its business. Higher purpose, he'd once said, was a cliché, and given what they'd been tasked to do, hollow and double edged.

He'd been right. And times were changing.

"We've got a bit of rope, maybe thirty-six hours," Midas said. "Even the brokers looking to the Palmers as the best remaining option won't go for a total clearing of the board. Not without securing more heavy concessions from Rawlings. They like to tell themselves they have standards and rules. Phillip was an original in good standing. Retirement or not, they won't like how this played out. Killing him in that fashion presents as a petulant move by a rogue faction. Which is why I'm also sure Jojo wasn't part of it. Despite what Kyle tells himself, Jojo's always taken orders from senior. Being that brat's minder was never his idea of a noble calling." Midas narrowed his eyes. "What did you make of Kyle the other night?"

"Furious," Mason said. "Wanted to pull his father's throat out with a grappling hook."

"And to be humiliated in front of Michelle, his new Girl Friday? Kyle didn't give a damn about what we all agreed to." Midas pushed out a harsh breath. "The last time I saw Phillip was at the zoo. On his way out, he mentioned he'd rather have gone to the aquarium. Someone I missed was obviously watching and listening." He slid away from the window to sit down. "Fuck me. Picked a bad time to lose my edge."

Mason leaned forward. "We don't have time for any of that," he said with a sternness he often used to combat his own palpable anxiety. "We need to make our move, generate some momentum. Kyle's off book. Hired a handful of those robots the Agency likes to use but never talk about. Psychotic specimens with motherhood issues. Think about it. He's a weasel and a worm. Somehow, he went around Jojo and his father because he figured he could. Rawlings is King Lear. Knows his son is a leaking warhead but refuses to dismantle him. Too many blue-blood mouths demanding their soft sheets and toy poodles."

Midas smiled half-heartedly.

Next to his bikes and the gym, books were what kept Mason grounded and open to interpretations beyond the obvious and the one-dimensional. He'd always believed he'd learned as much from literary fiction as he ever had from sports, street fights, or boots on the ground.

"Call the play, Mide."

A slow nod. "Phillip gave me one last lead I need to run down. It will take some time. Can you keep an eye on everyone? Wait for my call?"

"Carlo and his boys will do that. How about I shadow you?"

"Not yet. Just help me buy a bit more time."

Conor brewed his coffee surrounded by sterile fixtures.

The kitchen could have fit in a matchbox. A few feet away, an undersized flat-TV screen perched on the floor against a chipped desk. On its surface were three burner phones and a secure laptop that self-swept every half hour with one of Phillip's more ingenious apps.

Phillip. Hot tears rose in his eyes.

A twin bed sat made and unused. Afternoon light sluiced through strips of shuttered blinds. Outside the sliding glass door dangled a balcony too cramped for anything but standing and admiring what could be seen of downtown LA ten stories below.

This place would have been more functional as a large closet. Starter condo was what the brochure had called it, offering timely walks to upscale meals and entertainment. Urban living negating the need of a car.

Ridiculous concept, Conor thought. Living without wheels in this city was delusional.

This hidden shelter was one of three safe houses he ran, all purchased two years ago under one of his layered aliases. Useful craft he'd been schooled in twenty-five years after coming to the attention of Silas Whitten, one of his UCLA track coaches . . . and old buddy of Jasper DeMarco.

Now in the early seventies, Silas Whitten had been a decorated relay sprinter at UCLA, an Olympic alternate who'd used his legs and his savvy to distance himself from a tough neighborhood on Chicago's South Side, where he'd come of age as a Black teenager surviving the crush end of several encounters with then Mayor Daley's knuckle-scuffing, fat-assed cops.

Thirty years later, it had been Silas helping push Conor as a member of the UCLA track team. But the coach had also been an established member of another exclusive club known to only a few with the required clearance, overseeing a modest band of capable operators answering to Jasper DeMarco. Silas had been his right hand during the embryonic days when the Old Man was still in the field. To this day, DeMarco trusted him without reservation.

Conor Brennan hadn't been a tough sell for either team. His recruitment from the college track to operator had been so seamless, Conor couldn't exactly remember when Silas had appeared in his life. After a point, it had seemed as if he'd always been there with his pointed lessons that had soon become about more than running.

Midway through his junior year at UCLA, Whitten had sent him for a weekend in DC under the guise of a potential look at graduate schools. "Time for you to meet a few friends" was all Conor had been told.

The friends turned out to be an MIT overachiever named Phillip Gillis and the enigmatic Jasper DeMarco.

"I'm something of a team leader for a small group of civil servants," the Old Man had said after a cozy home-cooked meal and some convivial conversation.

The way he'd said it had made Conor and Phillip glance at each other and lean forward. Finally, they'd get some answers to this mysterious meeting.

"How and what we do is a discussion for another time," De-Marco continued. "You were both chosen by men whose judgment I trust implicitly. They will both be waiting when you return home. My only suggestion is to finish your degrees while spending as much time around them as possible. Listen to what they have to say and pay attention. We need young men like you, but what we offer isn't for most. If you should decide it isn't, I'd rather you let us know soon. With no hard feelings."

The three sat in silence for a few moments, the boys trying to work out what it all meant. It wasn't every day someone asked you to consider choosing a life you'd never imagined.

Phillip had asked, "Is this some CIA hard sell?"

"No. Now, if you boys will excuse me."

Phillip had headed for the front door, already skilled at taking orders.

Conor turned to follow, but DeMarco put a hand on his shoulder. "Silas says you might be the best raw prospect he's ever come across. We both have high hopes. And that, young Conor, *is* a hard sell. Also, the last time I will mention it." DeMarco walked back into the study, pausing just beyond the doorframe. They looked at each other one final time. This was the Old Man he'd come to know and revere, smooth and erudite, who didn't need parlor tricks or deception to have his commands followed. He smiled and quietly shut the door.

Conor and Phillip were driven back to the airport and onto red-eyes flying in different directions. When Conor had landed five and a half hours later, Silas was standing at the gate—one of many old conveniences later lost to 9/11.

These days, Silas was semiretired living in the Bay Area. Conor made sure they saw each other a few times a year.

Unfortunately, he was the man Conor needed now.

Silas was the only person he trusted for a measured read ... and possibly some assistance. It wasn't fair to ask, but he had no choice. Phillip was dead, and Midas had been sanctioned. Over the next few days, Conor would have to keep moving, never stopping anywhere longer than a few hours. Silas could help him figure out the terrain and what came next. To make that a reality, more useful craft would be needed.

Along with a bit of Irish luck.

CHAPTER 13

THE FOLLOWING NIGHT, MIDAS initiated his endgame.

The 405 freeway was sluggish, but he was in no hurry. Phillip's final text was stored on the burner. Midas could almost feel the numbers and words heating up in the tight darkness of his pocket, transforming the cellphone to a smoldering brick of kryptonite. But it wasn't any warmer than usual when he pulled it from his sweats and flipped it onto the passenger seat.

Thoreau had a line about the savage man, rage never fully erad-icated. Midas often wondered whether the philosopher had been riffing in the abstract or, more likely, had witnessed his own share of iniquity.

Midas inched the car along in the fast lane under another dark sky. Thankfully, he wouldn't be on this stretch for long. His target destination was only a few miles from the beach. He could have taken streets but hadn't been thinking much about the drive. Only about what was next on the list.

Like other cities in LA County, Carson was a mix of warehouses, office complexes, and a spattering of residential homes nestled between and divided by three freeways. Seventy-five years ago, it had been exclusively a storing center for freight shipped into the LA harbor through San Pedro and Long Beach. Part of the municipality remained true to its roots, but given the explosion of population in the county and the need for cheaper land, Carson had followed the trend and become a more sustained and functional community. Not much to look at, but self-contained and satisfying to homeowners and smaller corporations looking for alternatives to the exorbitant rents of the Westside, the Valley, and downtown.

The professional soccer stadium on Avalon Boulevard was now several years old, though still selling itself as a quaint and shining testament to English football. Its thirty thousand seats were all close to the field, or the pitch, as the Brits called it. The venue was run by a sports consortium and surrounded by high-level training facilities catering to all forms of Olympic events. Three multilane pools, track-and-field stations, and one of the only cycling velodromes on the West Coast. The complex was impressive, but the soccer field, the original jewel in the Carson crown, was now a poor cousin to its newer and even more quaint stadium downtown on the edge of the USC campus.

Midas reached the block he was looking for a few minutes later. A quiet street of modest post–World War II homes built affordably for returning GIs and dockworkers. In the decades since, some had been razed, replaced by typical urban refinements such as strip malls and grocery stores. But many remained untouched beyond cosmetic freshening, featuring backyards perfectly square and inviting for gatherings and barbecues.

The target address turned out to be an original structure, non-descript and on a corner.

Muted lights glowed inside behind closed shades. The garage door was closed, the driveway empty. Midas already knew the backyard bordered the Metro Blue Line, the LA railway system operating fuel-efficient trains that looked like fallen milk cartons. The fenced-off tracks in back offered the house added security.

He made a right turn and drove past at normal speed, eyes forward to avoid any cameras. Half a mile and two stop signs later, he turned left. A few hundred feet more and he reached a location where the Blue Line intersected a residential street, protected by wooden crossing arms straight up and motionless, ready to halt traffic whenever the boxy trains passed. Midas knew this happened in ten-minute intervals during rush crush, and every twenty-two or so minutes in the off-hours. The protective fencing ended at the sidewalks and the two-lane street that passed under the gates.

He flipped the car around and parked. And waited.

Ten minutes later, he felt a rumble under his chassis, followed by the screech of approaching metal wheels navigating the skinny rails. The train swayed as it rolled by with four cars, making him question whether these commuter convoys were all that safe.

He jumped from his seat, punching the alarm fob while picking up his pace to pursue the rolling train, ducking under the gates and along the inside of the fence. He stayed well left of the tracks as he sprinted behind the train's rear car, chasing the rabbit, as Conor called it. Before he'd gone a block, the wobbling cars had paced him and were far ahead, nothing but a pinhole and blinking red lights.

He evened his pace, rhythmically breathing in cadence with the scrape of gravel under his feet. He approached the chosen address again, this time from behind, unimpeded by backyard lights, hidden security, or guard dogs. He tugged his knitted black wool hat lower, just above his eyes, then vaulted up and over the fence into a backyard scattered with children's toys.

He sidestepped silently on the balls of his feet, cutting through a well-furnished patio with a sun-sheltering wooden lattice. At the back door, he paused. An older sliding version with tempered glass. Locked. The low hum of a television drifted from somewhere inside. Through that door would be the minders. At least one, likely two. The night was LA cold, so the windows would be shut and secured.

What was it Conor used to say? Use whatever was available and bank on stupidity.

A red fireman's truck stood out from the smattering of toys. He picked it up and moved next to a trellis off to the side of the glass door. Just enough so the slivers of moon wouldn't catch his shadow. With an underhand toss, the truck flew a few feet into the air, angled high and wide. The bright metal engine spun a few times before gravity took hold, dropping it back to earth with an abrupt *thunk* on the concrete terrace just inside the grass that ran to the fence.

Movement sounded from inside. Footsteps hesitantly approached. There was a *click*. Exterior lights flooded the yard in bright yellow, changing the colors of all things it touched. The door slid open too fast, the barrel of a handgun poking out to take measure.

Midas bolted from the shadows, grabbing the gun with his left hand while using his right to clamp down on the extended arm. He pulled outward forcefully.

The minder was surprised as he stumbled, keeping his grip but losing his balance.

Midas twisted downward.

As he lurched forward, the guard tried to brace against the momentum and free himself. But as he fell, he made the crucial mistake of taking a moment to lift his face and survey his attacker.

It was the only opening Midas needed, landing his fist an inch above the left eyebrow, packing the power of a metal press.

The man flopped to the ground, unconscious.

Pulling his own piece from the waistband at his back, Midas stepped over the fallen soldier and into the kitchen, rechecking that his suppressor was tightly screwed into the barrel. Old habits reemerged. He briefly surveyed the outdated electric range, sink, cabinets with crooked hinges, and a folding card table littered with plastic takeout cartons. He cut the lights from a wall switch and moved to a far corner. Hushed tones drifted from the front of the house, then went silent. Deliberate steps advanced toward the kitchen.

Midas squatted next to the cluttered table. The steps stopped just beyond the arched opening into the hallway, out of his sight range. A leg appeared first, followed by a figure, weapon raised and sweeping. Then came hesitation. The fallen partner was visible on the ground outside, breathing peacefully in the darkness.

"Drop it," Midas ordered from his crouch.

The man swiveled. Trained arms outstretched in a rigid silhouette. Midas's shot hit him below the nose, snapping his head back as blood sprayed from the rear of his skull and his shattered front teeth. He dropped to his knees before his body slipped forward and fell to the floor.

"Fuck." A third man stepped through the arch with hesitation, hands raised. "I'm unarmed."

"Slowly," Midas said.

The surrendering man leaned down to stare in disbelief at the man on the floor. His hands remained high as he turned, fear coursing through his expression. He looked to be about thirty-five, a six-footer, but thin and slight. Black fleece sweats were gathered around his ankles with Velcro cuffs above a pair of Nikes. His Liverpool FC jersey bore a crusty brown stain over his ribs. Thick dark hair was fringed around a sunken face bearing the aftermath of severe teenage acne.

No doubt this was the guy Midas was looking for.

"Anyone else?" Midas asked.

Fear and a vacant stare provided the answer.

"What's your name?"

Liverpool's diverted attention began to fixate. He shook himself out of his momentary stupor, summoning a weak but not uncommon rush of bravado. He was working through options. His hands dropped as he tried to relax with only the slightest tinge of panic, temporary adrenaline being a sturdy match for hovering unease.

Midas gestured to the prone lump on the stained linoleum. "He got his through the tonsils. How 'bout we give you a fresh opening in the prune bag?" The black eye of his gun dropped to waist level. "Usually makes things more interesting."

The man's face changed color as he wrapped himself tightly in his own embrace. His head started to shake and a high-pitched voice returned, repeating a defeated mantra. "This isn't right . . . isn't right."

Midas waited as it played through. When the gibberish ceased, he looked straight into the man's eyes, noting the lost eyes buried in the pocked face. "Again. What's your name?"

The world had gone quiet. Even the distant dogs were taking a break. The kitchen reeked of greasy Chinese food, cordite, and death.

"Must be something you want?" Liverpool asked. Bargaining. The stages of grief were coming at warp speed.

"Your name," Midas said.

"Do you know who . . . who runs this place?"

"I won't ask again." Midas clicked the hammer of his 9 mm for emphasis.

There was a small quiver. "Teddy. Teddy Sherman. Jake's on the floor . . . and that's Vinny outside. Is he still alive?"

Midas pointed to one of the two chairs next to the messy table. Teddy shuffled and sat down.

Midas kept his eyes fixed on him as he opened and backed through the glass door, pulling zip ties from his rear pocket. Teddy sat transfixed as Midas secured Vinny's ankles, flipped him over, and pulled the limp arms behind his back before securing the wrists. He then pulled a roll of duct tape from another pocket, tore a strip, and put it over Vinny's mouth. He pulled a plastic bag from his hoodie pocket that contained a small syringe, and jabbed the needle into the cold skin of the bodyguard's neck. A nasty kick under the ribs brought no response, satisfying any concern Vinny might be conscious and faking. Midas grabbed him under the armpits and dragged him inside, locking the slider behind him.

He held his gun up as if presenting it to a trial jury, making his point before putting it back into his waistband. "Get up."

Teddy rose on unsure legs but found some balance.

"Anyone else around I need to worry about?"

"No, it was always just the three of us."

Midas nodded. "Show me the rest of your house."

"It's not my house. It's—"

"Show me the house, Teddy."

The minder's stride lacked any bounce or incentive. Midas knew enough about panic stress to comprehend what Teddy was working through.

"You must be Midas."

He didn't bother to answer.

It tracked that they'd all been alerted a few days earlier, ordered to increase normal security measures. No doubt why Jake and Vinny had been in the house tonight, likely upgrades from the usual team. Midas assumed the neighborhood could be nosy. Mostly blue-collar families who had lived there for decades desiring a less troublesome nest between the gang patches of Lynwood, Gardena, and Bellflower. The kind of residents who paid attention. Slipping goons in and out of a corner address organically would have taken planning.

Midas followed Teddy through a short corridor that weaved between two bedrooms and a full bath into a low-lit living room hidden from the street behind dark curtains. A light-colored leather couch sat against a side wall facing a large TV with a paused video game on the screen. Two half-finished beers sweated next to the controllers on the coffee table. The other side of the room was cluttered with portable cameras and lighting stands.

Along with a child's race-car bed.

The boy sitting on its edge was wearing nothing but a pair of white underpants. He might have been seven years old. He stared up at Midas, the newest adult, with shame. At the foot of the bed rested a small round bag decorated with Captain America's three-colored shield and star logo.

Midas grabbed Teddy roughly, forcing him down to the floor.

He pushed his face into the carpet, securing his hands and feet with more zips. There was no resistance beyond defeated mumbling.

The look on the boy's face turned to fear.

Midas raised his hands reassuringly as he started to cry. "It's okay, little man. I'm gonna get you out of here and back home."

The boy heaved for a few moments, trying to believe the bald man's gentle words, and slowly calmed down.

"Do you have a shirt?"

The boy reached behind the hidden side of the bed, producing an LAFC T-shirt and kid jeans. The toes of a small pair of Pumas peeked beneath his bag.

Midas cautiously stepped forward to retrieve them, placing the sneaks on the bed next to the boy. "I like Pumas too." he said.

As the kid pulled on his clothes, Midas picked up the backpack, running a finger over the brightly painted Captain America star. Too bad the Cap hadn't come through for this kid.

Seemed like superheroes never played fair.

A few years back, Midas had been in a West LA coffee spot killing a few hours with Mason before a scheduled consultation. The lingering taste of dark Colombian beans had rested on his tongue, helping him appreciate a calm moment. He liked coffeehouses, the smells and pleasant strum from soft keyboards, polite conversation, and deliberate thinking behind the big windows steps away from the bustling, impatient world.

He and Mase were inconspicuously seated near a rack of mugs and T-shirts. Mase was leaning back against a shelf, almost dozing.

The glass door pushed open, ushering a *whoosh* from the street. The man entering was in his late forties, moving with a tic that bent his knees and pushed his center of gravity toward the floor.

Loose jeans whiffled in harmony with his squeaking, beaten-up sneakers. At the counter, he shifted a heavy weight from one shoulder to the other—a round backpack with the edges straining against its contents, proudly embossed with the Captain America logo—red hoops around a smaller circle filled with white and blue shading a five-point star. The man offered a salutation, eliciting a knowing smile from the young female barista, his frumpiness working in tandem with a pleasant charm, speaking to the status of a well-regarded regular.

Midas had found himself strangely touched. Sensing a different energy, the man turned, meeting Midas's look with a warm and crooked smile, his eyes going soft while nodding in the friendly shorthand for "How's it going?" No trepidation or inhibition, instead a healthy reserve of good nature and optimism. All from a middle-aged guy with a superhero backpack. The man turned back to the chatty college student working on his order, the two carrying on like lifelong friends.

As a child, Midas had loved comics. Batman, Green Arrow, Tony Stark, and of course, the Cap. They'd been a positive distraction for his curious and withdrawn young brain, trying to make sense of his family's fractured dynamics and ceaseless turmoil between destructiveness and decency. The skinny books with their lush panels and fragrant ink were his earliest lessons in morality and ambivalence, preaching stern warnings that all narratives eventually ended, and sometimes badly.

That damn backpack. Those damn colors.

Annoying that such incidental things could transport him right back to that best-forgotten world of a skinny kid with the funny name and remote parents. Growing up too fast, beyond the promises of off-limits innocence while others matured more naturally, blanketed in optimistic possibility. Midas's stilted childhood journey had been drawn from hardened attitudes and severe judgment along with survival training imparted to hone instinct and, when necessary, inflict damage. Others had toy soldiers and Little League. He'd had the precariousness of his father's rigid rules. Never assume and never trust.

"Are you all right?" Mason had asked, having woken up to take immediate note of his friend's faraway look.

That afternoon, Midas had suffered through an unwelcome epiphany. All because a friendly and decent guy had ambled into a favorite coffeehouse where he was known and appreciated. In those few seconds of panic, regret, and whatever else had worked him over, Midas had finally understood. This middle-aged man wasn't a poor soul at all. Who knew what his backstory entailed? And where he came from didn't matter. He'd made others smile. And while a colorful, superhero-themed backpack could deliver Midas to a dark, emotional edge, it had brought joy to its owner.

Something about that day had broken a part of Midas's heart.

The man in the coffeehouse was also the kind Midas would always feel a deep-rooted obligation to protect—the best he could offer those far more worthy than himself.

Tonight, it would have to be this young boy.

Midas would need him distracted, so he set the kid up to play video games in front of the big screen, handing him a bowl of snacks from the coffee table. Then with a shove he repositioned Teddy onto the small bed beyond the kid's sight lines, not sorry his hands were beginning to chafe from the zips.

Midas went to work on one of the anchored cameras, peering into the viewfinder while shuffling through the memory card. He flicked through images of this kid and several others, boys and girls in various states of being fully clothed and then not. Stills and video. Sprinkled throughout was a naked man in a bunny mask, working his role with detachment. Likely Vinny, or his partner Jake lying back on the kitchen floor with a new hole in his head. Fire crept into Midas's stomach, his shoulders tensing from the sudden lack of oxygen. The realization that he'd thankfully inter-rupted the meaner part of this session was no solace. The other kids hadn't been so fortunate.

He pulled away to study the rest of the room, moving to inspect a black plastic container hugging the foot of the wall. Inside was a trove of well-used children's toys . . . and bondage implements. He peeked around the big screen. The boy was still blissfully oblivious within the world of his game.

Midas walked back to Teddy, who was wide eyed and fidgeting on the undersized mattress. "You're quite the sick fuck."

"You think I want to do this shit? They made me." Spittle fleck-ed out in tandem with his weak reasoning.

"Nobody makes anyone do anything. Now you're gonna tell me about the farm."

Teddy's eyes closed tightly, his head shaking violently back and forth. The mumbles were beginning again.

Midas moved a step closer and slapped him hard across the cheek, grabbing his hair and pinning his head back, neck straining against the pressure. "I'm done with your inner turmoil and seanc-es," he whispered, inches from Teddy's pitted face. "You tell me what I want to know, or I'm going to use some gadgets from that hope chest to carve you a new mudhole." He punched him in the side of the neck to bring home his point.

Teddy sputtered out a few deep, coughing hacks. Midas eased his hold enough so the perv didn't suddenly choke or vapor lock.

The spasm finally ceased.

And then Teddy surrendered all he knew.

It was just after midnight. Midas took out his cell and sent a text. The short reply came quickly.

He pulled Teddy off the bed and walked him through a door that connected to the attached garage, empty except for an SUV parked on one side and the remnants of exhaust fumes. Midas jabbed a needle into Teddy's neck, not bothering to assist as he dropped to the concrete floor. Back inside, he sat on the couch to wait, watching the boy who'd fallen asleep peacefully against the side of the chair.

Before long, he heard the purr of two car engines. One pulled in the driveway, and the other parked at the curb in front. The boy had fallen asleep but woke when he picked him up. Thankfully he didn't struggle. Midas pulled his wool hat back on, again low enough again that his eyes were barely visible, then grabbed the Cap America backpack. The solitary streetlight was on the far corner, so he was able to maneuver under a decent cover of shadows.

Carlo stood by the nondescript car now idling quietly on the street. He pulled the passenger door open. One of the Shredders bartenders, Megan, sat behind the wheel, with another of Carlo's crew behind her in the back seat. Everyone wore black baseball caps and dark jackets.

Midas nodded at them, placing the boy onto the passenger seat and buckling him in. He took a final look at the Captain's shield, now resting between the boy's feet. Luckily, he'd found an address clearly printed on a card inside the zipper.

The boy yawned and looked at him expectantly.

"These are my friends. They'll take you home." He gently squeezed the boy's shoulder and closed the door.

The car accelerated slowly and drove away.

Midas and Carlo turned their backs to the dark street and walked briskly back inside, where they killed all the remaining lights.

"What does Megan know?" Midas asked, surveying the street from the window. He was surprised she'd been recruited.

"Nothing beyond the kid needing a ride home. I thought after all the men, a woman would be helpful with the kid. She's solid." Carlo's words carried his slight accent, spoken with a deliberate rhythm that could feel out of place around some Angelenos. He surveyed the room, muttering his disgust in clipped, guttural Spanish.

Midas studied the street for another few moments, then led Carlo down the darkened hall. The kitchen's visibility benefited from the almost-full moon seeping through the glass doors. The pair of minders was still on the floor.

"There's another one in the garage sleeping it off. How are we on the farm?"

Carlo squatted next to the laid-out figures, his gloved hands checking the restraints. "We're scouting it now. Looks like they've got heavy manpower inside. Not sure how many."

"Mason?"

"He's there. Waiting on us."

There were boxes of takeout chicken in the fridge along with bottles of water. Midas looked over his gloves for any tears before grabbing two bottles and handing one over. He drained his in a few short gulps. Carlo produced a plastic garbage bag from his pocket, snapping it open. Midas tossed their empties inside, along with the used needles.

Carlo went front to back one final time giving the house a fresh sweep, his movements barely a whisper, then returned to the kitchen.

Midas stood near the back door, erect against the wall, arms folded. "Listen, Lo. None of this is kosher. You and your boys should pull out. It's on me to finish it." Midas gave him a hard look from below the folded edge of the cap. The next move would bring a pelting storm of shit down on whoever was involved.

"We always knew," Carlo said. "Now we deal with what's in front of us."

Midas nodded reluctantly. "Give me five, and then signal your crew and have them back the wheels into the garage. It'll be tight, but there's enough room. See you in a few."

He opened the glass slider and slipped out. He ran to the back fence, vaulted himself over, and picked up another sprint along the darkened tracks, retracing the way he'd come. A dog howled in the distance, then another. It was colder now by several degrees. His quads were tight, but he fought through, adding pace. Like Mason, motion was his preferred state, slowing surroundings while centralizing focus. He was more effective when moving, running while others walked. Situations somehow made more sense, and better outcomes became more probable. Sometimes anyway.

The crossing rail rose in the distance. A new train was approaching.

Just keep moving.

Back in his car, Midas drove north.

Within a few miles, the tended neighborhoods gave way to small-firm retail, drugstores, fast food, and secondhand establishments. Also several locksmiths. Two more lights and he passed an oversize parking lot serving a clutch of grocery and big-box electronics stores, as well as outlets for Nike and Adidas. At the next corner he turned left, passing a couple of hulking distribution centers, deserted in the early a.m. hours beyond the few weak security lights flickering under a lowering sheet of fog.

Three long blocks later, he turned left again, passing between a pair of warehouses. The one to his right didn't cover the large amount of space that its neighbor occupied. Inside was likely one big, open area with a few offices in back corners. The difference was in the security, the perimeter holding a reinforced black metal gate at least ten feet high. From the street, the walls were not only hard to see, but also served as an obvious warning to anyone thinking about breaching.

The farm.

Midas kept his speed even, never too fast or too slow, so as not to alert any hidden sensors. He didn't see an entrance and assumed it was on another block, or on the opposite side. He cruised through an intersection, studying behind him with the side mirror.

Nothing moved.

Mason's text had directed him to a public park two miles away and nestled within a residential enclave. Tonight, the swings and slides sat motionless, anchored in soft sand. Metal benches had been placed below mature trees, separating the younger-kids area from a skateboard ramp. Probably a nice spot during the day.

He parked behind two other cars and walked to the Beemer in front, taking a quick scan of the surroundings before opening the passenger door and sliding in. Mason was behind the wheel, also keeping watch. The smell of tended leather mingled with a dusting of spearmint gum, Mason's flavor of choice. 1970s funk hummed softly from the radio.

"Carlo's ten minutes out," Mason said.

Midas remained quiet, Teddy's tableau still vivid in his mind. The boy should be home by now.

Mason glanced over, trying to gauge his mood. Carlo had doubtless updated him on the contents of the house. Backing off was no longer an option. As if it ever had been.

They'd shared many nights like this. Forcing solutions outside the norms of decency, sanctioned or otherwise. Both their fathers had been players dancing between such worlds, half-heartedly pretending they wanted better for their boys while, by example, encouraging them onto a murkier path. Mason exhaled, and Midas wondered, as he frequently did, what it must have been like growing up on the other side. The normals, enjoying all that childhood and teenage years should be, committed to nothing more than the enduring search for fun and personal gratification.

Mason had once confessed he'd occasionally felt that same optimism, playing ball or getting in the ring. Sometimes, he'd admitted, he could still access a bit of it when training, though such moments were transient and hard to hold on to. And once Mason's ankle and knee had been blown, physicality came with a steeper price. Filters and scratchy memories were all that remained.

A pair of headlights grew in the rearview mirror. They both straightened as reality returned, measuring the job ahead. The glare intensified. The lights were cut a few seconds before another car slowed beside theirs, Carlo sliding from the passenger side and into their back seat and waving his driver forward. It vanished around the corner some fifty yards ahead.

"The kid?" Midas asked.

"Home. Made sure he got into the house, which was full of people, probably the panicked family and friends. No cops, so I doubt they'd been called. He didn't seem too bad on the ride. Megan got him talking. He said two men had pulled up and offered a ride home. Told him they were work friends of his mom at the market, and they were going to pick her and his family up and take them all to a Lakers game. They knew her name, his, the whole family."

Mason snorted with edginess. "Lakers are off tonight." He jerked his thumb toward the car that had just disappeared down the side street. "Are the bastards still with us?"

"One is. Along with this Teddy guy. Both in the trunk sleeping off Mide's cocktail. The other is back at the house, which has by now been thoroughly wiped," Carlo replied.

"So what are we looking at?" Midas asked, eyeing the playground swings dangling from silver chains.

Carlo leaned forward, his gloved hands bearing a trace scent of gun oil. "Anyone of note is inside. One rent-a-cop on the gate, a small guardhouse you can't see from the street. We've got a handle on the building's power—it's in a hut against the rear of the property along a fence on the other side. That needs to be eliminated first."

A good break, Midas thought. Structures like this normally used power from underground, utilizing fiber patched from a hub miles away. Kyle had created his own source, a smart move given the nature of what was inside. For them it also meant a way to go dark without stirring up the neighbors.

Midas didn't ask how Carlo had gathered the grid intel. He

must have positioned someone inside the property, out of sight and evading cameras.

"Motion sensors around the outside rim," Mason added, apparently having already been given the brief. "Best play is snapping the juice and moving in from three of the corners. There's a vehicle bay on the northeast side. Likely a winch-and-chain activation. Built for trucks, so it'll take some time to open. Only other entrance is a double-steel number around the southwest corner." He held up his hand and touched fingers, simulating the edges of a box, two perpendicular lines. "Midas and I advance on the door while the boys around the corner keep an eye on the truck bay. Lo, you hold in the outer corner and watch everyone's backs. Once we're all in, you blast in behind us."

Nodding, Carlo handed a clear case the size of a business card over to the front seat.

Midas fished out two pairs of miked earbuds, handing one to Mason. Gotta love technology. Not like the old days with big, clunky headsets. They all fitted the slick devices into their ears. He reached for the duffel below his feet that held their NVGs and other essentials and began pulling out weapons.

Carlo jumped out and Mason started the car, his voice coming clearly through the comms. "We go in twenty. Spread the cars out and move."

Midas had always found peace in the lull before a mission. The centeredness, onset of focus, the clarity of vision. He felt his heart rate lowering. His legs loosened, pushing aside lactate and aging nerves. His vision became more acute. Even under the opaque sky he could have described veins in tree leaves or the exact color of ants frolicking in the gutters. License plates several yards away were readable, as was the shade of chrome on the fenders. It had been some time, but it was all returning, instinct fusing with necessity.

He was flanked several yards apart by the rest of the group. Silas Whitten had an axiom he'd once passed on to them all: To the naked eye, a small platoon with common purpose, though in reality, solitary practitioners with personal chits. Functioning as a core, but each step and action a singular choice.

Back when they'd all been pups, objectives had frequently shape-shifted, sometimes from hour to hour. Black and white rarely existed. And when clarity appeared, it was usually long after an op was over.

At least tonight there was no such ambiguity.

They approached the gated walls from various choke points and held position outside a cyclone barrier, nine feet high, just behind the property's rear corner. Mason was to Midas's left, Carlo farther away at the edge where the fence changed direction. Midas could see two other stealthy figures. Wagner, already inside, crouching against a steel-enforced shack protected with a secure bolt. Jarvis a few yards away, and still outside the perimeter. They were the best of Carlo's exclusive firm.

A whisper hit Midas's ear. "Thirty seconds." He took final inventory. HK53 snuggly positioned against his ribs, goggles on, Velcro belt bag around his quad securing the other tools.

There was motion from the shack. Wagner was at the door, shoulders hunched as he broke the lock with a cracking metallic *snap*. Behind a quick, hook-shot motion, he launched the heavy pair of cutters over the rear of the small enclosure, before rolling something inside, pushing the door closed, and scrambling away.

Midas hit the fence, scaling over and landing on the other side as a muffled explosion shook the shack from the inside out. Peering through a small warehouse window, he saw the lit interior turn black. Mason and Carlo came over the wall, and Jarvis hit the ground several yards away. The group fanned and pushed forward. Midas took a few steps and halted, HK up and trained to his right on the now-dark corner leading to the main gate fronting the street.

The first guard appeared, looking shaken by the noise and sudden darkness. He must have sensed movement and raised his rifle, making a fatally wide sweep around the compound and concrete. The side of his head shattered, viscera splashing the stucco wall. He landed on his back. Midas began to run, hopscotching flashlight beams someone inside was using against the sudden blackout. He joined Mason near the small metal back door, more than secure despite being intentionally designed to appear insignificant. Carlo remained far enough behind to provide eyes and cover to both. Jarvis and Wagner were out of sight somewhere on the other side of the building, waiting near the vehicle entrance.

Midas used a small charge secured with putty to blow the door's lock.

Mason dropped his shoulder, hitting the door with momentum and speed while rolling inside, sliding immediately to his left.

Midas followed in a low crouch as they sectioned off.

They were in an office of some sort with five desks haphazardly placed against various walls. All unoccupied. Each had a laptop glowing with screen savers, having defaulted to battery power in response to the outage.

Panicked voices barked from deeper inside the warehouse.

The air was loose, carrying hints of cigarettes and cheap cologne. Straight ahead another door stood open, swinging slightly as if someone had recently run through it.

Midas and Mason followed the path, flipping their goggles to night vision, lighting up everything in pale green.

They emerged within a huge cavern stacked with weakly blinking red lights and tall outlines resembling half-buried boulders in shallow seas. But these weren't rocks. They were racks of hard-drive towers spaced in multiple rows throughout the enlarged space. Obviously, there was a large generator just for these machines somewhere on the property. Kyle had created his own back-up power, enough to fuel a small city. Now the lack of windows made sense. Besides the office, the rest of the building's anatomy comprised this: about seventy-five square yards of climate-controlled space under a steel roof two stories high.

Motion came from their right, from the far end of the nearest set of towers. The *ping* of silenced assault weapons sent them to their knees below the eye-level barrage as the rounds flew over them. The guards were clearly shooting blind.

Mason leaned back and heaved a small canister in their direction. There was a rapid flash, illuminating their location.

Midas put both guards down with two shots each.

Mason touched his ear under the knit beanie. "Go," he whispered.

Another explosion sounded, this one larger and louder.

Behind the blinking drives, the semitruck-sized roll-down door disintegrated, blowing free of its chains. Wagner and Jarvis ran inside with Carlo on their tail, who broke left to cover the far wall. Mason and Midas skirted around the two closest rows of drives, and Wagner and Jarvis disappeared down two other aisles.

Ninety seconds later it was all over. Seven of Kyle's hired guns were flat and finished.

Midas met the team near the truck entrance. It was littered with chunks of the decimated metal door and smoldering shell casings. Jarvis and Wagner scooped up two fire extinguishers stacked outside the office door and set to putting out the few remaining flames.

Carlo whispered a few words of Spanish into his mic. A minute later, their two cars rolled inside followed by a Ford F-350. Two new men jumped out of the truck cab, grabbing an extendable ladder from the long bed. They raised it over one end of the massive hole left by the explosion, resting it at a tilt against the concrete above. One climbed the ladder and quickly unrolled dark plastic sheets, nail-gunning up enough to cover the jagged opening, protecting the team against wind and what would soon be cops and mayhem.

The overnight hours and the relative obscurity of the industrial area had allowed them to make their assault without much commotion. The blast had been loud, but the sound had been directed inside. Nothing seemed to have stirred in the nearby neighborhoods.

Ten minutes and ten rolls later, the gaping hole was crudely covered. It would have to do.

Teddy and Vinny had been taken out of the BMW's trunk, moved into the office, and trussed into two of the cheap chairs, still unconscious. Midas put another needle into each of their necks. Twenty seconds later, they both came around, jostling against the restraints. Vinny's eyes darted around.

The only illumination in the office was provided by the laptop screens. Wagner had fired them up on their battery power, along with a portable Wi-Fi receiver from his bag. He'd swiftly hacked into the hard drives, and all the portable computers now radiated the Windows screen saver. His keyboard taps gave the room a steady beat of inevitability.

Phillip would have been impressed at Wagner's efficiency.

Mason pulled the tape from Teddy's mouth, leaving Vinny's in place.

Midas leaned against a desk in front of them both. "Tell me about this place," he said.

Against the lethargy of the drugs, Teddy looked like a doughy freak from a bad dream. He stared back at Midas's shining head and grim, menacing smile. "I don't know where I am." He was muttering with thick words and slurred syllables.

Midas leaned over for a closer look. Vinny was recovering faster, fidgeting and somewhat clear eyed. Both had the acrid smell of unrestrained adrenaline and nerves. Teddy had pissed himself.

Midas looked out through the propped-open door at the multiple rows of still-functioning towers and software in the warehouse. Mason disappeared into the shadows and returned a minute later with a bottle of water from a minifridge they'd spotted. He held it to Teddy's mouth, letting him take a long pull.

Vinny stared over his taped mouth.

"You don't know, eh? That really the way you want to play this?" Midas asked Teddy with a mock sigh.

"Honestly," Teddy said, sputtering. "I have no idea where we are. Can you turn on some lights?"

Mason rolled his eyes at Carlo and shrugged. Always the hard way.

"It's almost two in the morning, and I'm tired," Midas said. "Been a long few days. Right, Vinny?"

The minder's glare was his only answer, his breathing heavy above the tape.

"We know most of it. Just need you to fill in a few blanks. This is your distribution hub for the Basmajian brothers, Rudy O'Shea, and probably a few others. You guys have a lot of hard drives out there, enough to make the *Boogie Nights* crowd envious."

"It's all legal," Teddy blurted out.

Despite the zips binding his ankles, Vinny tried to kick him, but instead tumbled over in the chair. Carlo picked him up and deposited him a few yards farther away.

Their focus returned to Teddy, now alone in the middle of the room. He had tears in his eyes, his situation having finally cleared what remained of the drugs. "What are you going to do with us?"

"Depends on what I hear." Midas took a few steps back and sat on the edge of the closest desk. "But since you brought it up, let's talk about legalities. Most of what you peddle through this place is, I'm assuming, within the letter of the law."

Teddy seemed to relax. He'd taken the bait, now thinking maybe he could get out of this.

Midas continued with a benign tone. "I'd rather talk about what you were doing back at the house."

Vinny grunted a warning.

Teddy just stared straight ahead, a slight tremor pulling at his cheeks. The foul air was turning heavy. He bowed his head, finally looking up. "I do what I'm told." His posture gave way, and he collapsed against his restraints. Condemned killers are said to mentally die well before they take their final breath in the electric chair or in front of a firing squad. The soul's dismissal a final betrayal.

"And now you're going to tell me. Everything," Midas said.

Teddy began to talk. About how Kyle Palmer had foreseen visionary potential for new twists on digital porn years ago. Quietly using the family name and trust to fund a burgeoning empire. His father, mother, relatives, and friends had looked the other way. In the process, Kyle had not only stopped the family's financial hemorrhaging, but also set the clan up for generations with a steady spigot of new revenue. All profits tossed into mutual funds and blind havens no one could ever trace back to their disgusting origins. Kyle had always hated his family's baked-in prissiness, but he still needed their connections and status. He was a wanton prodigal, but never truly left the roost.

"Kyle and I met at Princeton," Teddy said. "He was a strange guy with a taste for seriously deranged shit. And he really loved tweaking his old man. Problem was, the Palmer name opened too many doors for him to go completely native and off the reservation. His father took a flier and bankrolled his first few ventures. Wealthy assholes, right? As long as the heat and water stay on, they don't give a shit about the rest of the world falling apart."

"Spare us the sermon," Midas said.

"I was a film student," Teddy continued. "Had a few projects of note that got me some notices."

"Your mother must be so proud," Mason's voice drifted from the shadows.

Teddy looked his way, frustrated anger swelling his sweating face. "I've never tried to justify what I did. I was on a partial scholarship. Had massive bills when I graduated. Kyle offered me a way to get even on a much shorter timeline. Back then his business was tame, mostly soft-core. Not what it became."

"What it became?" Midas muttered. "How much are you worth, Teddy?"

"I do okay."

A subtle *squeak* chirped behind the two bound men—Carlo's palm squeezing the stock of his rifle.

"I'm sure you do. Okay. Now tell me about this place," Midas said. "It's no cheap setup."

"It cost a few million. The building was dirt cheap, but running the buried cables through the streets to a secure digital hub took some doing. We only got it up and fully functional about eighteen months ago. Could never trust Wi-Fi with this. Before that, it was all archaic. Portable hard drives and slower upload deliveries from various locations." Teddy took a breath. "The ability to deliver our products directly to other farms and homes on every continent has been a reality for years. But the quality upgrades we recently added make even the best of the current streaming services look like old VHS."

"Meaning what?" Mason said, stepping forward. "You can see circumcision scars on your actors' joints?"

Teddy shrugged half-heartedly. "We are the gold standard."

"Were," Midas said.

"Look, I realize the situation I'm in, but you can't shut down something that eighty percent of the world wants. Much less is willing to pay for."

"I don't care about the eighty percent. Just your part of it."

"It's not like you created something useful," Mason added. "Like the aqueducts, or the game of basketball."

"Usefulness is a relative term," Teddy said, locking eyes with Midas. "The writing might be on the wall for this enterprise, but I know Kyle. There will be others." His words hung with desperation, a last-chance Hail Mary.

The room went momentarily silent, letting Teddy muster a final shard of hope.

"Fuck." Wagner suddenly jumped up from one of the open lap-tops, swearing.

Vinny exhaled deeply under the tape, closing his eyes.

Teddy just sat, as if he'd been waiting for the last shoe to drop.

Midas gave them a both a questioning look as he and Mason moved to stand behind Wagner, who hit the Enter key. They all stared at the screen.

A loop began. A silent film. Men in masks and a young woman.

Midas's senses were still on hyperdrive, and he thought he could hear overnight traffic a few blocks off despite the heat rushing into his head and expanding it like an inflating airbag. He widened his stance, gripping the corner of the desk. The vertigo had arrived and would soon become a raging panic attack.

There was seemingly no end to this horror show. The depraved gift that kept right on delivering.

"That was all Kyle and his father." Teddy's pleading screech thundered in Midas's ears along with the dull roar of his own blood pressure. "It was a side gig that he produced and controlled. It had nothing to do with me."

"It's on your drives," Mason said, straining to find words.

The entire viewing took five minutes, any emotion hidden under the macabre masks. An exercise in indifference reserved for soft, flabby, aging men who'd christened themselves untouchable. Taking grisly games as far as they wanted. Because they could.

Midas steadied himself. Then he walked back to the center of the room, raised his gun, and put one shot into each of their skulls. The impacts pushed both chairs over as the dead men slammed to the floor.

The group began to clean and pack up, keeping clear of Teddy's and Vinny's leaking heads.

The first alarm came into fire station B24 in Carson at four a.m.

Within minutes, LA County Fire had rolled several trucks and called for backup from neighboring cities. Soon the warehouse's block was flooded with fifteen engines and a dozen black-and-whites. The city had no police force and was patrolled by the LA County Sheriff's Department.

The burning structure was large enough to get a battalion chief and watch commander onto the scene. Bleary-eyed residents trickled in from blocks away, awakened by the early-morning sirens and expanding smell of smoke. News vans dotted the perimeter and set up for a long morning, hoping for a news conference.

It would take hours to put out the fire, and another day before the nine bodies inside were sent to the morgue, mixed as they were with the destroyed remains of about fifty digital data towers. What had been on them would remain a mystery.

In the weeks and months to follow, no one would come forward to claim ownership of the warehouse. The resulting investigation of the property title would lead to nothing more than a financial hall of broken mirrors.

CHAPTER 14

CONOR WAS AWAKE WHEN one of his burner phones buzzed.

It was six a.m., and all the local stations were plastering their morning shows with some structure fire down in Carson that had apparently been raging for the past several hours. According to the captain holding hourly briefings, it would take some undetermined amount of time to get it under control, given the nature of what was inside . . . which at this point the smoke eaters either didn't know or weren't saying. Reporters doing live shots danced around the facts with nothing to add but ill-informed conjecture.

The text message he got was brief. Jojo summoning him to yet another meeting, this one at Kyle's place on Sunset.

Something must have jumped off. Kyle and his father were defying their own truce practically minutes after blessing it. Though after Phillip, what the hell did they expect? Poking a bear was ill-advised. Taking out one of their own was destructive vanity. Hubris had deluded the Palmers, who'd convinced themselves Midas would be forced to fold up and disappear. That his sense of survival would somehow balance in their favor, their sheer numbers over his formidable capability. As usual, they had fatally miscalculated. Their off-book army never stood a chance.

Conor picked up one of the other phones, scrolled, and punched in a number.

The answering voice was supple, belying many years of struggle. "Hey, kid."

"Kyle's calling an audible. Wants me at his place in two hours," Mason said.

"Pick me up on the way. You know where."

"You don't need to be there," Conor said. "I can handle it."

"Take me anyway. They'll think twice about being hasty or coloring outside the lines."

"If you think that's the right play."

But the call had already ended.

Hollywood had never been able to shake its desperation. Not with gentrification, paint, the added presence of LAPD riding e-bikes in shorts, or the trashy shops with cheap relics of bygone glitter. None of it could disguise the incessant churn of low-level, shuffling humanity or the predators targeting the weak. The city's marketing offensive at the end of the last century had been designed for television cameras and travel-agent brochures. Doctored and diminished crime stats had been circulated. And despite the proclamations of cleaning it all up, buffing the piss-infested Walk of Fame, and more importantly, the massive tax breaks gifted to the upscale hotels, serious crime had never dispersed. It had instead crawled deeper into the clammy alleys and condemned basements where ancient and authentic business was conducted, hidden within the municipality's tourist mirage.

Presentable, overpriced high-rise rentals and condos had popped up with regularity over the last several decades. Developers had no trouble filling their units with those seeking an asphalt underpinning in a once-famous zip code. But new residents learned quickly to keep a safe distance, sheltering a few stories above the historic and decaying landmarks, muting the street's angry growl with headphones and flat-screens. The grunge dwellers and thieves steered clear of this new form of social order, concentrating instead on the easier, vulnerable marks—visitors.

Conor was acutely aware of it all as he drove through those neighborhoods and into the more selective fringes of West Hollywood. He'd had his fill of Kyle's world.

He'd long ago learned to live with the constant anxiety and expectation of ambush, an ethos radically heightened over the past week. After parking, he punched in the code on the condo's ground floor and stepped inside, holding the door for the man behind him. They slipped into one of two open elevators.

On the top floor, they were halted outside Kyle's penthouse door. Another pair of new recruits.

"Supposed to be only you," one said to Conor.

"And now it's a party of two. Frisk us or fuck off. Your choice."

Both stepped to the side as Conor and his guest passed.

Conor walked in first, taking in an instantaneous shot of Kyle sitting on a living room couch looking shaken and smaller than usual. Michelle and Jojo were perched on backless stools in front of the breakfast bar, and Rawlings Palmer was on a chair in a corner, ever the puppet master. All heads ticked at their arrival, expressions rapidly turning apprehensive when they realized Conor wasn't alone.

"Lord help us," Rawlings said, grudgingly impressed. "Silas Whitten."

Kyle raised his eyes. He knew the name but had never met the tall black man scanning the assembly.

Conor had been pleased though not surprised Silas still looked so viable despite his never-ending tales of retirement and solitary camping trips around the globe. Advancing age or not, he remained fit, and like Midas, sported a shiny bald head. Though at six-foot-four, he was three inches taller, and with darker skin. Still lanky, forever the sprinter.

Tangible respect seeped from the Palmers and Jojo.

Silas held his gaze on Kyle, who dropped his eyes back to his lap. "Quite the little tussle you've started," Silas said, the voice fitting his appearance. Bass-deep and measured, slightly worn.

"Midas went off the reservation . . . as usual," Kyle managed to mumble.

"You should let the adults talk, little man," Silas said.

"Fuck you, relic," Kyle wheezed without raising his head. Obtuse and unable to read the board, as ever.

Behind him, Jojo shook his head while his father fought to keep any tell off his face. Michelle gripped her coffee tighter.

Kyle was so like his adopted city. Too many years of never being told no.

Silas simply looked bemused.

"Golden boy went way off the page tonight," Kyle continued, digging himself in even deeper. "Destroyed my warehouse."

Conor immediately flashed back to the morning news, the coin dropping. Of course. The fire in South LA. Unknown origin or contents. "The Carson fire?" he asked, apparently the only one in the room late to the party. "What the hell was in there?"

"Exactly," Silas said. As usual a few steps ahead, distance runner's mentality. Keep your eyes on the terrain and identify hazards before they were under your feet. "Tell us, *little man*. What was in your well-guarded storage closet?"

Kyle had apparently decided he'd said enough, though he visibly bristled.

"Rawlings?" Silas turned, facing Palmer senior, huddled in the corner.

Senior squirmed. A fine mist of sweat had appeared on his forehead just below the silver mane.

"It's your family business, right?" Silas said, pressing.

The room stayed silent.

Silas moved to Michelle. "Miss Kelly? I'm an old friend of Conor and his pals. Not sure whether you're in the know about *all* your boyfriend's day jobs. The Palmer family creates, produces, and distributes what they like to call high-grade adult entertainment. A clever way of labeling and marketing hardcore porn. Been at it for a decade, right, Kyle? Now, in fairness, we all knew this, even you, Michelle. So . . . let's stop pretending the boys blew up a corner of the Smithsonian."

"It was a private enterprise," Kyle's voice went high. "Had nothing to do with the Unit. We all have our side gigs. DeMarco never cared. You sound senile and out of touch . . . *old man*."

Conor took a step toward the couch. Kyle flinched, looking toward Jojo. But to his credit, this time the ex-ranger wasn't moving, momentarily holding his ground.

Silas reached out to put a stopping hand on Conor's shoulder. "You're half-right, boy," Silas said, making Kyle grind his teeth.

"J didn't care how we padded our accounts, as long as it was legal and didn't reflect badly on the group. But as your father will tell you, Washington is nothing if not fluid. Alliances change. Two administrations back, a new crowd decided to clip DeMarco's parameters. Enter the Palmers stage right. You brought along your backroom deals and history of forced favors. And DeMarco had no choice. He opened the books to your father, all while hoping to protect the rest of us, along with the work's integrity."

"Silas, you use words better than a Baptist preacher," Palmer senior said condescendingly.

"I read a lot."

"You also have too much fading brass in what remains of your scrotum." Rawlings let an irritated smile trickle forth. "Who the fuck do you think you're talking to?"

"Seriously? We're past dick measuring, aren't we?" Michelle blurted out, surprising everyone.

Senior shot Kyle a glance, implying she might be out of the will.

"Couldn't agree more, Michelle," Silas said.

Senior stood up, unsteadily making his way to a seat on the other end of the couch from his son, body language implying Kyle was well entrenched in his father's shithouse.

"We need to put an end to all of this," Palmer senior said. "For that to happen, Midas and Mason will need to stand down."

"Fuck them." Kyle bolted up, leaning over into his father's space. "They need to go."

Senior was momentarily taken off guard, the aging patrician for once looking toothless. He regained himself quickly, his fresh anger abrupt and abrasive. "Kyle, would you *shut the hell up?*"

The room waited for more. After a few beats, Kyle held his

hands up in mock surrender and sat back down.

"Now, can we talk sensibly?" senior asked.

For the next several minutes, employing a combination of self-righteous deflection and tone-deaf excuses, he unburdened himself with a long-shot effort to save his son, his family, and what remained of his waning influence.

Conor listened with unease. For generations, DC had catered to such families. Pedigrees were nice, but endless funds took precedence. At the same time, the aptly named East Coast elite was a closed society, operating as scoundrels above the fray, telling themselves only *they* held the right to do what was necessary to keep the country on track. Palmer and those like him had been losing the battle with social attrition for half a century. Now the old lions were desperate. Like two nights before, Rawlings Palmer was again playing for time, nothing more than a new diversion to ensure survival. After several minutes of a run-on monologue framing unseen objectives and moral duty, he'd finally played all his cards. "I expect Midas will be leaving town and won't be coming back," he said in conclusion.

"Good luck with that," Conor said.

"Precisely," senior replied, getting to his feet to portray authority and take advantage of the room's murky hues. "It's one thing to play a high-stakes game of Risk around the streets of this city. Quite another to play keep-away from the Justice Department."

The stab hit Conor hard, reverberating through his spine. He backed up a few steps, dropping into one of the leather chairs positioned against the wall. His head lit up in a cauldron of rising heat. He'd never had a stroke, but this sudden blurry vision and thumping heart had him wondering whether one was on the way.

Silas was watching him carefully. Jojo had a hand behind his back, strapped and ready to keep the peace if necessary. Michelle seemed unsure what was taking place.

Conor leaned back to better open his lungs and tried to think. He concentrated on the ceiling. "You reached out to the feds?" he managed to say.

"I made a phone call." Palmer senior looked pleased with himself.

Conor seethed. "To one of your gray-suited buddies."

"Not just any friend, the AG himself."

Conor brought his gaze back level with the room. Kyle was pushed so tightly into his cushion he couldn't have appeared any less menacing.

His father had stood and was almost bouncing on the balls of his feet in those ridiculous tasseled loafers. "Now, there is no need for anyone in this room to worry," Palmer senior added. "I would never share firm business with a competitor."

"Of course not," Silas said, picking up the play. "But you have given them the new goods on Midas. The Basmajian brothers? Rudy O'Shea? Now the warehouse? Lots of toes and multiple jurisdictions. Only the feds can bigfoot them all."

"Ledgers and chits, no doubt," Conor observed bitterly. "Kompromat on elected pedophiles."

"Deeper than you will ever know, Mr. Brennan."

"Call me that again and I'll put my fist through the back of your skull before Jojo can clip me."

Senior giggled nervously but took the warning, backing off.

Silas shot a look of warning to Conor that said, "Now is not the moment."

Senior's white hair bobbed as he calculated the terrain shifting back into his favor. "Your loyalty and skills have always been commendable, Conor. A solid soldier for the Unit and my son. We have no issues with you. Unfortunately, the Snow Leopard is feral and won't be called off. So, if our people can't shut him down, the FBI will. I gave them plenty. I even sweetened the deal with details on Guadalajara and Guatemala."

Kyle fidgeted, and Jojo appeared defeated.

"You've got nothing on those ops," Conor stated. "And Justice has no international jurisdiction. Besides, your son was also in Mexico. And we all know how that turned out."

But Rawlings Palmer had rediscovered his groove. "Don't be dense. I don't need them to prosecute, just be properly motivated to rid our theater of a bad actor. We all know they aren't above such things."

"Call them off," Silas said, sudden and firm.

Senior's new grin dropped a fraction. "You're out of the game, Whitten. You don't have those chips anymore."

"I need a laptop," Silas said.

Conor quietly exhaled, euphoric adrenaline moving through his system like a synthetic opioid. He'd seen Silas in this mode many times. He had his own cards to play. And the floor was about to drop out from under the Palmers.

Jojo reached into the nook behind him to a hidden shelf and pulled out a Chromebook. Moving off the stool, he handed it over.

Silas opened it where he stood, firing it up. With one hand he reached into his pocket. There was an audible *click* when the flash drive he'd retrieved locked into place, a sound that shook the room's nerves. Silas poked at the screen and placed it on the table in front of Kyle, who took a peek and said nothing, visibly deflated.

Everyone else, including Conor, moved behind the couch for a better view. Most of them had seen far too much during their lives, but this was a whole new realm. Overt brutality carried out on a trussed-up female who couldn't have been more than fourteen years old. The participants on the video all took turns, their faces concealed. Sagging men with weak hard-ons doing whatever they pleased. A few minutes in, Silas reached over and hit pause.

"Let's cut to the finale," he said brusquely, dragging his finger over the timeline to the last few moments.

The young girl remained center frame, the masked men now taking turns stabbing her superficially with ice picks. Her under-sized chest and groin became a mass of seeping wounds. None of the thrusts was fatal, just enough to inflict maximum pain. But the girl was no quitter, fighting against her restraints with disturbing courage. Conor wondered what she could possibly have been thinking.

The screen went black.

Michelle made a choking noise and ran out of the room. Down the hall, a bathroom door slammed.

Jojo moved to the window and stared out over Sunset Boulevard.

"Jesus." Rawlings Palmer's voice had gone hoarse as he continued staring at the frozen screen. "What have you done? You *fucking fool.*"

Kyle rubbed his face before reaching out to close the laptop. "Everything you wouldn't do." His tone was strangely even.

Conor wasn't positive but assumed the final figure had been him. The height and dimensions matched.

"You wanted more of a say in the agency games and decisions, *father,*" Kyle continued with a new-found, smarmy intonation. "That doesn't come cheap. Despite what you tell yourself, those assholes laugh at you. Why? Because you're an old fraud, a tight-assed, aging clown. And guess what, Pop? Saying no to them isn't an option. They wanted a fantasy and told me to up the ante. So I did it. For you and your fucking, *precious name*."

"Bullshit," his father said. "This was all about you. *For* you. You're a rabid dog, just like Midas."

Kyle considered this. "Probably," he admitted.

Silas moved toward the door. "Call off your bureau pals and we'll see what we can do about Midas. If not, I've got plenty of copies of the video already uploaded and ready to stream in places you'd rather it didn't. This ends *now*. And we all walk away."

Rawlings Palmer took a moment before reluctantly nodding.

Kyle said nothing and didn't move.

Jojo remained at the window staring down at the young women on the street below. Those fortunate to have no worries other than getting amped up over their next cold table reading.

Conor drove, pondering in silence.

Silas directed him to a corner in Venice near some new townhomes a few blocks from the famous beach. Once there, they pulled over.

"Midas and Mase will never stand down," Conor said. "Especially after they see your home movie."

Silas gave him an indulgent look. "Who do you think gave it to me?"

For an instant Conor was surprised, then he wasn't. It was all beginning to make more sense. The warehouse fire was Kyle's infamous porn farm. He'd heard some random rumors, but details of its existence had been buttoned down tighter than a Cayman

Islands vault.

"Besides, I have no intention of getting in their way," Silas said.

Of course not, Conor thought. He was here to fix, not apply a tourniquet.

Which meant word was already spreading around alphabet city about Kyle's dirty videos. How many more were there? How many more like that poor girl? And yet, Conor knew, in the final accounting none of that would matter. Doubtless too many high-steppers and shot callers on those disgusting flicks to let this fester or get any more exposed.

But Silas had his own mandate, and Conor could finally see the pieces that had eluded him for the past few days. He tried to shake off feelings of self-pity about being left out, but right now simply couldn't. He'd been a dupe all along, reluctantly staying in the fold these past years while convincing himself the Palmer family's skin empire was the going price for being allowed to do better work, taking care of actual, *serious* problems. For the first time in his life he felt disappointment for DeMarco and Silas, who'd knowingly motivated him with half truths, and then let him down. They were the real mandarins. Then again, if they were so damn wise, how could they not have anticipated how far Kyle and his father would go?

Then another bell chimed, somewhere deep in his brooding.

"You and the Old Man knew all along, didn't you?" Conor said with a grimace.

Silas leaned sideways, facing him while resting the back of his head against the closed passenger window, his eyes locked and clear. "We knew Kyle and his mates were trafficking heavy shit. Rough trade, pain-freak fantasies, twenty-four-hour bondage fests. But snuff? Little kids? No, Con, that we didn't know. I found out three hours before you did when Midas sent me a link to the video and some pictures from a photographer he iced."

"I'm supposed to buy that?"

"I ever lie to you?"

"Only by omission. Who knows how deep in the mud I've been? Midas and Mason got to walk away. Phillip, too. Why not me?"

Silas moved his gaze away, his eyes, surprisingly, filmed with moisture. Conor had never seen him even close to losing control. "I let you all down. Never will find a way to live with that. Truth is, Con, you were always the best of them, much better than you ever let yourself believe. Midas and Mason were superb ops, physical specimens, the ones you'd always want for tip of the spear. Phillip was a systems genius who could have been a billionaire if he'd taken the offer from Apple instead of us back in the day.

But you . . . you had a mastery. An ability to absorb the entire game and see the fringes of the board much better than anyone. *You* were the one we had to keep inside, the only one with the sensibility and the stomach to hang in for us, making sure things never got out of hand. Midas and Mason went over the line on those last ops. We had to let them walk away. They'd gotten too . . . *close* to the work. Phillip was adrift without them, so he too, made sense." Silas rubbed his palms over his strong quads. His voice dropped. "You were the only one we could trust around those Palmer hyenas. It was a raw deal. But if it means anything," he said, almost choking, "I don't have many... people. You were always more than just a coworker. I didn't want to lose you too. It was selfish."

Silas's mea culpa hit Conor like a cold brick, and his anger began to soften, dampening the cacophony of red pasting his brain.

Even so, the feelings of betrayal weren't going anywhere soon. Who knew when they would?

"You could have trusted me more."

"I could have done a lot of things," Silas said, distraction in his words. "The agencies of the sixties hated one another and needed someone to work outside the halls. They chose J because he had a righteous streak and despised authority. They knew he'd dutifully do what was needed, no matter how many obstacles the entrenched bureaucracies rolled into his way. Being an old soul lacking political survival genetics, he scared the hell out of all of them, though not nearly as much as some sociopathic military strongman or ex-Panamanian general lining his pockets while shrugging off civilian body counts.

DeMarco went against regs and chose me. Many years later, I chose you. We brought in Phillip, and later Midas and Mason. It was the best team I've ever seen because we never bothered or concerned ourselves with ass-covering permission. Which is why it worked. At least until Rawlings Palmer tried to tear it down." Silas reached for the door handle.

"So, what do you want me to do?" Conor asked, still the team player, defeated or otherwise.

Silas stepped out of the car, bending his long frame down for a final word. "Back Midas's play. It's long overdue."

The aging runner jogged away with a deliberate and arthritic stride, vanishing between a pair of driveways snaked between new-money condos, well below the highest floors hovering above the salty gray air.

Somewhere in the distance of a rough dream, Natalie could hear the faintest ringing. She labored to emerge from the mid-REM haze, rolling over while sluggishly waking to the realization she was in her own bed, and alone. Mason remained MIA, along with Midas. After a long night of making no progress in the case, she'd stopped by Shredders, only to be told by Carlo's new manager that the boys weren't around.

Any idea where they were? Not a clue, he'd said. *Well trained.*

She waited for her eyes to adjust. Early-morning stillness unnerved her, as it had since childhood. Most found it peaceful, but for her it was a nod to complacency. Experience had taught her that any lack of alertness was an invitation for predators and wickedness. Placidity was a floundering ballast for others to grasp in a staged and rickety diorama, blissfully unaware they were cruising into storms they'd never anticipated. It was an idiot's errand trying to control or make sense of the unexplainable fates.

The least she could do was bank a few chits of worthiness from the daily struggle to keep some of the worst away from civilian doors. The job made her feel useful, if rarely gratified. She could handle that, compartmentalizing the rest in a way her father never could. She was an effective cop, but not much else beyond the badge.

Amber light was creeping into her room. It was six a.m., and the alarm on her phone was still pinging. She turned it off, struggling to crystalize recent events in her tired brain.

Midas and Mason were in trouble. She'd felt it more with every passing minute of the ghosting silence of the past few days. Mason always stayed in touch, even during their more turbulent fights. So did Midas, she reminded herself. It was a nervous shorthand all three had nursed into adulthood. Very few could ever be trusted, and those inside the bubble required tending.

The thought sent a fresh flush of anxiety through her stomach.

She rose from the bed, heading for the shower. The phone's new *ping* stopped her at the door. She hustled back behind a hopeful flutter of expectation.

The screen name wasn't what she needed. She took the call anyway.

"Agent Fed," she said, trying to sound jaunty despite the hour and her mood.

"Natalie." His usual warmth was missing. "We need to meet, off campus. How about our beach in an hour?"

"What's going on?"

"An hour."

Mobile phones. Never that satisfying *click* of disconnection.

The first thing they taught in cop schools was to never present as nervous. An upper-hand attitude was vital when dealing with scumbags. As if the hardware, creds, and browbeating weren't enough.

She sat down on the edge of the bed, flecks of the morning peeking through the shades. The pleasant and healthy aroma of brewing coffee hit her sinuses. Automatic drip makers started off any day better.

What the hell was so important that Collins needed to talk offline and in person? She showered quickly and gathered her java to go.

Natalie hit the beach parking entrance fifteen minutes ahead of schedule.

Collins was already there, perched on the hood of his SUV facing the water, knees pulled in. His sweatshirt was bundled around his throat, head holding against a windy chill. She parked next to him, got out, and leaned on his fender to face him. They were quite alone. Too cold even for the seagulls.

Despite the overcast, his eyes were hidden behind black sunglasses. He looked all-in-fed, and troubled.

Her mood wavered from trepidation to dread. "You okay there, Collins?" Semiformality seemed necessary. It was hard to read anything behind those Ray-Bans. No doubt the point.

"You know a guy named Midas McKnight?" His mouth barely moved.

She hoped he'd said something else, that the wind was playing tricks with her hearing. She also knew he already had his answer, so she decided to wait. Didn't take long.

"How about Mason James? You two are close? I believe?"

Controlling her defensiveness had never been easy. At this moment, it would be impossible. She wound into overload, instinct screaming evasion. She straightened up, leaning in closer to his face, grabbing his knees with both hands to anchor and dislodge him away from his righteous, knowing tone and morally superior perch.

"None of your fucking business," she mumbled.

Collins ignored her, holding more still than the Egyptian sphinx.

She let go of his knees and turned, giving him the rear of her neck instead. Now they could both communicate without the benefit of reading expressions.

"Actually, Detective, it is very much my business. And yours."

The sandy parking lot was opening beneath her, sucking her

into an unknown underside with no foothold. Her mind whirled. Events were obviously in motion well above her pay grade.

"This is my last courtesy," he said. "They wanted me to bring you in, you and your chubby boss, Jay."

She'd never witnessed Collins's ungracious side and found it less than flattering.

"And why would that be?" she asked, lightheaded and convinced the waves were beckoning her to run right into them.

"The FBI director got a call this morning at seven a.m. Eastern. My SAC got a call twenty minutes later. So guess who he decided to call? At five a.m. *our time* I find myself in a meeting with all our stripes from the LA field office. Along with LAPD, SWAT commanders, some state bureaucrats, and a few city hall types. Everyone who's got skin in this case. Everyone, that is, except LA Sheriffs."

She narrowed her eyes. "You're going to need to use smaller words and paint your rhetorical bullshit with broader strokes. I have no idea what the hell you're talking about."

"We'll get to that. First I want to tell you about this call the director got from some old-school frat brother. A guy named Rawlings Palmer. Ever heard of him?"

"No."

"How about his kid, Kyle Palmer? No? Speaking of coloring, seems these two do a lot of it, outside the lines and heavily sheltered behind some important closed doors."

"So?" she asked, though she was beginning to have a reasonably fair and frightening idea where this was heading.

"So, Detective, it means the Palmers run a covert group of wet workers. All protected and assigned for the common good, of course. It's an autonomous, lone-wolf outfit called the Unit that works with, but not exclusively for, CIA, NSA, and at times DOD. All while never fully answering to any of them. I'm sure you know this is all classified?"

"Not so much if you know," she said. "And who does this Unit take orders from?"

"That is the question of the day. And not one I will ever get read in on. All we were given were a few bare facts."

She took a breath. "I'm Icelandic and a bit thick. Are you saying in your new and charming way that some government group is somehow involved with my case? And maybe all the murders?" She turned back around.

He'd pulled his hood up over his head and lost the glasses. The deep blue of his eyes studied her from inside the flaps with a weary, vacant look. "It seems the Basmajian brothers and that toad up in Boulder all worked for this group."

She couldn't hide the perplexed unease pulling at the corners of her mouth. Not that he was paying attention.

"Indirectly, of course." Collins moved forward. "Palmer's son, Kyle, is apparently the brains behind this . . . sleaze empire. Such side ventures are ignored but allowed for operators like them. By the by, the Palmers are a four-hundred-year-old New England family that spent the past several decades blowing through dusty and dwindling trust funds. That is, until several years ago when young Kyle found his calling and a way to keep the relatives awash in new money. His means might be disgraceful and a subject they avoid at picnics, but no one cares as long as accounts stay boosted. Making sense?"

Mansplaining? More like Fed condescension. "Sure, *Special Agent Collins*," she replied with bitterness. "Why don't you just tell me what you need me to know, or ask me whatever you think I'm withholding, and we can both get back to work. If that isn't too difficult for you."

The glare between them could have solved global warming.

Collins finally broke, exhaling as if he'd just surfaced after losing his scuba tank. His edge was gone. "I'm sorry, Natalie. Just got cornholed for two hours because I had no answers to give, which in my world is a bigger sin than lying. My guess is you don't know anything either."

"I'm not sure what I might know. This is all landing fast and hot."

He nodded at her coffee cup. "Can I get a hit of that?"

She handed it over.

"Thanks." He took a long slug, not seeming to mind the tepid warmth. He handed it back, wiping his mouth with a sleeve. "I was told that these guys, Midas McKnight and Mason James? Both were once a part of this Unit, and have been retired for several years. Rawlings Palmer told the director they were thrown out for liking their work a bit too much, along with another guy, Phillip Gillis."

She shot him a look. "Gillis was killed a few days ago," she said, her head spinning with the new information. "Pretty gruesomely."

"We know. Palmer's narrative has these two killing their old cohort because they wanted back into the Unit. But allegedly, Gillis balked. Palmer said he and his son were also approached and also told them no. Too much new oversight to let a couple of blood-simple, stone-cold killers back into the fold. The story we've been given is both went nuclear, refusing to take no for an answer, declaring war on the Palmer family. Beginning with the destruction of their assets. Which we now understand was Kyle Palmer's porn empire."

Natalie's thoughts raced in reverse over the past few days. Mason and Midas involved in these hits? It was all too much to contemplate. But, she had to admit to herself, not a scenario she couldn't imagine.

"And you believe that bullshit?" she asked, stalling as she tried to compose herself.

"On the face of it?" Collins said. "No. Too much we are not being told for me to form a sound judgment. It also doesn't sit right with my gut. A couple of sleazy pricks with white-privilege lineage calling in a dubious favor by asking *us* to hunt them down?"

"Is that the directive, hunt them down?" she asked with growing concern.

"Yes. Make them disappear. Off the record, of course."

"Thought you federales left that kind of finality to the other letter groups?"

Collins looked away, shaking his head. "I used to believe that too."

Though they were several yards from the beach, the roar was deafening. The El Segundo refinery was a few miles away, but its astringent dirty funk mingled with the salty fog, turning her stomach. As much as she hated the narrative, a bit of it made sense. She'd always assumed the boys had been off-the-books workers. She could smell it on them, the tangible despair both carried like Marley's chains. But stone-cold assassins? Making insane moves as part of some power play? And brutally clipping their good friend Gillis? That she wouldn't buy, ever.

She watched the sea churn, trying to settle her thoughts. Moving forward would require deliberate caution. Collins being here and offering a heads-up she recognized now as a true solid, because he'd need to bureau-up from here on out. She figured she owed him whatever she had.

"I've known Midas and Mason for a few years," she said. "Their bar was close to home, and I liked it. Despite what they might have once been a part of, both are decent souls. I seriously doubt a lot of what I'm hearing. Admittedly, I'm not completely unbiased. Mason and I have been together for over a year. Though truthfully, I haven't heard from him in a few days, and it's not for lack of trying. Not to mention, if they pulled off these recent hits, was it just Murphy's Law that I caught the case? Coincidence?"

"Sometimes that's exactly what happens, especially when you shit too close to where you eat. Sorry for the crassness. Maybe they weren't thinking it through. If you buy the jackets of their history, at least the few broad notes I've been given, you're talking about ghosts far too adept and smart to be cornered. We already know whoever killed the Baz brothers and Rudy was proficient. We have nothing, and probably never will. Neither did you nor anyone else. And now, out of thin air, this strangely timed gift from the Palmers."

"A bit too neat," she said, surmising.

"Doesn't mean it isn't true. What I'm more concerned about is what we don't, and probably never will, understand. We carry out this order and it's over. The Palmers will slide back into their wormholes, and we'll never learn the actual truth."

"What about that video? The discovery in Rudy's closet? Must have put the Palmers on notice. Porn might be legal, but tender-age brutality?"

Collins buried his head between his legs, shook it a few times, and brought it back up. "That video?" he whispered. "Has disappeared. Wiped clean from every phone and drive. I tried to bring it up this morning. Was told it never existed, and if I valued my life in public service, not to investigate its vanishing any further."

They both knew only a chosen few could make that happen.

"Jesus, Fed."

"I know," he agreed. "Those sickening fucks in the masks have to be on the inside, and well placed. Which is the real reason I'm not here and we never talked. I can stall my side for about thirty-six hours, pretend to play the tedious game of flushing your boys out. Maybe they'll surface for you and we can find out more. And Natalie, if it isn't already obvious, I have a real problem with the suits on this one. My only ask is you keep me in the loop. The more I know, the more I can help."

Her conflicted feelings were returning. She was angry they'd both come into this orbit without the benefit of serious intel, and about what they were up against. Collins was putting his neck in the noose for her, and she'd given him no reason to do so. It could get ugly for them both. She wanted to protect him. And while she continued to spin about Mason's and Midas's backstory, she needed to try and help them as well.

Assuming those two stubborn idiots would allow it.

"One of my LAPD pals slipped me this." Collins handed her a small sheet of paper the size of a Post-it. She glanced at the name and number. "Who is he?" she asked.

"From what I'm told, someone who knows all and can help us." Collins stood, finished for now. "You need o get lost," he said, half-heartedly motioning for her to leave.

She reached for his hand, holding it a moment longer than necessary. "You're a decent sort, Grant Collins. For a fed anyway." She gave him what was left of her smile and started to walk away.

His voice cut through the strong wind. "Doesn't do me any good, though, does it? Watch your back, Detective."

The contact Collins had given Natalie texted an address to a downtown dive bar along with explicit instructions on where to park and how to get in without being seen.

She pulled into a dank underground garage a few blocks away, driving down into the hidden bowels of subterranean level four. The text had told her which numbered space to park in along with which door to use. It was unlocked and took her into a workers area brightly lit with overhead fixtures.

She weaved around a few turns before finding the next mark she was looking for, a dead-end wall with a ladder leaning against it. She climbed up with skill, emerging on a new perch facing another entry, also unsecured. Once through, she entered another winding tunnel, walking up a slope another several yards to a final door.

On the other side, she had reemerged at street level in a banking kiosk with two cash machines. Who the hell was this guy?

Outside, Figueroa Street moved briskly with morning traffic. As instructed, she stepped between the machines and knocked twice. A piece of the wall swung open, and a hardened forty-plus-something in a white T-shirt and leather jacket gave her a practiced appraisal. Not the worst-looking guy, she thought, between the pronounced dimple on his chin and the dancing eyes.

"Detective Riiska? Conor Brennan." He offered his hand, which she shook without hesitation. "Thanks for the diligence. No one knows much about the miles of forgotten pathways underneath downtown LA. Those who do try not to ever think about them. You want some coffee? They won't open for another few hours, but it's on and decent."

"Thanks. I'd love some."

He guided her through a back storage room into a ground-level establishment, deserted at this hour, but suited to the beams of natural light from the street-facing windows. An ideal spot for people-watching or other forms of observation. The bar's counter was like none she'd ever seen, split into a pair of equal halves with access through the middle. No sliding under trap doors that raised up for those preparing or slinging drinks. Both sides of the bar held a dull shine on the varnished wood. Tall stools ringed the outer edges.

She took a seat on one, finding it more comfortable than it appeared. "Your place?"

"Know the owner," Brennan said.

What was it about these guys and their bars?

Above the assortment of sturdy green and brown bottles hung a TV tuned to one of the local morning news shows. A goofy-looking fiftyish reporter with a bugle nose, thinning hair, and ears the size of archery targets was standing in front of the smoldering Carson warehouse. Still the lead story everywhere. She'd run into the reporter on numerous occasions pushing his way into crime scenes. His inherent and clueless form of journalism included an on-camera delivery that could scratch precious stones. Thankfully, Brennan had the sound muted.

His back was to her, displaying the intrusion of a bald spot near the rear of his crown. He poured coffee while peering up at the nerdy reporter. "You hear about this fire?" he asked.

"Not much else for the past several hours."

He turned to set her mug down, sipping from his own with a small salute that served as an early-hour toast. It wasn't hard to see from his face that Conor Brennan was a man in some conflict.

The ropy tightness of his jaw, the slight creases at the corners of his mouth, his face set with forethought into a neutral expression.

Another pro. As advertised.

"That fire?" he said. "Was courtesy of our friends."

The statement took a moment to register. Despite her intention to remain measured, sadness and irritation began to rise.

He was watching her carefully. Having been in the virtual dark since being jangled by Collins out of a hibernated state, she was well past decorum. And done with being bumpered around like hired help.

"You know what, Brennan? My shock-and-awe quota is all used up." It came out too harsh, and she mentally kicked herself. This was a boys club. Coming off as a reeling girlfriend wouldn't help.

"Sorry," he said, looking tired and beaten.

She let her fibers uncoil a few degrees.

"Your bureau friend filled you in on all the—"

"Events?" she said, cutting him off.

He smiled. A good smile that did wonders for his face, shaving off fifteen years while masking secrets she could only assume would have filled a dumpster. The shadow left his eyes, which met hers with a determined, friendly gaze. "It's been a day, huh?" The weight behind those words hovered for them both, drifting alongside the stale remnants of last night's drunken promises and lingering cheap cologne.

"What exactly did Collins tell you?" he asked.

She considered the question. Right now, information was her only commodity. Midas was off the grid, and Mason had gone silent, likely doing all he could to watch his friend's back. Both had been marked for elimination, and the cavalry was getting its toys together to take them off the board. She tried to focus away from that scenario and take measure of the man in front of her. Brennan billboarded as pure spook. She'd known a few through her father, and later from her own cases. The best of them never got cornered, though this one seemed a man out of moves.

"He said you were part of this Unit," she said. "Someone I could trust."

"I'd like to think so."

"Then here we are."

He capitulated with a nod. "On the record, there's nothing to say. Big surprise, right? But for you and no one else? We were a tight-knit band." He paused. "That did some questionable things."

"For the right reasons?" she ventured, failing to completely dampen the recrimination.

"I really couldn't say." His fingers flexed, stretching over the polished wood. "We did what we did. Let's leave it at that."

"Why all of you?"

His bearing changed to one she'd seen many times, usually in a sepia-toned interrogation box. Suspects fixing her with smug silence that translated as "Are stupid questions really necessary?"

Brennan stared at her intensely enough that a needle began to sting her lower back.

"Because we? Were efficient." His growl came from a lower place.

It was her turn to stand down, somewhat ashamed. "Sorry."

"No," he said, fixating on the reasonably quiet street outside taking its break between morning coffee and the lunch rush. "I'm sorry. You've only been inside all this for a few hours. Must sound like some bad B movie."

"Not so much as you might think," she admitted. "I've watched

Mason and the boys take care of bar rabble. Skills like that don't come with colored belts and participation trophies."

Brennan smiled again. "Nordic people are some of my favorites. Missing very little while keeping it to themselves. Like the rest of Europe, you're comfortable in four or five languages and can shift from one to another in midsentence. To my ear, you've worked to sound moderately American and homegrown, Detective. Though your diction is more precise than the lazy inflection of normal rubespeak. How long have you been in the States?"

His curiosity seemed genuine. Still, she couldn't completely vanquish the reflex to measure the distance and hold back. Then again, at this point, what did it matter?

"Almost ten years. Seattle and then the last two here with Sheriff's homicide."

"Murder police," he stated before continuing for her. "Before that, England. Joined the Metro cops in London after college and a four-year tour. Father was a legend in Interpol."

The skin on the back of Natalie's hands started to warm.

"I'm very sorry," Brennan added.

She shook her head, fighting a sudden flush. "Checked me out, eh?" she said. "Guess I shouldn't be surprised."

"Mason gave me the broad strokes over a beer last year. Though nothing about your father. He's good that way. Once all this heated up, I needed to know all I could about you and Serena."

"Serena? From Shredders?" she asked, puzzled. The pretty bartender had disappeared awhile back. "What about—"

Brennan waved her off and cleared his throat. "A story for another time. Anyway. Like I said, we were a tight group. I owe them whatever I can deliver."

"Isn't it your *group* who's put out a notice on them? Aren't *you* the group?"

Brennan raised his mug for another long pull—she would have said bashfully if she didn't know better.

"I'm off the Christmas list on this one. But yes, people I work with. The details you got from your FBI pal came from me. As well as his promise to find me a bit of time. We are dealing with the final act of a lengthy game of chicken. Midas hurt Kyle Palmer badly several years ago, turning him into a barely functioning cripple. Until now we were able to keep the dogs off. Problem was, it was always a play for time and leverage. Both have finally run out."

Natalie had figured out most of this in the past few hours but needed more. "Why would an outfit such as yours even let the guys retire? My father used to say when it came to this kind of service, once in, always in."

"Most stay because where else can they really go?" Brennan shrugged. "Occasionally there are exceptions. Midas, Mason, and Phil Gillis were granted no-touch status by our boss, who back then still had the muscle to make it stick. About two weeks ago he took a bad fall as a result of the cancer he's been fighting. Been in a coma ever since. Word is he's dying, and it's doubtful he'll ever wake up. The Palmers saw their chance. Now Kyle, his father, and a few well-motivated subordinates are out to finish the job."

Behind Natalie a door rattled. A young Latino man of maybe twenty-two strode in, his full shock of spiked black hair the only part of him not moving.

Brennan waved him over, handing him some cash. "Go get yourself some breakfast, Miguel."

The younger man smiled at them, a toothy grin with touches of yellow on the incisors. He turned and was gone, closing the door without a sound.

"Good kid," Brennan said, watching through the windows as he marched off. "Used to mule opioids for a band of coyotes holding his family hostage down near Escondido."

"And now?" she asked, grateful for a small break.

"My friend? The owner of this joint? Found him on the side of the 405 one night beaten halfway to his bones. He'd gotten ripped off on a run and his handlers had taught him a lesson. They killed his mother and tried to sell his sister to some traffickers back home. My friend the bar owner brought me in. Those coyotes are long gone. *Fish food.* That was a few years ago. Now Miguel's got an apartment nearby and his sister waits tables here at night. She's going to junior college. From there it'll be on to UCLA."

Many years before, Natalie had suffered through her first truly bad day on her East London beat, responding to a young teenage girl who'd been raped, slaughtered with a serrated blade, and left in a dank dustbin. That night, Natalie's father had appeared at her neighborhood pub. Someone had made a call. He had friends everywhere.

Even now she could remember every word from that conversation, every moment.

Her father had slid in next to her, moving her third double vodka out of her reach. Always the adult. She'd flung some mean words his way while reaching to retrieve it, only to realize through the hazy quicksand of inebriation that he'd pinned her wrist to the bar. Then she'd quietly started to cry. Wailing cops simply didn't do in their world.

An hour later he walked her home and up to her flat. She was coming down from the booze and fighting the start of what would become a nasty night above the toilet. At her door, they'd faced each other for the first time as true colleagues. Never one for overt displays of warmth, he'd reached out to cradle her shoulders. "Natalia, we help those we can, and accept the rest. You're much smarter than I will ever be, and I have little doubt you will make your journey with distinction. But if you want to be fulfilled or satisfied, get out of this line of work now."

He'd backed away, turning to begin the four-floor descent down the building's stairs.

Before disappearing, he'd muttered, "This is why I wanted something better for you."

All these years later, she understood enough about her own scar tissue not to question why she was drawn to people such as Mason and Midas. Saving wounded lambs while searching for what the ancients called *justice*. Though truthfully? Nothing more than a feeble attempt to balance books and generate worthiness, all while usually falling short . . . on both counts.

"What can I do for them?" she asked Brennan.

"The Palmers have lost most of their help and muscle. The five or so that remain are formidable. They're not Midas or Mase, but advantage here favors the aggressor. If you can, find out what the guys need. They will tell you to stay as far away from them as possible. I wouldn't disagree. No one wants you losing your career or shield over this."

"Let me worry about that."

"I figure we've got a day at the most." Conor tried to smile some form of self-confidence, falling short.

She stood up, this time choosing the front exit. She stopped near the door. "I understand the Kyle Palmer-Midas dynamic. But what happened to Mason?"

Conor was washing their cups in a sink behind the bar. "Not a question for me. It was nice to finally meet you, Detective."

CHAPTER 15

GUATEMALA CITY, FIVE YEARS EARLIER

THE DUST AND SMELL said they were entering an abyss. The white smoke said they were too late.

Inside the city's borders, there was no shortage of tin-walled shanties, crude forms of villages and commerce, sweltering retail dens clumped in stifling rows. To the west a few miles outside the limits, roadside stands sold fruit and bottled water. Beyond sat red-hued emptiness promising desperation.

This dwelling was well outside of town. An aberration, removed from pavement, plumbing, and most other twentieth-century conveniences.

Mason had taken a rear position behind Midas and Conor. Behind him trudged the three spotters they'd pulled from a shaky bar near the center of a commercial neighborhood, men happy to take a well-paid break from bouncing drunken wannabe caballeros pawing at sagging strippers.

The men had been an easy sell. Mason and the team were obviously serious and well-heeled professionals. Loose cargoes, strong boots, long-sleeved lightweight Henleys, and a pair of reinforced black SUVs.

They were close. Their destination was about two hundred yards from where they'd left the vehicles, invisible within the choking smoke. The day before had rained, leaving muddy trenches. Mason tried to keep his mood in check as they trudged on.

The trail abruptly narrowed, sloping downward. They told the men to wait and shout if they saw or heard anything.

Fifty yards out, an adobe structure started taking shape, diminutive as it was remote, encased within a semicircle of mature fruit trees—lemons and figs. Despite what remained of the fire, the walls were holding. The roof was mostly gone, smoldering within the final remnants of flickering flames.

A splintered wooden box served as a stoop to what had been a ramshackle front door, now useless and broken on the ground. The farmer leaning against the crumbling frame was in his early thirties but could have passed for fifty. Leathery skin and conquered eyes told stories words never would. Like most of his countrymen, he was slight. Below his feet stretched a bloody mass of jumbled sinew and broken bones. He stared at the tangle of brown hair knotted above bloated lips and bruised cheeks. His gaze reminded Mason of too many others, occupying only time and space. Lost in his own tortured mind.

There was no acknowledgment or sense of fear as they approached. The farmer was beyond that.

Mason and the others passed a final row of trees and entered a sun-swept clearing. To the left of the home was a ground well, next to a horizontal rope strung for drying laundry, now sagging from the weight of hanging figures. Two small children and a charred dog.

"Oh, Christ," Midas whispered.

Conor walked toward the house and the one survivor. He attempted to use soothing words in Spanish. The little man looked up for a brief second before lowering his eyes back to the mangled woman stretched out before him.

Mason moved toward the dead children. The metallic smell of blood and burned flesh blew through his sinuses as a hammer started to bang behind his eyes and forehead. For a moment he was blind, colors appearing and vanishing. He felt weak and dizzy, forcing himself forward over those final few steps, each heavier and more paralyzing.

The last few yards he skidded and shuffled, needing to know and to see. It was the least he could do.

They were a boy and girl, likely siblings. Both had been gutted, the ground under their dirty suspended feet a repellent maroon soup of viscera, tissue, and undersized organs. Their faces had been left untouched, though the mottled eyes and darkened welts under the fraying ropes suggested they had been alive and struggled through the worst of it. The dog was a mutt of some sort. He'd simply been ignited, though not before being robbed of his genitals.

Mason stood lost in the acridly fragrant, sickening draft.

His throat tightened, and his torso started to burn in a helpless form of protest. Scenes such as this were nothing new in this part of the world, especially for those who refused to obey overlords. Later, he would wonder how long he'd stood there. Though it could never have been long enough. A weathered doll was locked between the girl's bruised, pudgy fingers.

Eventually his shock began to abate and the rage moved in, pushing tears down his cheeks.

There was a rustling, then a hand on his shoulder. Midas. Guiding him slowly back to the little broken man, another grim piece of business.

Conor had gently moved the woman's body from the doorway, laying her near a few wildflowers. He'd covered her with two weathered blankets he'd found inside that had survived the fire. Conor sat down on the small stoop, helping the farmer do the same. The small man's hands hung limply over his knees and dirty dungarees. His swollen feet had been beaten and strained against the sides of homemade huaraches. Other than that, he appeared physically unscathed.

Midas and Mason stood to one side out of his line of sight as Conor pulled a bottle of tequila from his bag and put it between his quivering legs.

Soon, the bottle was empty, and a numb flush was painted on the farmer's face.

He began to talk haltingly between fits of sobbing and heaves.

His name was Cobar. He told them the men had come at dawn, strangers to his family. There had been seven of them, fully armed though not military. They'd kicked down the door and eaten what little food the family had. They'd smoked crude, hand-rolled cigarettes, extinguishing them by flicking stubs at his children, who'd huddled silently with their parents in a corner near the tiny kitchen. The taunting had continued. They'd pulled out their dicks and pissed on the floor, all the while laughing like fools. They'd kicked the dog a few times and then shot it. The children and his wife had begun to wail.

A few minutes later, a man Cobar knew only as the Colonel

had arrived, heavy with purpose, blistering hate hidden behind mirrored glasses. He'd been given a fast appraisal, followed by bone-crushing slaps to the faces of the farmer's wife and children. The Colonel's gut, cinched over a nylon belt trussing baggy fatigues, had jiggled when he laughed. His men kept laughing as well.

Begging for the lives of his family caused the men to laugh harder.

The Colonel had barked an order, short and precise.

Cobar's children were grabbed and taken outside. His wife stood to protest and was beaten before being shot. Cobar had lunged for the Colonel, getting a crack to the side of his head from one of the men's pistols for his trouble. With blood flowing into his eyes and unable to walk, he'd been dragged outside to watch. The children were strung up, along with the dead, limp dog, which they doused with gasoline. Their small-lunged shrieks battered his brain as the strangers' nonstop cackles pitched into animalistic howls. Hunting knives appeared and were used to slice them open. Cobar had tried to crawl but was beaten repeatedly with the butt of several rifles. There was a *whoosh* of a lit torch and another blow to his head that had mercifully pitched him into darkness.

When he woke, the men were gone. What was left behind was the potent smell of death, and his own sense of futility.

The little farmer put his head into his hands. He was finished talking.

Conor pulled a satellite phone from his bag.

Three hours later, back in the city the sun was beginning to go down. Red grit hit their windshields, mashing into dusty paste.

The ebony SUVs were constructed like testosterone-infused Hummers, barely flinching as they cruised over the raggedy streets at a paced clip. Trolling wagons of death with enough toys to wage a serious assault. Avoiding the street vendors, they rolled through the back routes, steering away from dead ends and checkpoints. The lead vehicle took a hard, screeching right and snapped to a stop a few miles northwest of the main downtown drag.

It was an off-the-path neighborhood, one of the worst-kept secrets in the country.

The Colonel owned three square blocks, some of which he'd been given but most of which he'd simply taken, if strong-arming and hostile occupation could ever be considered simple. His true backstory was of a hack-level prison official just smart enough to read the signals of change festering within his impoverished country, hooking up with the right side, reinventing himself as indispensable to the imprisoned leaders of a burgeoning coup and facilitating their escape to take over the country. For his efforts, the former prison guard was given the nickname phrase Colonel of the Revolution. Two years later, the fickle Colonel had reached out to sympathetic allies in the United States, his political exploits and malleability having gained attention throughout the alphabet agencies.

DeMarco hadn't been fooled, having gathered several of his own troubling reports on the man. Reading the leaves, he'd sent three of his favored Unit down to the Central American city for a sitrep. His brethren at CIA, NSA, and the Pentagon had long coveted returning Guatemala back to the fold, along with its drug corridors, hidden training camps, and jungle landing strips. But the Old Man wanted to know more about this figure known as the Colonel.

Today they'd learned all they needed to know. After dropping off the spotters near the outskirts, the team had returned to the city for the prearranged meet, the carnage at Cobar's farm lodged like lead in their minds.

Mason thought the bar chosen as a meeting place looked as ratty as the rest of the city. A pair of the Colonel's henchboys were kicking at the hot pavement outside, rifles across their backs, winking at the gringos as they walked past without paying them any notice.

Inside, the walls were black and barren, a slight refuge from the dusk-tinged glare and oppressive heat. Chipped tables in need of varnish swayed on the buckling wood floor. The team made its way toward the rear. The Colonel sat surrounded by a handful of his men. The underlings scrambled to get up and make room for them as Mason, Midas, and Conor approached. To the right, a lone old man stood behind the bar nursing a beer and watching with practiced apprehension.

The rest of the place was empty except for a pile of rifles lined up and standing in the corner. The three of them sat down across from the Colonel, who was filing his manicured nails with an emery board. He asked whether they wanted a drink.

"Just got back from your garden party outside of town," Conor said. "What was that all about?"

It was one of the few times Mason could remember when Conor wasn't smiling or genial with his small talk. Midas was heaped into his chair like an aging fighter, knuckles white under the dirt on his hands, the veins in his arms pulsating as if they might explode.

Like the farmer, none of them was in a talkative state.

The Colonel's black sunglasses hadn't been removed. He smiled through crusty, graying teeth, taking an extended pull from a bottle of cheap tequila. He wiped his full, sloppy-wet lips with the back of his cuff.

"Your reputation precedes you, Señor Brennan, as it does for your friends. I was pleasantly surprised that they sent men of such . . . significance. It signals an understanding of how serious I am about trying to save my country. With your government's help, we can accomplish great things here." His English was good.

"I asked about your visit this afternoon. To a small farm outside of town," Conor said, clearly unwilling to let it go.

The Colonel's cheek twitched. "Cobar's farm, yes. He inherited that sinkhole from his peasant father. They've grown coffee and a bit of sugarcane for forty years. A few fruit trees as well. But for my plans to work and to make your American politicians happy, such farmers will need to rethink what and how they grow. You must understand what I mean?"

"Sure," Conor said through a clenched jaw. "A few poppies? Maybe a bit of those smelly green weeds?"

"You see the future because you are educated," the Colonel said. "Most here have accepted reality and fallen into line. Cobar had no interest in becoming any more than what he'd always been, a small-time nobody. Lacked . . . ambition. Wanted no part of what I needed him to do. It sends a poor message to other stubborn, grubby farmers."

"And his wife? Kids?" Conor seethed.

"How about his fucking dog?" Mason leaned in with a low snarl, slowly, so as not to alarm the torture-happy henchman a few tables over.

The Colonel took another quick swig, not processing the danger he was beginning to sense.

Mason could feel his temper slipping precariously. He was done with these types. The Colonel was nothing but a treacherous, scheming survivor, one who'd built a burgeoning empire on exploited opportunities and homicidal indifference.

The Colonel's brow began to unfurl. He'd probably sized it all up and convinced himself he had nothing to fear—even if he had gotten a bit overzealous at the farm. He tipped his head and studied them. "As I said," he continued, "when you are trying to facilitate great change, disobedience cannot be tolerated. I'm not a bad man, but this country has been a war zone for decades. Sacrifices must be made if we are to succeed."

"Ri-ight. Sacrifices." Mason drew the words out, giving himself a five count before hitting his feet and reaching across the table in one blindingly fast motion. He took hold of the Colonel's ears in each hand, tearing them from their moorings as he yanked the man's torso onto the table. Mason had beaten his face into the surface three times before the stunned room could react and the men at the next table jumped up to reach for their rifles.

Too late.

Conor stood and whirled, taking out two of the Colonel's men with a pair of shots from his .45 m. At other tables, hands shot up in immediate surrender. Midas had moved, deploying himself near the front door. The two men from outside stumbled in because of the noise and never saw the blows coming. They fell, kissing the floor like broken furniture.

All attention returned to Mason.

He held the Colonel's battered face by his hair up to gain eye contact. The nose and forehead were shattered, mouth ballooning in a purple swirl. Ears swung from the sides of his head dripping a steady stream of thick blood. His eyes were gauzy, and he looked poised to pass out. Smears on the table had already darkened. For a would-be soldier, he'd offered no resistance.

Mason used his free hand to reach for the empty tequila bottle, which he broke in half against the side of the splintering table. Neither Conor nor Midas moved to stop him. It would have been futile. Mason drove the jagged end of the bottle into the side of the Colonel's face, pushing until most of it disappeared into his skull.

There was a twitch, and then it was over.

"And these guys?" Conor asked, waving his muzzle at the horrified men still holding their arms high above their heads.

"Please." One pleaded, using badly broken English. "The Colonel would have killed us and tortured our families. We had no choice."

Down the block a juice vendor was shaving ice when he heard more extended gunfire.

He knew enough to look away when the three men emerged a few minutes later, driving off in a pair of black SUVs.

LOS ANGELES, PRESENT DAY

Mason stared through the window in his office, looking almost diminutive in his desk chair. Natalie had listened to his story about the incident in Guatemala without comment. All she felt now was emptiness.

"That's all of it," he said.

She'd called an hour ago demanding they meet. Mason had responded angrily, arguing it wasn't safe. She'd insisted, and he'd relented, reluctantly guiding her to his gym, the only place he felt such an ill-timed get-together would be moderately secure.

Expecting evasiveness, she'd been shamed by his surprising willingness to talk. His words had run over her like tractor treads.

"Is there anything else you need to know? Or anything you feel the need to say?" he asked.

"Nothing that would be worth a damn," she said. "Other than I'm so sorry."

"Phillip and Serena deserve your sympathy," he said. "Not me."

"Why not you?"

He reclined as much as the chair would allow, taking stock of the ceiling. For all his constant introspection, moments of pointed humor, and stoic strength, Mason was a shy man, frequently avoiding eye contact.

One who reacted to troubling events defensively. And while being all too capable when his number was called, he would never get past the haunted aftermath of his self-judgment. In some ways he seemed to her a young boy, trying to understand a world that twirled in ways he couldn't remedy or explain, even while his rigid rationality told him such searching was a fool's journey. Mason would always be the first in and last out securing an objective. And then later kick himself for flaws in his own character. It broke her when he drifted inside those solitary prisons, never trusting anyone to share his burden.

"Conor . . . Midas and I? We were all too young to know any better," he said. "It's no excuse. Not an excuse, but a fact."

At least he was talking again.

"Philly was our tech, and we purposely kept him away from the heavy stuff. But like I said. We were all kids, impressionable . . . stubborn, and unfortunately, too damn good at what we did. Dumb enough to delude ourselves that it was sufficient to be on the righteous side of the ledger, no matter what we were asked to do. That mindset isn't sustainable and eventually starts to disintegrate. Early on, you don't know what to make of it, so best to mentally box it for another day. Kick the turmoil in your head down the road as long as you can. With age, it all becomes harder to push aside. Real soldiers go through the same thing and deal with much worse. We aren't special."

"You can't blame yourself for decisions made all those years ago," she said. "And made above you."

"No? Who should I blame? Conor for recruiting us? DeMarco? How about my old man for not being an adequate father and sending me in search of something I've never understood? No. Nobody forced me to do anything. I won't speak for Midas, but I was an angry young man who'd lost a decent shot at a baseball career. I was nineteen when I took up journalism and started freelancing. Spent the next several years trying to prove I mattered, to my editors and the Unit. I cultivated so much rage. Most of which remains. Back then buying into a virtuous narrative was heavy tonic for a pissed-off soul. Was it the wrong choice? Probably. So if there's blame, it begins with me."

"But when and where does it all end?" she asked. "Two nights from now after more bodies drop? Maybe you and Midas? There will be plenty more time for self-immolation. Right now we need to get through this. And I need you to let me help. Otherwise, I call a few uniforms and my new pal from the FBI and put you on ice for forty-eight hours."

He sat up, shooting her a hard stare. Then he relaxed with a sad smirk. "You'd do that?"

"Try me, asshole."

He tipped his head down, studying his hands. The shy boy had returned. "I couldn't live with getting you hurt, slugger. This isn't your problem."

"Not your call," she said, fighting to keep her voice even.

Mason kept a garage-sized storage unit a few miles away in El Segundo, a block south of the 405. It took the overflow of equipment from his gym and extra supplies for the bar, along with some more dubious items. The rent was written off yearly under a no-trace LLC.

He was sitting on a box he'd pulled near the front of the roll-down door so he could surveil while waiting.

Midas pulled up, parking the car across the open door for cover. Old habits.

The two looked each other over, both agreeing the other looked like hell.

"Conor mentioned you were on the calendar for a come-to-Lucifer with Natalie," Midas said, lips quirked humorlessly. "How'd that go?"

"Only way it could."

Midas shook his head grimly. "Some bills never get paid. She shouldn't have gotten in the middle of this. I never considered the chance of that happening, not for one second. What a fucking idiot. I'm getting old and stupid."

Mason shrugged. "Had to happen eventually."

"No philosophy today, Mase. Just smack me in the mouth. You've got the right."

"Maybe later."

Mason's nose was picking up the familiar El Segundo odor, the slight taint of sewage from one of the treatment centers out near the water. The reason homes in the sleepy city went for about forty percent less than their cousins to the north and south.

"She wants to help," Mason said. "Told her you'd let her know." Midas nodded, and Mason looked away. "So where are we?" he asked.

"Just about there," Midas said, his low voice full of fatigue. "Wonder if you can handle something for me? Got summoned to a meeting. A one-on-one." He paused for a moment, rubbing bloodshot eyes. "Said I'd show, but truthfully, I can't handle it. It's clean, outdoors, crowded. Too many civilians for any sandbagging. But have Carlo shadow just for the hell of it. Of course, I'd rather you say no. Lie low for a few days."

"Text me the details," Mason said.

Midas nodded, distracted but present.

"Don't drop the craft," Mason said, as ever the vigilant warrior. Regret and doubt notwithstanding. Wind snapped at the cheap plastic pennants on the storage facility's roof. "And check in, every hour. Nonnegotiable."

"You got it," Midas said. "I grabbed some coffee. It's in the car. Can we sit for a bit?"

An hour later, Mason pulled the door closed and hit the code. After clearing the security gates, the two cars pulled away using opposite routes.

Neither had uttered another word. At least the coffee had been solid.

Mason rolled into Beverly Hills, a pin in the county of Los Angeles he normally avoided. Being a unfussy type lacking the disposition for overpriced retail and fundamentally aggressive shopping clerks, he'd never quite seen the point.

That said, there were several decent places to get a meal if one could stomach charcoal infusion or the liberal shame of occasionally eating less than organic. Tonight, he avoided the cramped few blocks constituting the city's center, instead taking Santa Monica Boulevard off the 405 freeway with its moderately straight line to the corner of Wilshire.

To his left rose the Waldorf Astoria West, a luxury appendage to its Park Avenue namesake. The wedge shape blended well with the topography, its design a not-so-subtle nod to New York's famous Flatiron building. Mason passed the hotel's driveway entrance, crossed the four lanes of Wilshire and circled back a block down. It was seven thirty at night, and there were plenty of open meters on the street. If things went bad, he didn't want to risk an undermotivated valet or the underground maze of a garage.

He left the car and crossed Wilshire from the opposite direction, striding in a measured pace down Little Santa Monica, the shorter side street parallel to its congested cousin. He then diverted two blocks before turning north.

Back on Big Santa Monica, he chose angles and darted through the speeding traffic to the other side. An eighties song once claimed that nobody walked in LA. Mostly true, and especially so along multilaned streets. Early evening meant the sidewalks were mostly empty, leaving Mason feeling far too exposed. He traced the south side of the hotel's exterior along the street side. At the midpoint was a metal door with a keypad. A sign read EMPLOYEES ONLY. The door should have been locked flush. But it easily swung open with a tug on the metal handle, and a small wedge of white paper fluttered to the ground. He kicked it aside and closed the door behind him.

Carlo had been efficient, as always.

Mason made his way through a battlefield of scattered bellboy carts and room-service trays. Having memorized the floor plan, he slipped inside the men's staff changing room. It could have been a dance studio, though with much lower ceilings and papered with rows of stacked lockers. A hotel this size employed an army of help. He walked between the rows of low benches to the opposite end, emerging into another poorly lit area revealing six freight elevators. Several yards away, a festive off-reddish hue beckoned, seeping through from the main entrance along with a low hum of patrons and soft music. Carlo's recon had been precise.

Mason stepped inside one of the service lifts and punched fourteen.

For patrons and guests, the rooftop bar was a destination accessed from the lobby elevators.

Mason emerged behind the revelry in a back area where waiters were digging through boxes. None seemed interested in him, paying little attention as he made his way past them and detoured to the bar's entrance on the hotel's north side. Despite the winter temps, two short-skirted twentysomething women with generous curves and heaps of mascara-driven makeup appraised and welcomed him from behind practiced greetings. He visibly softened his posture and expression as he walked past, pleasantly signaling with a friendly gesture that said he was meeting a party already seated.

The women returned the smile and immediately lost interest, looking back to their phones.

The terrace was expansively laid out, stretching around the roof and featuring elegant patio seats, heat lamps, and pristine views. Under tonight's clear skies, the lights of Los Angeles stretched below, almost touchable. A miles-long glistening blanket of twinkle from the Griffith Park Observatory to downtown, through the hills of Laurel and Coldwater Canyons to the beaches of the Westside.

Impressive. He wished he had time to appreciate it more thoroughly.

The crowd was mostly entertainment-industry types, money managers, and various other varieties of social climbers. Plexiglass barriers rimmed the five-foot-high stucco walls, enclosing the customers, tables, and the bar within a pleasant, lucent fortress. Necessary to ensure a bad day chased with expensive drinks wouldn't end with a long plunge into the traffic below.

Mason's meeting was positioned with her back to the city's night, disregarding the scenery to instead watch the rhythms of the drinkers.

Michelle Kelly's mouth was drawn in a semifrown of disappointment. She looked tense, but not overly so. As she watched him approach, she switched gears and sat up, stiff and rigid. He chose a chair to her side where he could study the bar's margins. Somewhere in the buzzy throng Carlo was watching, well hidden.

"Didn't ask for you," she said.

"Life remains a series of disappointments."

"Asshole."

She raised her arm for service. In the months since he'd seen her last, Michelle hadn't lost her luster of impatience. Her dark eyes reflected in a glaring shine against the speckles of the clear night sky, one of two signs she was already floating. The cruel smile being the other. As her former boss, Mason was well acquainted with both.

A waiter appeared. She ordered a double Chivas, a repeat for the empty glass sweating its final few shards of ice. She held it nervously.

"And for you, sir?" the young man asked.

"Nothing, thanks."

Her glassy eyes tracked him as he walked away. She could have been a cornered cat, or just another Angeleno paying too much for a watered-down short pour of Scotch. They sat quietly until the waiter returned. She raised the glass half-heartedly, toasting something unseen, then frowning again against what he assumed was a welcome burn descending past her heart and lungs.

"I needed *him* here," she said.

"He's a little tied up. I'm sure you've heard."

"Screw you and your high-minded sarcasm."

Mason let himself breathe out, hoping the appearance of relaxation would get her to the fucking point. "Okay," he said. Not sure whether she was hearing him over the alcohol, the crackling propane lamps, and the rising conversations from nearby tables.

There was a screech of brakes from the darkness of the street below, the whining howl of tires gripping asphalt. Thankfully it wasn't followed by the sickening *crunch* of bumpers, only a short symphony of horns.

"I didn't know about Serena," she said at length. "Only supposed to be a snatch and grab. Put her on ice for a few days."

"Yeah?" He leaned forward, refusing to give an inch or mask incredulity. "What the fuck did you think would happen?"

She took another heavy pull of the Scotch, fighting something. "Not that."

He stared at her over the glass she held to her mouth. As if she could hide. "How the hell did you get involved with *him*?"

The glass dropped back onto the table, her expression sliding toward rueful. "Would you believe at that dive around the corner from Shredders? The one that serves those awesome late-night omelets?"

He did believe it. Not a stretch. Kyle had certainly targeted their bar for surveillance.

"Point is," she continued, "he found me . . . at the right moment. Seemed like a nice guy. Money, his own club." She held up her glass, pointing at it while making eye contact with the waiter, who started to walk their way before Mason waved him off.

"Hall monitor," she grumbled, draining the last of what she had. "After those final few months of constant griping with Midas the detached statue, Kyle was like a warm bath. Easy, sunny disposition, funny. A good listener. He told me right away he was an old friend of all of you. Actually, more old acquaintance. Early on, I asked him how he'd gotten so banged up. And you know what? He told me. The whole story. In gruesome detail. I felt bad for him, and we started seeing each other. A few weeks later, he told me about his plan to settle things. By then I was telling myself I hated Midas and loved Kyle. It wasn't hard. I was all in."

"Bully for you," Mason said, sarcastically.

She slammed the glass down, drawing a few glares from nearby tables. "Fuck you, Mason. And fuck him as well. If these last few days have taught me anything, it's you're all the same. Simplistic as that may sound."

"Kyle's a sociopath."

"And the two of you aren't?"

"No," he replied, momentarily easing. "Though admittedly, not much better."

Michelle's head fell back as she aimed a wicked wave of laughter toward the sky, more of a primal howl laced with heaving cackles. Then she stared at him with no shortage of malice. "God. You two and your self-wounded, narcissistic guilt. Wasn't it all government work? What's the term Kyle taught me? Sanctioned? Get over it, already. You know another thing I appreciated about him? He never punished himself like you two mopey schmucks. It was just a damn job."

Mason moved swiftly, grabbing her wrist. So quick she hadn't seen it coming. He could feel the anger creasing his face.

She tried to pull away but was locked up. "Let go," she said, almost snarling.

He pulled her closer, increasing his pressure. "Kyle's countless faults," he whispered, loud enough to ring in her ears, "now seem to include a nondiscerning mouth. Do yourself a favor and forget every word he ever told you. About anything. Do you hear what I'm telling you?"

The fear rising in her eyes said she did. Even as she continued trying to yank herself free.

"Michelle," he said, his tone gaining urgency. *"Do you understand?"*

"All right," she blurted, pulling her hand back when he finally let it go. "You don't have to be a fucking ape."

For a moment she'd begun to warm to the joust with her old boss. Now she looked as if she wanted to be anywhere else. The Scotch was wearing off, and his intense pivot had delivered the intended effect. Small shudders rippled through her shoulders. She forced herself to look away from the severity of his eyes. Several stories below, the city continued to gleam, blurry at the edges—like its inhabitants, Mason thought.

"Kyle never should have made you a part of this." He tried to soften his words, her fresh tears having an effect.

She stood up. "I'm getting another drink. Then I'll be back. You can either let me go or tackle me in front of all these people. Not like I have anywhere else to be." She cut through the tables with little hint of any boozy tightness beyond the deliberateness of her steps, which were somewhat slower than he remembered. She returned with two glasses, placing one in front of him. A rounded ball of gourmet ice floated in a shot of Jameson.

"I'm celebrating," she proclaimed, half-heartedly. "Sort of anyway. Need someone to toast with, and you'll have to do. Drink it or don't."

Mason lifted the weighted tumbler in a weak-hearted salute, which she returned. "What are we celebrating?" he asked.

"The next chapter. Moving on. Whatever makes the most sense." She took a short pull after warming it with both hands. "I lost something this morning." Distance had crept into her words. "Crazy thing is, the only person I wanted to tell was Midas. It's why I called him. Figured I'd add another file to his misery index."

"What are we talking about, Michelle?"

"Not what . . . *who*." New tears fell without restraint. She bowed her head, anchoring herself against the table, trying to calm a wave of trembling. "I was only three months along, but I knew it was going to be a boy. My boy."

A cherry bomb ignited in Mason's brain.

He stayed silent, ensuring her a few moments of as much privacy as the setting allowed. The bleak energy now emanating from their small table drew nervous gawking from nearby patrons. He matched the looks with a well-trained glower, forcing their attention in other directions.

After a time, her shaking began to diminish. She studied him with something wedged between anguish and forbearance.

"What happened?" he asked.

"After this morning's meeting at Kyle's, I left. Couldn't handle the video that Whitten guy showed us. Started throwing up as soon as I got home. I ran a bath, stepped in, and realized I was bleeding. Somehow, I got out and dressed and got to the ER. Doctor says I hemorrhaged."

"Michelle. I . . ."

"What, Mase? You're sorry? Or should we just chalk it up to that damn karma you so love to believe in?"

He looked away. A coward's response. The chisel tapping at the back of his skull was gaining ground. "Did Kyle know?"

Her head shook no. "Three-month rule, right? I was close to telling him. Now I just want to disappear."

Why the hell she'd ever considered, or wanted, to have Kyle's child flickered through Mason's thoughts, framed in discolored projections. It wasn't a worthwhile topic. Not now or probably ever. Relationships, however toxic, would always be the ultimate equalizer. Punishing someone for a commitment to the wrong person was a nonstarter.

Lest ye be judged.

"We've got a nice place up north," Mason said. "Near Santa

Maria. I want you to go up there with one of our people. In a few days you'll be able to head wherever you want. I'll help with that."

He went to stand behind her chair, gently helping her up. As they began to walk, it wasn't hard to discern what she was thinking, gazing out and over the wall of Plexi to the streets below.

He slightly tightened his hold as he guided her out of the bar. "We've lost enough the past few days. I don't feel like losing you as well."

"He won't care, but will you tell Midas I'm sorry? About Serena?"

"Sure."

Mason put his arm around her and headed for the elevator where Carlo would be waiting.

Natalie sat in the darkness of her car, knowing she couldn't ask Collins for what she now needed.

At the very least, she owed him distance and deniability. For many of the same reasons she also couldn't put this in front of Jay. It was all well outside the boundaries. The fraternal order of no-man's-land. *Damned if you didn't, and damned worse if you did.*

Inevitable accountability worked for some, but Natalie had never been one to test the fringes by outrunning the rules. Arcane procedures and assholes with nameplates lived to knock those like her down a few pegs when less-than-by-the-book activity went off the rails.

The rain had returned, loaded drops landing with muted thumps on her windshield, bursting before rolling away. She couldn't think of any city that didn't smell better after a nice soak, including this one.

She forced herself to stay focused.

It made little sense, but she'd called the one person her gut told her she could trust, even if his presence could induce nausea.

Movement in the side mirror turned into a milky figure walking more briskly than he was used to as the fresh drops splashed off his head and shoulders. He reached for the door handle as she cued the lock, then he swung down into the passenger seat. He reeked of beef dips and bar grease, though the sweeter smell of crisp precipitation mitigated some of the foulness.

Dooley Dolan gave her a big smile, two racks dotted with archaic silver fillings.

"Detective Riiska. I realize I'm appealing, but a meeting a bit less . . . *clandestine* would have meant so much more."

They were sitting on a mostly deserted street in one of the sketchier areas of Venice, which still existed despite the best intentions of the gentrification gypsies.

"Dools," she said, already doubting her questionable choice. "Appreciate you coming."

"Well, it was either you or an old movie. No hockey or hoops on tonight, so you won out. Barely." The smell of strong beer wafted with his words. His tone playful, even welcoming. Something of a departure from their usual terse shorthand.

Damn Irish. They had their moments.

"Your sacrifice is noted," she said through a small smile.

He gave a slight bow and burped.

"Classy," she said, trying not to smile.

"You feel like telling me what's going on? I like old flicks, and TCM's running *The Third Man* tonight."

A pulling twinge radiated in her chest. Mason loved that movie, too, and had made her sit with him one night and watch it. She hadn't been prepared for the haunting vistas of the black-and-white noir flickering off the crumbling city walls of post–World War II Vienna. Orson Welles inhabiting the charming rogue with no guilt who killed children because he traded in tainted food and medical supplies. The rest of the cast conflicted and somewhat tainted, themselves. It was, she had to admit, a masterpiece of filmmaking. Today's movies were men in tights, all computer-generated editing. HGH bodies with weak scripts and less-than-worthy dialogue.

"I'm in something of a jam, Dools." She felt weak and small saying so, especially around him. But she was also out of moves.

He turned in the seat, giving her a new measure of attention. He cleared his throat. Any lingering breeziness from happy hour vanished with his smile. "Lay it on me, Detective."

An hour later the rain had ceased. Pale mist was all that remained of the storm, along with a cold, jagged breeze.

They climbed from her car. As was her habit from childhood, she pushed her hands hard into her jacket pockets, fighting the anxiety and uncertainty.

Dolan leaned over the top of the roof. "We'll figure it out," he said, shooting a half measure of his normal grin as he turned and departed.

She couldn't be sure, but it almost looked as if he were jogging.

CHAPTER 16

THE DEEP SAN FERNANDO Valley was an outpost of Los Angeles deliberately ignored by the entitled and their lip-filled housewife shows. Strip malls featuring Central American food and discount stores gave way to noncommercial buildings and storage facilities. It was nearing midnight, and traffic had dissipated. Distance between the streetlights began to stretch, such desolation common to back-end counties throughout the state.

It reminded Midas of that silly song Mason was always humming. W*alking in L.A.*

Once off the 118 freeway, his halogen headlamps carved a path through neighborhoods where orange groves had sprawled many decades before. Midas was headed to an enclave hidden within the cramped streets of small-business office parks, never more than two stories and inexpensive compared with similar areas closer to Ventura Boulevard. These were the venues of family-owned trucking, Hollywood prop shops, and nonperishable food supplies sold to stores such as Walmart.

Having ditched the large streets and traffic lights of Roscoe Boulevard, he maneuvered past a barely lit trailer park bordered by a few vacant lots, several other smaller roads, and cul-de-sacs of single-family housing tracts. A few well kept but most in need of facelifts.

Homes in this part of the valley had several drawbacks. Frigid in winter, wilting sweatboxes in summer. Not to mention the constant creep of badly nourished migration from the south, or the fentanyl and other assorted synthetic death labs pushing through the concrete edges of the city like determined weeds.

Midas kept one eye on the mirror, having doubled back to Roscoe. He cruised down the big street for a mile. Convinced he had no tail, he made another hard right and headed under the freeway toward the low mountains northwest of the highway. After a mile and a few more turns, he was crawling down another side street reserved for indiscreet warehouses, enclosed with several hulking 18-wheelers lined up like listless boxcars. Drivers sleeping off the overnight hour in extended cabs.

He passed the trucks and made a right, parking on the edge of another blighted residential neighborhood. His presence elicited no reaction from the dwellings. Behind these living room windows protected with iron bars, nothing was moving.

He waited in the silence, letting his mind and eyes adjust to the shaded, crystallized surroundings of night.

This was the only option. No matter what, or who, was waiting.

Underneath his seat was a hidden custom drawer, accessible from a button on his key fob. From it, he pulled out his Browning 9 mm along with an extra clip. The car door whispered open. He closed it with a subdued, slight *tick*, the silent alarm arming automatically. He then skirted back to the corner he'd just passed, weaving through the slumbering trucks.

Kyle's studios were settled in a nondescript structure. A driveway on either side led behind to an area for private parking. Choosing the left side, he eased around the building, hugging the walls to avoid cameras and motion detectors.

There was none, which he found strange.

He stopped momentarily, crouching to peer around the back corner where the driveways converged into an uncovered parking area marked with the usual white lines. Four cars sat in the lot.

Midas straightened his posture and waited.

A few minutes later, Natalie pulled off the same exit from the 118 freeway, turning right off the bottom of the ramp.

Dooley's headlights followed several yards behind.

She'd last been out this way as part of a task-force sting. That night's haul included a hundred barrels of laced smack and stacks of cash, all hiding in an air-conditioned basement some industrious thug engineer had dug out beneath a moderate-sized home that looked like any other from the street. A week after the raid, LAFD had been called back to investigate a foul smell seeping from beneath the foundation.

Four corpses, minus heads and hands, had been discovered inside a separate vault underneath the home, a steel-enforced crawl space where they had been torched alive.

Drug runners didn't appreciate inefficiency.

Natalie drove on heading west off Roscoe Boulevard, tumbling to the same thoughts she always had out here. Beyond the canyons that took you over the Santa Monica Mountains toward the beaches, or the nightlife and eateries along Ventura Boulevard, the San Fernando Valley was a locale better left to others. Soul-destroying heat augmented by an abundance of dirty crime. Latino gangs plying for turf with opioid chefs and the eastern-European mafias.

Make America great again? That pumpkin-faced idiot should spend an afternoon out on this patch, where red-faced Anglo anger stood no chance.

She veered off onto smaller streets as she approached the address, holding to a moderate pace.

Dooley's headlights were dual specks in her rearview. She felt oddly reassured by his company.

From his hidden position at the back of the building, Midas scanned as much of the exterior as possible. The office was modest, scaling well below what they'd faced a few nights back at the Carson warehouse. The roof was sheathed in brown shingles, construction around fifty years old. There were no windows, only a glass door at the understated entrance off the parking lot a few yards away.

The dark silhouette of a lone guard leaned nearby, smoking. The rain had passed, and the wind had died. The air was quiet, other than the occasional distant thresh of mashing gears from the night-owl trucks on the nearby freeway.

The silhouette tossed his smoke, pulling his phone from a rear pocket, and walked a few steps to perch on the hood of the nearest car, a 750 Beemer. He leaned back to light up another cigarette, probably why he never saw Midas coming. Though he must have sensed a threatening energy, because he turned in a crouch just as Midas sprang to his feet, aiming one elbow at the man's sternum and the heel of his other palm at his throat. The guard's hands rose in defense too late, and he hit the ground, unable to resist but vigilant enough to attempt a weak leg sweep on his way down.

Midas hopped over it, closing his forearms around his neck, rapidly putting him to sleep. He pulled the limp figure behind two junipers beside the back door, lifting the entry badge from his breast pocket.

He paused for a final scan of the surroundings, then slid the card over the nickel-sized sensor. A small *click* flicked the lock open.

Reception consisted of cheap, functional seating along with a transparent desk and a dim lamp. Recycled air circulated mustiness. Behind the desk was a hallway so dark beyond the first few feet that it may as well have been underground. He started to walk down it, using his small mag light to help him trace the perimeters. There were no other doors or exit signs.

After a hard left he approached the first floor's back corner and an unmarked door. A narrow strip of light painted the floor beneath it. He silently opened it and moved in low to the ground. The space was open with a concrete floor wide enough to host a full-court hoops practice.

In the back, a solitary man in a folding chair was watching hockey on a wall-mounted screen. The rest of the room was empty and clean as a surgeon's table.

Midas took several steps forward. The man didn't move or look his way.

"Jojo," he said, not surprised.

"Did you hurt my buddy?"

"He'll be fine," Midas said, scanning the room more thoroughly. Something wasn't adding up. "Not much of a welcoming committee."

"No," Jojo replied, disgust in his tone. "I'm a little surprised by that myself."

"Kyle?"

"In there." He gestured over his shoulder to a wide silver door with the dimensions of a restaurant freezer.

"Is he expecting me?" Midas asked.

"He never figured you'd get this close. Me either, once the old man sicced the feds on you." Jojo gave him a weak grin, scrolling through his TV choices with a remote. "Thousands of channels and nothing but shit. And in case you're wondering, his little fuck studio in there is soundproof. Whatever he and his latest flavor have going, they can't hear a thing."

Midas nodded, letting the gun fall to his side. "Jo, I want you to do me a favor."

"Sure." JoJo stood, coiled and taut. Always the capable customer.

Midas took a few steps forward. "Walk away," he said.

Ten years earlier, they'd all been in a barbecue joint thirty miles north of Atlanta, JoJo playing host. The Unit was sharing a glutinous meal after dropping in to visit a group of survivalists planning to firebomb the student center at the University of Georgia. Midas's appetite had been elsewhere that night, and hadn't been helped watching JoJo and Conor make impressive work of the chicken, ribs, beef slabs, baked beans, coleslaw, and mac and cheese. All served on platters the size of boogie boards.

Between large bites and drool flecked with sauce, JoJo had

dropped his philosophy on them. Admitting he "Couldn't give a shit about the school's faggy, pampered-ass, Faulkner-revering pansies." But the ex-army ranger, who'd grown up an hour from the Athens campus, had been worried that if the cracker shitbags had been successful, they also would have somehow blown up Uga, the revered and sweet-natured bulldog that served as the university's mascot. "Cruelty to animals is beyond my realm of acceptance," Jojo had added, mumbling with two fingers in his mouth while he attempted to dislodge an embedded piece of twelve-hour pork from between his molars.

Conor had laughed the hardest. "But Jojo," he'd said. "*You're . . . a cracker shitbag.*"

"So I know of what I speaks," Jojo had replied.

Midas suppressed a smile at the memory. The big man now, as then, was equal measure contradiction, proportion, and ability.

"Why would I walk away, Mide?"

"For old time's sake?"

Jojo smiled toward his feet. "You and your damn *Godfather*. I always preferred *Apocalypse*." He squeezed his hands into fists at his sides, shoulders stiff beneath the fitted waffle crew. "Besides. You know I can't."

"I do know. But had to try." Midas tapped his fist to his chest in a small salute to journeys past. "I need to talk to Kyle," he said, motioning with the gun.

Jojo pulled his own in slow motion from behind his back, holding it out in suspension with a thumb and index finger. He shook his head, flipping the .45 Colt gently on the floor. "Still using that peashooter? Fuckin' chick's gun."

Midas recognized Jojo was assessing limited options and searching for time. Both of which had run out.

"I warned him," Jojo said. "Too many times to matter. Told him never assume Midas was finished until we pulled out his heart and watched it stop thumping."

Midas motioned him back into his chair, moving forward to kick his gun aside. The cannon spun and skittered across the floor well out of range. Midas pulled a skinny capped syringe from his pocket. Golden liquid danced sluggishly inside with a weak fluorescence. A full dose.

"You *have* to be kidding," Jojo said, making a face.

"A bit of Propofol. Enough to put you down for a few hours. You never liked him, and I choose to believe a smart soldier like you was never privy to his plans for Serena. So make this easy. They'll think I got the drop. Even *your* ego can handle that."

Jojo's expression said he knew what came next, that Midas had moved into another phase. Determination with no sense of compromise or self-regard. And he was also clearly troubled that the added freelancers had been grounded without his knowledge. Jojo would be wondering who the hell had made that call?

He stood, for the second time. "I'm a *capable* soldier, Mide. *Good* soldiers would never sign up for what we were asked to do. But I learned to live with it. Pity you couldn't."

Midas nodded, uneasy with backhanded compliments, even fractured ones wrapped in questionable logic.

The big man started coming, shortening the space between them with resolved purpose.

Midas moved his gun behind his back, sliding it into his belt band, and stepped forward.

Jojo threw his initial punch too early, hoping to take advantage of Midas's millisecond of indecision. Midas slipped it, just enough to watch the calloused fist fly past while holding his own position in balance, feet planted shoulder width apart and closed off. The western stance favored by those who weren't Hollywood types on invisible wires, and instead looking for a quick end to a street conflict.

Jojo pulled his arm back, mistaking Midas's lack of a counter as a sign of capitulating.

Midas raised his arms, pulling his elbows close to his torso while taking a half step forward, dipping slightly to his left and squaring his shoulder.

Jojo read it as he should have, throwing another straight right toward Midas's face while ducking to avoid the telegraphed hook.

Midas straightened up in a flash and Jojo knew he'd made a mistake, overcommitting. His punch traveled forward, meeting nothing but air. Midas pivoted again to his left, raising his right foot slightly and snapping off a lightning stomp against the side of the bigger man's knee.

Jojo howled, instinctively reaching down for the injured joint, pitching forward on his good leg, arms instinctively grabbing below the thigh to mitigate as much of his dead weight as possible.

Midas twisted his waist like a dancer, resetting balance as he spun again on his weakened adversary, pooling years of technique and strength into a hammer fist that caught Jojo flush in his right cheek, the force almost lifting him off the ground. He spun and sprawled backward, hitting the floor face down. Ranger training kicked in as he rolled to his side and kicked out with the leg that still worked, creating a bit of distance while trying to regroup. He strained, attempting to rise vertically from his knees.

Midas took a step back. "It's enough now. Take the needle."

"Fuck you, goddamn quitter." Jojo's breathing had become short and whistly.

Midas realized his last shot must have caught part of the nose.

Even so, Jojo willed himself to stand, unsteady and swaying like a palm tree, bending but never snapping. They were once again inches apart. "The three of you were always better than I ever was," Jojo sputtered. "I could live with that. But all of you, Conor too, lacked the ability to do what you were told. It was just our *fucking job*. It should have been enough."

"It was never a job, Jo. And we're too old to bullshit each other."

Response came in the form of a slow and looping overhead haymaker, more a half-hearted joust. Muscle memory from teenage brawls in the Georgia humidity. Years of high-level training meant nothing when the body was broken and severely incapacitated.

As his hand came down, Midas slipped the opposite way, pulling his own forearm inward into a horizontal line in front of his chest, following with a targeted elbow into the exposed throat.

Jojo fell back for the second time, hands reaching below his chin reflexively to combat a sudden inability to breathe. The physics of his tumbling weight and wounded body made it impossible to brace himself as he slammed into the wall, his head snapping back to meet it with a nasty *crack*. He slid slowly to the floor, legs rigid and straight. The disabled knee was already the size of a small cantaloupe.

Midas stepped forward, tossing the syringe into his lap.

"Just know this," Jojo said through his wheezing. "We're not done. I'll be on your ass. In your rearview. Until one of us is gone."

He viciously pulled the cap off the needle with his teeth, driving it into his thigh, thumb suspended over the plunger. He smiled and pushed, taking it all. The effect was immediate. Glass filled his eyes as he offered Midas a one-finger salute. His head bobbed to rest at one side.

Less than fifteen seconds.

"Sleep well, Jo. You've earned it."

Natalie and Dolan marked the moments quietly, staked out and drinking the lukewarm stale coffee Dooley had grabbed from a 7-Eleven.

Midas's directions had been as true as his word. They were now waiting on a corner around a corner from his parked car, keeping watch on the two routes he would likely use to leave the targeted building.

The idle 18-wheelers in her mirror made her uneasy. Burly semis had frightened her as a child, the radiator grates looking like demonic grinning clowns large enough to swallow her without a trace. Even now, immobile under these sparse streetlights, they still struck her with dread.

Dolan was proving more perceptive than she'd been ready for, not only securing the coffee, but also keeping mute. No whining or probing of their current surveillance's visceral contours. Despite the trouble it could bring down on his own head he was here, backing her play. And removed from his cackling chorus of office knuckleheads, he'd begun to remind her of another old-school cop she'd once admired.

"Dools?"

He turned his head slightly, sheepishly giving her some attention while keeping watch on the street.

"My father was a cop. Big surprise to the Freudians, huh?"

There was the slightest drop under his eyes. Sympathy? Regret? The darkness of the SUV's cab rendered a pure read impossible.

"Jay told me. Back when you joined up."

"Chief of the Reykjavik Police Department," she said. "Then we moved to London for an Interpol posting when I was twelve."

"Sounds like he was good at what he did."

"I was twenty-three when he died. He'd been suspended, officially under investigation for turning rogue in service of a Serbian drug militia. The story was he'd employed international resources to keep them a step ahead of various task forces. For a month he sat around his flat. A cliché in sweatpants and bare feet watching TV with no sound and drinking vodka without a glass. He'd refused to defend himself, and I've never known why. One night I came home from playing pickup soccer with some cop friends and found him, as usual, stretched out on the couch. And I lost it. Screamed at him." There was a catch in her throat. "He just sat there. Never said anything or looked at me. Not once. So of course, I felt guilty. I left for a few minutes to buy some groceries. I wanted to make a nice dinner. Children can never say they're sorry. Instead they try and make amends with a good deed. When I got home, he was dead. Big needle in his arm, belt still cinched above his elbow. Door locked, nothing else touched. No signs of a struggle. Ruled a suicide, even though he'd never touched a drug in his life."

"Jesus," Dolan said, powerless to offer anything of greater substance.

She gripped the steering wheel with one hand, blinking hard. "Don't know why I told you that. Haven't talked about it since it happened. Maybe one day I'll figure out *why* it happened. What he wasn't saying. Who he was protecting."

"He was protecting *you*, kid," Dooley said evenly, probably assuming she'd already worked that out for herself.

"Hard to get past that night." she added, looking away. "Guess I just needed to find a cop worth sharing it with." She paused. "I'm about to be in some serious trouble. And I don't want you getting burned. I appreciate you being here, but would feel better if you got out now and walked away."

His laugh came softly. "Obviously, you've never seen *my* file. Blew all my chances years ago." He warmed to the change of subject. "I've always hated the suits and their chickenshit pandering. And as you know too well, never learned to keep my mouth shut. Never really wanted to either. They keep me around because I do decent work. Plug and play. Close enough cases. If I'm good at anything, it's doing my job while making them uncomfortable. And I'm talking about those nitwits downtown, not guys like Jay. Which means I continue to fail the cardinal rule of any gig—don't make the bosses feel dumber than they are. But so what, right? I've taken perverse joy being someone who pisses on them before they feel it rolling down their leg. Call it a character flaw.

You're a serious detective ... Natalie Riiska. And I respect that. Just don't ask me to repeat it in front of those pension-chasing idiots. I've been circling the drain for years and hold the title for office asshole. Tonight? I have nothing better on my calendar. So, if it's all the same to you, I think I'll just hang out. But one other thing: Don't sell Jay short. He's a real cop and will have your back." His conspiratorial grin widened. "By the way, since we're being so ... confessional? I've always had a major Jones for you. Even with that skinny Nordic ass."

For a moment she said nothing, then rendered a moderately courageous smile that he would later admit almost broke him.

"Do me a favor?" she said. "Never walk behind me again?"

"That, I cannot promise."

Midas ca`utiously opened the metal door.

Unlike the spacious area where he'd left Jojo sleeping off the cocktail, this was half the size, walls lined with soundproofing padding that looked like seat cushions and filled with various questionable production sets. One was kitchen with a bay window opening onto a phony garden. Faux bedrooms corresponding to certain age groups lined another corner, along with a sparsely furnished living room.

Kyle hadn't heard Midas come in, too busy in an overly lit bathroom with only two walls, running a small camera shooting over a chest-high, glass-enclosed shower spitting actual water. A naked figure stood behind the beveled glass. The girl might have been sixteen, red blond with patches of troubled adolescent skin. She saw Midas first, gasping at the intrusive presence of another man seeing her undressed.

Kyle turned, stiffening with confusion.

The girl turned off the water and covered her shivering body.

Midas picked up a black silk robe from the floor and lobbed it over the glass. She gratefully wrapped herself in it as if time were a factor and stepped out, wet hair dripping on the collar. She didn't try to hide her apprehensive look, wavering between Midas's intense posture and Kyle's now-forced, quivering smirk.

"Why don't you get out of here," Midas suggested.

She skirted past him as if she'd been grounded for coming home late from a concert.

He willed his heart to take a slow and tranquil dive, fresh burning in his gut and brain. The girl stopped at the door, unsure of what came next or what to do.

"Assume one of those cars out back is yours?" Midas said. "Get in and drive away. Our friend outside is napping, so I'd appreciate it if you don't stop to bother him. Can I trust you with all that?"

She nodded with wide eyes and slipped out.

Kyle limped to one of the nearby beds and lowered himself slowly onto an edge, sweat beginning to streak his face, likely tumbling to the fact that there was no one left to hide behind.

Midas stood and waited.

"I realize we already had a reunion a few nights ago. But no salutations for an old comrade?" The words fell from Kyle's twisted mouth.

Midas began to battle the opening waves of new fatigue. He too wanted to sit. Wanted more to sleep. What he didn't want was more useless talk.

"We both know what this is about." Kyle's desperation was taking over. The stiltedness of his rambling revealing mounting terror, something Midas knew he'd rarely ever known or cared to understand.

"Do we?" Midas eventually replied.

"Piss off." Brittle. High pitched. Kyle was playing for time, trying to convince himself his saviors were closing in. Born to understand that someone was always around the corner ready to shield him from harm. "You've been a liability since you walked out on us," Kyle went on to say. "DeMarco's motherhood issue. Everything I did these past few weeks was approved."

"I doubt that."

"And I *couldn't give a shit.*" Kyle was now almost screaming. "You tried to *kill* me, then walked away. Remember? You don't have privileges anymore."

"That, at least, is true."

"So what, then? I'm still in the tent . . . hell, I *own* the tent. A valued leader and member of an elite unit. At least to those who still matter. The revered Snow Leopard? He's all finished. Nothing now but a fucking nuisance."

"Can't argue with that either."

Midas's acquiescence and unwillingness to spar only spurred Kyle's desperate infuriation.

"You had a home, a purpose. Enabled to be the brutal bastard you are. And you blew it all up. Over some South American *whore*."

Midas ignored the pressure thrusting behind his eyes. "I remember a very young and tortured girl," he said. "Certainly no whore. And she was Mexican."

"Pious fuck. As if you have any room in your closet for self-righteousness." Kyle grabbed a handful of the cheap bedcover, his plump hand squeezing into a fist. His face had gone pale. "They would have chosen you over me. Any day of the week. All you had to do was ask."

Midas shook his head. "It was over for me. You helped me understand that."

The heavy camera lights had warmed the room considerably, and the heat was almost smothering.

"And what makes you *so-o* much better?" The bravado was fading. Kyle was reaching for anything he could bargain with. "Tell me, have you seen Michelle recently?"

"No." Midas clamped his jaw, refusing to react.

Kyle took a moment, putting that together. "I figured she would have run straight back to you. Far away from the evil sperm donor."

"She called. But we didn't talk. Mason is taking care of her. She didn't think you knew."

Kyle held up his hands in weak surrender, tears mingling with the sweat in his eyes. "I would never have hurt her. Or the baby."

"Just other people's kids." Midas caught himself parrying hard-wired impurities with impulse. He was ready to quell his own guilt by inflicting a necessary dose of physical suffering. For Serena and Phillip. But he also knew words were often far more damaging.

"She lost the baby. Miscarried. Earlier this morning."

Kyle's eyes moved to the floor. He started talking to himself, though it was indecipherable, all mumbling and gibberish. Rawlings Palmer's son was beyond exposed, trying in that moment to make sense of a lifetime of internal weakness.

Then he went silent, steeling himself for a final stand. "Michelle and I both got what we wanted," Kyle said.

Midas was tired of the rambling but asked anyway. "And what was that?"

"For a pro, you can't read leaves worth shit." Kyle's head came up as he leaned forward. "I didn't even have to convince her. Michelle really hates you. Doesn't know why, but she does. Probably had something to do with your girlfriend. Believe what you want, but she isn't clean in all this. We took a piece out of you, and that was satisfying. For both of us."

Midas felt the fire returning. "Serena and Phil?"

"You expected a gentlemanly game of hearts? What you did to me doesn't get taken back. Phillip? That geeky shit? And your pretty girlfriend? So much more…poetically clinical, don't you think? As opposed to having JoJo break your back and knees before putting one in your crown. Truth is, I'm not sure he would have done it."

"He tried. For your father, I assume. He's in the next room asleep." Kyle rolled his eyes. "Save it. Volunteers. Never victims.

And Conor will be dealt with. He promised I'd be covered."

"Daddy got overruled," Midas replied. "You're in the cold. No tin shoulders left to stand on."

Kyle was smacked by an abrupt onslaught of spasmodic shudders. If he hadn't already been seated, what remained of his legs would probably have given out.

Midas didn't care. "Time to leave."

"All you're missing is a hooded robe and scythe," Kyle muttered.

Midas approached the bed, using Kyle's collar to help him stand. He put his hand between the fleshy shoulder blades and pushed him toward the door. The smaller man's shuffling was somewhere between injured animal and a terminal patient pulling an IV bottle.

After a few steps, he paused. "Where are you taking me?"

"I haven't decided yet," Midas replied, cheapened by his own weakness.

As they waited, Natalie's mind wandered.

Despite the grander illusions, she had come to appreciate that most of Los Angeles, even the better areas, was loaded with streets like this—hidden and strange.

Dickens had framed his Victorian power plays against such backgrounds. Within his prose, old English streets became tragic corners, camouflaging menace. The LA she worked was a hunting ground for rapists and serial killers, and a haven for drug labs.

Cops avoided the fringes, as petrified of the shadows as everyone else.

Sitting with Dolan behind the no-peek windows of a fully secured black Escalade should have made her feel less tense. Strength in numbers, and all that. But the only tangible comfort tonight came from the warm weight of the Glock cinched at her hip.

Finally, there was movement in her side mirror, from behind the building.

Dooley saw it as well. Two figures had appeared. They turned and headed to the corner, crossing behind the Escalade to the opposite sidewalk. Midas stalked behind another man she couldn't quite see, who seemed to be stumbling. The pair walked under one of the flickering lamps, passing parallel to where she and Dooley were positioned across the street.

Midas signaled to her with a dip of his chin while steadying the shoulder of his companion. She recognized Kyle Palmer from his DMV photo. Even in the muddled blue of the early hour, she could see sweat strafing the point of Palmer's chin.

She wasn't surprised Midas had spotted her, considering he'd told her where she'd be able to find him.

In some ways, this remained a simple equation. Bringing them all in was the only play—careerwise, anyway. The two men continued to move through the darkness, then vanished around another corner. It had become that kind of night.

Natalie mentally ran through what she'd learned in the past twenty-four hours. Kyle Palmer was the bank and the raj of one of the most prolific erotic entertainment empires in the country. Or so Brennan and Collins would have her believe. There was always more to a story. Though everyone, including her, had good reason to want this finished and swept away.

A minute later, the cell on her hip vibrated. She eyed the number, momentarily hesitating. "Midas?"

"Hey, slugger." Mason's pet name for her. The boys who kept each other's secrets.

"So much for stealth surveillance," she said.

"A Hummer might have been less conspicuous."

"Yeah."

"You getting pulled into all this was simply bad luck, and bone-headed prep on my part," Midas said. "Sorry isn't enough, but it's all there is. I used to be better at these things."

"So I've been told. But what I need now is a reason not to bring you both in."

"There isn't one," he replied, exasperated. "Do what you think is right. No one will hold anything against you, least of all me. We'll wait in my car for fifteen minutes."

She flashed back to the aquarium. The corpse with a bloated arm. Viciously poisoned. She'd met Phillip last year on the Fourth of July when he'd invited Mason and some other friends up to his stunning, glass-encased home in the Palisades. Sight lines to the ocean from almost every angle. He'd proved a skilled host, talking to her over the grill while others had cooled off in the pool. Thinking back on that day now, she realized what Mason had told her was true. Phillip had not been in the restitution end of their business.

"Did Kyle Palmer kill Phillip?" she asked.

A hesitation. "He was there."

She let that float above them both, longer than she probably should have.

"I can't let you just... drive off," she finally said. Above her, one flickering streetlamp took its final breath and went dead, turning the night a straighter shade of black. She wished she could hit some button and turn it back on.

"Natalie?" Midas said, out there somewhere… still close.

"I'm here."

"Don't blame Mason. It was an impossible situation." Then the call dropped.

She tossed the phone onto the dash.

Dooley sat silent, no questions or judgment.

The next several minutes passed in moderated suspension. It felt as if everyone were waiting on her.

Though it was Dooley who offered the solution.

"I think we should go check inside that office. Thought I heard someone scream."

"Okay, Dools. If you think that's best."

He squeezed her shoulder and opened his door. "I do." He walked behind the vehicle and waited. She gathered herself to join him. Together they scouted around the grounds, finding the beaten guard unconscious behind a bush.

Dooley called it in, and they waited for the troops to arrive.

Just before making the call to Natalie, Midas had guided Kyle to his car.

He put a hand on his shoulder, unlocked the passenger door, and reached to open it with his other hand. He stood back to let him settle in. As Kyle leaned down, Midas moved forward, putting both arms around his neck from behind.

Kyle struggled, thrusting his head backward, trying to scream while losing air. "Don't do this," he pleaded over the forearms tightening around his throat. He thrashed against his own jerky spasms.

Midas leaned close to his ear. "You deserved worse."

There was an abrupt *snap* from the cervical vertebrae. Kyle collapsed, and Midas gently steered him into the seat, reaching down to push his feet in before closing the door.

Then he walked around to the driver's side, flipping open his burner.

CHAPTER 17

MASON ON HIS PORCH, dawn still an hour away.

He was empty, blue eyes washed of their usual, alert crispness. His legs stretched out over the damp wooden rail, a loose zip hoodie the only defense against the chill. It was nearing five a.m., the distant breakers pulsing out the minutes. He'd never looked more tired. Or broken. She made enough noise to let him know she was there before taking refuge in the chair next to his.

"Hello, Natalie."

She was taken back by the formality, then recalled their conversation from a few hours before. Boundaries had been shattered. Nothing could ever be as it had been. What that would mean in a week or more, she had no idea.

"What have you heard?" she asked.

"Nothing, really."

She settled herself against the brace of the salted wind. "I stepped over the line this morning, Mase. Never thought of myself as that kind of cop. But here I am."

His eyes filled. No longer any need to hide or camouflage the emotion he'd always been so careful to conceal.

She looked away, trying to offer a measure of privacy. "It was my choice," she whispered, more to herself than him.

"Doesn't mean it was the right one." He was fighting a catch in his throat. "I backed you into a corner. Took advantage of what we had. It wasn't right."

"I'm a grown woman. No one has ever made me do anything." He didn't argue.

"Our taint compromises another decent soul," he said wearily. "How many does that make?"

She had no answer, so instead went with what she knew. "A few hours ago, the two of them walked out of Kyle's building. They got into Midas's car and disappeared. Before they did, Midas called me, said he'd wait a few minutes if I wanted to scoop them both up. But as far as anyone will know, my partner I worked a tip and arrived after the fact, finding a studio and a few beaten-up associates of Kyle Palmer. Who are saying nothing. There were a couple of thumb drives and laptops, but they'd been wiped. That was the extent of it. I gave my report to Jay and Collins an hour ago."

"Midas?" he asked after a hesitation.

"The case remains open, with an APB for a bald, fortyish-something Black man, from an anonymous description given to the FBI. Off the record? Everyone agrees nothing can be pinned on anyone, and that all this will ultimately go down as a power-play turf war between rival porn lords. Kyle Palmer is missing and looks to be out of the game. I assume that will be enough to satisfy all those masked types on that gruesome tape. Kyle's father is apparently already proclaiming ignorance, alleging he had no idea what his son was wrapped up in."

"His father will regroup," Mason said. "This weakens him, but he still has plenty of chits. At some point . . ." His voice trailed off.

"That's a problem for another day."

She could feel the air shifting around her, the oxygen growing thin.

"It would be smart if you forget about all of us," Mason said. "Your cops and new FBI friend can't ever prove we were ever more than casual acquaintances. As far as they know, you came into the bar occasionally for a glass of wine. That should be enough. It won't be you they want. And I don't see them running the risk of mussing a decorated detective. But they *can* make your life uncomfortable. So better for you if we all keep some distance."

"Can I ask you something?"

"I'd say you've earned the right to ask me anything," he said.

"You mentioned your cover in those days was as a journalist. Freelance reporter sending dispatches from various hell holes. Surprising to me your Unit bosses allowed that? Cover name or not, dispensing facts from inside those missions?"

He took this in, for a few moments.

"The Old Man? DeMarco? He was never thrilled about it. But having been through it himself, he understood the need for decompression. Writing helped me process what we were doing. I wrote what I could from the ground level, keeping certain aspects protected, of course, and then sold it to serious magazines and papers that printed that flavor of dispatch. The *New York Times*, *LA Times*, the *Atlantic*. Back then I also thought, naïvely, that getting something out there might make a difference to the *right* sort of people. That perhaps someday we'd stop throwing our money and might behind the greedy, dangerous leaders. Again, in retrospect, it was stupid and wide eyed. But I was still young enough to have a jaded optimism, and that budding hope gave me the permission I needed to keep working those missions. Went with a nom de plume, as novelists call it. Phony byline."

"So . . . what happened?" she asked. "No one believed the reporting? Political pressure? Behind-the-scenes discrediting?"

"Nothing so organized or lofty," he replied, the look of defeat returning. "I was too thorough. And no one could ever challenge anything I wrote for veracity." He brought his legs down and sat forward, rubbing his knees. "The truth was they just didn't care. Those *right people*? Couldn't be bothered." He shifted again, stretching one leg back onto the ledge and taking a deep drag of the wind, picking up momentum and swirling over the sand.

"That's disheartening," she said.

"But with hindsight, not a surprise. Ours is a nation that likes to pretend it's open minded and sympathetic when it comes to suffering, inhumanity, and strong-arm regimes. But honestly? We're driven by materialism, fear, and a pathological need to follow. Missing almost everything that matters because our heads are forever buried in our phones.

Over the past several decades Americans have become risk- and confrontation-averse. We like to tell ourselves we care. That a momentary, visceral reaction to an AP photo of a dead father and infant daughter drowned while trying to cross the Rio Grande makes us part of some . . . *enlightened community*. Same with going to church, coffee klatches, and emotional encounter groups. Share a few tears and then head home, deluded in a belief that you're woke"—he made air quotes—"or you've done enough to label yourself as worthy.

Right wing or left, most let themselves off the hook by never asking too much of themselves. My take? Most Americans are indifferent, settled, or petrified. Hoping and expecting someone else will tell them what to think and do. And praying that people such as me will keep the true chaos away from their front yards and comfort zones."

She turned her chair to face him. "But isn't that what we do, you and me?" she asked. "Stay vigilant for those who can't do it themselves?"

"Certainly what the mission statement says," he replied.

She nodded, hating herself for accepting his cynical framing of humanity, though she couldn't deny she'd had similar thoughts. "It's never easy though, is it, Mase? Committing yourself to bettering a world where the worst people usually win."

But he was done with this subject.

She wanted to say more, to talk herself into a future that included him. Somehow commit to making it all work. Or at least promise to try. But their moment had passed. If it had ever truly been there. For them, there would never be a safe harbor. Still, she found herself lacking the strength to do what was necessary, and completely close the door.

"I'm going to need some time," she said, hating the sound of her torn selfishness.

"I know." He didn't seem surprised. Or thrown. In the past few days, she'd been exposed to someone he'd hoped to keep buried from her. A wayward drifter fit only for an existence of abeyance, bearing scant resemblance to those more conventional. But she also couldn't stop from wondering . . . would she really be better off without him?

Tears had returned to his eyes. He looked to be fighting one of his stubborn migraines. "My dad's having some problems," he said.

"I need to head up north."

She could see through his ploy. Like her, hedging when he knew better.

"Is he okay?" she asked, figuring part of this was probably true.

"You never know with Max. But all the same, I need to lay eyes on him. Now seems like as good a time as any. For everyone. Carlo can run the gym and the bar while I'm gone."

A few minutes later, Mason stood up and walked behind her, not trusting himself anymore to look into her face. The woman he'd failed to protect. The friend he'd have to learn to live without.

But how?

He wrapped his arms around her, resting his head against the back of hers. She shuddered at his touch, silently starting to cry while grasping his arms with her strong and delicate fingers. They held on to each other for a long time before he straightened up and opened the slider.

"You're better than all of us, slugger," he said. "And you'll always be the best of me."

He walked inside and closed the door behind him, making barely a sound above the crash of the rolling surf. Disappearing without hesitation under the pale slivers of a fading night.

If Conor believed at all in any form of therapy, he supposed this would be it.

Five in the morning, hunched over the guts of his Lionel *Civil*

War General. More conventionally known as a model 4-4-0 steam engine.

When it came to scale, his taste slid to HO, but for engines like this, Lionel didn't disappoint. Despite the asshole's best intentions, the damage done by Palmer's henchboy wasn't as bad as Conor had initially thought. The wheels had been an easy fix. Now, it would just be a bit of paint and a new bulb headlight. He was going with a yellow lamp, which most old-timers and collectors considered cheating. He didn't care. Yellow looked better moving around the tracks.

An old-school dialer phone on his desk started ringing. Quaintness aside, the landline was secure. He'd put it in himself and swept it every few days. He delicately placed his tiny screwdriver next to the others and picked up the bright red receiver, something he'd always felt was a nice touch. The Bat Phone.

"Go," he said.

"Conor."

"Hello, Mide."

"Still doing your best work in the vampire hours? What is it tonight?"

"Locomotive. Civil War era. Poppa Palmer's goon roughed it up."

"How badly?"

"Bent the wheels. Headlight and some paint. He got schooled for it. You know what a bad idea it is to touch my trains."

Conor heard an extended exhalation laced with genuine remorse. "That wasn't cool," Midas said. "Sorry it happened . . . sorry about all of it, Con."

"So am I."

Conor ran his index finger along the bottom of the engine's

chassis, pulling off a few drops of lubricant. He rubbed them against his thumb and held the scent briefly under his nose. The fragrance was pleasant, hobby oil mingling with the metallic and painted varnish.

"Where is he?" Conor asked.

"Where he should be."

Conor took a drawn-out sip of the black coffee at his elbow. His own, brewed fresh. The shop next door wouldn't open for another hour. "It shouldn't have gone this way."

"Except it did," Midas said, added resignation seeping into his words.

Conor leaned against the back of the high stool. This had always been his favorite time to work. Silence and solitude, forgiving partners. "I'm going to have to pretend, Mide. Gather the scalp hunters. No stone unturned. You know the drill."

Because there were still a few scenes yet to play, Conor would be ordered to lead the search for their old compatriot. Agency quacks and Rawlings Palmer would demand no less.

"I always wondered, back then. Why didn't you jump with us?" Midas said, encroaching on a subject they'd avoided for years. "But then again, you had Silas's and the Old Man's backs. We all understood. Never said so, but that was awful decent of you, taking the hit for the rest of us."

Warm moisture invaded Conor's eyes, pressure pushing inside his chest. Like his old friends, he really was ... *well past it.*

"Con?"

"Sorry. Zoned for a second. What can you tell me?"

"Jojo's laid up for a couple of weeks. Kyle will reappear... shortly."

Conor knew better than to ask.

"You'll be okay, Mide. Mason too. Eventually. DeMarco came around just in time. He's getting out of the hospital in a few days, but he's all done. And after fixing this mess, he deserves some rest. Strange, though. He didn't meet as much resistance as we all would have assumed. Truth is, none of the b-crats and meeting takers were ever fans of the Palmers, no matter how many secrets father and son held over them. They'll sit down in their back rooms and chart the after reports. Then they'll rule it all a wash. It's what nervous ass-coverers in power do. But someday soon, Rawlings Palmer will move on you. And Jojo will be running point."

"I'm more concerned he'll move on you, Silas, and the Old Man," said Midas.

"Predictions are a sucker's game. Worry when necessary. None of us will be caught flat footed again. In the meantime, for the sake of appearances, I'll be looking for you. Though it will have to wait. The Old Man ordered me to take a few comp days. Something he can document to keep them quiet while giving you a head start." Conor started to laugh, for no real reason other than he knew Midas would be smiling as well

Cubicle pukes took their 401(k)s and comp days as seriously as they did Jihadists.

"Speaking of beyond the playbook, why Natalie and her FBI friend?" Midas asked.

"Because I would never have been able to cover your back. At least not in an efficient way. Given her ties to Mase, I figured no matter what she thought philosophically, she'd come through. The feds had nothing but what Palmer had given them. He only made that call because after the fire he was petrified you were coming for him as well as Kyle.

So he gave them everything he knew, assuming federal reach

and manpower would slow you down enough to ensure him and his son some kind of escape. Reaching out to her, through Collins, was my only move.

I hoped with her help we could make sure the right side crossed the finish line first. Collins came through as well. Good to know all feebs aren't hermetically sealed at the rectum. Though when I met her, I realized why Natalie was already under his skin. She's the real thing. And with guys like us, it's always about a woman, right?"

"I'm not arguing," Midas said, softly. "Reaching out to her was a smart play. And of course she came through. I fucked up by getting her involved in the first place. She didn't need any of this heat. None of you did."

There was more to say, but they'd run out of time.

Theirs was a species that struggled with what others took for granted, communication and emotions frequently positioned beyond reach.

"I'd drop you a line, but . . . ," Midas said.

"Someday, I hope," Conor replied.

"Keep an eye on Mason and Natalie for me."

"No problem. Though they're more than capable."

"Oh. And one more thing . . . ," Midas said.

Conor hung up twenty seconds later, allowing himself another small smile as he reached for his keys, locking up on his way out.

The morning sun was still an hour away, and Conor was surprised to find one of the side gates unlocked. Good help would always remain at a premium, especially when it came to city jobs.

The gift shops were dark and quiet. He paused briefly to study the map and arrows, choosing the route up a moderately steep knoll offering views of a variety of species.

The first he passed were the florid Chilean flamingos, whose tropical burnt-orange hues stood out in the predawn pitch. Conor's pace was deliberate and measured. He trudged to a higher altitude along a tree-lined concrete path, passing several man-made habitats with residents hidden somewhere inside, having long ago adapted to human hours and circadian rest patterns.

Animals were good that way, he thought. Better than humans had ever proved to be.

Near the top, he traced his direction from a long yellow arrow painted on the ground. The walkway opened to a featured domicile fronted by a rustic amphitheater and a single row of benches.

Someone had arrived first, sitting alone on one of the hard oak seats.

The perimeters of the amphitheater reached twenty feet into the air. The enclosure was half the size of a small apartment building, protected with a chain-link fence. Inside was an island of rocks and weeds rimmed by a small moat, made to simulate the Himalayan terrain. Ten feet behind the fence sat the two youngsters, early risers. A few feet away their mother kept watch.

The snow leopard twins had been born four months ago. The LA. Zoo had acquired the entire family as part of a well-publicized rescue mission, with the blessing of the Dalai Lama.

The female had been saddled by her trainers with the grandiose moniker Esmerelda. Her twins were Jason and Lucas, named by an elementary school class in Eagle Rock after winning an essay contest. Esmerelda stretched out and yawned while her offspring wrestled in the forgiving weeds. Conor could have taken a seat and watched them for hours, delaying the unavoidable while soaking up their stately energy.

Instead, he made his way closer.

Kyle was, as always, well attired. Dark slacks, long-sleeved black shirt, and soft-soled loafers. Italian, of course. His clothes appeared to be carefully pressed and remarkably clean.

Especially given he was dead.

His head rested oddly to one side as the cubs in front of him continued their tussle. A slight breeze materialized, sweeping his parted bangs. The eyes were closed, hands placed in his lap.

Kyle's interloping presence should have caused some form of residential panic, animal sensitivity being precise and acute even under confinement. Except these intrepid specimens with the long, thick tails were different, revered and celebrated for centuries throughout the world. In their natural setting, most carried through an entire lifetime without ever being seen by a human. They were worshipped by some and, regretfully, hunted by others. Diminishing numbers spoke to their endangered status. The ones who survived somehow understood that, keeping their own counsel while remaining a few steps ahead of those who lived to do them harm.

Esmerelda was silver with deep-set black spots like small map drawings. She had wrapped herself within her fluffy rudder of a tail, head held high to behold possible dangers in the shifting air. Her boys had the same markings, with more of a tan flush to their fur. They would one day share the same muted steel coloring of their mother.

Conor smiled at the small family, wondering how the hell his old friend had gotten Kyle up here? A golf cart maybe, from the nearby public course? Easy and mostly quiet.

He chuckled. Midas would forever be a puzzle, making moves within a box of self-imposed discipline. Driven by an unyielding code.

It was time to leave. The zoo's morning staff would arrive soon.

Conor took final appraisal of the magnificent cats.

Jason and Lucas continued to frolic while Esmerelda and Kyle both sat still, each contentedly enjoying the show in their own way. Something Conor would later remember as oddly touching.

Perhaps snow leopards *were* a higher form of reality.

Who was he to dispute existential truth?

THE END

NOTE FROM
THE AUTHOR

THOUGH THE IDEA AND story for this novel have been ceaselessly bouncing within my thoughts over many sleepless nights, it was only in the past few years I realized the time had come to get serious.

And there is no way I could have done it without a great deal of support and guidance.

To Nina Bruhns, my eternal thanks for running point through the minefield of issues presented within my first draft. Her steering and polish were invaluable to the final narrative. Christian Storm designed a striking cover that took hold the minute I saw it, equally sinister and subtle in all the right ways. He was also an active and complete pro in the shaping and formatting of the finished work. Steven Tu for his expertise and diligence in building an arresting site which brings Midas to the next level. Ben Galley for walking me through the curveballs of publishing. I also could not have confidently finished without the final look and experienced eye of Leigh Wingate.

Again, my everlasting thanks to you all.

Most importantly to my wife, Mika, who continues to be my fearless source of eternal optimism and hope. The one who, when it's needed, helps me get out of my own head with steadfast, tangible strength, and an abundant reserve of positive grace.

I am proud of you, always, and forever fortunate that you came into my life.

— SLC

ABOUT THE AUTHOR

S.L. COOK is an Emmy-award winning news and sports producer who enjoys discovering compelling stories. He has traveled extensively throughout his life to find them.

His career began as a Producer for *NBC Nightly News* and the *Today* show, living both in Los Angeles and New York for several years. After being hired away by CNN, he soon became the network's Managing Editor in Los Angeles, where he oversaw and produced coverage during some of the most turbulent years in the city's history, including the Rodney King beating, the subsequent trials of the police officers, and the 1992 riots. He also ran point on the massive Northridge earthquake, as well as the heartbreaking and wide-ranging destruction from several turbulent fires and floods throughout southern California.

After returning to NBC to help coordinate coverage of the OJ Simpson trial, he was named a lead producer for the launch of Fox Sports News. From there followed several years as the Executive Producer for Sports at CBS in Los Angeles, the largest such broadcast department in the nation.

Along the way, he published short stories and Op-eds for various papers and sites around the country.

Today, he continues to produce television sports – when he's not too busy writing, or working the stubborn aches and kinks out of a complaining and aging ex-ballplayer's body.

His passion remains striving to present and tell stories with an unencumbered voice. He is currently at work on his next novel.

www.ingramcontent.com/pod-product-compliance
Lightning Source LLC
Chambersburg PA
CBHW030235120726
47903CB00005B/1489